A
RECKLESS
SOUL

ALSO BY ELIZABETH COLE

Honor & Roses

Choose the Sky

Raven's Rise

Peregrine's Call

A Heartless Design

A Reckless Soul

A Shameless Angel

The Lady Dauntless

Beneath Sleepless Stars

A Mad and Mindless Night

Daisy and the Duke

Heather and the Highlander

Rose and the Rogue

Poppy and the Pirate

A RECKLESS SOUL

ELIZABETH COLE

SKYSPARK BOOKS

PHILADELPHIA, PENNSYLVANIA

SkySpark Books
Philadelphia, Pennsylvania
skysparkbooks.com
inquiry@skysparkbooks.com

Publisher's Note: This is a work of fiction. Names, characters, places, and incidents are a product of the author's imagination. Locales and public names are sometimes used for atmospheric purposes. Any resemblance to actual people, living or dead, or to businesses, companies, events, institutions, or locales is completely coincidental.

Ordering Information:
Quantity sales. Special discounts are available on quantity purchases by corporations, associations, and others. For details, contact the "Special Sales Department" at the address above.

A RECKLESS SOUL / Cole, Elizabeth. – 2nd ed.
ISBN-10: 1-942316-25-9
ISBN-13: 978-1-942316-25-1

A
RECKLESS
SOUL

ELIZABETH COLE

SKYSPARK BOOKS

PHILADELPHIA, PENNSYLVANIA

SkySpark Books
Philadelphia, Pennsylvania
skysparkbooks.com
inquiry@skysparkbooks.com

Publisher's Note: This is a work of fiction. Names, characters, places, and incidents are a product of the author's imagination. Locales and public names are sometimes used for atmospheric purposes. Any resemblance to actual people, living or dead, or to businesses, companies, events, institutions, or locales is completely coincidental.

Ordering Information:
Quantity sales. Special discounts are available on quantity purchases by corporations, associations, and others. For details, contact the "Special Sales Department" at the address above.

A RECKLESS SOUL / Cole, Elizabeth. – 2nd ed.
ISBN-10: 1-942316-25-9
ISBN-13: 978-1-942316-25-1

Chapter 1

$$\underline{\Omega}$$

London, August 1806

Sophie wondered if she should just kill the man.

She stretched to full length under the sheets. Beside her, the man in question lay deeply asleep. She glanced at him to confirm that he was out cold, then rose from the bed in an easy, fluid motion.

Her body was like a dancer's, narrow-framed and sleek. Growing up, Sophie had often been mistaken for a boy. Though she was now five years past twenty, it seemed her hips had filled out only within the last few years. But she had a natural grace to her movements, bolstered by years of ballet and theatrical training. Despite her less than lush figure, she knew how to attract attention. The recent encounter proved as much. She'd seduced her mark with little more than a smile.

She gathered her clothes from where they lay on the floor and put them on without any particular hurry. Her dress was in a cut common for a lady's maid, but Sophie wasn't a lady's maid.

She was a spy.

Her job was to retrieve a false seal used by her mark, Garrett Mourne.

Her cover identity was Sara, a French-born servant for one of London's wealthy families. As Sara, she'd been close to Garrett for weeks—he was involved in the hostilities between France and England, passing information and rumors between players in exchange for cash. Managing his romantic advances was simply part of the game. The previous night had been typical. Garrett was a dull lover, which suited Sophie perfectly. She pretended a delight in his attentions, and was never in danger of actually feeling the passion she displayed.

She checked her appearance in the small mirror by his wardrobe, so she could adjust the blonde wig she wore— her own hair was quite dark, and unfashionably short. Thin, straight brows arched over her large eyes, which were a light brown that held flecks of hazel, and she knew how to catch and hold any audience with them. She grinned at herself as she turned from the mirror. With Garrett still dozing from the mild dose of opium she'd slipped into his drink, it was time to get to work.

Sophie slipped out of the bedroom and walked through the silent house. Garrett had been renting it for months, but hospitality wasn't a priority for him. Time and neglect took away most of the charm of the once-grand place. Dust gathered everywhere, and only the most used areas were kept clean.

Sophie paused at the door of the parlor, which Garrett

used as his work room. She waited to be sure she was undetected—the few servants he employed would be up and about soon. After a moment, she turned the knob. The door was unlocked, and she sighed in relief. One more thing she wouldn't have to disguise.

Early morning light had barely begun to filter into the room. It was outfitted with a large table and several chairs. Papers, stacked haphazardly in piles, covered the table. Stolen jewelry and coins lay on the floor. She ignored all those things, her eyes scanning the desk.

Shutting the door behind her, Sophie went into action. She walked over to Garrett's table, searching among the piles. Nothing on the top. Methodically, she lifted every stack and sorted through the papers. She riffled through the collection of pens and inkwells, hoping to find the object she sought. Still nothing.

Sophie turned to a set of cabinets and repeated the search. Cursing softly, she opened drawer after drawer. "Where is it?" she breathed.

A floorboard creaked in the hall. Sophie froze. She listened for more sounds, not even breathing. Another creak. She moved one hand outward toward a slim letter opener left on the desktop. As a weapon, it wasn't intimidating. But Sophie had won fights with no weapon at all before. And if she were seen, a fight would be inevitable.

Someone moved again outside, and then spoke. "I said bring the wood in first, dolt, *then* sweep. What's the point of cleaning first?" The voice continued to scold the other servant, and footsteps faded down the hall.

Sophie breathed out. Just the household waking up.

She had a little while, but she'd have to be twice as careful leaving the room.

Though she hoped Garrett would sleep for some time, there was no guarantee the opium would work as expected. If he found her pawing through his things, no amount of persuasion—verbal or physical—would appease him.

She continued her search. Finally she found a locked drawer. She made short work of the lock with a pin from her hair and the drawer rolled open soundlessly. It didn't take her long to find what she was looking for.

It was a seal. She examined the design on the bottom—a lion standing up on its hind legs, with claws ready to attack. Stars surrounded the creature. It looked authentic, but Sophie knew it was an excellent forgery. Garrett had been using it to send false messages across the Channel, confusing the recipients and therefore hindering the war effort. Garrett didn't care who won the war. He was merely interested in tilting little things his way to profit from the confusion.

Sophie, however, *did* care who won. She pulled an object from the pocket sewn into her shift. It was a seal that looked nearly identical to the one Garrett possessed, though his had a few wear marks she could only replicate when she had both in hand. She scratched similar markings in the new seal. She even smeared a bit of red sealing wax on the new one to complete the illusion. Then she placed the new one back in the drawer.

Her work was nearly done. Smiling, Sophie tucked the first seal into the pocket of her dress.

She could have snuck out of the house at that point,

but Sophie thought her act required an encore. She inched the door open and peeped out into the hallway. She waited until she could hear nothing, and slipped out of the work room. Gliding up the stairs in her slippered feet, she returned to the bedroom, breathing a thin sigh of relief.

She reached the bed and stared down at Garrett, her eyes cold. He was a thin, tough man. He'd worked his way up through the ranks of the London underworld, and it wasn't hard to imagine how he did it. He could not be called handsome, but there was something compelling about the man. Sophie knew what it was. Power. Garrett controlled several gangs in London, and he was shrewd.

In all honesty, she'd be doing her adopted country a favor if she killed him. He was indirectly responsible for the suffering of so many people: families and shopkeepers who paid protection to his gangs, the soldiers who fought in the wars he helped prolong. But if she eliminated him, another enemy would simply take his place.

I suppose you have your uses, she thought, *and who knows when you'll be useful again?* She removed her clothes and slid back into the bed. Sophie took a certain pride in seeing a job done properly, which in this case meant tricking her mark into believing nothing unusual had happened.

She let a sweeter expression settle on her face. "Garrett," she whispered, shaking him lightly. "Garrett."

He opened his eyes, blinking slowly. He was groggy, but not too badly off. Sophie hated the idea of using more opium than necessary. It was risky. He might notice the unnaturalness of his sleep.

"Sara?" he muttered.

"We both slept late," she said. "I have to go, or I'll be thrown out."

"You're still here?" he asked, distracted. "What time is it?"

"Time for me to leave."

"Oh, but you're delicious, Sara. Stay here." He ran his hands up and down her body, feeling the heat of her. He lingered over her breasts, and then moved to her hips and her bottom. He looked more alert than she expected at that hour.

"Garrett," she said in warning. "I can't stay, and you know it. My mistress hardly lets me out as it is."

"Come back tonight." Garrett leaned in and kissed her, his lips warm, but his breath sour from the aftereffects of the drug.

Still, Sophie returned the kiss, as if hungry for him. He wasn't terribly skilled, but she'd experienced far worse. She opened her mouth and moaned a little, letting him think she enjoyed it. Then she broke it off. "I must go back now. Trust me, I'd stay if I didn't have to work for that harridan."

He laughed, and she did too. *The best trick is to make your victim fool himself.* She got out of bed once more and dressed, feeling to make sure the seal was safe in the tied pocket in her skirts.

Garrett looked at her appreciatively. "Come back as soon as you can."

Don't wager on that, she thought smugly. But she gave him a smile that would have to serve as the only farewell he'd ever get from her. Then Sophie ducked her head and hurried out of the room.

She left the house and emerged on the street. She ignored the carriages and conveyances for hire, walking tirelessly until she reached a new section of the city. Here, tidily dressed gentlemen hurried from place to place, looking important, although more than one pair of masculine eyes followed her progress down the street.

Eventually, she reached a large building of marble and brick. It was already busy, for several private firms had offices inside. Instead of entering through the imposing front doors, however, she sidled down an alley at the rear of the building. She found a small door that appeared to be a tradesman's entrance.

Sophie made her way through a warren of rooms and hallways, climbing several staircases to get where she was going. At one door, she knocked quietly. Another woman opened it. "Yes, miss?" she asked in a disinterested voice.

"I have a delivery," said Sophie.

Glancing quickly up and down the corridor, the woman allowed her inside.

When the door closed, she turned to Sophie and nodded in recognition. Sophie had reached the headquarters of the Zodiac, the most secretive group in the already secret world of espionage.

"Hello, Miss Chattan," Sophie said. She knew some things about the Zodiac, but they didn't include this woman's Christian name. Though a fixture in the private headquarters, the woman was a mystery.

Chattan nodded back curtly. Her eternally messy ash

blonde hair was barely bound, and her plain, practical gown sported several ink stains. She surveyed Sophie's wig and her outfit with a disdainful eye, then said, "He's been expecting you." The other woman gestured to an inner door, then returned to her own desk, dismissing Sophie from her mind.

"And a very good day to you as well, Chattan," Sophie remarked under her breath, just loud enough so the other woman heard it.

Sophie didn't wait for a response. She entered the inner office with a breezy greeting. "Morning, Aries. I got the little item you fancied." Though French-born, Sophie never lost a chance to sound as British as possible. She considered it her duty to master such things.

The man who ran the office had been standing at a window, staring out at the streets below. Now he turned and looked Sophie over. Julian Neville, also known as Aries, was nominally Sophie's superior. To her, though, he was much more. Julian was the man who taught her how to be a spy. He was also the man who practically ran the elite espionage group known as the Zodiac. He reported to the Astronomer, who was truly the head of the group, as far as anyone knew. Sophie didn't even want to guess the true identity of *that* person. She was much safer not knowing.

Julian smiled. "Well, my Libra returns." Libra was Sophie's code name, and her most closely guarded secret. Of the twelve agents who made up the Zodiac, she was the only woman. "Did you run into any problems?"

Sophie shook her head. "It went like clockwork. Garrett Mourne thinks he's a mastermind, but he's got the same weaknesses as any other man." She bunched up a bit of her skirt and held it out toward Julian, carelessly revealing slender legs nearly up to the top of her thin stockings. "Feel this. As if any real maid would wear a weave so fine! This dress wouldn't last a month in service. After weeks of sleeping with him fairly regularly, you'd think he'd notice."

Julian fingered the fabric, eyebrow raised. "I see. And it does allow your figure to be a bit more…prominent, doesn't it? Clever." He dropped the fabric.

"I thought so. I sewed it myself." Sophie had many skills, not all of them learned in her training as a spy. She'd practically grown up in a theater, and learned how to sew from the seamstresses there.

"Was it tolerable?" he asked, sounding concerned.

"Garrett Mourne, you mean?" Sophie asked. "Yes. Garrett's a thief and a turncoat. But he treated me well enough."

"Even in bed?"

"I've had worse and better." She shrugged. "What else is there to say?"

What else could they say? As a spy, he'd done the same things she had over the years. Sophie viewed her body as a tool. She had long ago learned to attach no emotion to physical intimacy. It was a means to an end. Some women used it to secure the attention of husbands or lovers. Sophie used it to gather information.

"I worry about you sometimes."

She shot him a look. "Julian, we've had this discussion before. I knew exactly what was required of me when I joined. The fact that I'm a woman should make no difference."

"It shouldn't," he agreed. "But I have this lingering sense of chivalry."

"Put it to rest," Sophie said. She returned to practical matters. "I have what you're looking for."

She handed him the seal. He took it, not hiding his eagerness. He peered at the design for a long time, then put it down on the desk and let out a breath. "That's a very good copy. No wonder everyone was fooled for so long."

"No more. The replacement has one extra star around the lion's head. Garrett won't notice the alteration until his missives go unheeded a few times."

"And now that we have the forger under lock and key, he can't get another seal of that quality. Good work, Libra."

Sophie straightened up at his mild praise, knowing that for Julian, it was the equivalent of a salute.

"I'm afraid," he went on, "I have to send you on another assignment immediately."

"What is it?" she asked.

"Read this." He handed her a letter.

Sophie read it over, her eyebrows slowly knitting together until she was scowling at the end. "From this, it appears someone within the government is selling…not secrets. But support, perhaps? To the French cause?"

"Very likely. It's another breadcrumb on a trail I've been following. You recognized the sender, of course."

She had. "Volange," she said, her voice flat. A mysterious man named Arceneau was the most dangerous criminal in Europe, but his lieutenant Alain Volange was far more vicious.

"So you know how bad things might get," Neville said, watching Sophie carefully.

She nodded. While Sophie was still living in Paris, she had worked as a petty criminal—mostly pickpocketing—and she had seen firsthand what Volange was capable of. The man was unforgiving and had an affection for pain. Sophie used to have nightmares about him. Years later, she got the opportunity to work against him, which suited her far better.

Sophie knew broadly what Arceneau's interests were. He was a businessman, cold and calculating and willing to deal with virtually anyone with the funds to pay his asking prices for goods like gunpowder, ships, and war machines. He also dealt heavily in blackmail, trading secrets around the continent like cards around a gaming table. Arceneau was dangerous precisely because he had no interests other than money.

Julian took back the letter, and explained, "This confirms what we've heard in a few other quarters. Someone has been making secret alliances, or at least promising support. In short, there is a traitor in the British Cabinet."

She inhaled. It was a serious accusation, and Julian would never even suggest such a thing unless he was convinced of it. "Who?" she asked quietly.

"That's what you're to find out, Sophie."

"Excellent. Tell me what to do."

"I will tell you all about it tonight, when you meet me and my guest in the Oak Room at the Whitby Club."

"That club doesn't admit ladies inside," she noted. "So I gather I'm to find my own way in."

He smiled, and his implication was clear. *Impress me.*

"Who's your guest?" she asked, knowing he wouldn't tell her outright.

"Someone who will help you."

She raised her chin. "You trained me to always work alone."

"This time is different."

"Will he understand what I am?"

"I expect you'll make that quite clear yourself."

"So what is he, then?"

"Someone you'll need to know in order to complete this assignment. And that is all," Julian said, irritation making him curt. "Eleven o'clock tonight, Sophie."

She stood up. "Well, I do like to make an entrance. I'll see you then."

Chapter 2

♏

Bruce Allander, Lord Forester, was six feet three inches tall, and every inch of him was in pain. He winced as he removed his boots. He was too disgusted with his state to wait for his valet to get started.

It was mid-afternoon, but he felt as if it had been days since he sat down, not mere hours. He was sweating from the hot summer sun, and his bones ached from the day of physical labor. His skin, naturally prone to tanning, was nearly olive at this point in the summer.

"Good God, what was I thinking?" he asked, groaning.

It was a rhetorical question, but that had never stopped his longtime valet, Lawrence, from replying. "You were thinking, my lord, if the field wasn't cleared by autumn, it would be another year before it could yield a successful crop." The man, almost ascetically thin and a foot shorter than his master, did not look the least bit intimidated. He had no reason to be, having known Bruce from an infant.

"It seemed like such a good idea this morning," Bruce

said. He leaned back in the chair for a moment, feeling his spine protest. He couldn't be getting old, he thought. Not yet. He was only thirty-three.

"As an idea, it was perfectly sound." Lawrence offered his employer a clean towel to wipe the worst of the sweat from his face. "But I don't understand why you had to clear it yourself, sir."

The last word was stressed lightly, a reminder that Bruce was indeed lord of the manor…specifically, a viscount. Such labor was beneath the dignity of his station. Bruce didn't care. He did plenty of things ostensibly beneath his station, and most of them were far more demeaning than working the land.

He wiped his face with the towel, inhaling the clean, slightly harsh smell of laundry soap. The move made a few strands of midnight black hair fall into his face. Lawrence would soon be hounding him to see it was cut. Bruce often avoided the task, never wishing to sit still longer than necessary.

He handed the towel back to his valet and said, "You know why I do it. I want to run this estate well. That means being out there, working with the tenants, seeing the problems. Not merely sitting around collecting all the rents."

"Yes, sir." Lawrence had the gift of agreeing with his master in a way such that his complete disagreement was clear. He was a perfect valet. "Oh, this arrived while you were grubbing stumps out of the dirt." He felt in his pocket and handed Bruce a folded, sealed letter. "Came about an hour ago. I would have sent one of the boys out to find you, but I knew you wouldn't last much longer out there."

Bruce looked at the seal, a rough outline of a goat's head. *Aries.* He ripped the note open and read it over. "Well, there goes my evening of leisure. I'm going into London. Leaving within the hour if I'm to be there in time."

"I'll prepare your things." Lawrence sighed. "I do recommend you make use of the bath that's already been drawn. Unless you're heading to some dank part of London." Lawrence held the opinion that all of London was rather dank. The valet much preferred the bucolic world of Old Harrow, the Allander family's estate. He walked away to assemble what Bruce would need.

Bruce ripped up the note and silently cursed his decision to work in the fields that day. Even with a bath and a change of clothes, he'd be tired and barely presentable for his meeting with Aries. But then again, Julian had seen him look worse…much worse.

As promised, within the hour Bruce was in his coach, being driven to London. That was one thing about working for the Zodiac…it was never dull. Bruce tossed around potential ideas for the assignment Julian would give him. He liked to guess as many scenarios as possible, though he was still often surprised at the real assignments.

Some were strange, some required months of planning, and others only took the space of one evening. But none of them were trivial. That was all that mattered.

The coach made good time. He didn't have the opportunity to stop at his townhome, but he arrived at the Whitby Club a little early. The club was housed in an under-stated, gracious building of red brick. Inside, he was directed immediately up to the top floor, where Julian awaited him in a small but richly furnished private room. The chamber was paneled in oak, and the upholstered leather chairs and rich appointments made it clear this was a haven for gentlemen only.

Julian nodded as Bruce entered. "Ah, you were able to make it after all," he said, as if they were merely wasting an evening in town.

With admirable timing, a man in butler's attire appeared in the doorway as soon as Bruce seated himself. Julian caught the man's eye. "Did you want something to drink, Forester?" he asked.

"Scotch." Bruce sat down in a leather chair opposite Julian, noticing another chair had been moved nearby. Someone else was joining them? That was unusual.

"Scotch for the gentleman." Julian gave the order and the butler nodded before closing the door.

"Sorry about the short notice," Julian said then. "Did I drag you away from anything?"

"Only a farm field."

"What were you doing there?"

"Mostly clearing out boulders and tree stumps," Bruce said, his muscles still hurting. "I suppose I should thank you."

"Don't thank me yet. You don't know what I'm going to ask you."

"Ask away."

Julian shook his head. "I prefer not to repeat myself.

We're awaiting one more person…who I hope will arrive soon."

At that moment, the door opened again, and Julian waved a hand for silence. A young man in servant's clothes entered, bearing a tray holding a decanter of fine scotch and a few glasses. He poured one and silently handed it to Bruce.

He tossed half of it back, and the warm liquor instantly banished some of the ache from his body. "Ah, that's better."

Julian was looking hard at the waiter, who had not yet left the room. Instead, he was pouring another glass, despite the fact that both men had their drinks. Bruce frowned. The *Whitby Club should supply a better class of servant*, he thought. Then the young man turned around, smiling lazily.

"How do you like my entrance, Julian?" The voice was feminine and suggestive. Bruce was at a complete loss. The waiter was no boy at all. It was a woman.

Julian just laughed, his face losing years of tension at the woman's question. "*Very* good," he said approvingly. "Even I had to look twice." He held out his glass. "Actually, even though it's not your real job, would you mind?" The woman refilled it without taking her eyes off Bruce.

His own eyes narrowed as he examined her from head to foot. It was undoubtedly a woman. A beautiful woman, at least from what he could see. The men's clothes fit her well. She was tall, perhaps only a half foot shy of his own considerable height, which aided her deception. She was on the slender side, but the fine shape of her legs was now obvious through the fabric of the breeches, and he could see the outline of her calves under the thin stockings. Her jacket and ruffled shirt were cut just a bit large, presumably to conceal feminine curves. Above the collar, her slender neck rose up to a face that was lovely, now that he was looking properly. He wondered how he'd missed it when she first arrived. High cheekbones. Patrician nose. Lips far too full for a boy. But her hair…

Short, dark hair was cut close around her head, nearly as short as a man's, but still oddly feminine. Was that her real hair? Had she actually chopped it off to impersonate a young man as a prank? What sort of woman did that?

He looked into her large, light brown eyes and found his answer. There was a challenge there. A dare. Bruce was intrigued.

Julian was actively enjoying his discomfort, or the woman's attitude, or both. "Scorpio, meet Libra."

Bruce couldn't hide his surprise. "She's a sign of the Zodiac?" *That* changed things.

"I am," Libra replied. "And it is perfectly acceptable to speak to me directly."

"Sophie, be kind. You do astound, after all."

Astounding was a good word for her. Bruce had no idea what to say. He began, "I never thought the Zodiac would hire a woman as an agent…"

"No one ever does," Sophie said. She tilted her head up proudly. "Which is why I'm so effective."

Bruce didn't doubt that.

Julian explained, "You can see, Forester. Libra will be a valuable asset in this assignment, where the element of surprise will be the most vital weapon you have."

"It's been very useful to me so far," Sophie said. She frowned at their superior. "So why are you bringing him into our confidence?"

Julian said with the formality of introduction, "Bruce Allander, Viscount Forester, is the fifth person in the world to know your code name. I chose him for a reason, and not without due consideration."

"Hmm." Sophie walked over to the other empty chair in the room and sat down, letting the servant's deference slide from her bones though without regaining the customary mannerisms of a lady. Bruce could still see the outlines of her body. It was damned distracting, and highly improper for any woman.

Her next words, however, brought him back to reality. "I know what I'm capable of. So what…assets will his lordship bring to the cause?" she asked, disdain and contempt dancing in her tone. There was the tiniest hint of a foreign accent in her voice. He wondered where she came from, and why the Zodiac would hire someone from abroad. Or was it a distraction as well?

Julian explained his plan. "Forester has been in the field for over a decade as a Zodiac agent, and has done extremely well. You seize opportunity, he plans down to the minute. You have a gift for improvisation, and his gift is experience. Further, he never forgets a thing."

"True," Bruce added quietly, looking down at his drink. And he planned to remember everything about this woman.

Julian went on, "His skills complement your own.

Without his knowledge and expertise, you cannot hope to succeed in this next assignment."

She snorted delicately, but said nothing more.

Bruce said, "What is this, Julian? You'd better explain why we're both here."

"You're both going on an assignment. Together."

Bruce recoiled. "We don't do that. I always work alone."

"I seem to remember a time in Calais, not that long ago, when you and Sagittarius worked together," Julian retorted.

Sophie's eyes flickered at that statement, with what Bruce presumed was curiosity.

"I was doing a favor for a friend," he said dismissively. "An unusual situation."

Julian would not be dissuaded. "So is this one."

"But why do I need a penny stage actress to tag along?"

"Penny stage actress?!" Sophie sat up straight in her chair and glared at him. All pretense of laziness was gone. That had gotten a rise out of her. It must be true, Bruce thought.

Julian held up his hands and stopped them both before blood could be drawn. "For the love of God, listen to me. Sophie, I told you how urgent this is. Now let me fill Bruce in on the details."

He turned to Bruce and told him about the rogue cabinet member.

Bruce was troubled. "How could such a thing happen? Surely all the cabinet members are trustworthy."

"Sophie said much the same thing. And yet, someone has promised to support the Emperor in exchange for money...and presumably protection. We need to know who it is. I'm convinced the answer lies in the house where you'll be going in order to complete the assignment. A name, a document. As quiet as all this has been kept, there is proof somewhere. Countries don't change allies on a handshake. Someone has kept records, made some payments, or carried out promises. I want proof."

"I'll find it," Bruce assured him.

"It gets worse," Sophie added.

Julian mentioned the specter of Arceneau meddling in politics.

Bruce knew the name. "If he's involved, we have to assume he'll kill to get what he wants."

"Oh, he has people who kill for pleasure," Sophie said quietly.

"You know of him?"

"More than you do," she returned, her expression lofty.

"Enough," Julian said. "There's going to be a gathering hosted by a man named Thomas Theriot at a place called Carterhaugh Manor."

"Never heard of it."

"That's because it's in the middle of nowhere in the north. A vast estate that once rivaled the palaces of Europe, but it's been long past its glory."

"What sort of gathering?" Sophie asked.

"A number of wealthy and socially influential people—a few British-born citizens, but largely French expatriates who have since claimed to be loyal to Britain. They have been invited for a month-long house party. You'll join them."

"And do what, exactly?"

"Your task is two-fold. Find out whether the guests intend to join any sort of plot or conspiracy run by Theriot. And get your hands on whatever documents Theriot has identifying the cabinet member."

"That sounds like quite a lot of information to gather," Bruce noted.

"Precisely why you're going to be there, Scorpio. I know you're the best man for this sort of work."

Sophie glanced at Bruce again, more inquisitively. "And while he's playing clerk, I'm to distract Theriot?"

"You're both responsible for every aspect of the assignment. Retrieving proof of the traitor is the first priority. Work together."

She leaned forward. "I agree it's important to find the proof, but I don't understand why it must be *two* agents. I could easily get in on my own."

Julian held up one hand. "Doubtless, except the guest list is very exclusive. So you'll both be replacing someone already on that list. Sophie, you'll impersonate the woman: Madame Marianne Cassou. I have her description, as well as her wardrobe. You'll be able to mimic her very well with a proper wig and clothing. Bruce has the right height and look to pass himself off as the other guest. And you both speak French fluently. That's vital. With the sort of people who are expected to attend, you'll likely have to conduct yourselves entirely in French at least some of the time."

"Not an issue for me," she said, confirming Bruce's guess that she actually *was* French.

"And you both must be very careful. Arceneau is smarter than the average man. His proxy will be intelligent as well, and the number of guests means you can never let down your guard."

Julian pulled something out of his pocket. He presented each agent with a small object. "Take these."

Sophie looked at the gold ring with an expression of revulsion. Bruce was no more pleased at the ring in his hand, clearly the match of the one she'd been given.

"Exactly what are these for?" he asked.

"What do you think? You'll be masquerading as a married couple."

"You can't be serious," Sophie said, eyeing Bruce.

"I agree," he said. "What man in his right mind would marry *that*?"

Sophie's eyes narrowed dangerously.

"Forester, you'll be acting as Theodore Cassou. The Cassou couple were the only potential guests the Zodiac could make use of. And together, it's far less likely either of you will be thought a spy."

Bruce was annoyed to discover his ring fit perfectly.

Sophie slid her ring on as well. "It's a bit loose," she said to Julian, shaking her hand experimentally.

"That's because you still don't eat enough, Sophie." His offhand comment needled Bruce for some reason. Why would Julian even know how much Sophie ate?

From the look that flitted across her face, the comment

flustered her. She must be sensitive about her size. And her stage actress past. Bruce filed those items away to think about later.

Julian described his plan in detail. Bruce saw a significant flaw in it, namely that he'd have to work with Sophie to accomplish the goals.

"As I say, you're going to impersonate a couple with links to the conspiracy. Madame Cassou seems to have maintained some correspondence with Theriot, thus securing the invitation. We need to know what he thinks she'll provide him."

Sophie's eyes were intent. "And is her husband a willing partner in this endeavor?"

"We're not sure," Julian admitted.

"Oh, that's grand," Sophie muttered. "So we don't even know which of us is supposed to be the traitor?"

Julian shot her a dark look, but said, "We got the best information we could, dear Sophie."

Bruce broke in, "Speaking of Cassou, where is he? The real one, I mean?"

"Abroad—quite safe and out of the way. I called in a favor to delay the couple with some bureaucratic nonsense in Austria. They won't be able to travel for at least three weeks. That's your opportunity to finish the assignment."

"I still don't see the need for two of us. Let me go alone," Sophie told Julian. "Scorpio can stay home…and out of my way."

"No," Julian said flatly.

"Better yet, send the lady back to the stage and let me

get to work," Bruce said, keeping his voice low. "I'm using the term *lady* as a courtesy, of course."

Sophie got up, glaring at him.

"I'm done here," she snapped. She walked to the door, then turned back. "This is a bad idea, Julian."

With those words, she glided out of the room, leaving a faint scent of perfume and scotch in her wake.

Chapter 3

♏

AFTER SOPHIE SHUT THE DOOR, Bruce said to Julian, "She doesn't appear to like your plan."

"I'd say she doesn't appear to like *you*," Julian noted. "I thought you'd both get on better than that."

Bruce shifted uncomfortably. "Surprise, maybe. She'll get used to the idea by the time we leave." He hoped. Sophie as an antagonist would be hell on a man.

"I hope so. Sophie's a practical girl. One of the reasons I like her so well is because she has no illusions."

"So she won't be confused by the roles we'll be playing?" The last thing Bruce needed was a woman playing at marriage and misunderstanding the reality.

"Sophie? God, no."

"Then why not send her alone, if she's so skilled? It could be explained away if her husband didn't join her. Not that I'm begging off the assignment," he added.

"Sophie has always been remarkably independent, even more so than other agents," Julian said. "It's a point of pride for her. But for a few reasons, I'd feel better this time if someone else had eyes on her—and vice versa."

"I see," Bruce said evenly. "Well, I have two days. I'll get to work now."

He left the briefing fuming inwardly. Libra would be a problem. Julian's plan, as it was outlined, did require them to act together. But Bruce would see another path once he scouted out the situation. One that would work on his terms. He could send the woman back with instructions to go play at being a spy somewhere else, where the stakes were not quite so high.

A fine mist was falling from the sky when he hit the streets. Bruce was so lost in thought that he almost walked past his own house in town. He turned in abruptly at the gate, and stalked through the front gardens. He decided to go round back and let himself in with his own key. No need to rouse the house's servants when he was perfectly capable of tending to his own needs.

He had just reached the glass door to the conservatory when he heard a small, out-of-place sound. Every danger sense he had clamored at him. He whirled around, ready to strike at whoever was there.

It was Sophie, though she looked nothing like before. Now she looked rather like a ghost in a pale gown and long, dark tresses just visible beneath a very ladylike hat. Struck by her unexpectedly feminine appearance, Bruce just stopped himself from delivering a blow—though she probably deserved it, stalking up behind him like that. She should know how fast a trained agent could be.

For her part, Sophie stepped back, but looked smug. "I

see you noticed me at last."

"How long have you been following me?"

"Since you left the Whitby Club, of course. I changed, and then watched for you to leave. Of course, there was no guarantee you would head directly home."

"What are you doing here?"

"We need to talk," she said calmly.

"So talk."

"Perhaps you would be so kind as to invite me inside?"

She had a point. He hadn't a care for the light rain while walking home, but now he felt it beginning to cling. "Very well." He turned the key in the lock and opened the door, ushering Sophie through first.

The conservatory was a haven of luscious smells and quiet, damp earthiness. "This is much better," she said, looking around the darkened area. He took note of her socially acceptable garb: a light cotton gown and little soft leather slippers. Ladies would not walk the distance he just covered. Yet Sophie had. She took off her hat and held it delicately in gloved hands, looking for a place to put it down. Everything about her now suggested a well-bred woman.

"How did you…change so quickly?" he asked, curious despite himself. Sophie had been dressed as a footman, and now there was no trace of her former persona. The hair had to be a wig, yet he would have sworn it was real.

"It's not such a trick." Her voice held a slight accent, hinting again at her French heritage. "It's second nature to me now."

He wondered what her first nature was. What lady willingly went into his Majesty's service, leaving all normal life behind? Forester found himself searching for her eyes in the darkness. "Take my arm. I wouldn't want you to trip. There's a bench over at the end of the row. We can talk there, So...I can't call you Sophie. What's your family name?"

"Bertrand," she replied. "But you *can* call me Sophie. It's not as if I'm a lady." Her tone was both amused and a little bitter.

"Miss Bertrand," he said firmly. Just as if they were at a society event, he led her to the iron bench, cushioned comfortably for anyone who wished to sit and admire the plants. The conservatory had been a pet project of his late mother's, and Bruce kept it up as a sort of memorial to her. He rarely set foot in it himself.

Sophie let her eyes adjust to the dim light and sank to the bench, laying the hat to one side.

"You wanted to talk," Bruce said coolly. "I'm all ears." With nowhere else to go, he sat beside her on the bench, closer than social convention would dictate.

"You resent me," she started. "I feel the same way."

He said nothing, but he immediately tensed up. How dare she tell him what he was thinking?

Sophie went on, "Let's begin again. Aries has a flair for the dramatic. He was the one who suggested I make a surprising entrance. But I see now that's not the way to deal with you. We're both used to working alone. I'm still not sure this assignment requires us to act together, but Aries planned it that way, and he has never steered me wrong before."

"Nor me," Bruce admitted. "If he wants us to work together, I'll trust him. For now."

"Good. Now, to cut line. You don't trust me."

He pulled back, offended. "What did I just say? If Aries…"

"I mean, you don't trust me because I'm a woman." She held up a slim, gloved hand. "My methods are different. You don't know how to treat me because in your world, either among the gentry or in the military, there are no women in a position quite like mine. True?"

There were always female informants and the like, but a long-term, professional spy in a group like the Zodiac? He doubted it. "I suppose you're correct."

"Good," she said. "Now, I'll tell you this once. I am a sign of the Zodiac. Think of me like any other agent. Not as a woman. Not as some vaporish lady. There's nothing you can do that I can't, understand?"

Bruce was conscious of a heat rising from her agitated body, of a pleasant scent—half liquor, half perfume—floating on her skin. In the dark, he couldn't see her eyes well, but he could feel her gaze on him.

He caught her hand in the middle of an empathetic gesture. "I'll admit, I have difficulty thinking of you as just another agent."

"What are you doing?" She struggled to free herself from his hold. Bruce felt the veneer of civilization slide away, replaced by something far more primitive set off by her intoxicating scent. "You say there's nothing I can do you can't? Prove it to me."

"How?" Sophie asked, a bit breathlessly.

"If you are an agent, and you are captured," he said as he tightened his grip on her hands, "how will you get free, for instance…if I kissed you?" He found her mouth in the dark, and claimed it.

She didn't recoil. Instead she leaned into him, seeking more of him. Her lips parted. His hands shifted to catch her waist, pulling her closer. She wrapped her now freed arms about his neck, not breaking the kiss.

Bruce forgot his challenge. Sophie was a dream come to life. He grasped her slender waist, lifted her so she sat on his lap. She met him willingly, even eagerly, twining her arms around him, giving him her mouth, letting him taste her sweetness. Her weight settled comfortably across his thighs, and he felt the warmth of her body through the flimsy gown. He hardened at the thought of her beautiful legs wrapped around him. It would be so easy, here in the dark, damp warmth of the conservatory.

She took her arms away from his neck for a moment. He felt her stroke down the length of him, questing, feeling the muscles ripple under her quick, light fingers. A teasing, almost hesitant touch, even through the heavy woolen fabric, made him groan. He blinked and saw her eyes glittering in the dimness. Then he felt a cold blade against his throat.

"I'll get free by using your weaknesses to my advantage," Sophie hissed, holding a knife expertly against his skin. *His* knife. The witch had pulled it from his boot.

She didn't move the blade, even as she climbed off him, shaking her skirts free with one hand. "Well, I am disappointed. You're so proud to be a sign of the Zodiac, but you're no different from the rest. French, German, English…just men after all."

She stepped back, still holding the knife at the ready. "Here's my proposition." She drawled out the double entendre. "We have the target of the assignment. We have the same information. We're on the same side. Are we not on perfectly equal ground?"

"I'll show you ground," Bruce growled, yet not moving toward her.

"I propose a race. Whoever brings the information back to Aries first wins the prize."

"What's the prize?"

"Why, the honor to continue in his Majesty's service," she said. "The loser will resign, and everyone who matters will know why. Agreed?"

"You're digging your own grave," he warned her.

Sophie's lips curved into a strange smile. "I've already done that, my lord." She stepped back again. "May the best spy win!" She dropped the dagger at his feet, and was gone.

Chapter 4

♎

Sophie fled the greenhouse, emerging into the near-darkness of the city night. Her heart was racing, only partly due to the fear that Forester would follow her outside and respond to the more violent part of her challenge. She shouldn't have threatened him with the dagger. But she'd been so…angry.

"*Enfer et damnation!*" she muttered. She had hoped this man would be different. From the way Julian talked about him, he was remarkable. And at first, when she examined Bruce, she liked what she saw. His thick hair was jet black, meant to be short but in need of a trim. The sharp planes of his face were compelling, and without really being handsome, he still rated a second look. Then she saw his eyes. Hard and dark, they were the eyes of a man who did things his own way. Like her. She thought she might have found an ally.

Then he opened his mouth.

Obviously, the initial meeting hadn't gone well. Sophie was irritated by Lord Forester's…well, lordliness. He called her a penny stage actress! He might as well have called her a prostitute, for all the contempt in his voice. True, she *was* a lowly actress's daughter, and an actress herself sometimes. But he didn't have to insult her about it. He seemed not to have any respect for Sophie's abilities.

Still, she knew she was partly at fault, considering her flamboyant entrance. People didn't like to be made fools of, and she'd forced the issue with her too-clever disguise.

The thought of their private encounter brought her back to the kiss. He knew what he was doing in that respect, at least. Feeling him kiss her, hold her, Sophie was initially transfixed. She felt her body respond to his kiss even while her mind struggled to find an answer to his challenge. How would she get free? Did she *want* to get free? She had kissed many men before, but not like this. He was different.

Then, of course, the answer came to her. He wasn't any different. She regained her equilibrium even as she continued to respond to him. He didn't even notice when the seduction shifted to her control. He probably thought he was winning right up until she put the blade to his throat.

She walked on. The rain drizzled down in a fine, light mist. The sheen of water turned London into a dark, glistening onyx carving of a city. Most streets weren't lit, but those that were gleamed in the night, the puddles mirroring the lights and adding to the glow. Some carriages were equipped with lanterns, and those lights floated by like fairies in the dark. She wasn't in a mood to appreciate it.

Sophie kept her head down, returning to familiar streets. So disappointing! Yet why had she really thought he'd be different? She'd felt him looking at her when he realized who and what she was. She knew he wanted her.

"*Enfer et damnation*," she repeated. This time she'd really made life difficult. Was it smart to antagonize him as she had? Especially when the world was so uncertain? No. The war would get worse, not better, over the next few years. The Emperor would never rest until he conquered everything Caesar had before him—or until he could be stopped. Arceneau and other criminals like him would always look to take advantage of the chaos. And Sophie, who had lived through the Terror and seen the worst of what could happen as regimes changed, knew she had to do everything she could to prevent such a thing from happening again.

The rain stopped by the time she got home. Her rooms were on the third floor of a boarding house quite close to the Pavilion Theatre, where she sometimes worked. Most of the boarders were actors and actresses. Sophie was the longest-running tenant. Because she always paid promptly (thanks to the Zodiac's support) and because she never invited men over, she was a favorite of the landlady. Mrs Duckett always saw to it that Sophie had a bit of cold supper—no matter what strange hours she kept—and that none of the other boarders ever bothered her or invaded her rooms.

Sophie sometimes felt sorry for the landlady, who didn't even know Sophie's real name—only her stage name of Sarah Finn. But she did want to be as invisible as possible.

Her rooms looked more like a storage closet than a

place where someone actually lived. Wooden crates and leather-bound trunks were stacked upon each other, and hatboxes competed for space with carved wooden forms of heads, each topped with a wig. The wigs alone cost more than her annual rent, for they were elaborate works of craftsmanship. Most featured thick brown hair in varying shades, but there were a couple of blonde heads as well, and even one ginger. Sophie smiled at them, remembering each assignment she'd used them on.

The cascading chestnut curls bound up with a gold circlet...she'd worn that one when she had gatecrashed a debutante's ball and snuck into the study of the young lady's father, who had been embezzling funds from the Navy. She left out the window, but with the evidence she needed.

The wavy blonde locks she'd once worn with a liberty gown...that time she'd charmed a portly minister who blabbed to the wrong people. She soon learned all his secrets, and she never laid a finger on him.

And the auburn curls. Sophie only wore that wig for one assignment, when she spent a full week working her way into the confidence of a shrewd lady who nevertheless had a weakness...for redheads. Sophie learned a *lot* on that assignment, only some of it related to the state secrets the woman held. And as usual, she came away with the information the Zodiac asked her to get.

There was no assignment Sophie couldn't complete in one way or another.

However, impersonation, theft, and seduction were far from her only talents. She had a public life as well, in part to distract people from her real calling. As Sarah Finn, she appeared quite regularly on some of the less prestigious London stages. She was known for her ability to play both breeches parts and comic roles, as well as for her skills in costuming. Most of the people in the boarding house knew Sophie as either an actress or a seamstress making costumes for theaters.

Certainly, the wigs and the many outfits and odd props in her rooms bolstered that impression. The rare times Sophie was available to eat at the common table, she regaled the others with tales of her theatrical exploits both in Paris and in England. Most of those stories were absolutely true.

Sophie had grown up in theaters, among the actors and playwrights and characters who populated that world. They accepted young Sophie into the loose family of the theater. She played many child roles on stage, even when the play didn't actually list such a part. Sophie was clever at making even non-speaking roles compelling, just by the way she stood or moved on the stage.

Her mother had been an excellent actress herself, playing aristocrats and beauties on the stage in Paris. She had admirers, rich men who supported her with gifts. Sophie knew full well what happened when her mother left her night after night to join a gentleman for supper and then in his private rooms. *I'm doing this for you, my love,* her mother would say, giving Sophie a new jewel or a bit of money to keep safe. *When we've saved enough, we'll leave and travel wherever we want. We'll dress like princesses and everyone will call you Lady Sophia, you'll see.*

But then the king was killed, and his queen. Young Sophie watched as revolutionary fervor took over the city of Paris. As a child, she didn't understand why so many were deemed enemies of the state. But she knew things had become dangerous.

Even so, nothing prepared her for the day when her own mother was taken. Sophie watched in horror as her mother was declared an infiltrator, a royalist sympathizer...even one of the hated aristocrats herself. "No!" her mother had screamed. "You don't understand. I'm an actress! They are roles I play! Please, let me go!"

They did not let her go.

And young Sophie was soon left to fend for herself, living on the streets and in the theaters of Paris. She survived by her looks and her wits.

Until she met *him.*

Sophie sat lost in thought, remembering the most important evening of her young life. The man had seen through her act and invited her to London. Sophie closed her eyes, recalling the evening as if in a dream...

She was startled by a knock on the door. She sat up, finding that she'd actually fallen asleep fully clothed. It was already early morning, to judge by the light in her room. "Hello?" Sophie said.

"Miss Finn?" the landlady called. "There's a delivery for you downstairs."

Despite the early hour, Mrs Duckett smiled at her favorite when Sophie opened the door. "A number of trunks were brought up to the door. Starting a new show, are you?"

"Yes, I am," Sophie said, thinking quickly. "The northern circuit, so I'll be gone for a few weeks. Let me see the delivery."

Sophie shook off her grogginess and accompanied the landlady downstairs, to find someone she didn't expect. It was Chattan. "Hello, Miss Finn," she said, speaking to Sophie as if she were a stranger. "I have the items you'll need for your next production."

Sophie nodded back. "How many trunks?" she asked.

"Three. Mostly costumes and a few props. You can be assured of their authenticity, as they came from the source."

Sophie raised an eyebrow. Did Chattan mean someone had actually stolen some of Madame Cassou's clothing? "I hope there was no trouble acquiring the items," she said.

"None at all." The other woman handed Sophie a thick packet. "The script and such. You're to look that over."

"I know what I'm doing," Sophie said. She was constantly annoyed by Chattan's insinuations that she was not up to snuff—the woman had never warmed to her. But Sophie knew how to study for a role, and she would dutifully read up on everything Madame Cassou was known to do: appearance, habits of dress, even food preferences. "I'll be prepared by the time I need to leave." As if this was her first assignment! She'd been doing this for years now.

"Remember, you will not be traveling alone," Chattan said then, her expression smug.

"I can take care of myself."

"It's not you I'm concerned about." With those words, Chattan turned around and left. Sophie watched her, wondering what she meant. If she wasn't concerned about Sophie, who did she care about? Forester?

Sophie surveyed the massive trunks. She had less than two days to become someone else and begin an assignment that might end a war. And she had to drag a lord along with her. Unfortunately, the strapping Viscount Forester did not look like he'd be easy to drag anywhere.

Chapter 5

♏

After the damnable Sophie dashed off into the night, Bruce remained in the conservatory. He was furious, both at her mockery and his own behavior. He'd meant to prove a point, and instead got completely distracted.

Bruce eventually retired, but his night was restless. He didn't dream of Sophie. But he had far too many questions about her and the assignment to sleep well.

The brilliant summer dawn in no way improved Bruce's attitude toward the assignment or the woman he was supposed to work with. He couldn't keep all his thoughts to himself.

He went into the city to search out one of his most trusted friends. Sebastien Thorne was a peer like himself, as well as a member of the Zodiac. A second son with few expectations, Sebastien had indulged his vices for years, gambling and relying on his wits to get him through life. But a few events had forced him to grow up quickly, and now he was as reliable as he'd once been scandalous. Not that Sebastien would be particularly pleased to be told so. He still affected the airs of a careless rake, using his good looks (considerably better than Bruce's own looks, he could candidly admit) to get what he wanted.

Bruce, on the other hand, relied far more on preparation beforehand, and at the last ditch, on his physicality.

He was taller and broader than nearly all his friends, and he knew he could affect people's dispositions merely by standing up. And if that didn't work, he knew how to fight. Though he was not violent by nature, he understood violence as a tool. It was one of the first lessons he'd learned in life.

But violence was the furthest thing from his mind when his saw his friend in the small room at the club where they were both members. The other man looked up at Bruce's greeting and a smile spread across his face. "Forester! I thought you were out of town."

"I'm about to be, actually. I paid a call to the Quince Street house and they told me you were here." He paused. "Shouldn't you be up in Cheshire?"

Thorne's smile grew beatific at the thought of his estate, where his wife no doubt waited. "I would like to be, but some business intervened." He looked carefully at Bruce. "Is, ah…business why you're here?"

After verifying that no one would hear the two talk, Bruce nodded. "I got a new assignment. I can't tell you much—"

His friend waved a hand to indicate he understood.

"But it's unusual, and I'm not sure why Julian's doing it this way."

Sebastien arched an eyebrow curiously. "How so?"

"This isn't a solo assignment. It's me and another agent."

"I'm listening."

"I know you left the field after we went to Calais this spring." Bruce had actually joined Sebastien for the last part of the job, when they retrieved a vital asset of British intelligence—a captivating woman who became Thorne's wife shortly thereafter.

Sebastien nodded. "I was of two minds about it, but it's for the best. I'm going to train new agents. We're a bit short of men at the moment."

"We are?"

"Did you know Capricorn is dead?" Sebastien said the words calmly, but his hands were clenched.

"When?"

"Last week, in Paris. And Pisces nearly lost his life a few months ago. *And* our newest recruit isn't ready for the field yet. We can't stand to lose more men," he said. "Aries is worried about what's happened. If you're to work as a pair, it's for protection."

Sebastien's use of the word *men* made Bruce ask, "You don't know with whom I'm assigned to work?"

"There's no reason for me to know the tasks for active agents." He gave an eloquent shrug.

"That doesn't bother you at all?"

"The secrecy? Sometimes. I wonder how much is necessary, and how much is tradition. But I'm not in charge. My job is to find new men to bring in as potential agents and train them. Thank God I know you're out there working. I can trust you to be careful."

Bruce nodded, slightly reassured. Of course, even if *he* were trusted, that still left the French-born Sophie, who might very well have conflicting loyalties.

The discussion with his friend left Bruce with even more questions. He returned to his townhome, knowing he had plenty of work to do before actually traveling to-ward Carterhaugh Manor for the assignment, with Sophie in tow.

Fortunately, Bruce didn't need to return to Old Harrow before embarking on the assignment. In truth, he was nearly always ready to leave the place, even though he'd grown up there and loved the land dearly.

It had become disquieting, his time at the estate. Since the death of his mother, he was the only Allander left in the house. After a painful scandal, his brother vowed he'd never set foot on the property again, and Bruce never ran into him in London. Unlike Sebastien, who had a loving family and now a new wife, Bruce had no one to think about other than himself.

Old Harrow was home, but it no longer felt like home. The people were always welcoming. Many of the servants he'd known from childhood, and they'd lived on the same land as long as his own family had. But it wasn't the same. Bruce strived to make it a stronger, more profitable estate. He wasn't sure why, though. He had no heirs to pass it on to. His younger brother Ashley hadn't mar-ried…and honestly, no proper lady would have him. So the honor of the family name remained for Bruce to hold. He'd make Old Harrow a model of modern agriculture, and when he eventually left the Zodiac, surely there would still be time to start a family. It was, after all, his duty. He'd fulfill that duty some day, but not until he was done with his current work.

His house in town was modest. Bruce never enter-tained, so he didn't require much space. His servants were very few, although he did maintain his own equipage and horses in town, thus requiring the additional services of a hostler and a stable boy. But other than that, he made do with very few trappings of wealth. Only his work as an agent, as well as his impatience with the idea of always hiring a ride, kept the house in town looking active at all.

He was greeted at the front door by the housekeeper, a woman of deceptively severe appearance. "Welcome back, my lord," she said, after closing the door.

He nodded briefly, preoccupied. "I plan to work in my study for a while. I'll ring for supper later."

Satisfied that his household would run as smoothly as ever, he went upstairs.

As was his practice, he shut himself up in his study. It was a small, square room on the upper floor. The room was specially designed to reflect the perfect symmetry of classical architecture. The fireplace occupied the precise center third of the wall, flanked by equally wide book-shelves on either side. A window opposite was the same width as the fireplace, and two landscapes of the same dimensions hung on either side. A desk sat directly in front of the window, facing out to catch the light. On the other end, exactly one chair faced the fireplace, with a square side table at each arm. Nothing was out of place, and everything was in balance. Bruce liked it that way.

Bruce went to the desk and spread out all the papers he had relating to the assignment. He began reading me-thodically, committing fact after fact to memory, even those that seemed—at first glance—to be totally irrele-vant. His household knew nothing of his work with the

Zodiac, but everyone knew better than to disturb him when he closed the door to the study, even if hours elapsed before he came out.

As he read, he put a hand in his pocket and found the gold ring. He slipped it on. The metal was cool at first, the edges of the ring catching on his skin. He twisted it around his finger, trying to get used to the feeling. The raised pattern of stylized stars was unremarkable, but it brought his thoughts back to the Zodiac. Would Sophie find her own ring as strange as he did? Could he really pretend such an odd, recalcitrant woman was his wife? And could she possibly be such a talented actress that she could pass herself off as a titled lady?

True, she had looked ladylike in the conservatory, at least at first. But it hadn't taken long to show her true colors as a duplicitous woman…who wasn't the least bit seduced by him.

Bruce refused to admit his dislike of her might have something to do with that. He wasn't that petty. Or egotistical. Was he?

He shook his head. Sophie's seductiveness had worked only because she was so unexpected. He knew about her now and wouldn't have the same reaction again. Besides, she wasn't that attractive. Too skinny, too tall. Too disdainful.

He abruptly yanked the ring off his finger, concealing it in his pocket again. Yes, convincing anyone he'd married a woman who looked like Sophie was going to be the most challenging part of the assignment by far. Everything else would be simple.

Chapter 6

Ω

ON THE DAY SHE WAS to leave for Carterhaugh Manor, Sophie dressed in an elegant traveling costume from her new collection. The weave of the gown was mercifully light, appropriate for hot summer days, and it was dyed a rather pretty sky blue, which contrasted with her brown eyes and the light brown hair of the wig she now wore. Her hat was stylish, bleached white straw covered with fine cotton and a hint of lace that shielded the top half of her face. It softened her appearance and gave her anonymity, which she preferred. Sophie was always happier when most of her was concealed in some way.

Her shoes were her own, but the white leather matched perfectly. She kept the diamond necklace she would wear as Madame Cassou safe in her reticule. It was expensive, and Sophie didn't see the point in provoking any possible theft. She would wear the necklace when she arrived at Carterhaugh Manor.

The last thing she packed was an ornately carved wooden box, which she slipped into the small case she would keep in the carriage next to her. She smiled, remembering the day she met the person who gave it to her.

Young Sophie knew the elderly man who brought the big trunks to the theater was different. He was not an actor. He was not a playwright. He was not a dancer or a lecturer. He was a magician.

She hid on one of the catwalks above the stage and watched in awe as the man ran through magic tricks in the otherwise empty theater. Seeing the work behind the magic in no way lessened her astonishment.

At one point, the magician tossed a live bird into the air and it flew up, up into the rafters. The wings beat so near Sophie's face she could not suppress a yelp of surprise.

"It won't hurt you, dear," the man called from below. "But if you come down, my little dove will not stay up in the rafters when I have work to do."

Young Sophie asked indignantly, "You knew I was here the whole time?"

"A magician must always be aware of his audience, my dear...even when his audience is one hidden little girl." The old man laughed delightedly.

"Is all your magic just tricks?" Sophie asked, even as she began to climb down the ladder to the stage.

When she stood before him, the old man looked her up and down. "Not tricks. *Illusion*! It's an art." He made a sound like a kiss then, and the bird fluttered down onto his arm.

"Will the bird fly to me?" she asked.

He said, "Perhaps. Would you like to learn a bit of magic? I've been working on a piece, but I need a little person to hide onstage for a long while to make it work.

You've shown you can do that."

"Oh, yes! I can hide forever!"

"Ah, my child, no one can hide forever. But I wager you'll be a fine assistant with practice. My stage name is Barharam the Magnificent, but you can call me Abraham."

"I'm Sophie," the young girl said.

"Sophie?" He shook his head. "Sweet, but too simple for a magician's assistant! You will be...Serefina the Brave! Do you like that, little dove?"

She liked it very much. Soon, she began to assist the magician onstage for his evening acts, and the brave, charming Serefina became a draw at the theater. With her cut of the receipts, Sophie was able to buy an extra hot meal every day of the week. And the dove flew to her every time she called.

The grown woman now sighed. If only things had remained so simple. But fate had other plans for Sophie. Recalling her current task, she looked around her rooms, checking that everything was in order. Who knew when she'd get back here again?

By arrangement, a carriage came to the boarding house to pick her up. The driver's eyes flickered over her as he helped Sophie into the coach before loading the few trunks. There was no sign of Scorpio inside. She allowed herself to hope that Julian had ordered him off the assignment after all.

"We should be off in a few moments, ma'am," the coachman said. "My name's Jem, by the way. Call out if you need anything."

She settled into her seat, waiting to be off. A few minutes later, Sophie heard the coachman talking to another person outside, though she could hear no distinct words or voices.

But when Bruce suddenly opened the door of the carriage, she wasn't terribly surprised. "Good day, my lord," she said, using her poshest accent.

"*Bon jour, madame*," he replied, just as easily. "It appears we have the same goal."

"The same destination," she corrected coolly.

Sophie hoped she appeared at ease. The proximity of the man seated across from her made her skin tingle. She had forgotten how big he was, filling the carriage with his height and bulk.

She had hoped to rest a bit on the journey. Now, she wouldn't sleep a wink. She pursed her lips. Really, he was most inconvenient. She said, "When I entered this coach, it looked like I'd be alone."

"I just needed to stretch my legs." Bruce was unfazed by her cool reception. "Jem must have neglected to tell you I'd be joining you."

"I wonder how he could have forgotten that," she said dryly.

"Well, he's employed by the Zodiac—indirectly—so that might have something to do with it."

Sophie leaned back. She was annoyed by his hint that he knew more about the workings of the assignment than she did. "We'll see. The only thing I'm sure of now is that I'm stuck with you for several hours."

He gave her an unrepentant grin. "True. Any wagers

on who will jump out of the carriage first?"

She shot back, "You will, of course. And I'll lay any stakes you suggest."

"Your real name," he said. "And if I lose, which I won't, I'll pay you fifty pounds."

"Done." Sophie smiled at the ridiculous sum. An easy wager, since he already knew her real name. What sort of secrets did he think she was keeping?

The coach finally jolted into motion, advancing through the crowded city streets. Sophie watched out the window, determined to ignore Bruce for as long as possible.

After several minutes, he broke the silence. "You're not going to even speak to me?"

"What would be the point?" She looked him over. "I already know what sort of man you are."

"Based on what?"

"Our first meeting. And our second. Nothing I saw persuaded me that you'd be of assistance in my work. So you'd best stay out of my way," she warned him.

"What if I don't?"

"I'll remove you myself," she said.

"Are you threatening me?"

"Yes," Sophie said, catching his gaze and holding it. "I am. If you can't help me with the assignment, I'll make sure you don't hinder me."

His eyes hardened. "Likewise."

With that exchange, both spies fell silent again, each gathering their strength for the next fight, which appeared inevitable. This would be an impossible assignment.

* * * *

It was a long way to travel by coach—at least two nights on the road—and while hiring a private vehicle made it far more comfortable, they still had to stop frequently to rest the horses. At the first stop, Bruce exited the carriage and then offered a hand to help Sophie down. She took it, and smiled dazzlingly at him. "Thank you, my lord." As she stepped onto solid earth, she turned back and said, "Oh, you owe me fifty pounds."

He blinked. "What?"

"You jumped out of the carriage first," she explained sweetly.

His eyes narrowed, but he didn't blow up as she expected he would. "So I did," he said quietly. "You won't win the next wager so easily, though."

"We'll see," she retorted. He was more tolerable when he owed her something.

They continued on the road, the novelty of private travel quickly wearing off for Sophie. She studied Bruce from under her lashes. He read from a stack of papers for a time, then watched out the window. He didn't say a word to her, and Sophie knew that they were both behaving ridiculously.

"Can we talk?" she asked, finally.

He looked at her. "I thought you didn't want to speak to me."

"I meant is it safe to talk," she clarified.

"Oh. Well, our driver is known to me. Odd boy, but trustworthy. Even if he could hear us, which I don't think he can. Why?"

"We should discuss our approaches. If we're to do this together, we should know how we tend to work."

"Yes, we should."

"Don't you trust me?" she asked, her annoyance returning.

He laughed a little. "I'll be honest, Sophie. I don't trust you any further than I could throw you."

"How far would that be, as a practical matter?"

He paused, as if truly considering the question. "About ten feet."

"How do you figure that?"

"I'm, what, half a foot taller than you…and close to twice your weight."

Sophie conceded with a nod.

"And I'm used to physical work," he went on.

Of that she had no doubt. His broad back and the solidity of his frame allowed no other possibility…unless he was actually made of stone.

"So you think you could toss me about ten feet," she said slowly.

"Possibly more, if you weren't struggling."

"Don't count on that," she warned him. "I don't see myself blithely allowing you to toss me anywhere." She allowed him to think what he liked about the double entendre.

"Yes, Aries said that. *Sophie has always been remarkably independent. It's a point of pride for her,*" Bruce said, his voice coming out completely different from his previous tone.

Sophie blinked in surprise. "That's astonishing."

"He said it only two days ago. I'm not senile."

"Not the words," she said impatiently. "How you just repeated them. You sounded *exactly* like Julian."

Bruce shrugged. "I've always been able to do that. I just remember where I was and what I was thinking when I heard it."

His gift for mimicry was enviable. She knew professionals who spent years perfecting the art, and Bruce seemed to be able to do it without a second thought. Was that one of the skills that would be so useful on this assignment, according to Julian? Who would Bruce need to mimic?

"What is it?" Bruce asked, looking at her curiously.

"Nothing. I was just wondering what other talents you have."

He grinned. "Many, sweetheart. Hope you don't get to see all of them."

"I'm sure I wouldn't want to," she said tartly.

So much for getting along.

Sophie's mind drifted off, back to her childhood. She tried thinking of her mother. Picturing her face was becoming more and more difficult in recent years, which worried Sophie quite a lot. She had hazel eyes, that Sophie was sure of. And lighter hair than Sophie's now, almost blonde. Or was she remembering her mother in a wig? Maybe she was darker. And did she have a wide smile? Or was she a little sad? Perhaps Sophie wanted to remember her as happy. Maybe she was making it all up. How could Sophie's memories be slipping away?

Her hand drifted up to her chest. Absently, she touched

the spot where her mother's locket would have hung.

"Sophie?" Bruce's voice startled her back into the present.

She whipped her head back to focus on him. "What?"

He shadowed her move. "Did you lose a necklace?"

She was startled he knew what she was thinking. "Um, yes." She pulled her hand away and laid it carefully in her lap. She didn't like the notion that she could be so transparent to a stranger.

"What does it look like?" His gaze dropped to the floor of the carriage, looking for a telltale glint of metal.

Despite herself, she laughed softly. "Don't bother. I lost it a long time ago." The necklace she lost could never be recovered.

"I see." He sat back again. Perhaps he did see, but he was also the last person on earth Sophie wanted to confide in. He first ignored her talents, then tried to seduce her, and then attempted to outmaneuver her for the assignment. Scorpio was nothing to her.

Chapter 7

♎

THEY STOPPED AT AN INN called the Plough & Stars. The coach arrived while there was still plenty of light in the sky, but Sophie was glad enough to be out of the vehicle. Even the best coaches were bumpy, and the road had steadily worsened as they drove further and further away from London.

The inn itself was well kept. It was built in a horseshoe shape surrounding a mostly enclosed courtyard. The stables were easily identified by the smell, just as the main public room was obvious by the noise coming from the open doors and windows. The other parts the building were all guestrooms.

Jem said, "This inn has a suite on the upper floor. Likely empty now, but quite well done, they say. I've heard even some members of the royal family have stayed here once or twice."

"Well, it should do for us," Bruce drawled.

Sophie almost snapped at him before she realized he was joking. His humor would take some getting used to.

"My lady?" he asked, apparently deciding to play his role to the hilt.

She took his arm, and he escorted Sophie inside. Even

if the well-appointed coach hadn't alerted the innkeeper of well-paying customers, their clothes certainly did.

Bruce demanded the best room—the suite if available, as well as a private dining room. Sophie admired the way he did it, until she reminded herself that, for Bruce, this was no pretense. He was a lord.

The innkeeper said, "We do have a suite, sir. But I'm afraid all the private dining rooms are spoken for this evening."

Sophie scanned the perfectly pleasant main room, but sniffed like she had smelled something appalling. "I will not dine in a common room like some farmer's wife," she said to Bruce. "We must press on." He wanted a real lady? Then he'd get one.

Bruce in turn leveled a dark look at the innkeeper. "Are you *quite* sure all the private dining rooms are taken?"

The innkeeper heard his tone and quailed. "Ah, let me check." He disappeared for a moment, and reappeared just as quickly. "A mistake on my part, sir. Forgive me! There is indeed a private dining room available. The best one, as it turns out."

"Show us to the suite then," Bruce returned, carelessly adjusting his cuff. "My wife is fatigued."

They were taken to the suite, which boasted a large sitting room and not one but two bedrooms with dressing rooms. Sophie was pleased. She'd have a bit of privacy while she adjusted to playing Marianne Cassou.

"Give me a moment before we go down to eat," she said to Bruce. She took time to unpack a few items from her trunk, which had been brought up almost instantly. She made sure her wig was in good form.

She also changed into an evening gown. Even on the road, the prejudices of the upper class had to be observed. A lady would never dine in the same gown she traveled in.

Sophie adjusted the bodice of her gown, then opened the door to find Bruce standing there as if he were about to knock. Startled, he stepped back. "That was quick."

"I don't waste time," she said shortly, ducking around him.

"That's clear enough," he muttered. In a louder voice he said, "Shall we go to the dining room?"

"Our private dining room that you no doubt snapped away from someone else? Certainly. I'm famished."

He led her there, and seated her as if she were his wife. He kept looking her over from the top of her head to her waist, where the table blocked further perusal.

"What is it?" she asked at last. "Why do you keep looking at me as if I'm a mare?"

"Am I?" His eyes crinkled at the corners when he smiled.

"Are you looking for some flaw?"

"You said you wouldn't dine like a farmer's wife," Bruce said in a low tone.

Sophie's lip quirked. "I've nothing against farmers or their wives. The word *peasant* would have been laying it on a bit thick, don't you think? But I wanted to establish myself as a useless toff. Did I fool you?"

Bruce leaned back, appeased. "I think you might look

into dining like a farmer's wife, at least occasionally. You ought to put some meat on your bones."

"What does it matter to you how I look?" Sophie asked.

"I wouldn't like anyone to think I'm starving my wife."

"I've always been skinny."

When the serving girl entered with more dishes, they both stopped talking, since the conversation wasn't exactly typical of a married couple.

The serving girl did her job well enough, but Sophie didn't like the way she told Bruce to let her know if he should need anything later on. But she also didn't care to get involved. If Bruce wanted the attentions of some slattern, he was welcome.

If he noticed Sophie's annoyance, he said nothing. Instead, Bruce started to discuss politics. Sophie responded with her own opinions, knowing he was testing her to see how much she knew.

He mentioned a recent pamphlet, lauding the author, who recommended a stronger stance against both France and the young American nation that seemed far more sympathetic to France than her old master.

"Well, are you surprised?" Sophie asked. "Why should the States rush to reconcile with Britain? Their war for independence nearly ripped the colonies apart, and France's aid was vital."

"Vital, you say. You admire that?"

She wondered what was he driving at. "I don't have an opinion. It wasn't my war."

"So you think they'll come to the aid of France this time?"

"They're far more likely to if Britain stirs up another conflict on the seas. I think we should leave the States well alone. President Jefferson *hated* Ambassador Merry, by all accounts. Fox was smart to recall him. But unless the new ambassador has a better relationship with the man, we have little expectation that America will be anything but an enemy. You know Jefferson is thinking of echoing Napoleon's idea to embargo British goods."

"That will hurt America far more than it hurts Britain," Bruce said.

"Perhaps." Sophie shrugged. "But it sends a message, too. How many places can British ships be turned away before we find ourselves fighting over trade once again?"

"You're well informed."

"I read the newspapers," she said. "Plays and politics are all I read."

They held off discussing anything regarding their own assignment until they reached the privacy of the suite. Once inside, Sophie declared that she had to immediately change into her dressing gown, again testing out the mannerisms of a lady. She drifted into the bedroom she claimed as her own, and shut the door firmly behind her.

She changed into a loose-fitting dressing gown. Though it covered her fully, it was still far more intimate in style. After a moment of indecision, she removed the wig. In general, she didn't like for people to see her real hair, short and unfeminine as it was. But it was unlikely she would be able to maintain that practice at Carterhaugh, where Bruce and she would definitely have to work closely together. She may as well get him used to the look. Her shorn hair was tousled, but it drew attention to her face and made her large eyes look even bigger.

She stepped out into the main room, and watched him take in her new appearance.

"Interesting," Bruce said.

"You saw it when I was in the Oak Room."

"That was different. You were still in costume then. But now you're not."

"It's Madame Cassou you see, not me."

"The outfit perhaps, but not the person underneath. Anyway, it's interesting."

"You're attracted to short-haired, lanky, boyish types?" she asked archly. "Not that I'm judging."

"Stop it," he growled. "I thought I made it clear you're not in any danger from me, no matter what your hair looks like."

"That wasn't the impression I got in your conservatory."

"I was just proving a point."

"You got quite impassioned in proving your point."

"A mistake I'll certainly never make again," he said. "I know you better now."

Sophie frowned, but dropped the subject.

Bruce was happy to change it. "We have this evening to discuss our roles as the Cassou couple. I want to lay out a plan for what to do at Carterhaugh, with contingencies for anything that might go wrong," he said.

"Contingencies? Is that even possible? We won't

know much until we get there. We don't know anything about the surroundings or the specifics of what we're expected to do."

"We have a general idea. Planning never hurt anyone. And we do need to understand our roles, so neither of us is sleeping until I'm satisfied we understand each other. Did you look at the materials Aries gave you?"

Sophie was offended. She studied for all her roles, and she devoted the most attention to her roles for the Zodiac. "Of course," she returned coldly.

"Then tell me about your cover identity, please." Bruce sat back on the chair near the fireplace. Even in summer, the nights were sometimes cool, and a small fire had been lit that evening.

She took a breath, sitting down opposite him. "Madame Cassou was born Marianne Laforge, though she hails from Burgundy—I'm Parisian. She's actually thirty, so five years older, but I don't think that will matter too much. She emigrated to England about a decade ago. She married Lord Cassou about three years ago, and they live in London most of the year. It seems one of them doesn't care for England very much."

"Or one of them needs money badly," Bruce added. "Sometimes greed is the only motivator a person needs."

"Perhaps. Either way, Marianne Cassou is known to be a snob, always hinting she has royal blood and she's better than everyone else. I can play her easily," Sophie said.

"Because you think you're better than everyone else?"

"I'm a better agent, certainly."

"We'll see, Madame Cassou," he said.

"Very well, tell me all about you, my *dear* husband."

Bruce looked up as if reading invisible words on the ceiling, then he spoke, and his voice shifted subtly, becoming a little more lazy. "Born in France, near Paris. Came to England when the Revolution abolished his family's title. Established himself in the social circles of London to a slight degree. That's where he met his now-wife. They married and immediately went on a tour of Europe, and in fact they travel frequently.

"Cassou excelled at fencing while at school, as well as riding. He professes a great love for the English hunt—I have my doubts. And he banks at Child's, though his main account is not very large. So he either keeps some money elsewhere, or he's borrowing heavily."

Sophie raised her eyebrow. Bruce did do his reconnaissance. "Do you think they're in on it together…whatever it is that's bringing them to Carterhaugh?"

Bruce nodded slowly. "I think they are in each other's confidence, at least to a point. My information said he is described as being extremely attentive to his wife…very French, that. He must know what she's up to. If your spouse didn't know you were working as a spy, why drag her along on journey after journey?"

"Is that what you would do?"

"If I were Lord Cassou?"

"No, you. Would you leave a wife at home on an assignment like this?" Sophie asked. "Do you *have* a wife? You never said."

Bruce shook his head. "No. I can't imagine marrying

any woman while I'm part of the Zodiac. I know at least one agent who did, but it was difficult for him to balance his obligations."

Sophie said, "Like acting, but you can never step out of the role."

"You *are* an actress, Sophie, is that right? It's your profession?"

"Occasionally," she answered, warily. "It provides a useful cover. No one wonders when I leave town for weeks or months on end. I say I'm acting on another circuit and all is explained away."

"Useful," he echoed. "And I assume you are not married either."

"Certainly not." Sophie laughed. Who could she ever marry? "I am happy on my own."

"Are you?" he asked.

"Why shouldn't I be? I can support myself, and I have meaningful work where so many others do not. I answer to no one."

"Except the Zodiac."

"Of course. I thought you were referring to my personal life."

"You don't seem to have a personal life."

"What do you mean?"

"Well, you don't speak of family or friends. Do you have any?"

Sophie stood up abruptly. "We're wandering quite far from the subject."

"I think it important to know who I'm dealing with," he said.

"You're dealing with Libra. What else do you need to know?"

"Much." He shifted on the chair, and she was again aware of his sheer size. If he wanted to, he could subdue her, no matter how much warning she had.

She said, "Let's get back to the Cassou couple. How will they act toward each other?"

"With more sympathy than we do, I hope."

Sophie ignored the jibe. "As you say, Cassou dotes on his wife. She must behave in a manner to maintain that devotion."

"All the more reason to feign affection then," said Bruce. "Whether she returns his feelings or not, she keeps him interested."

Sophie smiled slyly. "Is that what you think?"

"It's a possibility," he said, his eyes narrowing.

"And how do you think she interests him?" Sophie stretched luxuriously. The thin fabric of her dressing gown tightened across her chest. She had his attention. She knew it.

"Don't," he warned.

She ignored him. "I thought you wanted to practice our roles." She leaned across the space between the chairs. "I have a lot of practice, you know."

"I already guessed that," he said. Though he tried to sound final, Sophie could hear the curiosity in his voice.

"A husband would know what it was like to kiss his wife," she went on, not entirely sure why she was goading him, other than because she could. "No one should doubt we're a couple."

Abruptly, Bruce snaked out one arm and pulled her to him. Sophie found herself tumbled over him on the chair, her legs straddling his as the fabric of her skirts hiked up. His hands slipped to her waist, holding her just firmly enough to make it clear that she wouldn't be moving unless he let her.

He kept her there, glaring. "I've already kissed you, Sophie. Remember the time you held a knife to my throat?"

"Keenly," she whispered, but with a smile that ought to take the sting out of her gloating.

He wasn't moved. "But that was not a particularly wifely sort of kiss, was it?"

"I might be an unusual wife."

"No doubt. Do you even know how a wife would kiss her husband?"

"Of course." Sophie inhaled. She knew he'd give in. Men always did.

"Then kiss me like that."

She leaned forward with a knowing smile. An inch away, he stopped her, his hands moving to curl around her shoulders. "No. On the cheek."

"You're joking."

"Not in the least," he said. "A *real* lady would show restraint at all times."

"I am restrained."

"You don't look it, with your skin so flushed and your breath so quick."

"My breath is not quick! And besides, you're not ready to lift my skirts." She rolled her eyes. "What a hypocrite."

"You forget, a man isn't supposed to control himself. That is the province of women, who are so much more refined and modest," he teased.

She leaned back. "I'm going to be sick."

"Play the part, Sophie. Kiss me. Like a good wife."

Sighing, she leaned over to the side and laid a brief peck on his cheek. His skin was warm, and the stubble of beard scratched her lips just slightly. "There, my darling husband. How's that?"

"Passable, my devoted wife," he said coolly.

"Passable?" Sophie struggled out of his embrace. He let her go, and she scrambled back to her seat. "This will never work," she said. "Aries was mad to think it would."

He watched her, his face impassive. "You have a better idea?"

"Other than you going home to your own grand estate and leaving me free to get into the house on my own terms? No," she retorted.

"You certainly do want to get rid of me," he said quietly.

"Imagine that, with you being so charming and helpful."

"Darling," he said.

She blinked at the non sequitur. "What?"

"Or dear, I suppose."

"Have you lost your mind?" Sophie asked. "Why did you just call me that?"

"Once we're there, we can't use our real names within earshot of anyone else," he explained. "Even when we're alone, we should avoid it."

"Ah." That made sense to her. "So you'll call me darling?"

"Or dear. Which do you prefer?"

"I don't care at all, *dear*." Sophie paused. "Dear is boring."

"And English," he admitted. "Any ideas?"

"Cherie?"

"That might be better. I wish you had a distinctive pet name though. Something I can use to get your attention without alerting anyone else."

Sophie thought for a moment. "You could say *dove*."

"Is that what your mother called you?" he guessed.

"No," Sophie said shortly. "It's just a word. Unusual, but not too remarkable."

"Yes, dove." Bruce didn't smile, but everything about him suggested he was laughing inside.

She rolled her eyes. "It's time for me to sleep. We can plot our assignment details tomorrow in the coach." Sophie retreated into the bedroom, noting with annoyance the absence of a lock. She considered whether to barricade the door with a chair, but then shrugged. Tonight would be as good a test as any. If Bruce didn't enter her room with the assumption that as an actress and an obviously worldly woman, she was free for the taking...well, she might give him another chance.

However, she slid a sheathed knife under her pillow before she went to sleep.

* * * *

She was woken a few hours later by sounds that would have scorched the ears of a more gently bred woman. Steady knocking of the bed posts against the floor, gasps in a rising volume, and then unabashed cries of pleasure soon had Sophie gritting her teeth. From the nearness of the cries, it could only be Bruce and the serving girl. He must have found her and invited her up to the room as soon as Sophie went to sleep.

She lay on her bed, fuming. How could he be so insulting as to bring the girl into the very same suite? They were allegedly a married couple staying at the inn. What wife would endure such offensive behavior?

She sat up, suddenly grinning. A real wife would go find the couple and give the slattern a piece of her mind. Sophie could likely get the innkeeper to sack the girl for her behavior—though he'd undoubtedly hire her right back. But catching Bruce in the act would be the coup. It would put him in his place, which was not between the legs of some village slut while they were on the eve of an important assignment.

Sophie got out of bed silently, and put her dressing robe on over her shift. The couple seemed to only have increased in their passion for each other. The woman suddenly moaned in a way that made Sophie raise her eyebrows. What was he doing to inspire such a display?

Sophie left her room, ready to play the offended wife. She started to storm across the common room toward Bruce's closed door...which she suddenly realized was *away* from the sounds of the noisy couple. In her half-awake state, her anger had got the better of her and turned her sense of direction—and proportion—completely around.

She lurched to a halt, then noticed something else. Bruce hadn't gone to his bedroom at all. He was sprawled in his chair before the embers, a few papers still clutched in his hand, though how anyone could sleep in such an awkward pose was beyond her.

Before she knew what she was doing, Sophie moved toward Bruce, intending to wake him and send him to bed for a proper rest.

She paused to look him over. Sleep softened his features, erasing his skeptical, searching expression. His hair was mussed, the waves starting to get unruly. The subtle light of the embers caused shadows to deepen the contrast of his eyes and cheeks, and gave his mouth an interesting definition. He was more attractive when he was unconscious, she thought, and almost laughed out loud at the idea.

He'd taken his coat off after she went to bed. His shirt was untied at the neck so that it draped open, and the well-formed chest made her a little—just a *little*—breathless. Combined with his impressive height and natural grace of movement, he'd be something to look at in bed. Perhaps that was one reason her frustrated brain turned her around and made her think that the sounds of sex were his doing.

Just then, a woman's loud cry of release penetrated the walls of the sitting room. "Lord," Sophie muttered.

Bruce twitched, about to wake up.

Sophie quickly put her hand on his arm to wake him

fully. "Bruce," she said in a low voice. "Bruce?"

His reaction wasn't what she expected. Bruce whipped one hand around to clamp down on hers. His eyes flew open as he stood up, ready to fight whoever snuck up on him. The papers he'd been holding fluttered down to the floor like white leaves.

"It's me!" Sophie yelped. "It's just me."

Bruce held her wrist tight in one hand. His other hand was balled into a fist, about to strike.

"Bruce, it's Sophie," she gasped out. "We're here in the inn. You fell asleep in the chair."

His eyes narrowed. Then, as suddenly as he grabbed her, Bruce let her go. He took a deep breath, and stepped back. "I…forgot where I was."

Sophie rubbed her wrist where he'd grabbed her. "Yes, that's obvious. You move *fast*."

"Did I hurt you?" he asked contritely.

"Of course not. I'm tougher than that." She stooped to gather the papers on the floor. "But you should go to your bedroom now. No one should sleep in a chair like this one."

Bruce nodded, watching her pick up the papers. "Why are you awake?" he asked.

Sophie blushed, remembering how she'd been planning to humiliate him with his doxy. She explained, "There's a couple…enjoying themselves in the room adjoining mine. I couldn't sleep."

Bruce listened until he heard the now much fainter sounds. He glanced at her. "And that bothers you?"

"It was louder before," she said, defensive. "And I

was much closer."

"Would you like my room?" he offered. "The bed is undisturbed."

She shook her head, unaccountably embarrassed now. "They can't possibly keep that up all night. It was just annoying." She put the messy stack of papers on a nearby table, then wondered what to do with her hands. Such indecisiveness was unusual for Sophie.

He was still looking at her. "Did you think it was me?" he asked.

"Of course not!" she snapped, irritated that he'd somehow guessed her thoughts. "Why should I? Your room is over there." She pointed to it, quite unnecessarily.

"Because I wouldn't do that," he said. He picked up the papers she just put down, and subconsciously straightened the pile. "Not with you nearby."

"What you would or wouldn't do is of no concern to me," Sophie said.

"If you have no concern for me, why did you wake me?"

"Because I don't want to deal with an irritable travel partner tomorrow!"

"As irritable as you are now?" he asked, with far more amusement than the situation warranted.

"Fine, go back to sleep in your chair. I leave you to it."

"Sophie," he began.

"Good night, Bruce," she said firmly.

"I thought you couldn't sleep."

"I'll put yet another pillow over my head. If it doesn't

drown them out, maybe I can hope to suffocate by morning." She turned and walked to her doorway.

He hadn't taken his eyes off her. "Now I'll have to check on you, dearest," he said.

"You're not invited," she snapped.

"Go to bed," he returned. "I hope to see you alive in the morning."

"I seriously doubt that," she muttered.

* * * *

Bruce watched her retreat before he entered his own bedroom. Sophie might be able to play a lady, but she was truly a foul-mouthed guttersnipe. If she got any more antagonistic, she might as well report to Napoleon directly. True, she hadn't harmed the assignment yet. But she wasn't helping. And Bruce couldn't talk to her without the conversation ending either in an argument or a seduction designed to drive him mad.

Sophie knew she was irresistible. It wasn't fair. He let down his guard for one moment back in his own conservatory, and now she knew he desired her. Or rather…a woman like her. Her seductive behavior might be something he could ignore if she didn't match it with a contempt for him that was unavoidable. That was what stung. She didn't even consider him worthy of a conquest.

But his reaction to being woken up might have finally warned Sophie not to play with him. He hadn't meant to scare her—he had no idea who she was for that split second after waking. But he could tell she *was* scared for a moment, before he recognized her. He wasn't sure if he ought to be relieved or upset. He didn't like the idea of frightening a lady unnecessarily, but if that's what it took, then so be it.

Of course, he felt like a heel for grabbing her. She was a woman, agent or not, and Bruce had been trained from birth to treat women as one would treat fragile glass. Was that the real reason why Sophie confounded him? She defied every expectation of what it meant to be a woman. She was fierce, independent, and certainly didn't require protection.

So what am I doing here? he thought. He recalled his instructions to watch Sophie. Watching Sophie would likely drive him insane. He hoped they completed the assignment before that happened.

Chapter 8

♎

SOPHIE SLEPT SOUNDLY FOR THE rest of the night, roused only by Bruce knocking lightly on her door. They got ready in near silence. Soon, Jem was steering the coach onward to Carterhaugh Manor.

The atmosphere in the coach was much quieter the second day. Both Sophie and Bruce were tired yet strangely anxious, in a manner peculiar to actors and spies, to begin their roles.

Sophie sat lost in thought for a time, staring out the window as the landscape of the countryside rolled slowly by. She had to put herself in the place of a lady. A high-born aristocrat who believed the world existed to serve her. Sophie had played ladies before, but never with an actual lord at her side, who would doubtless be watching her performance with a critical eye. She'd done well enough the previous night at the inn, but simply existing at Carterhaugh Manor would be a far more demanding role, with a harsher audience. Uncharacteristically, Sophie was nervous. And the presence of Bruce, a man who embodied what she had to pretend to be, wasn't helping her confidence.

To be fair, he didn't seem a typical aristocrat, even

beyond the fact that he was a spy. Sophie looked across at Bruce, wondering how he'd ended up in the Zodiac. She knew little about his real personality.

"Tell me about yourself," she said finally, to break the silence.

He looked at her as though surprised to see her there. "What do you want to know?" he asked.

"Anything. Where did you grow up? Do you have brothers? Sisters? What are your interests?"

"Lord Cassou?"

"No, *you*. Forester."

He shrugged. "I grew up at a place called Old Harrow, which you have no reason to have ever heard of. I still live there for part of the year, when I'm not working for the Zodiac, or getting stuck in London for the parts of the Season I can't avoid."

"You don't like the usual diversions of society?"

"It's a contest of inanity," he groused. "Hundreds of petty souls all staring at each other, gossiping and watching for the slightest weakness or misstep. Then they swoop down on the victims and glory in their misfortune."

"But they are your peers," she said, though she couldn't help laughing at his characterization.

"Only by the chance of blood and the ties of family."

"When did you join the Zodiac?"

He closed his eyes, remembering. "I bought a commission in the army nearly fifteen years ago. Then I met Julian Neville. He offered me a role doing something worthwhile, and I was in the mood to accept. Haven't regretted it. I suppose it must be over ten years. You?"

She counted on her fingers. "Eleven since I came to London, I think. It was the autumn of 1795."

"That was when you met Aries? You must have been quite young."

"Yes, Aries," she said hastily. "We met at a party. For some, life was nothing but parties, a *beau monde* from dusk till dawn. But I asked about you. Tell me more. How do your parents feel about your disdain for the *ton*?"

"My father is dead. I never really knew the man," Bruce said. "He was very cold, and very concerned with the honor of the family." Bruce trailed off for a moment. "I have a brother," he said suddenly. "Ashley. Younger by five years."

"Are you close?"

He laughed, though he didn't look happy. "Not any more. Ash nearly drowned himself in scandal several years ago. Himself and our family name. I haven't seen him in a long time."

"What did he do?"

"He seduced a married woman," Bruce said shortly. "And her daughter."

"Forgive me for noting that isn't a terribly unusual sort of scandal."

He laughed, a dark sound. "Both at once? Keep in mind he was nineteen, and a divinity student at the time."

Sophie raised her eyebrow. "That *is* a bit more unusual."

"He was serving at a church in a small town where he was supposed to be learning how to tend a flock of the faithful," Bruce continued.

"He got too invested, I take it."

"He shocked a whole county. Drummed out, of course. And a field day for the gossips. He should have been ashamed of what he'd done. But what did he do? He ran off to London and immediately took up with none other than Regina Fox. Have you heard the name?"

"The Golden Lady?" Sophie nodded. She'd never met the woman, but the courtesan Regina Fox was infamous. She was said to be a dazzling beauty who favored gold and yellow in her wardrobe. She was one of the most sought after, and most expensive, ladies of her class. "What sort of wealth does your family have that a second son could afford her…if I may ask?"

Bruce shook his head. "We're not that wealthy. I don't know how he paid for her attention, and I don't want to. But Ash somehow saw her exclusively for over a year. They still see each other occasionally, and not simply because both are part of that world. Anyway, now the Honorable Ashley Allander is one of the more notorious men in the demimonde of London. A rake and a scoundrel. In fact, I don't want to talk about it. I don't even know why I'm telling you this."

Sophie guessed he hadn't spoken about it to anyone for years. "And you have no other siblings?" she asked, keeping her voice gentle to draw him out.

"None. And my mother died soon after Ash's descent into scandal."

"He broke her heart," said Sophie.

Bruce shook his head. "I wish I could say that, but it

was consumption, pure and simple. She had never been a robust woman."

"So no parents to hound you, and no siblings to run with. No wife or family to think of. You really don't have many distractions from your chosen path as an agent." Sophie realized from this glimpse into his life that he had virtually no one to tell him what to do.

"I keep care of my estate," Bruce said. "Other than that, I can do whatever I like. But the Zodiac is my life."

"How dedicated."

Bruce focused his gaze on her again. "And you?"

"What about me?" she asked. "I don't even have a title or an estate to care for like you do. The Zodiac is all I have."

"So tell me how you got here. Why work for England when you're French?"

She put up a warning hand. "I'm *Parisian*, not French. I have no love for Napoleon, nor for the regime before him. Just because I speak the language doesn't mean I endorse a madman who grabbed the crown and named himself Emperor."

"That still doesn't explain why you fled to a different country entirely."

"I'd had enough of Paris, and Aries offered me a choice." She leaned forward. "Don't forget when I was there. I saw what the Revolution did to the people I knew in Paris, people I loved. Innocent people died on the altar of liberty. Good people. And now this Emperor thinks to rebuild Rome, and he doesn't care how many people die to make his own dream come true. Yes, I was born in

France. But my loyalty is to England, the country that sheltered me after the chaos descended. And the Zodiac, and what it stands for."

Bruce looked at her for a long time, considering her words. "Tell me about your most difficult assignment," he said then.

"Why?"

"Why not? We've got hours."

Sophie thought about it seriously. There were several contenders, but she picked the one most likely to shock him. "In 1800. I had to seduce someone with a direct line to the general, as Napoleon was then. If I were exposed, I might have imperiled the Zodiac as well as myself."

"But you successfully seduced him."

"Her," Sophie corrected with a smile.

"You seduced a woman?"

"Yes. To be precise, I let her think she was doing the seducing. After that night, she had no secrets from me."

"And how exactly—"

"Curious?" She shrugged. "It was not that different, really. Less pain, true, and no concern about...consequences. It was a little strange for me, but I would do it again."

"Hmm," he said.

"I take it you've never been in a similar situation."

"Seducing a woman?" he asked, with a wry grin.

"Seducing someone of the same sex," she clarified.

He shook his head. "No."

"Do you think you could?" Sophie asked. She half-hoped to make him uncomfortable, but he didn't seem shocked.

"I don't know," he said, thoughtful. "It would depend on how high the stakes were."

"But so often we don't know," said Sophie, thinking of several assignments that seemed quite simple, only to be revealed later as vitally important.

"That's true." He paused. "I expect it would be easier for a woman."

"Why?"

"Desire, or lack of it, is more easily hidden."

"Men are more obvious," she agreed, with a laugh. "And predictable."

"Predictable?"

"What man doesn't want to have every woman he can?"

"Isn't it the same for women?" he asked, looking a little offended.

She laughed. "You don't understand anything, do you?"

He straightened up in his seat. "So enlighten me."

"Oh, I will," Sophie said. "I'll tell you a secret that will change the way you see women, if you're smart enough to understand it."

"Why would I not understand?" he asked. "Are you going to tell me in Latin?"

"I'll tell you in English or French…your choice. But it will be up to you to comprehend its significance. If you do," she paused and smiled, "you will know more about women than ever before. It will make you a better spy."

He shrugged. "You assume I don't already know this

secret."

"From what you just told me, I *know* you don't know this one."

"Very well. Humiliate me with your greater wisdom. But don't expect—"

A shout came from outside the carriage. Jem yelled something, either a warning or a curse. Then the carriage lurched to the side.

Sophie gasped in surprise as the carriage threatened to overturn. Bruce moved toward her, his arm thrust out to come between her and the window. She knocked into him, unable to stop her slide toward the rapidly tilting side. Her head nearly hit the glass, saved only by the fact that he'd reacted so quickly.

Before either could speak, Jem yelled again. The horses whinnied and the carriage lunged forward. The carriage righted itself, but their forward motion suddenly halted. Sophie landed in a heap on the floor of the carriage, half on top of Bruce.

"Bloody hell," Sophie muttered, disentangling herself from Bruce's arm. "That could have been very bad. Jem?" she called in a louder voice. "Are you all right out there?"

"In one piece, ma'am!" his voice came back.

Bruce pushed Sophie gently back into her seat. "Are you all right?" he asked.

"I'm quite safe. Let's see what happened."

Bruce found the door still worked perfectly well, and he climbed out just as Jem jumped down from his perch to calm the skittish horses. "What's the matter?" Bruce asked.

"Sorry, my lord. A fox ran across the road. Fool creature! It spooked the horses. I'm afraid we veered a bit off course when I tried to get them under control again."

Sophie turned to look at the carriage. "The wheels aren't broken," she said hopefully.

"True, but they are stuck in that mud," Bruce added. Jem's attempt to control the horses meant forcing the carriage to the side of the road, where sticky mud claimed the wheels.

"We'll get it out in no time," Jem said confidently.

However, it was not so simple. The weight of the carriage caused the wheels to sink further when Jem tried to steer it out.

"Wait, wait," Bruce called. "The corner's stuck. It's pulling everything down. Let the lady mind the horses. We'll have to lift that part of the carriage out of the mud."

"Lift it?" Sophie echoed. "You mean, by yourself?"

"Unless someone else comes along to help." Bruce took his jacket off. "Hold this, please."

Sophie took it without a word, placing it carefully over her arm. She was so surprised the lord was willing to do the work himself that she couldn't think of anything to say.

Jem quickly unhitched the horses and handed Sophie the reins. "Keep well away, ma'am. This may be messy."

That was an understatement. The two men were besieged by mud as they worked to free the carriage from the puddle. Bruce provided most of the power, while Jem used his wiry strength to slowly inch the carriage out of the mire.

Sophie looked on from the other side of the empty road, feeling helpless. Bruce, now wearing only his loose-fitting shirt, was already sweating and dirty from the heat of the day and the strain of such work. Jem didn't look any better, and he let loose strings of inventive curses.

His temper short, Bruce reprimanded him about his language, reminding him there was a lady present. Jem apologized to Sophie, who merely nodded. Neither man was in the mood to hear her say she was not a lady and had muttered all those curses herself at some point or another.

Eventually the men got the carriage back on the road. Jem rehitched the horses and frowned at the sun.

"We lost some time," Jem said, "and I'm wary of pushing the pace, lest we break a wheel under the strain."

Bruce told him to stop at the nearest decent inn, then clambered back into the carriage, where Sophie already waited.

"Sorry for the delay," he said. "I can take my jacket back now."

Sophie made no move to return it. "Are you insane?" she asked, surveying him. "Your shirt is ruined. You can't put this clean jacket over it."

"I can't not wear a jacket," he said. Indeed, a gentleman *never* went out in public without a jacket.

Sophie could tell he was uncomfortable appearing as he did, but she remained firm. "You must endure, my dear. You're safe in the carriage where random passersby will not be offended, and we'll be at an inn soon enough."

She was correct. The inn was not so fine as the one

from the previous night, but it looked quite clean, which was all Sophie cared about at the moment. In her most ladylike way, she ordered the best room, and insisted the hot water be brought up as soon as possible. Bruce had stayed with Jem to see that the coach was indeed fit to travel the next day.

Sophie was shown to a large, bright room. The water was heated and brought up with remarkable efficiency by the innkeeper's children. Sophie hoped it wouldn't cool too quickly.

Fortunately, Bruce came in then, worn down by the effort of final repairs to the carriage. "Good news," he said. "There's only minor damage. Jem will handle the rest of it, and we can continue on in the morning as scheduled."

"I ordered you some hot water," Sophie said, pointing to the pitcher and basin.

He grinned. "Of course, you're going to stay with me while I clean up."

"What wife wouldn't?" she retorted.

Bruce stripped to the waist without so much as a warning. Sophie, a little stunned, watched him as a wife might…though in a society marriage, it was entirely possible that a woman might never see her husband half-naked save for in the darkness of a bedroom. And many proper ladies would never dare look more than they absolutely had to.

He was…impressive. His face was not exactly handsome, not in the way that made younger ladies sigh. His features were not quite regular, and his deep-set eyes were too direct. But he didn't need to be handsome when he had that height and musculature. Still, Sophie wasn't defeated by the situation, even though she was positive Bruce intended to discomfit her.

He started to wash the mud off his face. "Tell me the secret," he said, as if they were having a normal conversation. "The one you were taunting me with before we got stuck in the mud. I'd say I've earned the answer."

Sophie was glad to have a topic to focus on. "So you did. Here's the question: what's the first thing a woman thinks when she meets a man?"

"All women, any woman?" he asked, dipping the cloth into the hot water and wringing it out. He didn't even glance over at Sophie.

"Yes," she said. "It's the same thing. Guess what it is. And then I'll tell you the true answer."

He echoed, "When a woman meets a man…she decides whether she wants to bed him," he finished crudely.

Sophie thought he was trying to shock her. He'd have to try harder than that. "No. Guess again."

"She decides how much money he has, or if he's worth her time."

"No. That comes a bit later. Try once more," said Sophie.

"She…I don't know. She assesses whether he has something she wants. People always see others as a way to get what they want."

Sophie shook her head. "You're not trying. Those things all happen. But I said I would tell you the very *first* thing a woman thinks on seeing a man."

"I give up. Tell me what a woman thinks on seeing a man."

Sophie said, with deliberate calm, "She thinks, *How can he hurt me?*"

Bruce stopped what he was doing, the washcloth falling into the basin with a splash. "That's not true," he said instantly.

"I promise you it is," Sophie said. "It is the first thought to cross a woman's mind, no matter how young or old, rich or poor, powerful or desperate. Maybe not all women even realize they think it—but they do."

"Honestly?"

Sophie nodded. "She thinks: Can this man hurt me? How much could he hurt me? In what ways could he hurt me? How can I escape? How do I fend him off? How do I survive this?"

Bruce stared at her, his previous task completely forgotten. "Is that what *you* thought when you first met me in the club?"

She nodded again.

"But Julian vouched for me, did he not?"

"What does that matter?" Sophie asked. "Believe me, all women share the same fear. Only after she asks that question and makes those dozen small decisions can she move on to what *you* think of as normal thoughts."

"That's mad."

"That's life for a woman. Understand this, and how can you go about treating half the world in the same way?"

He frowned. "You make me sound like a monster."

"Not at all. I merely acknowledge you're a man, and as such have never had to ask yourself the same questions."

Sophie paced to the other side of the room, then stopped in surprise at what she saw. Along the back of Bruce's shoulder, there was a long, ugly, raised scar. The skin around it was puckered red, while the scar itself was bone-white. The whole thing ran about nine inches from the edge of his arm to near his spine. The peculiar straightness of it showed that it had been a most unnatural accident, but Sophie couldn't think of anything to cause such a wound.

He glanced over with a smirk. "Are you watching me? What are you thinking now?"

She'd be damned if she would let him think she lusted after him. "You have quite a scar," she said.

"Burn," he said shortly, looking away again. "Happened when I was young."

"It looks painful."

"It was."

"Does it hurt when you move? Does it restrain you at all?" she asked.

"Not anymore. If you want a closer look, make yourself useful." He held out the washcloth.

Sophie bit back a few choice words about the level of usefulness he could expect from her, and stepped forward to take the cloth. She did have to get used to being near him, after all. The nervousness she was feeling would fade as soon as she conquered the unfamiliarity of working with him.

She let the warm water run down his broad back, not paying particular attention to the scar, other than to keep wondering about its cause. A burn, he said. Perhaps a stick? A burning branch or beam? But it was narrow, and perfectly straight.

"A poker," she said, thinking out loud. "One that had been held in the fire deliberately."

Bruce's body stilled. "Good guess," he said. He didn't offer anything more about the incident.

Maybe he'd been struck as a child at school. But by a poker? Who would do that to a child? Swayed by the uncomfortable image of Bruce as a young boy, suffering such a thing, her touch gentled. "I am sorry," she murmured, without intending to.

He didn't reply, other than to ask, "Am I free of mud?"

Sophie dipped the cloth in the water again, and ran it over his shoulders and neck, carelessly this time. "You look clean enough to me now. You should put a shirt on before you get cold."

"You're remarkably uncurious for a woman," he said.

"How so?" she asked, thinking that she had been peeking at his body more than she should.

"You didn't ask who held the poker," he said, inadvertently confirming her guess.

Sophie stepped back. "It's not my business. In fact, with the exception of those people who I am hired to spy on, I do respect others' privacy. Just as I guard my own." Sophie headed to the door. "I'm hungry. I'll request some supper after I check on Jem." She was absurdly glad to get away from the room. The less clothed Bruce was, the more he affected her, which was not something Sophie usually encountered.

They ate supper in near silence and turned in early, tired out from the day. Bruce took a few blankets and stretched out on the floor, leaving Sophie with the bed. She thought his refusal to sleep next to her was a bit too conspicuously chivalrous, but she didn't complain. She much preferred to sleep alone. At Carterhaugh, she'd be able to retire to her own room, which would be a relief.

They both rose early the next day. Bruce muttered quiet curses as he worked the kinks out of his back. Sophie packed her trunk swiftly, again reminding Bruce that she wasn't a lady by birth. Finally, Sophie seized the blankets from the floor and flung them onto the bed.

"What's that for?" he asked.

"Precaution. Let's not give anyone a reason to think we're not sleeping in the same bed every night. All it takes is one person to get suspicious and ask around about us."

"I see," he said. "Good thinking."

Sophie was careful not to smile. As victories went, it was a small one, but she'd take it all the same.

Chapter 9

Ω

THEY WERE ON THE ROAD well before the sun rose above the trees. They were behind schedule now, and wanted to get to Carterhaugh Manor as soon as possible.

After talking a bit more with Bruce about the particulars of the assignment, the monotony of travel lulled Sophie into a doze. A touch on her arm brought her awake again instantly. Sophie's eyes flew open, and she saw Bruce leaning over her from across the carriage. "What is it?" she asked. "When is it?"

"Relax, Sophie. We're getting close to the village outside of Carterhaugh Manor. I thought you might want to see the lay of the land."

She nodded, still a bit drowsy. Automatically, she smoothed her outfit and checked that everything was in place. More than once, men had tried to take advantage of her while she slept. However, she didn't think Bruce would try such a thing. She was quite in order. Irritatingly, the new ring she wore caught her attention when she adjusted her gloves. It still did not feel right.

"Problem?"

"No, I'm quite well." She touched the hilt of her blade she always wore under her skirts.

"I didn't rob you, my darling wife." He paused. "Nor

did I touch you."

"Of course not," she said. "I would have known if you tried." She tried to affect unconcern. "If we're getting close, I should become Madame Cassou now."

"You weren't already?"

"Before, I was just wearing her clothes," she said. "Now I have to wear her mind." Sophie pulled the diamond cross from her reticule and fastened it around her neck. Bruce watched with interest. "Where did you get that?" he asked.

"Julian gave it to me," Sophie said. She saw the flash in his eyes before she explained. "Madame Cassou is known for always wearing a cross of great value. It was necessary for the deception."

"I wonder how he explains the bills to the Astronomer," Bruce said.

Sophie smiled at the image. "I'm sure he has *carte blanche*."

"So long as we keep bringing back the goods."

"Oh, yes. As we will this time." Sophie almost corrected herself to say "as I will this time," but it was pointless to argue with him so close to Carterhaugh. She'd discover the best way to get the information once she got inside. If Bruce stayed out of her way, she'd be in and out like lightning, and then they could both go on to other assignments.

As she watched out the window, the coach passed through the village, and then a while later by the gates of the vast, isolated estate. Towering stone pillars flanked the driveway, and a fence backed with tall greenery marked the division between the estate and the outside world. Sophie sensed a shift in the air around them.

She looked over to Bruce. "Are you ready?"

They finally reached the lands claimed by the estate of Carterhaugh. To Sophie's eyes, the whole countryside was gorgeous. Pockets of old forest divided patches of farm fields and grazing lands. The terrain was softly rolling hills, and the shortened horizon was compensated for by the charming, peaceful picture.

As a child who grew up in cities, Sophie had no memories of such scenes. To her, they were always a little magical…places that existed only in stories.

It was also lonely, and Sophie knew the house was chosen for that reason. Very few people would be able to wander this area without being seen. Their host wanted a secluded spot. He'd certainly found one.

Bruce had been looking out the windows as well. "Shameful," he said. His brows were drawn together in a scowl.

"What is?" Sophie asked.

"The land around here."

"What do you mean? It's lovely!"

"The country is beautiful, but the land of the estate is horrendous. Can't you see it? Nearly half the fields are fallow, and those that have been sown are still choked with weeds. The man in charge of this place has no idea what he's doing."

"He just doesn't care," said Sophie, knowing instinctively she was right. "The house will be beautiful inside but…People like Theriot don't care about anything they can't see themselves. I wager he's hemorrhaging cash to maintain his lifestyle, because he's never learned how to make money off land."

Bruce didn't appear to hear her. He stared out at the fields. "I'd have planted wheat along the road, and vegetables along the stream, where the water will run down the slope," he said. He pointed at one field. "They're grazing sheep on the stretch most likely to be the richest soil. Stupid! I'd pasture them upland."

She laughed at that. "Are you a viscount or a farmer?"

He gave her an injured look. "I know how to run an estate, Sophie. As you guessed, the income is what provides for *my* lifestyle. My duty is to see that the land is used in the best possible way, and that the tenants are equally well-treated. It's my role in life…well, one of them."

He sounded confident. But something about his words rankled her. "Well, it must be reassuring to know you'll have something to fall back on once you leave the Zodiac."

"Who says I'm leaving? You're not still proposing that wager, are you?" he asked. "Sophie, are we doing this as planned? Because if you won't cooperate, I need to know right now. You won't sabotage this once we step over that threshold. I can't let you." His eyes bored into hers.

She took a breath. "I'll follow the plan. But I don't have to like it."

The carriage drove up along the main road leading to the manor itself. At close range, the neglect that bothered Bruce was more obvious. The current owner didn't help his tenants with their cottages, and only a few people in poor clothing could be seen working in the fields.

The house itself was impressive though, Sophie had to admit. A bit run down, true. But the sheer massive bulk of the great house of Carterhaugh Manor as outlined against the afternoon sky forced one to admire the glory of the place.

She remembered what Aries had written about the estate. Once the property of a now vanished noble family, Carterhaugh had been empty for a long time. It now housed the dubious Mr Theriot, who had the valuable papers Sophie needed to get. Any beauty of the house would only be a distraction for her.

At last, the carriage reached the front entrance and rolled to a stop. At the door, they were greeted as if they were royalty. A man who could only be Thomas Theriot stood in the open doorway. Obsequious servants, dressed in fashions about one generation behind their master, all bowed and scraped…and watched the newcomers carefully. *They've been warned to watch for anyone out of place*, Sophie thought. *I must never give them a hint about me.*

Bruce's plan called for them both to be circumspect on arrival. They'd hold back until they could see how things worked. Only then could they decide on how to proceed and what to say.

But when Sophie saw their host's eyes linger on the neckline of her dress, she decided Bruce's caution could be damned.

Just as Bruce was helping her down, Theriot himself addressed them. "Ah, Monsieur and Madame Cassou, is it?"

Bruce turned and bowed a little stiffly, "Yes." He looked their host over with a critical, cool gaze.

Sophie, however, wore a wide smile. "Monsieur Theriot, your invitation came at a most opportune time. London in the summer is hideous."

Theriot said wryly, "Is there a season in which London is not hideous?"

Sophie frowned at Bruce. "Darling? What do you think?"

He pretended to consider the question. "Usually, one or two afternoons in October prove tolerable." He gave her a look, probably wondering what she was about.

"England is not tolerable at all. I cannot wait to find a new home back in Burgundy," Sophie purred to their host. "It's been too long."

Theriot laughed. "Well, we can talk about that notion later. For now, let my humble abode do. We have been expecting you. Please come in, come in."

Sophie latched onto Theriot before Bruce could stop her. "I hope we have not kept you waiting. I myself detest waiting for nice things." She flirted shamelessly with the man.

"You are worth any wait, madame," their host said, with a quick glance at Bruce. Sophie noted his bland expression, and knew he was seething at her inside. Oh, well.

Then Theriot continued, "Allow me to show you around Carterhaugh personally. I have a few moments to spare."

He led them into the halls, and Sophie put on her dreamiest look as she surveyed the interior. *"C'est belle,"* she murmured over and over. *"Magnifique."* Playing the snooty aristocrat was easy for her, and it made her feel closer to the memory of her mother, who had done it so well in plays.

As they walked through the mansion, Theriot showed off his treasures. Sophie felt an acute sense of dislocation. The inside of the house was astonishing. Furniture in the latest style graced every room. Portraits and landscapes hung on the walls, including images even Sophie recognized as the work of famous artists.

"Is that a de la Tour?" Bruce asked at one point, stopping before a painting in which one brilliant candle flame illuminated shadowy figures.

"Yes, it is," Theriot said, looking back.

Bruce stepped closer to examine it. "The linseed," he muttered, "And the brushstrokes..." He spent a moment looking at the image. "Remarkable," he commented at last.

"Rather lovely, isn't it?" said Theriot. "I had many such works shipped over from France...rather than let the rabble destroy them."

"And thank God you did," Sophie murmured. Theriot smiled at her, apparently ensnared.

"Madame Cassou, you are not only as beautiful as rumor has claimed, but as cultured as well. I knew from your letters that you would be a most charming companion, but meeting you at last..." he trailed off. "Your sympathy for my position is most encouraging."

"Yes, I am eager to hear your latest thoughts on our discussion," Sophie said smoothly. Inside, she felt a jolt of anxiety. If Cassou and Theriot had corresponded so much, they had surely been in each other's confidence. There were so many things Sophie didn't know!

"Oh, I shall tell you all about it when the guests are assembled. That is, after all, the point of this retreat."

She murmured, "But you can give me a tiny hint now, can you not?" She leaned slightly toward Theriot, disregarding Bruce's presence entirely. "You must indulge a woman's curiosity!"

"I will indeed, madame." He glanced back at Bruce, who'd wisely dropped behind, ostensibly to study more of the art. Theriot whispered, "I have some curiosity about you as well, my beauty."

Sophie allowed her eyelids to drop just a bit. "We must discuss that a different time, Thomas," she said huskily. Her confidence returned. Theriot's interest was obvious. He *wanted* to be seduced. She had him. Any mistakes she might make in terms of past information could be smothered with a kiss or a caress. And the information they came for could be secured with a promise of illicit pleasure. She was back in her element.

* * * *

Bruce wanted to *throttle* Sophie. How could she take such a risk? They'd barely stepped through the doors when she tossed all his planning aside and directly confronted their host. They knew so little about what was going on, yet Sophie spun lie after lie with no care for what she might do if she were caught out.

He'd have some choice words for her once they were alone again.

As they continued on, Bruce watched the lady at their host's side. He was torn between wanting to excoriate her for recklessness and wanting to see how she worked. She was infuriating, aloof, condescending…utterly perfect. She charmed Theriot by exploiting his desire to be seen as important and well-heeled. She also plied for information in a subtle way, wringing the names of several other guests and their connections to him with enviable ease.

The man was obviously smitten with her, and just as obviously willing to take her right from under her "husband's" nose. Bruce tried to ignore a sense of masculine ownership. In fact, he should encourage this development—subtly, of course. If he were Theriot and had a woman like Sophie clinging breathlessly to him, he might say more than he ought to as well. In fact, even when he knew about Sophie, he'd still almost done that the first night, when she overwhelmed him in the conservatory. She was a remarkable woman. He didn't fully trust her, but he couldn't deny her appeal.

Was it because she was actually very similar to him? A solitary person, really, who lived by her wits. True, she was maddeningly impulsive where he chose to plan, but their outlooks were not that different.

She glanced back once, smiling at Bruce and giving him a tiny wink. He realized with a slight shock that nothing in her expression was challenging. She was reassuring him, even as she clung to Theriot's arm.

He noticed the same thing again when Theriot completed the main tour and released them to the care of the housekeeper. Sophie accepted Bruce's arm with a relaxed smile. In fact, Sophie's antagonism toward him seemed to recede completely, and they started to respond to each other's unspoken communication. Perhaps it only took that final step for Sophie to put on her chosen role. In a very real way, entering Carterhaugh was like stepping on stage.

* * * *

After the tour, a pixie-sized maid showed them to their room. Sophie was elated after her first encounter with Theriot. She could handle this assignment after all.

But when they reached their room, she faltered. The room was just that, a room. It was not a suite. Sophie hadn't expected that their plan would require them to share a bed over several days or even weeks. Unlike the inns, they could not sleep separately here and expect it to go unmarked.

"I am used to my own room," she commented to the maid in her loftiest tone.

The maid said nervously, "I do apologize, madame, but it is all we have. The guest list is quite large. At the master's orders, all the married couples are sharing."

"I see. Of course, I shall need an attendant. I hope *that* is not too outlandish an accommodation."

The girl curtsied automatically. "I'm to be your lady's maid too, ma'am." She looked even more nervous. "My name's Maggie."

"And your family name?" Sophie asked. Ladies' maids were customarily referred to by their surname only.

"Sawyer, ma'am. But I'm not a proper lady's maid, so Maggie it is."

"Very well…Maggie," Sophie said, letting doubt color her tone.

The trunks were there in the room, all of them still locked. The housemaid apologized for not unpacking them. "I didn't know where the key was, ma'am."

"I have it. I prefer to direct the unpacking," Sophie answered distantly. "I like everything just so."

"Yes, ma'am. Just ring when you're ready to do so." The little maid left, closing the door behind her.

The two spies stared at each other. Before Sophie could utter a word, Bruce stepped up to her and leaned to whisper in her ear. "We have to assume that everything we say will be overheard, even in this room."

"Do you think they're listening? Are they *watching*?" she murmured back.

"Not watching. They shouldn't take such steps unless we make them suspicious. So let's not give them a reason to watch." Bruce's breath tickled her skin.

"What should we do?" she asked, a bit breathless. He smelled good. There was no reason he should, after traveling all day, but he still did.

"Unpack our mysterious locked trunks so the help can examine all our things?"

"I have a better idea." She fluttered her eyelashes and whispered, "Will my adoring husband escort me on a walk through the formal gardens? I am weary, and want the solace of nature." That last phrase was from one of Sophie's recent plays.

"I would be delighted," he murmured back.

Bruce slipped a possessive arm around her as soon as they reached the gardens. Sophie responded by leaning into him. Anyone watching would think they were a couple.

As they walked, Sophie asked, "How did you know that painting was a de la Tour?"

"I did study a bit in school," he said, shrugging.

"Well, that's lucky. I had no idea. Until you mentioned the name, I didn't know I should be impressed."

"Don't be too impressed. It's a fake."

"You're sure?" Sophie asked.

"Fakes. Almost all of them. You can smell the linseed oil once you get close, and the paint is barely dry. They're good reproductions, but they aren't the real thing."

"I wonder if Theriot knows, or if he got taken. He sounded impressed with himself," Sophie said thoughtfully.

"And you sounded like you knew what you were talking about when he was escorting you around," Bruce added.

Sophie said, "There's an art to talking about things you don't know. Mostly, you ask a few questions and let other people show off their knowledge, which they're happy to do."

"So you don't know about art?"

"As I told you before, I know plays and politics," Sophie said. "On nearly every other matter, I make it up as I go along."

"I should have expected that," he muttered.

Sophie's plan to flee outside, where they could speak without being overheard, was slightly marred by the fact that only a small portion of the gardens closest to the house were tended with any degree of care. But Sophie noticed a small hill with a crown of trees at its top, and directed Bruce to walk her there. The view would be excuse enough.

On the hilltop, she sat down on the grass and he followed suit, remaining close by her to maintain the fiction of their relationship, should anyone be watching from the house.

Sophie smiled as she leaned over to him. "What do you think so far?"

Bruce smiled back, but his hand clamped down on her arm. "I think you're reckless."

"What do you mean?" Sophie felt a sting from the unexpected criticism.

He continued, "We had a plan, yet you ignored it completely. You had no idea what you were walking into!"

"I trusted my instincts!" she hissed back. "And it worked. He'll be eating out of my hand by this time tomorrow."

"Not if I have anything to say about it." He leaned closer to her. "Making it up as you go along! Do you have any idea how close you were to getting both of us exposed? One wrong phrase, and there wouldn't be anything I could do to save you."

"I'm not looking for a savior!" Sophie snapped.

"Well, you've got one whether you want it or not. My job is to protect you, dove. And I do that by thinking ahead. When you go off on your own, both of us suffer. Do you know how many times in that conversation I nearly had my heart stop, wondering if your answer was the right one?"

Sophie had been worried too, but she didn't think Bruce had been. "Look, it all ended well enough. Don't you think we learned something?"

After a long moment, he nodded and released his hold on her. "I think we know the nature of our host, and why the Cassous were invited. You're the prize. He wants you as a lover."

"He didn't waste time, did he?"

"But you won't seek his company tonight?"

"Far too early," she said. "He'll not value the conquest if it comes without effort."

"You did well to draw all those names out of him," he admitted grudgingly.

"Did any of them sound meaningful to you?" she asked.

"A few. Known sympathizers of the old monarchy in France. Interestingly, I don't think any are vocal supporters of the Emperor."

"Which doesn't make them allies to England."

"God, no. Staying in this house will be like sleeping in a snake pit."

"There's a pleasant image," Sophie said, shuddering. She put one hand on his. "Let's discuss what precisely we should do at dinner. I know you like a plan."

He glared at her, his eyes still stormy. "What's the point of making a plan if you dance off the nearest cliff each time?" His face was tight with anger and—she was stunned to realize—disappointment. In his eyes, she'd failed him. Sophie wasn't used to failing.

She also sensed something else beneath his anger: concern. He genuinely worried that she'd put them both in physical danger, which would destroy the whole façade.

Sophie at last felt a twinge of regret. "I should have given you some warning."

"You bloody well should have." His expression didn't change, but some of the darkness in his eyes retreated. "There will be plenty of time to risk our lives, dove. Don't go looking for opportunities."

He *had* been concerned for her. Sophie felt a tension rise in her chest. She didn't know how to deal with Bruce's concern, so she pushed it aside for the moment. "Tell me your plan for tonight. I'll stick to it. I promise."

"Once we go down to dinner, we can split up. Flirt just like you did before. It seems to be effective. We should each talk to the other guests and find out exactly what everyone is doing here. Did Theriot invite them all? What has he told them…if he told different stories, why? And why is he planning such a large party? Who is here for other reasons?"

"And who might know the Cassou couple?" Sophie added. "So many guests. I don't like it. We don't know if any of them has actually met 'us'. If so, someone could expose us in a heartbeat."

"Oh, now you recognize the dangers! We'll deal with that when and if it comes. Just get through dinner tonight and get back safe to our room. We can compare notes then. Later on, I want to get the layout of this whole house down. I'll slip out of the room tonight to map it."

"A likely story," Sophie said, playing up her role as a jealous wife to lighten the mood. "I saw how that maid looked at you."

He was startled for a moment, then laughed. "I doubt it. I'd try to seduce the lass if I thought it would do any good at all. But she doesn't seem like a font of knowledge."

"Nonsense. She's a local girl, and she's obviously intimidated by the quality of the guests. A few kind words from you would have her spilling every secret in the shire."

He shrugged. "Perhaps I'll try, if the opportunity arises."

"You should. If nothing else, your attention might thwart a previous order to spy on us."

"You think she got such instructions?" he asked.

"Remember how upset she was when I said I'd be there for unpacking! I'll wager anything the entire household staff has orders to report anything odd."

"Which means Theriot is expecting trouble. Well, perhaps I should pay a bit more attention to the maid after all," Bruce said.

"Let's go back," Sophie said, standing up again. "I want to rest before we have to get ready for this evening. The prologue went well, but the first act starts tonight."

Chapter 10

♏

BRUCE AND SOPHIE RETURNED TO the house, where he saw her to their room. Then he took advantage of the lull to orient himself as soon as he could. The first floor of the house had been completely redone, as had the main wing of the guest rooms. But as he walked into the upper floors and further wings, the appearance of the house got steadily seedier. It was clean, but not new. Old paint and paper adorned the walls. Curtains had a certain stiffness of age about them. Theriot spent plenty of money on first impressions, but he didn't have unlimited funds.

Bruce didn't have time to go further. He made his way back to the main wing, and encountered the maid Maggie again. She was walking down a hallway, going from bedroom to bedroom to check that all was ready for the guests. She curtsied nervously when Bruce sighted her.

He thought of Sophie's words of the other day. A woman first thinks *how can he hurt me*. The maid might be scared of a lord cornering her. He blinked, seeing himself in that position for the first time. Of course she would be! Bruce had to calm her down.

"I am terribly embarrassed to admit this," he said to the maid. "but I've lost my way. Which wing was the small library in?"

She relaxed a bit. "You're in the wrong part of the house, sir. You need to retrace your steps to the grand staircase and go down one flight. The small library is in the east wing."

"Thank you," he said. "You know your way around well. Have you worked at Carterhaugh very long?"

"Oh, no sir. The staff was all hired last month. Over twenty people from Bromthorpe alone! This house was shut up until earlier this summer. We never thought it would open again. But the new owner has spruced it up."

"You mean, he hired plenty of fair maids to spruce it up for him," Bruce corrected with a smile. "I doubt *he* swept all the floors."

She giggled at the image. "No, sir. We didn't even see him until this week! He came up from London, I think."

"Just in time to meet all his guests. He asked you to keep an eye on us, didn't he?"

Maggie couldn't hide her reaction to his question. Her eyes widened and she choked out an inane response. "Oh, no. That is, yes. To see that all was proper...well, that is..."

"I see," Bruce said. He'd got what he wanted. "Your shoes are quite worn, Maggie," he said, looking down.

She shuffled so her skirt hid the tips of the shoes. "I apologize, sir. They were my sister's before me."

"Nothing to apologize for, Maggie. I imagine shoes don't last long when you work on your feet all day."

The maid's eyes flashed warily, anticipating a crude offer of how she might work "off her feet."

But Bruce merely handed her a coin, saying, "Buy yourself a new pair. A small thank you for keeping me from wandering the halls for weeks."

She ducked her head as she accepted the coin. "Thank you kindly, sir. I must return to my work now."

"So you must. I retrace my steps, and one flight down to the other side. Correct?"

She nodded. "Yes, sir."

Bruce followed the maid's instructions to the small library, though he'd known where it was all along. Maggie had dropped a few interesting pieces of information; what was more, she wouldn't regard him as an instant threat in the future. Sophie's strange revelation had been useful after all.

Sophie rested while Bruce prowled the house, and said she felt much better when the time came to dress for dinner. At Sophie's suggestion, Bruce headed down to the main floor while she completed her lengthier preparations. Her arch, flirtatious comment about not having his advantages didn't fool him. Sophie had already shown that she could change her dress and appearance like lighting, if need be. He thought the real reason for why she wanted solitude was because Sophie needed to be alone to truly prepare for her role. The persona of Madame Cassou was so far from Sophie's own philosophy and demeanor that maintaining it had to require immense concentration.

Downstairs, Bruce was pondering the idea of how actors conceived of their work when he caught sight of someone he absolutely did not expect to see: a narrow-faced, blond man with a ready laugh. It was Charles

Wolverton, the Zodiac agent known as Pisces.

He must have been under some sort of cover, because he was dressed in a flashy manner that was unlike his usual sober attire. He wore a tight-fitting green coat over a rather too ruffled shirt, but every piece of clothing he wore was obviously expensive. A lady hung nearby, eagerly listening to whatever doggerel Charlie spouted. She was impressed by his appearance, his intelligence, his made-up persona, or all three.

Charlie glanced around the room at that point. When he caught Bruce's gaze, he stilled for a split second, then made the most minute shake of his head. *Come here*, he seemed to say.

Bruce obliged. He sidled slowly toward the other agent, first greeting a few other guests.

Charlie, as the son of wealthy gentry, had no need to prove himself, but he'd served in various diplomatic capacities almost from the moment he left school. He had joined the Zodiac shortly after Bruce. Charlie, one of the few agents he knew personally, had briefed him before a few key assignments, providing information that probably saved his life.

When he reached Charlie, the other man nodded to him in a friendly fashion. His expression was neutral, but Bruce knew he was taking in virtually every detail around him. Charlie was quite frequently the smartest man in the room. "Cassou," he said, keeping to Bruce's cover.

"Been a while," Bruce said laconically. He wasn't sure what name Charlie was using, and he didn't want to trip up. He was still recovering from Sophie's improvisation earlier.

Charlie turned to the lady he had been speaking to. "Will you excuse me? I have a very dull item of business to discuss with this gentleman here, and then I shall fly back to you."

The lady tittered and assented even as Charlie steered Bruce away.

"I'm glad I caught you early. I have a message for you," Charlie muttered.

Bruce looked around and gestured toward the staircase. "We can talk on the stairs. We'll hear someone coming either way."

Charlie followed him. They reached the stairs and took a few steps up. Just below the landing, Bruce stopped and let Charlie take one more step than he did, because he towered over the other agent.

Bruce looked over his friend. "Interesting outfit." It was an example of pure dandyism. Rich fabrics were cut tightly to emphasize just how tailored the outfit was. Only a rich man could afford such a look, no matter how ridiculous it might be.

Charlie grimaced at the back-handed compliment. "Don't say a word. I feel like a sausage in a casing, but this was the best I could do on short notice."

"What's going on?" Bruce tried to keep calm. Surely Charlie wasn't there to replace him! It was far too late for that. Theriot had already met him, and Sophie.

The other man leaned forward and lowered his voice. "I have to tell you something. You know about Arceneau, correct? Aries told you?"

Bruce nodded. "I've run into some of his underlings before."

"Well, things are going to get complicated for you. He's sending one of his closest associates here, to this house. Which was…unexpected."

"Do you know who?"

"A man by the name of Volange."

That name was familiar. Sophie claimed to know the man. "What does that mean for the assignment?" Bruce asked. "Does it shorten the timeline?"

Charlie shook his head. "No. In fact, you need to stay to discover what more is being planned here. Arceneau rarely shows his hand, so this is an unprecedented opportunity. Theriot isn't acting on his own. He's got involved with Arceneau on some very deep level. But you need to be circumspect and not take any risks. Volange is a dangerous gentleman."

"Aries sent you to tell me that?" Bruce asked. Charlie must have ridden like hell to have gotten here so soon after he and Sophie did.

Charlie nodded. "He found out just after you left, and didn't trust a written message. He's extremely concerned that this assignment go flawlessly." He glanced around. "Is Libra here at the house?"

"Yes."

Charlie winced at that revelation. "Then I have one other thing to tell you. Don't trust Libra."

Bruce's chest contracted in shock. "Aries didn't tell you that," he said in disbelief.

"I overheard him talking to Chattan," Charlie explained. "She's unflappable about everything else—I couldn't help but notice when she made a remark about Libra. Something about Aries having a blind spot."

"Noted," Bruce said slowly. "Do you know when Volange is expected?"

"Two or three days, most likely."

Bruce ran a hand through his hair. "This is not what we bargained for."

"Aries sent *you* for a reason, man. You'll think of something. I heard about what happened in Calais. Brilliant work."

Bruce shook his head. "I was barely involved..." He broke off, wondering if he heard footsteps. But there was nothing. "Just tagging along, really," he concluded.

"Don't be modest. I knew that with the three of you on the case, the *Andraste* plans would be found..."

Bruce had stopped listening. His thoughts lingered on what Charlie said. Chattan's distrust, together with Sophie's disregard for his plans, and her desire to be alone suggested only one thing. She was not who she appeared to be.

* * * *

Upstairs, Sophie spent a few minutes contemplating her choices. She'd sent Bruce down ahead of her, knowing the last thing a man wanted to do was stand around waiting for a lady to get ready for dinner. And she wanted to maintain some semblance of privacy, which all women needed.

Physically, she was pleased with the overall ensemble.

As Madame Cassou, she wore a fancier look than she'd choose for herself. This dress was a lightweight silk, dyed a brilliant green. She wore the sparkling diamond cross pendant on a chain around her neck.

She checked her final appearance in the mirror. The wig fit perfectly, and no one would guess the color wasn't her own, as the brown curls harmonized with Sophie's natural complexion.

But would they know what she really was? Sophie was used to living two lives. She also had plenty of experience pretending to like what she hated and to care about things she had no interest in. Madame Cassou was no different from those other roles. The character was just a means to an end.

"I can do this," Sophie murmured. "I am the part I play."

Feeling stronger, she headed to dinner after locking the bedroom door. She was certain there were multiple keys to all the rooms, but she had to keep up the pretense. She walked down the hall to the ground floor, feeling the assignment was going smoothly enough so far.

However, she stopped short at the head of the stairs when she heard Bruce speaking in a low voice to another man.

She backed up against the wall so they wouldn't see her.

The stranger was speaking. "...I heard about what happened in Calais. Brilliant work."

"I was barely involved," Bruce said. "Just tagging along, really."

"Oh, don't be modest," said the other voice. "I knew that with the three of you on the case, the *Andraste* plans would be found."

There was a pause, then Bruce said, "We were lucky."

"That's a good thing to be. Speaking of luck, I can't press mine further. Message delivered, so I'm leaving now. Be careful."

"Always am, Charlie," Bruce said.

Sophie heard a set of footsteps departing. Charlie? It sounded like another agent met with Bruce. Was there new information? Why had Bruce alone been told, and he'd not waited for her to arrive?

She took a breath and moved forward, making no more attempt to be quiet. Bruce heard her and was looking up at her when she rounded the top of the steps.

Sophie pasted a smile on her face. "Did you wait for me, darling? That was sweet." She didn't mention the conversation.

Neither did Bruce. His expression was a careful mask. If Sophie didn't know better, she would have said he was sizing her up.

But then he said, "I thought we should go in together. A husband wouldn't let his wife out of his sight in this place, would he?"

Sophie laughed lightly, concealing her annoyance at his behavior. "One can imagine all sorts of clandestine meetings here, can't one?" she asked slyly.

He refused to be baited. "It's the perfect house for hiding in."

"But I wish to be seen, dear," Sophie said with a careless air. She would be a perfect Madame Cassou if it killed her.

Sophie tried to put the odd exchange Bruce had with the other agent out of her head. She'd wrangle the truth out of him soon enough…whether by seduction or sword point, she didn't care.

But for now, she had a job to do.

Chapter 11

Ω

THE DINNER THAT FIRST EVENING was extravagant, even
by aristocratic standards. About ten guests were at the
house—more were expected to arrive within the next few
days—but the food would have fed a battalion. Four cour-
ses, featuring over twenty dishes each, occupied most of
the table. Roasted game lay next to delicately spiced fish,
and the smells were unquestionably divine. The host
bragged of his all-French kitchen staff, though the visible
servers were decidedly British. Sophie joined the other
guests in praising the superiority of the meal. She picked
at most of the dishes, though. She was too consumed with
identifying all the guests.

First, there was Mr Marc Deverall, a dandy and rake.
He was quite an appealing man…at least as a dinner
guest. He was witty and attentive, and furthermore possessed blue eyes that more than one woman had succumbed to over the years. He was English by birth, unlike
many of the guests. But it was an open secret that his family had made a fortune in smuggling, so the host's interest
in him was clear. A business alliance to smuggle goods
between England and France would be valuable to any

group hoping to influence the war. But precisely what goods would be shipped? And where would they be shipped? And would Deverall even survive the house party? Considering the sheer volume of wine he drank, Sophie had her doubts.

Then there was Lady Danielle Randolph, who sat next to Deverall and was already falling prey to his charm. She possessed wide-set green eyes and soft, light blond hair that haloed around her head. Unbound, her hair would surely make some men think her an angel. And even if she were not a beauty, her income (estimated at well over thirty thousand a year) would keep any man's interest. Deverall himself appeared to be making a serious play for her attention. Theriot, too, had already made a comment that caused Sophie to prick up her ears; she guessed he wanted some kind of payment from Danielle. Could he be blackmailing her? Tricking her?

At present, Lady Danielle appeared to be taken with Deverall, though she also paid compliments to Theriot and to the false Lord Cassou. Bruce kept his interaction with her to the level of politeness and nothing more. After all, his role was to appear most interested in Sophie. She tried to watch his eyes to see if they strayed to Lady Danielle more than usual. But she couldn't tell.

Further down the table, the older Madame Baden was as outspoken as Danielle was subtle. A matriarch with silver hair and a stentorian voice, she pronounced everyone's greatest assets and flaws as she saw them, and offered her services as matchmaker to anyone in need. She promised Danielle she'd see the girl "settled" by the end of the week. Sophie took pleasure in seeing Danielle's skin turn a faint green—the lady knew very well that her power lay in her eligibility.

Mr Baden was a non-entity compared to his wife. He was short in stature, and his slight frame and wispy hair only served to make him less noticeable. However, he was well-connected politically. He called several members of the cabinet personal friends, and knew most of the more influential members of the House of Lords. Sophie would not discount Baden as a major player in whatever Theriot had planned.

There were a few other guests who Sophie noted in passing, mostly French expatriates and refugees of the Terror. The Comte de Marche—almost certainly not a real Comte—was a dealer in art and likely a fence as well. His companion was the voluptuous Mademoiselle Eugenie, a woman best known for her association with several famous artists on the continent. She posed as a model for many paintings. Some were astonishing works of true artistic significance. Other paintings, Eugenie explained with a wink, were of a more whimsical and intimate nature, to be found only in private art collections. De Marche and Eugenie lived together without the benefit of marriage, and showed not the slightest shame about it. A few men at the far end of the table remained mysterious to Sophie. She didn't see anyone who looked like he might be another agent. She wondered if the man called Charlie had fled the house entirely.

After dinner, everyone moved to a large drawing room. Drinks flowed freely, and hired musicians, including a comic opera singer, performed the latest music. The songs got more suggestive as the night went on.

Sophie spent her time flattering other guests. Men surrounded her quickly enough, and she dazzled them with well-timed barbs and quips. She decided she could twist Deverall around her finger if need be. And Theriot's eyes were frequently on her.

She learned a little more about why these people came all the way to Carterhaugh Manor. A few murmured about the hostilities, but nearly everyone expressed interest in the many illicit diversions Theriot had promised them. Even the most jaded libertine would be impressed by what was coming in the next few days: dancers, drugs, and other diversions.

"And until the surprises arrive," Deverall noted, "there's enough wine to fill the North Sea."

"Not after you've been around the bottles," another man said.

Everyone laughed. Sophie watched Bruce out of the corner of her eye. He looked like a different person altogether when he smiled. He held a half-empty wine glass in one hand. Sophie didn't know how much he drank, but perhaps that was the reason for the shift in personality.

After Sophie glanced his way, Bruce worked at not appearing too obvious as he kept an eye on *her*. Bruce thought about Charlie's warning all evening. He watched Sophie with colder eyes, trying to see whether her actions betrayed her. He couldn't tell anything, though. Sophie was practically a stranger. How could he know if she was being herself, or if something was afoot?

Was it significant that she was French, like so many of the guests? But if Sophie were working for the French side, surely she would have been eliminated by now… unless the Zodiac was waiting for proof. Perhaps that was the real reason Bruce was there. He was to find incontrovertible evidence of Sophie's betrayal so he could take her back to Aries and the Astronomer. He just had to find the link between her and Theriot.

It would be a little like a seduction. He looked around at the crowd in the room, all getting tipsy, both on the copious amounts of wine and on the promise of hedonism. A seduction would fit right in. The only problem with that was that Bruce never felt particularly comfortable when he had to use seduction. He could do it. He had done so on several occasions for other assignments. But he hated the whole process. There were few feelings less desirable than tricking a woman into bed just because she knew something useful. The women he'd seduced were largely bystanders in the secret wars of espionage, holding secrets they didn't know were valuable, or providing access to the people he was really after.

Sophie didn't appear to have the same qualms. Bruce watched her flirt and wink at nearly every man around the table. She wasn't a bystander. He shouldn't feel guilty about seducing her if he could expose her as a double agent. *And what if she's not?* he thought. *How will I justify it then?*

Then again, Sophie wasn't a lady. She'd told him so

herself.

* * * *

The evening dragged on. Sophie had never been handed so many glasses of wine, and managing not to finish them was a challenge in itself. She received no less than three offers from men to slip away from the festivities. She declined them all, though with the sort of coquettish laugh that suggested *later*, rather than *never*.

A female singer with a throaty alto voice sang songs that no proper lady should hear. Yet the guests just laughed giddily and allowed the farce to continue. Lady Danielle shot a furtive look at Bruce after one particularly suggestive line, her eyes betraying a most unladylike interest. Unexpectedly, Sophie felt a twinge. How dare that so-called lady consider Bruce for a dalliance! *Wait,* Sophie told herself. *You don't know when that might be useful.* And really, what did she care if Bruce bedded Danielle at some point?

Sophie glanced at Bruce again. She could see why Danielle might be interested. He was striking. In his current persona, he was more approachable than he was as himself. Cassou was a lazy, careless aristocrat who clearly lived for pleasure. Bruce himself was dull, obsessed with details and duty. Danielle wouldn't like the real Bruce at all. Even if he did know how to kiss a woman rather well.

Sophie felt her cheeks heat at the memory. She snapped open her fan and used it, then kept it open to serve as a shield. Still, it took her a few moments to cool down.

Madame Baden cornered Sophie during a lull in the entertainment. After chatting idly for a minute, she said, "Tell me of your family. You must be connected to the Garniers."

"Not to my knowledge," Sophie said, cursing herself for not knowing more about the Cassou relations. "My maiden name was Laforge."

"But you look just like the Comtesse de Garnier! The hair! The eyes!"

"I don't know who that is," Sophie said with finality. Since she was currently wearing a wig, she doubted Madame Baden was correct.

It didn't stop the lady. "No, no. You're the spitting image, I'm sure. Robert, look at Madame Cassou here. Does she not make you think of the Comtesse de Garnier?"

Her husband, the older gentlemen she addressed as Robert, looked over. He took in Sophie's appearance with appreciation, but no recognition. "Not especially," he declared.

"Oh, you men are blind! Blind!" Baden regarded Sophie again. "The height! The nose! Those cheekbones! You look as though you merely await your crown, dear. That is the mark of a true aristocrat. No commoner could hope to match the bearing of someone of really pure blood."

Sophie murmured a suitable reply. Inside, she wanted to laugh. Pure blood? If Baden knew who Sophie's mother really was, she'd run the other direction.

Madame Baden, fortunately, was called away by other

guests. Sophie breathed a sigh of relief. Then she turned around, and saw Bruce had joined her. "What was that all about?" His hand slipped around her waist in a familiar gesture.

"Apparently I look like someone else," Sophie muttered. "An old acquaintance of Madame Baden's."

"Well, you do look like someone else." Bruce kept his voice low, so only she could hear him over the din in the room. He smiled down at her, and Sophie was struck by the warmth in his eyes.

"A different someone else," she clarified. "Some French noblewoman. She thinks I lack only the tiara!" She made a dismissive gesture. "It doesn't mean anything. People are always telling me I look like someone they know." But rarely with such unwavering conviction. Who was this person, and why would Sophie look like her at all?

Before she could think on that further, Bruce leaned in and brushed a lock of hair back from her neck. His fingers grazed her skin, and Sophie felt a distinct frisson, even though they were in full view of everyone.

"What are you doing?" she asked in a low voice.

"Appearing enamored of you." He dipped his head lower, murmuring, "Humor me. If we look as if we're about to rip each other's clothes off, we can escape to our room and get the hell away from this crowd."

Escape? *That* was the best idea she'd heard all evening. Sophie laughed suggestively. "Do you really think so?" she asked in a louder voice.

"I'll convince you," he replied, smiling in a way that

actually made her stomach flutter the tiniest bit.

He led her out of the room, accepting a few risqué comments from other guests about how they would spend their evening.

Apparently to keep up the pretense, Bruce kept his arm around her even after they left the main room. Sophie didn't protest, and in truth she no longer minded his proximity.

It was only when he closed the door to their room that he released her. "I thought I'd punch one of those idiots if I stayed," he growled.

Sophie had heard a few of the opinions of the men regarding the English militia and its quality, and she was indeed surprised at Bruce's restraint. "You didn't let your feelings show," she reassured him.

The room was illuminated by a single candle, lit by Maggie so the guests wouldn't stumble in the dark. The dim light made Bruce mostly shadow, and emphasized his scowl.

"I *can* manage as long as I have to," he said. "But sometimes wish I could—"

Sophie heard a strange sound, like a quick patter in the hallway. Was someone out there listening? She put her finger to her lips and jerked her head toward the door.

Bruce understood instantly. He stepped up to her, pushing her closer to the wall next to the doorway. "I wish I could send all them away so I could make you scream the way you did in Austria," he said, just loudly enough to be heard by someone outside.

Sophie let herself give a throaty laugh, even as she

started at his unexpected words. She hoped if there was a maid listening, she'd have her ears burned by their talk. She winked at Bruce. "As I recall, you began at the top and worked your way to the bottom." She drawled the improvised words in her warmest voice, and fancied she heard a stifled gasp from outside.

Then she didn't listen for the eavesdropper any more, because Bruce was there, keeping her against the wall with his hands. His kisses traced her neck and chest, leaving Sophie free to moan in pleasure.

And she did moan. It was easy, because it turned out she had remembered his skill correctly. Sophie heard some words between the kisses, and she gasped in response, leaning into him as he worked his way from one shoulder to the other.

"Beg me for more," he demanded in a low tone.

She did, quite honestly.

"Louder, so our audience can hear you," he prompted.

Audience? Oh, yes. Sophie raised her voice and begged prettily for more, and hoped her words would work on him.

They did. Sophie knew there was an excellent reason why she was letting him do this to her, but her skin was warming under his touch, and she didn't particularly care if anyone could hear. She slipped her hands under his jacket, feeling the strength of the body underneath.

Dimly, Sophie heard voices in the corridor, and the sound of footsteps retreating. She should tell him it was safe, that his touch was no longer necessary. She should... but when his breath warmed her neck, she sighed with pure pleasure, her body flaming yet calming at his whim. If only…

"You can stop now," she whispered.

He pulled back, watching her with a calculating expression. "Do you want me to?"

Sophie watched Bruce with narrowed eyes. Had he not been affected at all? The last time they kissed—at the inn—he'd also pushed her away. Only once did she draw any kind of reaction out of him. Perhaps he wasn't as susceptible to her as other men had been.

She refused to believe it. "What do you want?" she asked, putting a little purr in her voice. Surely if she strung him along a bit, she'd discover more about him.

He didn't say anything, but moved to be close to her again. He dipped his head to kiss her neck, just below her ear. His kiss was softer this time…he was doing it for her benefit now, not an audience outside. His hands came up around her neck, grazing her skin gently.

She lifted her chin and finally kissed him, her lips tickled by the first signs of stubble on his face.

He shifted, and then a weight fell away from her neck. Bruce drew the necklace away from her and carefully let it drop to the carpet. Sophie hadn't even noticed him undoing the clasp.

"That's the only one I have," she warned. "I need it."

"You don't need it now," he said.

"It's part of my role…"

"I'm uninterested in your role, dove. I want to see you. The hair and dress…take them off."

Sophie took a deep breath. He wanted to see her?

Well, she had to change at some point anyway.

"I'll take care of my hair. You can help with the dress." She deliberately kept her tone light, though she was now nervous.

He sat on the edge of the bed, and watched as she carefully loosed the pins that held the mass of curls in place. She rarely felt shy when taking off a costume or a wig, but then, she never did so with such an attentive audience. Bruce didn't take his eyes off her, and she flushed under his gaze.

The wig came off, leaving her short, dark hair in an untidy mess. But Bruce only smiled, and said, "Come here."

She did, not thinking twice about it.

Still sitting, he ran his hands through her hair once. The action relaxed her, but made her feel vulnerable, so she took refuge in mockery. "You like the short cut, don't you. Boyish enough for you?"

He only drew her closer. "Stop pretending you look like anything other than a beautiful woman, dove. It's disingenuous."

"Don't flatter me. I have the figure of a willow twig."

"I don't have to flatter you. You have the figure of a nymph, and you know it. Your beauty is all in the way you move. When you walk, when you lift an arm…no man can look away."

"Like this?" She lifted her arms and twined them around his neck. She saw his eyes close briefly, and reveled in his reaction.

"Exactly like that. When I look at you, I can tell you

never just let your body be still. You wrap yourself around a man."

She did. Sophie had never considered it before, but she always did that. How the hell did he know that? She leaned into him. "I could do that now."

His breath quickened. "Let me take your dress off first."

She shrugged, smiling a little. "If you like."

"Turn around, dove."

He took his time undoing the back of the gown. He laid a simple kiss on her bared skin after he undid each button. The first few kisses made Sophie laugh softly, but by the time he slid the gown off her shoulders and was halfway down her spine, she waited in anticipation of the next kiss, since each one made her shiver with pleasure. Each interval grew longer, as he waited an inordinate time to slide the fabric of her dress and the chemise underneath lower down.

She wanted him to reach the small of her back, knowing somehow that she'd love his touch there. But why was it taking so long?

"Are you teasing me?" she asked. She began to twist around to see him.

His hands quickly tightened on her waist, keeping her in place. "You object to the pace? Tell me, then."

"No...I like it," she said, remembering she wanted to see what he considered seductive. At least, she thought that was what she wanted...she couldn't quite recall her reasoning at the moment.

Bruce finally slid the fabric down past her hips, and

Sophie did turn around then. She reached for his shirt, and tugged it loose. He let her, and discarded it quickly. Sophie had seen him half naked before, but not in a candlelit room, not when she was already nude.

Before she could decide what to do, he gently pulled her toward him, and kissed her again, this time starting in the exact center of her chest. Then he moved to one breast, and Sophie gasped when he took one nipple in his mouth. He didn't rush, and as she slowly warmed at the touch of his mouth, she had more than enough time to doubt the wisdom of her plan. Why was it important to know how he'd treat her in bed? She already knew he wouldn't force her into anything. He had the opportunity before and let her alone.

Oh, admit it, she told herself. It was because most of the men she had to seduce didn't look like him.

Because he was precisely what women dreamed of. Remembering his earlier words, she reached up and curled her arms around his shoulders. She heard him sigh in response. Could it really take so little? She hadn't even tried anything really scandalous yet.

She felt the urge to touch the scar on his back. She saw how he held his scarred shoulder slightly differently, as if he was still anticipating another strike. Sympathy was not what she wanted to feel, she reminded herself. She only wanted to learn about him.

Except she was really only learning about herself, specifically that she liked Bruce's attention far more than she expected to. He continued to kiss her breasts, with the same delightful and maddening pace. Sophie's breathing quickened, and she couldn't hide her reactions. She wasn't pretending to be pleased. Everything he did to her felt lovely, and she didn't want it to stop.

This whole diversion could quickly get out of hand. She knew how aroused he was, and he hadn't even finished taking his own clothes off. It was a powerful feeling, but alarming too. It meant he was attracted to her, to Sophie…not to someone she pretended to be.

Well, he can't have me, she thought, suddenly angry. That was not something she offered anyone. She had to stop this before it went further. She wasn't someone's mistress, she was an agent. An agent…she recalled the event earlier. That was what she wanted to know from him.

Sophie didn't blurt out the question. She would ask in her own way.

She moved her hands to push Bruce all the way back on the bed, and then she moved above him, her legs on either side of him. She smiled coyly, then bent down to kiss him lightly on the lips, judging his reaction. From the way his hands drifted to her hips and held her against him, he was thinking of nothing else but lust.

She shifted so she could whisper in his ear. "This is what you want?" she asked softly.

"It's an excellent beginning," he said, his voice tight.

"Ah. Speaking of beginnings," she asked, sitting up. "Who's Charlie?"

He blinked, then focused on her. "What?"

She crossed her arms over her chest. Though she was still naked, she felt far more in control than she had a moment ago. "Don't pretend you don't know what I'm talking about. You spoke with someone you called Charlie earlier this evening. I overheard you from the stairs. It sounded like he was giving you a message."

"He was…" Bruce began. Then he seemed to wake up completely. He sat up, forcing Sophie to come face to face with him. His hands, still on her, suddenly pushed her off him. "Bloody hell, you did all this to ask me about that conversation?"

She found her footing and stood up next to the bed. She threw him a superior glance. "I wanted to know how you…worked. And how difficult it would be to get information out of you."

"Really."

She found her chemise and quickly slid it over her head. "Yes. You didn't think I was seduced, did you? Utterly undone by your kisses?"

"You didn't object," he said, watching her narrowly.

"I had to give you a few minutes to lose your head."

"You didn't, in fact. You could have simply asked."

"And you could have simply told me," said Sophie. "If you trusted me as a partner, you would have informed me…at the beginning."

"As we went downstairs? There wasn't time, and too many people to overhear." He slid off the bed, and moved away from her. "The way you played along…I should have known you were up to something." Shaking his head, he found his shirt and put it on. "Well, at least you didn't threaten to cut my throat this time."

Sophie glared at him. Was he laughing? "You're treating this as a joke?"

He lost his faint smile. "That's essentially how you treated all…this," he said, gesturing to the bed. "Frankly, I'd rather you hold a knife to my throat than pretend you feel something you don't. It's…well, if you wanted to know how to repel me, now you do."

"Noted." Sophie sought the comfort of the open window, where a night breeze entered.

Bruce joined her there after a minute, holding something in his hand. "Your necklace, darling," he said, his tone perfectly cool.

She took it, resolutely not looking at him. "So. Who is Charlie and what message did he give you?" she asked.

Bruce didn't say anything for a moment, and Sophie added, "Since we're speaking of *trusting* each other."

"Charles Wolverton. A man I've known for years."

"And…one of ours?"

"Yes. He's Pisces. He had a message for us, and I took it. I'm sorry I didn't wait for you, but he didn't want to linger."

"As long as you tell me what he said, I'll forgive the lapse."

"One of Arceneau's lieutenants is coming here within the next few days. We'll have to be careful when he arrives, and see what more we might learn."

"Did Pisces say who it would be?"

Bruce paused, then said, "It's unclear."

"Well, that's not terribly useful in the end, is it?"

"At least we know someone more important than Theriot is planning to join the group. That's not insignificant."

"I suppose."

She watched as Bruce turned around and picked out some new clothes. He changed into a dark outfit, one that lacked any distinction. In dim light or at a distance, he might be mistaken for a number of other men, or just ignored completely.

"What do you intend to do now?"

"I need to finish learning the house," he said. "I didn't have enough time before."

"We should both go."

"It's more dangerous for both of us to be out," Bruce disagreed. "I can explain it away by getting 'lost' or pretending to search someone out. Besides, I think we could do with a separation."

She rolled her eyes, but said, "I should know what the house looks like though."

He nodded. "Of course. I'll describe it to you once I get back."

"That's not the same at all. If you won't let me join you," Sophie said, irritated, "I'll just go on my own."

"No, you won't." Bruce had been relaxed, but now he pulled himself up to his full height again. "I won't let you."

"*Let* me? How will you stop me?" Sophie put her chin up.

Bruce frowned. "I'll...I'll lock you in."

"You're welcome to try." She'd been getting past locked doors since she was nine years old.

"God help me." He sighed. "Stop fighting against everything I say."

"I think you're wrong," she said, "but if you insist, go alone."

He looked at her suspiciously. "You're giving up?"

"Shouldn't that make you happy?" she asked, crossing her arms. "Now, are you going or not?"

"Consider me gone."

Chapter 12

♏

BRUCE WAS ONLY TOO HAPPY to escape the bedroom. Sophie continued to surprise him, and he seemed to lose face every time. If she hadn't said anything, he might have been completely ensnared by her. And he thought he had a chance of seducing *her*?

Bruce had to stop thinking of the incident, especially if he was to sleep next to her every night. That would be a unique form of torture. Why the devil did Julian insist on sending them together, again?

Enough, Bruce thought. His task was to understand the layout of the whole house, not just the places he'd seen before. Bruce was methodical where Sophie was not. In little more than an hour, he managed to walk down nearly every hallway and at least poke his head inside most of the unoccupied rooms. The notable exception was the wing where Theriot's private rooms lay. That part of the house was blocked by a rather dramatic entryway featuring the rood screen of an old church. A servant guarded the small door at all hours, so no one could enter or leave Theriot's apartments without being seen.

As Bruce continued to explore, he found something else odd. All the guests were crammed into one wing of the house. He found his way through an unlocked door to another wing where he discovered a number of bedrooms, all in adequate repair, but unused.

Why had the maid suggested there weren't enough rooms for everyone? Granted, these rooms were not lavish. But most guests wouldn't need much more than a modest bedroom. It seemed more likely that Theriot wanted to keep an eye on everyone by confining them to one part of the house.

After seeing all he could inside, Bruce slipped out a side door into the gardens. A half moon was just rising, and he breathed a sigh of relief that there would be light for him to navigate. A white stone path led away from the house. He reached the end of the path where a small brick building stood, probably a gardener's workshed. Larger trees kept the ground in dappled shadow, but a small movement made him stop.

"I thought you'd never be done." Sophie's voice came low and clear as she stepped closer. She was once again dressed as a boy, with slim black pants and a dark shirt. Her hair was short again, tucked underneath a cap.

"I should have known," he growled. "What are you doing out here?"

She said, "Being useful. I tested the latches on all the windows and the locks on all the doors. It might be very helpful to know how to get in or out in a hurry."

"And what did you find?" He tried not to notice— again—that her legs were too exposed by the costume she wore. He stifled the thought, but not before his stubbornly stupid body began to react to it. He moved to stand deeper in the shadows.

Sophie was now between him and the house. Blessedly, she didn't face him as she gestured. "The lower windows at the back of the house seem to be locked only sporadically. The doors leading to the servants' quarters and the kitchens are locked, but the doors toward the main staircase and the center of the house aren't."

"The servants tend to their own domain, but ignore the master's," he said. Now that he wasn't staring at Sophie, his own body was returning to normal. "Good to know."

"And you?" she asked.

"I went through the whole house, except for Theriot's quarters and a few locked rooms. I'll draw you a map later if you like."

"Give me the essentials now," Sophie ordered, turning around.

Bruce gave her a verbal sketch of the house's layout. Sophie's eyes gleamed in the rising moonlight, her expression intense as she absorbed his words. Her face was narrow, and her cheekbones high. When she turned to the side suddenly, looking at something in the trees, Bruce had a sense of déjà vu. He'd seen that face before. Not Sophie, but some boy who looked just like her…where?

"What's wrong?" Sophie asked, looking at him.

"Nothing," he said. "I see why people always think you're familiar. I just got the same feeling."

For some reason, the expression on her face was amused, knowing. "Tell me."

"I can't…I don't remember…" he trailed off. "I must be imagining things."

"Perhaps," Sophie said, her smile growing wider.

He reached out and held her by the shoulders. "You're making fun of me. You do know what I'm talking about."

"As I said earlier, people always think I look like someone they know. Perhaps you're thinking of the first time we met in the Oak Room. I was dressed like this then too."

But he knew that wasn't it. It was the cap, and her face below the cap. Sophie was warm beneath his hands, and he knew he should let her go before he started thinking the wrong sort of thoughts again. No, it was too late for that. Sophie already knew what he was thinking. Of course she did. She stretched lazily, provocatively, her unusual clothing showing the shape of her body underneath. "Something on your mind?" she asked.

"Stop it."

"Stop what?" she purred.

"You know what." Annoyed by his own reaction to her, Bruce pushed her against the brick wall of the little garden building.

"Am I so distracting?" she asked, breathless but unafraid.

"Your body is. What do you want to prove? Will it help if I admit that you know what you're doing when it comes to seduction? I admit it."

"Yet I can still do my job while you boil underneath your clothing. Why don't you just go home and admit I'm the better agent?"

"What if seduction alone won't solve this?" he retorted. "I'm staying, dove. And you will stop your constant teasing."

Her eyelids lowered and she looked away at last. In a dull voice she said, "I understand."

"You'll stop, then?"

"I already have."

Indeed, there was little about her that was provocative now. He realized he had pinned her against the wall, but she wasn't playing with him anymore. Her body was still, her expression cool. He suddenly felt like a heel for touching her, a fact that only made him angrier.

Bruce released her. "We need to trust each other," he said, in an attempt to regain his equilibrium. "No matter what you think of me as a man, at least respect our superior's choice to put us together on this assignment."

That seemed to have a salutary effect. Sophie nodded, her dark eyes serious. "I admit Julian usually knows what he's doing." It wasn't an apology, but it would do. If only she hadn't used Aries' first name, reminding him of the special relationship they apparently shared. He remembered Charlie's warning again. Julian had a blind spot when it came to Sophie. Perhaps because he loved her?

"We should get back to our room," he said. On the way, Bruce indicated the windows of Theriot's rooms as he walked with Sophie though the gardens. "Bastard keeps a sharp watch on everything. There's no way we're going to get inside his rooms without him knowing."

Sophie considered the situation. "Well, I see two options."

"Which are?"

"First, I could try to enter the windows from the roof."

Bruce looked at the height of the roof and shuddered. "That's impossible."

"Not at all. I just need a rope and a little time to myself."

"Isn't that what suicides say?" He shook his head. "This job isn't meant to be done by a common thief. What's the second option?"

"Theriot will invite me into his apartments himself."

"Why?"

Sophie looked at him in amusement. "For the usual reason."

Bruce liked that option even less, even though Sophie's success was all but assured. "You assume that you'd have time to yourself after…entertaining him."

"Oh, he'll sleep," Sophie said. "I can bring a bit of opium to ensure it. Then I can search the rooms at leisure after he's snoring away. The information's there somewhere."

"Unless he hid it somewhere else. Let's say you run out of time. What if you have to take more drastic steps?"

"Such as?"

"Killing your target."

"Then I kill him." She shrugged.

Bruce said, "You may find it more difficult than you think."

"You assume I speak as a novice."

The way she held her chin up and kept her gaze so steady made him nearly miss a step. "You've actually killed someone?"

"Why so surprised? You have."

"Yes, but in war."

"We are engaged in a war. I don't wear a uniform, but this is still a battle. Aries picked me because he knows I'm capable of doing whatever I have to do."

"Including killing?"

"Signs are selected for their potential as well as their past. Are you suggesting that he apply an arbitrary rule to all recruits? Two confirmed kills before you can join the elite agents…something like that?"

"It's not a bad idea."

She rolled her eyes. "Only a man would think that."

"Let's see what we can accomplish with talk first," he muttered. Bruce didn't like to think she would risk more than him to get the task done.

And, deeper in his mind, he had to admit he didn't like the idea of some other man hearing her make the sounds he'd heard earlier that night. *Well*, Bruce thought unhappily, *at least I'm in character*. Cassou was reportedly obsessed with his wife, and Bruce was starting to understand the feeling.

Chapter 13

Ω

THEY RETURNED TO THEIR ROOM without being seen. Sophie hurried to the one trunk she hadn't allowed Maggie to unpack earlier. She unlocked it with the only key, which she kept on a ribbon tucked into her clothing. She pulled out several boxes. One of them held the wig she wore earlier, which Sophie double-checked before replacing the lid. She couldn't afford to ruin the wig. She pulled her shirt over her head, then glanced over at Bruce. "Don't list this under provocation. I have to change out of these clothes and pack them away so no one sees them."

"I assure you, I'm not provoked."

"Then what happened in the garden?" she asked.

"You started it, dove."

Sophie grumbled something rude in French, but changed hurriedly. She soon had all the incriminating items of clothing locked safely away, and was clad in a simple shift.

When she finished, Bruce invited her to join him near the window again. She went, a little wary now. "What's on your mind?"

"What do you think?" he asked. "I mean, of Carterhaugh and the whole party so far?"

"You said something about a snake pit earlier," she said. "You were absolutely right."

"I wish I weren't," he replied. "And I wish we knew more about the real purpose of the gathering—I hate surprises. Who are these people? What are they truly doing here?"

"Other than eagerly anticipating saucy music and drinks they could swill down anywhere?" Sophie asked, contemptuously. Then she shook her head. "Unfortunately, we'll just have to wait until everyone arrives. Then Theriot will speak."

"What do you think of Theriot? A few words, quickly," he instructed. "Don't take time to reason it out."

Sophie closed her eyes and summoned an image of Theriot. "Weak. Swindler. Desperate," she said, using the words that surfaced first. She opened her eyes again. "Interesting."

Bruce nodded. "Interesting, indeed. Why *swindler*? Did he ask you for money earlier?"

"No," she began, "not directly. But I'm sure he will. There was something he said to Danielle over dinner that made me think he needs money. Maybe much more than he's letting on."

Bruce nodded again, slowly. "So he throws an extravagant party to soften up his marks? Possible."

"Or to get them in a position of weakness for when he asks for a favor," Sophie said. "Remember, there's a reason these people in particular were invited."

"Of course. They're all idiots with no thoughts for anything but their own pleasure."

"No! All of the guests—every single one—have some sort of real connection to the regime that existed before Bonaparte seized power, before the Revolution, even."

Bruce's expression grew interested. "You think so?"

"I'm sure of it. Madame Cassou herself would have been extremely well-placed in the French court, if the Revolution hadn't come along and destroyed her family. Trust me, these people aren't here to help the Emperor. They hate him."

"So?"

"My guess? This little party has been called to get them all into one place to discuss the possibility of restoring the old world."

"That's mad. The republican experiment didn't work out, but Bonaparte will let France burn before he allows any hint of the old kings to come back to power."

"These fools think otherwise. Most of them truly believe they can turn back the clock and take over old titles, old estates. And Theriot is encouraging them to indulge those beliefs. The food, the entertainment, the wine…all of it has been designed to loosen inhibitions and encourage the most indulgent, grandiose thinking."

"And our host is going to exploit their dreams."

"Somehow, yes. And it fits with what we've seen in the house. It's all a set," Sophie said.

"Exactly like the forged art. Theriot doesn't have nearly as much money as he's pretending. So much looks good on the surface, but there's nothing below it."

She nodded. "Think of the servants, too. Maggie said over twenty were hired from the village. She's a bright girl, but she has no training as a lady's maid. Why didn't Theriot hire a number of servants up from London, those with the skill to serve the aristocracy?"

"Rural people are far cheaper to hire," Bruce said.

"Assuming he'll pay them at all. The trappings—curtains, bedding, wallpaper, all the decor—all put up over a crumbling structure. My guess is that as soon as this house party is over, Theriot will disappear. Anything that can be moved will be carted away and sold…or used for another scam like this one."

"The scam being what, exactly?"

"It's two scams, really. The first is a simple grift. A fabulous promise of wealth and honor for a modest investment in the scheme. Theriot has been spinning lies around all the guests for months via letter and other means. You should have heard what he promised Deverall! But in case that doesn't work on everyone, he has a back-up plan. Virtually any intoxicant is available here… and there are ample opportunities for vice. The servants have been told to watch the guests. Once an indiscretion is committed, the servants will report to Theriot, who will proceed to blackmail the person in question. Either way, he gets the money."

"It seems too elaborate," Bruce said skeptically. "That's a huge effort to put into any endeavor."

Sophie shook her head. "That's the heart of illusion. No one appreciates the lengths a magician will go to achieve a very simple effect. Take a card trick, for example." She held out her hands as if holding an imaginary deck. "I have an ordinary deck of cards, fanned out and face up. You can see them all, everything looks correct. I collapse the deck and flip it over. I'll tell you to pick a card, and keep it hidden from me. Then I will guess which one is in your hand."

"I've seen this one before," he said.

"Then you know the pitch. If I guess right, you'll pay me a certain amount of money, nothing less than a guinea, but as much as you stake. But if I'm wrong, I'll give you *ten times* as much. You're excited. These are good odds!"

"I'm not a gambler, but I take your word for it."

She smiled. When thinking about illusion, she was in her element. "Now, I ask the audience how much you should wager. You hear suggestions, you banter with the audience. Let's settle on a guinea. I hold out the deck. Draw a card, I say. Hide it from me. Keep it with you, stash it in a pocket if you like. Just be sure I can't see it. I take a few steps and put the rest of the deck on a nearby table.

"Then I walk back and tell you what you've picked… the seven of diamonds. You know I'm right."

"How do you know?"

"Magic," Sophie said.

"No such thing," he retorted. "What if I take the deck from the table?"

"Oh, I'll tell you do so in order to put the card back. You'll find an ordinary deck, with all the cards but the seven of diamonds, which you pull from your pocket. The audience will see and verify it."

"But you didn't just guess. What's the secret?"

"It's barely a secret, the trick is so old. There are *two*

decks. The first one is ordinary, except that it lacks the seven of diamonds. Fanned out, there are too many cards for a person to notice the absence of just one, particularly a non-face card. But when I told you to ask the audience how much to wager, your attention—and the audience's— was distracted. A discussion of money will *always* distract people. While you faced the audience, and they were looking at you, I performed a simple sleight of hand, swapping the original deck with another I had concealed. Trust me, it takes only a second. Even if you were suspicious, even if you only glanced at the audience, it would be enough time."

"But how do you know I'll pull the seven of diamonds out of the second...oh. The second deck is *all* sevens of diamonds."

Sophie smiled, pleased with his quickness. "Precisely. Who would purchase over fifty identical decks of cards simply to pull a single card out of most of them? No one in their right mind. It's ridiculous! But a magician doesn't think like an ordinary person. And while you look at your card and put it in your pocket...you're distracted again. I walk to the table and place a deck on it...the first deck, with another sleight of hand trick. If you look through it, and I'll encourage you to do so, you'll see only what you expected."

"And that's exactly how illusion works. I see what I expect to see."

"And I'm one guinea richer." Sophie grinned.

"So you're saying Theriot's scam is a very elaborate illusion designed to trick the guests into seeing what they expect—and taking their money after it's too late."

"You're catching on."

"This is going to be an interesting house party, dove." He actually laughed. "Where did you learn such things?"

"Paris." Sophie wandered over to the table near the bed and picked up the puzzle box she'd placed there when she unpacked. She always brought it with her, no matter where she went. It was small, made of some exotic, richly grained wood that glowed chestnut and red in the light. More remarkably, it was carved all over with the motif of leaves and vines. Fanciful flowers bloomed on every panel. On the top of the lid, a tree growing on a tiny island was carved in exquisite detail.

It was a gorgeous object. It was also impossible to open without knowing the secret.

Bruce looked over. "I saw that earlier. What's inside?"

"Open it and find out." Sophie handed it to him.

He didn't even try, instead turning it over and over to peer at all the decorations. "You know I won't be able to. Isn't that the point of a puzzle box? It's beautiful, though. I can't imagine having the patience to create such a thing. Where did you get it?"

"I've had it for years."

"Not quite what I asked," he pressed.

"A magician gave it to me," she said, "when I worked at the theater in Paris." Sophie was sensitive about the circumstances of the giving. Then again, Bruce was the first person who ever held the box without trying to pry the thing apart before giving up in frustration.

"Did he use it in a trick?" Bruce asked, interested.

"Not on stage. One could, but the box is more compelling at close quarters."

"Indeed," he murmured.

Sophie paused, then said, "He had to leave the city, and that was his parting gift to me."

"You must have made an impression. This isn't a toy."

"I often performed with him as an assistant. My stage name was Serefina…the Brave." She stopped, embarrassed. What a childish thing to say.

But Bruce only smiled. "You've had more names in your life than most people."

"And?" she asked.

"I once made a wager that you would tell me your real name."

"A wager you lost."

"Just as well," he said. "I'm not sure you could tell me."

"I know exactly who I am."

"And who is that?"

She said, irritated, "I'm the woman who owns that box. Give it back."

He handed it back to her without hesitation. "Someday I'll find out, dove."

"What does it matter to you?"

"Questions need answers," he said.

"How lucky you are to have lived a life where you can find answers." Giving up on the discussion, she climbed into bed, watching Bruce across the room. He was still fully clothed and was looking at something he'd written down earlier.

"Just as a friendly warning," Sophie said as she lay down, "what happened earlier wasn't an invitation. If you so much as graze me with a fingertip, I'll kill you."

Bruce broke off from reading to smile at her. "I love you too, dear," he said sarcastically. "Now go to sleep. And remember: technically, we're on the same side."

Sophie turned her head away, annoyed. She drifted off to sleep, wondering if she *could* kill him. Not the best thoughts for happy dreams, but she never remembered her dreams anyway.

The next day, Sophie woke up early. She'd slept soundly enough that she had no idea when Bruce came to bed. She was sure he heeded her warning though, since a few feet of cold, empty bed separated them. He definitely hadn't tried anything.

Sophie determined to keep whatever fragile truce she'd made with her partner last night. He *was* right. They were already in a struggle against France. It was foolish to make Bruce an enemy as well.

The second day at Carterhaugh proved to be less nerve-wracking than the first. Odd as some aspects of the house party were, in many others it was quite typical. The guests mostly slept late, and then devoted their time to leisure and idle chatter. Sophie and Bruce agreed to stay separate for most of the day, hoping to glean more information from the guests, or—if the opportunity presented itself—search for the necessary documents, wherever they were hidden.

As more guests arrived and the false Cassou couple met more people, the nature of the gathering became clearer. As Sophie deduced, everyone present the first night had some sort of link to the aristocracy that held power in the *ancien regime* of France, and *all* of them loathed the new Emperor.

However, beginning on the second day, a number of rowdier guests began to arrive—rakes, courtesans, and hellions up from the city, lured by promises of wild entertainments in a location where nothing would leak out. Sophie decided they were mostly there to provide cover for the real purpose of the gathering. Of all the guests, only ten or perhaps fifteen could be of interest to Theriot and his still secret plans.

Guests drank like swine, and the supply seemed never ending. Snuff was taken at every opportunity. Opium was readily available. The result was a collection of personalities devoid of rationality or self-control.

Sophie despised them all.

A conversion with the Comte de Marche that afternoon left her reeling. The man first flattered her, then attempted to seduce her, all without seeming to care that he was doing so in full view of a dozen other guests. Sophie put him off with words, but she dearly wanted to demonstrate a more physical reproof.

Bruce came across them and heard the tail end of the exchange. He steered her back to their bedroom and shut the door.

"You have to be more careful for the rest of this visit," he warned her.

"How so?"

"You're letting your contempt show."

"Excuse me?"

Bruce said, "You hate the aristocracy. And it shows through in your performance of Madame Cassou."

"I do not hate…"

"You do," he said. "With every fiber of your body. You hate them for being idle and stupid and still able to command the people *you* grew up with."

"You don't know that."

"I know you hate me. You've hated me since the night we met and I pointed out your origins. I'm a lord, and despite all your efforts, you can't get rid of me."

"Don't pretend to understand me," she hissed. "I don't care for the other guests, that's true. But they all like *me*. Or who they think I am."

"Please. You obviously despise all these people for what they are. You're charming enough and beautiful enough that they haven't quite sensed it yet. But they will. So tamp it down."

She glared at him. "You're imagining things." How dare he evaluate her performance as if he had the authority to do so.

"I can see you, can't I? I hear what you say, and that little edge you put on all your comments about the aristocracy."

"They don't care about anything but themselves and their own pointless lives. You heard that Baden woman at breakfast. She thought if the local fishermen couldn't keep Carterhaugh adequately supplied with mussels, their village might as well burn to the ground."

Bruce put a hand on her arm. "Calm down."

"I am calm."

"No, you're not."

She tried to step back. "Let go of me."

"Not until you promise to listen. Our two little point-less lives depend on you being convincing."

Furious, Sophie wrenched her arm away. "If you don't like my methods, you can leave."

"You keep suggesting that," he said, his eyes narrow. "Why?"

"Because I don't need you here! You're only getting in the way."

"*This* is what me being in the way looks like." He shifted so he blocked her from moving, from even seeing around his body. "When I tell you your performance needs work, I'm helping you."

She strained against him. Unfortunately, Bruce was both bigger and taller than she was, and he already had leverage against her. She couldn't push him away, so she stopped trying. "What would you know about it?" she asked. "I am a professional, Bruce. I was practically born in a theater."

He didn't budge. "Then you should recognize the dif-ference between criticism and a personal comment."

"And you're offering professional criticism?"

"From one professional to another, yes."

Sophie seized on his comment. "Ah, so you admit I'm a professional."

"Oh, yes." He let her go and stepped away. "Though I won't say what profession."

Sophie moved like lightning, but he still caught her

wrist before she slapped him.

His grip wasn't tight, but Sophie might as well have been clamped in an iron ring.

"That's not a very ladylike thing to do…trying to hit me." Bruce let go of her wrist, but didn't move away. He plainly didn't think she was a threat to him.

"Why wouldn't I? You all but called me a whore."

His eyes flickered. "No, I didn't."

"You implied it."

"I was referring to you being an actress," he said quietly. "Rather than an agent."

"Oh, were you?" As if that were really less insulting, Sophie thought.

"Yes. You're quite good at it. Except for the little thing I mentioned."

Sophie glared at him. "Don't mention it again."

"Then don't give me a reason to."

She stalked past him. Moving around him was rather like having to move around an ox. What an oaf! Her heart was beating far faster than she liked. Anger always did that to her. She sat at the vanity and looked into the mirror. "I hope you haven't ruined my hair."

He turned to watch her. "Technically speaking, it's not yours."

Sophie whipped around, ready to strike again. "Oh, is that a problem, too? Should I have anticipated this excursion and grown it all out in the right shade to please you?"

Surprisingly, Bruce now held up his hands in a gesture of defeat. "Sorry. It's very lovely hair. I don't think I touched it."

"Good," she muttered, turning back to the mirror. "It's not as if I have a stockpile of wigs here. I need to be careful about what I do have."

"Are you in need of anything? I mean to say, were you able to bring everything along? We were forced to prepare rather quickly." He sounded contrite.

"I'll manage," she said, her irritation subsiding a little. She focused on the mirror. Luckily, the wig endured the latest spat without damage. She adjusted some of the curls and arranged some others to fall around her face, framing her eyes and cheekbones. Then she pulled the cross pendant back into place. "I do wish I had another necklace. This is the only one fancy enough for Marianne to wear. I hope no one notices she's always wearing the same one… it's a bit odd."

"A lady like her would have more in her jewel case," Bruce agreed, looking at Sophie's reflection in the mirror. "And from what we know, she'd never wear a cheap necklace."

Sophie shook her head, causing the curls to bounce pleasingly. "If anyone remarks on it, I'll make up some story about how the stone are terribly rare…perhaps they were first set in a reliquary or missal or something."

"That could work." Bruce smiled. "You're good at making up stories on the spot, aren't you?"

"Improvisation is a necessary skill, both on the stage and in the streets."

"And how long did you live on the streets?" he asked.

"Only two or three years," Sophie said, as she reapplied a touch of color to her lips.

In the mirror, she saw Bruce's eyes darken at her words. She didn't have to tell him that a few years on the streets was more than a lifetime. He didn't ask how she endured it.

Their fragile peace restored, the agents returned to the gathering below. Sophie kept up her banter with the other men, and true to her word, restrained herself from making any jabs that might betray her true feelings about the guests. She kept her own thoughts low, down in the dark. It was the character of Madame Cassou who came out. All the jokes, all the teasing…that was a series of lies she spoke as naturally as she laughed at the others.

And it worked. Whenever she walked into a room, at least three gentlemen surrounded her, offering her libations and liberation from whatever might trouble her. She strung them along as if they were her toys, and gathered a fair amount of information along the way.

But whenever Bruce entered her vision, or she heard his voice, Sophie found herself hesitating, slipping out of character. She realized she was afraid he'd be too convinced by her act, and think her as empty as the part. And yet, she had to play her role. So she giggled, she cooed. She accepted the attentions of men with the skill of a courtesan.

Later that afternoon, Bruce interrupted a small gathering where Sophie sat with a few other gentlemen.

"Going for a ride before it gets too dark, dove," he said carelessly to Sophie. "Theriot said there was good fox hunting around here, but I want to see for myself."

Before she could say a word, one wag broke in. "Excellent, Cassou! You play with the foxes, and I'll stay here and play with your wife."

The temperature in the room suddenly dropped.

"I hope I misunderstood that remark," Bruce said, very quietly.

"I thought it clear enough," the man snapped back, anticipating a round of laughter.

Bruce turned to face the man. The few early laughs were silenced immediately. Bruce was a big man, and the look on his face was perfect for an outraged husband. "Do you impugn my wife?"

The other man looked rather chagrined. "A joke, sir. Merely a joke."

"You may play with other men's wives, if they permit. I won't tolerate my own becoming fodder for your weak efforts at amusement. Do I make myself clear?"

"Perfectly."

Bruce waited about two seconds too long before he relaxed his shoulders, which had the effect of drawing attention to him. Sophie knew that was what he intended. If anyone doubted they were truly a couple, his somewhat embarrassing display should put such doubts to rest. She smiled at him tremulously when his gaze flickered over her. He was actually a fine actor himself.

"*J'taime*," she whispered, loud enough so he and a few others around them would hear it. Her tone wasn't sensual. It was proud, adoring. If he could make others believe they were in love, so could she.

Chapter 14

m

BRUCE HEARD SOPHIE'S WHISPERED WORDS and felt them at the same time. *I love you.* The perfect phrase for a grateful wife to utter. And she made it sound so sincere. He hoped he hadn't overplayed his part. He didn't even have to feign the rage. He was furious at that fop insulting Sophie…even if it wasn't really Sophie he was insulting.

As he walked to the stables, he calmed down. It would be good to escape Carterhaugh Manor, if only for a little while. Theriot had created an atmosphere of decadence. Bruce, however, wasn't particularly drawn to decadence, and he already felt as if he were drowning in it.

Soon enough, he was riding away from the house on a borrowed horse, one of several Theriot kept in the stable for guests to make use of. He felt better as soon as he was moving. Bruce had always been a good rider—it was one of the few things his father actually praised him for.

Bruce had lied to Sophie earlier. He remembered his father with perfect clarity, the details of so many of his words and gestures sharp in his mind as if they happened yesterday. The elder Forester watched the education and development of his two sons like a hawk. And like a hawk, he recognized weakness and pounced on it.

Nothing Bruce could do seemed to please him. But as he grew up into what his father termed "an adequate specimen of man," some achievements drew grudging respect. Thus, he learned to become an excellent rider and a good hunter—his father adored all things related to hunting. Because of his greater size compared to most boys his age, Bruce was also quite good at fighting, whether it was boxing, wrestling, or fencing.

He thought by buying a commission he might prove himself in the military. Surely that would at last impress his father.

It didn't. Bruce advanced in rank as fast as possible, with commendations along the way. No achievement on the field or off it impressed his father. *Not killed yet, I see* was the kindest phrase Bruce could remember.

If his efforts didn't impress his father, however, other people took notice. When a man named Julian Neville asked Bruce how he felt about recognition for his efforts, Bruce had answered honestly: he didn't care at all.

Good, Julian had responded, because he had a position open in a rather important group. Members defend the country against the worst threats imaginable…but they can never speak a word about what they do.

Bruce was in exactly the sort of mood to say yes.

He had no idea what he was getting into.

"Hold up," he murmured to the horse, suddenly drawn back into the present. He had instinctively ridden to high ground, and he now turned the horse about in a tight circle, surveying everything. Carterhaugh lay below, the rambling structure surrounded by gardens in various conditions, from adequate to nearly wild. Beyond the gardens, the fields spread out, also tending toward wild meadow more than carefully tended plots. At the very edge of his vision to the east, he thought he could discern blue-grey water…the sea.

But more interesting to Bruce was the nearby forest, a dark fringe of trees beginning at the edge of the fields. A forest could hide any number of things, and Bruce did not care for surprises. He was sure no one was watching him, so he rode down the slope toward the darker green.

As he approached the woods, he thought again of how he ended up where he was. Bruce had been extraordinarily lucky. He didn't have his father's affection, but the man didn't try to hold him back.

But however indifferent Forester had been to Bruce, it didn't hold a candle to what the old man thought of his second son, Ashley. Bruce was older than Ash by five years, and he did everything he could to protect his little brother. Ash had been a frail baby, and then a thin, pale child. Knowing instinctively that he'd never match his brother's qualities, Ash turned inward.

He learned to read with astonishing quickness. He sat in on Bruce's French lessons and quickly surpassed his older brother in the language. Tutors in German, Italian, and Latin soon found Ash picked up languages the way other children picked up toys. He adored logic and argument. He could convince anyone of anything…except their father. Ash was terrified of Forester and could barely open his mouth in the man's presence, which only made Forester more disgusted with his younger son.

It was perhaps not surprising that Ash turned his attention to spiritual things. He was a smart and attentive student, and he enjoyed theology as much as poetry and language. He entered a well-regarded seminary. It seemed he had found his vocation.

Until everything fell apart. Bruce didn't know if Ash always had a dark streak, but the scandal he caused destroyed the reputations of two different women, enraged a whole village, and got Ash drummed out of all reputable society.

Bruce, who had always protected his brother, suddenly discovered that not only could he not save Ash, he didn't even know how to go about confronting him. Who was this young man Bruce thought was his brother? Ash changed so much in a few months it seemed impossible he could have been the boy Bruce grew up with.

Even their mother told Bruce to leave Ash alone. *He's chosen his path*, she warned Bruce. Their mother had never been a strong woman—physically or mentally. She was a mere background fixture at home. She'd done her duty in presenting two sons as potential heirs. Her husband recognized her contribution by conferring a generous amount of annual pin money on her, and also by never visiting her room again after the birth of Ash. It must be admitted that he was quite discreet in his affairs, far more so than he needed to be. He cared about appearances, even if he didn't care about people.

Still, Bruce's mother had been a lonely woman. She delighted in her sons, but never found many friends. After Ash's fall, she dwindled further, and succumbed to consumption within a matter of months. Bruce's father died the next winter, of a seemingly inconsequential illness. Bruce refused to visit the old man before his death. The next time he set foot in the family home, it was as the new Viscount Forester.

But he never felt the title was his. No matter what he did to the estate, no matter how he tried to modernize and innovate, he always felt like an impostor.

Perhaps that was why he didn't ever mind slipping into roles like that of Cassou. Bruce was already pretending to be someone he was not. Why not make himself useful at the same time?

He reached the edge of the woods, and found a narrow path leading into the trees. He wasn't sure what he was looking for, but he wanted to be aware of everything on the estate. Even so, he was surprised when he followed an even narrower trail for a time and suddenly found himself in front of a tiny cottage, which was so well-hidden among the trees it was amazing he had seen it at all.

"Hello?" he called out, dismounting.

There was no smoke from the chimney, nor any sounds. Yet the home was in good repair. Someone must live there.

Bruce approached the door. "Hello?" He knocked, and when there was no answer, he waited. A peculiar silence filled the area. Curious, he reached for the latch and opened the door.

Stepping inside, he found the place was uninhabited. The few shelves of the main room were bare. There was furniture, all of which looked too extravagant for a cottage. A few chairs and stools flanked a table at one end of the front room. A bed was tucked into the opposite corner, with the fireplace in the middle of the long back wall. He suspected the furniture all came from the great house. Someone must have raided the place during the long time it was abandoned. Perhaps he—or she, Bruce supposed— lived in this cottage until Theriot took ownership, then fled, fearing discovery.

But the roof was sound and the frame solid. Bruce peered into a smaller room near the bed, and found it empty. It looked as if it had been used for storage at some point. He liked the little place, and he wondered if Theriot even knew it existed. He liked it even more when he saw the door and windows had solid, working locks and shutters.

"I'm coming back here," he said to himself. It was too bad that Jem had to go back to London immediately. The boy would have been a good person to quietly outfit this place in case anyone needed to stay close to Carterhaugh without being seen. But Bruce could take care of such details too.

Feeling he'd found a small treasure, he left the house and rode back to Carterhaugh as the long afternoon faded to early evening. He wouldn't tell Sophie straight away, but he felt better now that he had a contingency plan.

His optimism lasted exactly as long as it took to return to Carterhaugh. A stabler relieved him of his horse, and he walked toward the entrance to the great house. Nearly at the door, he heard a carriage arrive. He turned, curious to see who the newcomers would be.

A woman in a gold gown stepped out with the grace of a princess, and Bruce knew he had a problem. Regina Fox knew who he really was, and the shrewd woman would never be fooled by the meager disguise he sported.

As if to prove that fates were aligning against him, Regina took in her surroundings and saw him. She looked puzzled for a moment, then surprised, then curiously delighted. She sent him a smile that promised a future meeting, but said nothing.

Hoping to delay the inevitable, Bruce stepped up to her. "Miss Fox. You may not remember me. Theodore Cassou at your service."

"*Monsieur Cassou!*" she said, without missing a beat. "I barely *recognized* you. It has been far too long since we have seen each other," she went on. The implication in her rich, naturally seductive voice was unmistakable.

Bruce was acutely relieved Sophie wasn't present at the moment.

"Miss Fox," he said. "You look as astonishing as ever." It was the simple truth. Though older than Bruce by indeterminate years, Regina somehow grew more alluring with time. She would never be mistaken for a young lady, but the knowing look in her eyes could be devastating.

She smiled. "I am amazed to see you here, at the ends of the earth! I think we should take a few moments to, ah, catch up." Again, her tone raised the surrounding temperature several degrees. Regina Fox could likely seduce an angel...and she knew how powerful secrets could be.

"Whatever you wish, Miss Fox."

"Just what I like to hear." She watched him, and her

smile turned ironic as her patron joined them. "Have you met Freddie…Lord Reardon, that is?"

"Not yet. How do you do?" Bruce nodded politely, and the other man gave him a wary perusal.

Regina said, "It's lovely to be out of that carriage. Would you be so kind as to take me for a turn around the garden? Freddie can greet our host while I recover from travel."

He nodded, grateful for her discretion.

They walked to the gardens. Regina scarcely looked at him as they strolled slowly down the paths. "I suppose," she began, keeping her voice low, "that there is something going on beneath the surface here."

"You are as intelligent as ever, Miss Fox."

She sniffed. "It doesn't take a genius to realize something's amiss when the staid Lord Forester shows up using another man's name."

"I wasn't sure if you had actually recognized me. Or if you knew Cassou personally."

"I have met him, though not in a professional capacity. And I have reason to remember you, of course," she murmured. "How's your brother, by the way?"

"You doubtless have seen him more recently than I have."

"Sadly, you're probably correct." Regina paused to look at a lily blooming near her feet. She glanced sidelong at him. "Perhaps I associated with the wrong brother. Should I have regrets?" She laughed, in such a charming, wistful way that Bruce almost regretted it too.

"I was never in your class," he said. He hadn't intended a double meaning, but Regina heard the implication anyway, and merely shook her head.

"No, you never were. It appears you are in a very different class." She squeezed his arm slightly. "But I seem to have an advantage. You need my assistance now, true? Tell me what you desire."

"First, your silence on my identity."

"Naturally," she said. "What else?"

"In all honesty, I'd like you to leave this house. For your safety as well as mine. Something will happen here…it would be better to not be involved."

"I have no choice but to believe you." Regina watched him for a moment, then said, "Very well. That request is within my power. I'll bring Freddie around, and we'll be off by tomorrow."

He sighed in relief. "Thank you."

"Of course," she said, smiling again, "my services always come at a price."

Bruce nodded. Regina was a consummate professional, and she did not work for nothing. "What is your fee?"

"You're a friend, so my fee is low. When this business—whatever it may be—is concluded and you return to civilization, you will look up your brother and speak to him."

Bruce recoiled. "He doesn't want to speak to me."

"Ah, well," Regina sighed theatrically. "Then Freddie and I remain at this house party, which promises to be most diverting. I do hope I won't lose my head and slip up when addressing you…"

"You're a bully," he accused.

"No, I'm practical." Regina paused on the path and turned to face Bruce. "Believe me, family reconciliations are not much in my line. But I know your brother very well. I spent over a year doing my best to make him *extremely* happy."

"I have no doubt," Bruce murmured.

"He would have traded that whole year in a heartbeat in exchange for a few kind words from you."

"Now, that I do doubt."

"You have my terms," she said. "Do you accept them?"

He took a breath. "If that is truly what you want in payment, I'll do it."

"How lovely to hear." Regina took his arm again, and resumed their stroll. "Do you know, my dear Monsieur Cassou, I am not at all sure this northern air agrees with me? I should hate to languish with some sort of malaise… or worse, get spots." She held out one arm and looked at a patch of exposed skin quite critically.

"It would be a crime to deny London the pleasure of seeing you," he agreed. "I don't know if you'll be appreciated the same way up here."

"Quite so," she drawled. "Fortunately Freddie is such a dear about acquiescing to my whims. I think our time here must be curtailed."

"A regrettable but necessary conclusion," he said, with mock sadness.

"Just be sure to look up our mutual friend when you return to the city," she said as they neared the house again. "I assure you I keep apprised of events."

"You have my word, Miss Fox," he promised.

"And you have mine," she said, giving him a smile as bright as the sun.

Freddie was waiting for them when they returned. "Regina," he said with a frown. "Where have you been?"

"Why, I could not pass up the chance to reminisce with my dear friend Theodore…Monsieur Cassou, that is," she said. "And what could I do, after you ran off and left me alone?"

"You told me to…oh, you tease," Freddie said, all smiles again. Regina knew how to deal with her latest patron.

Bruce saw Sophie watching them as well, and excused himself to join her.

"So that's the infamous Miss Fox," was all she said. Bruce compared her cool reaction to Freddie's own excitement. "You spoke to her?"

"I did. She is discretion itself," Bruce said.

"And the whole room witnessed her confirming your presumed identity." Sophie nodded to him. "Well done."

Praise from Sophie? Bruce blinked in surprise. "Thank you."

"You can tell me the details tonight," she murmured.

He nodded. For some reason, that line was far more alluring than anything Regina had ever said.

* * * *

As soon as she saw Regina Fox, Sophie was curious about the woman. From Bruce's account, Miss Fox was nothing more than a friend, but Sophie doubted that. Surely a such a woman drew all men's eyes. She was everything Sophie was not: curvy, luscious, carefree. A woman who didn't hide any part of her personality from the world.

Sophie left Bruce to his own devices for the remainder of the afternoon. Without truly intending to, she observed Miss Fox. Sophie wasn't jealous of the courtesan, naturally. She didn't care if Bruce slept with every lady of the demimonde. But if Regina knew something about Bruce's past…well, that would be interesting to hear.

Sophie found Regina and her patron later on. The couple sat on a long chaise. Freddie was smoking something that smelled far sweeter than tobacco. Regina was laughing at some story he just told. The sound bubbled through the room, drawing Sophie closer.

Regina saw her and raised one eyebrow. "Hello, there. I don't believe we've met. You're the wife of Theodore."

"Marianne Cassou," Sophie said, deliberately putting even more of a French accent into her voice. "You know my husband?"

Regina's brows knitted together slightly, as if she was unsure of how to proceed. She knew Bruce was an impostor. But who was this Marianne? "Please join us," she said at last. She smoothed the yellow silk of her skirts as she watched Sophie approach.

"Yes, do," Freddie added, giving Sophie a once over. "What brought you all the way up here?"

"I was invited by Thomas…Monsieur Theriot, that is. The same as you."

Freddie shook his head. "I'm just trailing in my darling's wake."

"The invitation was issued to me," Regina explained.

Sophie was surprised, but even more so when Regina went on, "Thomas wanted me to come because it would confer that extra *soupçon* of debauchery to the event. If the Golden Lady is there, it must be scandalous. But I should not shock you by discussing my business, dear."

"You'd have to work hard to shock me," Sophie replied, speaking as herself. She realized immediately she should not have said that, but Freddie and Regina both laughed out loud, pleased with the audacity of her response.

"What an original woman," said Freddie. "I like this crowd."

"I like *some* of the crowd," Regina countered. She looked at Sophie, "Including your husband, of course. He's such an interesting gentleman. He has so many… unexpected sides."

Freddie said, "I don't like when you talk about other men, Reggie."

"Then why don't you leave?" Sophie suggested, her tone sharp. "I'm rather fascinated by the turn of conversation."

"Well," Freddie huffed. "That's what I get for letting a lady drag me up here. I *will* leave." He stood up and walked unsteadily out of the room.

"Mind your step," Regina called after him, affection in her voice. "That leaf is rather strong." She turned back to Sophie. "Don't be annoyed by Freddie. He's rather a dear, in fact."

"More so than…my husband?" Sophie asked.

Regina's voice dropped. "Well, let's discuss that, shall we?" She gave Sophie a hard look. "Your husband looks remarkably like another gentleman I know—the Viscount Forester. Isn't that a coincidence?"

"I've been told I also resemble several other ladies," Sophie said blandly. "So it can't be such an interesting coincidence. But since you bring it up, do tell me about Forester."

"You know what I am." Regina lifted an eyebrow. "So what do you wish to know?"

"Why doesn't he speak to his brother?"

"Ah." Regina immediately lost her superior expression. "Not what I thought you'd ask."

"Indeed?"

"I thought you were curious about the more…intimate aspects of our friendship."

"Why should I be? Viscount Forester is not my concern," Sophie said, nevertheless feeling a twinge of envy. "But I heard a little bit about his brother, and I wondered why he never reconciled with him. I would have tried harder."

"Why?"

"Because—" Sophie checked herself, debating how much to reveal to the courtesan. "Because I never had siblings. I can't imagine casting one off, no matter what he did. Wouldn't it be cruel?"

"Cruelty is hard to define," Regina said. "What his brother was accused of doing was much worse than what he actually did. But reality doesn't stand a chance against rumors."

"That's all too true," Sophie agreed.

"Forester, you must understand, was something of an ideal for his younger brother. And when Ash fell from grace....well, he didn't fall so much as he crashed to the rocks below. He said things he should not have, all for the sake of appearing to be unrepentant and untouchable. I think Forester didn't quite realize that, and he said things *he* shouldn't have."

"He thought his brother really didn't care about what he did?"

"Or who he hurt. Forester cares about that sort of thing very much, so he couldn't forgive Ash for his sins. Even though Ash regretted his actions much more than he let on."

"And now they haven't spoken for years," Sophie said sadly.

"Yes," Regina said, her tone more matter-of-fact. "But they're both still alive, and they could reconcile, if they both acted like men instead of boys."

"Well," said Sophie, "I hope they do...though of course it has nothing to do with me personally."

"No. How could it, Madame Cassou?" Regina gave her a smile as she said the false name. "You're just interested in the gossip, of course."

"Of course."

"I wish—" the other woman began.

"It's boring out there," a voice cut in. Freddie had returned. "Are you ladies quite done talking about Cassou?"

"As a matter of interest," Regina said, "we didn't talk about him at all. Just old gossip."

"So I wandered around for nothing?" Freddie collapsed down on the chaise by his mistress. "How terrible."

Regina put out an arm and drew him closer. "I'll make it up to you."

Sophie stood. "I shall leave you two to reconcile." She smiled at Regina as she left. The courtesan was rather like her after all. She used her wits as much as her beauty to handle her marks. The only difference was that she didn't hide what she was.

"I do hope we can speak again sometime, dear," Regina said.

Sophie wondered if that would ever happen. First, she'd have to survive this assignment.

* * * *

The rest of the day was uneventful. That night, as Bruce and Sophie lay in their bed, not touching, he mentioned the most confounding aspect of the party.

"There's something so different about this place, this particular gathering," he said, struggling to put his thoughts into words. "I've seen all these things before, but...."

"Not all at once?" Sophie asked in a low tone. She shifted in the bed so she faced him, and she propped her head on her elbow.

"It's not just that. It's a mood. I can't describe it." He lay on his back, and balled his hands into fists.

"I think I know what you mean," Sophie whispered.

Bruce turned his head to look at her. In her simple shift and without the mass of the wig, Sophie looked much more fragile than she really was. Her short hair made her face more prominent, and her eyes were huge in the dim light.

She took a moment, then said softly, "I've seen something like this before."

"When?" he asked.

"During the Revolution, and then during the Terror. I didn't understand it at the time, but people behaved very strangely. It was as if all the rules went away, because no one knew who was in charge. It was also…I don't know, a little bit like the end of the world."

"You mean people thought they were going to die?"

"Why not? People were dying all around. The king was killed, and in his place was this zealot. Soldiers and townspeople alike went to fight. How many came back? And the guillotine took plenty more lives. Everyone knew any day could be their last. It made them…"

"Crazy," he supplied. Intrigued by her explanation, he shifted to prop himself up against the headboard. "That might be it. But it still doesn't make sense for the people here, today."

"It might. Everyone here seems to have a connection to the old world, before the Revolution. And they miss it —or rather, they miss what they imagine it must have been like. This party might be the only time they have to play queens and kings."

"Eat, drink, and be merry…" he murmured, thinking

of the possibility.

"For tomorrow we die," Sophie finished. Her voice had a desperately sad quality. Bruce realized with a shock that for her, the situation wasn't theoretical. He was pondering the idea. She was reliving it.

"How did you stand it?" he asked. "Growing up in that hell, I mean?"

Sophie looked down, and then gave a little shrug. "I don't know. I didn't have a choice…"

"But you knew something was wrong," he said, his voice unconsciously growing a bit louder.

Sophie laid her free hand on his arm. "Quiet," she whispered. "Of course I knew. My mother told me to be careful and guard my tongue. I stayed close to the theater, where I knew who to trust. But life went on. I worked backstage. I performed a little bit more. The house was packed most nights, you know. People wanted to forget. I was Serefina the Brave all the way up to…" she trailed off.

"Until what?" he asked, curious but unwilling to press her to remember something too painful.

"Up till Abraham had to leave."

"Abraham?"

"The magician. The best magician in all of Paris. No one knew as much about stage magic as he did! So many tricks and acts! There was one he worked on for twenty years, he told me. A mirror stands alone on the stage…" Sophie began to describe the trick, and she sat up, growing animated. "It can be rotated. There's nothing behind it. It stands a foot off the floor, so no trapdoor! Abraham selects a woman from the audience, usually a pretty one. He has her walk all the way up to the mirror…and then she keeps going. She steps inside! He spins the mirror around, and when the glass faces the audience again the woman is gone. All you see is a dove fluttering behind the glass!"

The combination of Sophie's excitement and her whispered tone gave her words a sense of wonderful intimacy. Bruce was drawn into the tale as much as he was drawn to the teller. "Go on," he urged.

"Then he spins it again, and the woman reappears. She steps out and doesn't even know what happened!"

Bruce frowned. "So how does the trick work? Where does the woman go?"

Sophie's tone grew mysterious. "Oh, I can't tell you that."

"The code of magicians?" he asked.

"Yes…and the fact that I don't actually know," Sophie admitted. "Abraham was very secretive about his work. I knew some of the tricks, the traditional ones and the ones I worked on. But there was so much more to learn."

"Except that he left."

Sophie nodded, sobering instantly. "He got frightened, because there were rumors of attacks on Jews. He was very popular as an act, but he knew…He lived through such times before, he told me. He said when things went badly, people looked for a scapegoat. He said it was time to go."

"And you missed him," Bruce guessed.

"He was my friend," she said. "My teacher and my

friend. When he left, he took all the tricks and cages of doves. And he said I couldn't go with him. So all I have left is the puzzle box. He was the one who gave it to me," she finished in a rush, her whispers fading into silence.

Bruce reached out to take her hand in his own. He wasn't sure any words would be welcome, but he said, "I'm sorry."

She bowed her head a moment, but then looked up. "Don't be. It made me stronger."

"How?"

"I learned how to lose people."

"Not a lesson a young girl looks forward to," he guessed.

"One better learned early than late." Sophie pulled her hand away from his and shifted so her back was to him. Bruce saw the curve of her silhouette and the way her head was tucked close to her chest. She wanted to hide from the world. Including him. She was planning ahead, he realized. She expected nothing from him, because at some point she lost everyone close to her.

Chapter 15

ɱ

WHILE SEVERAL GUESTS WERE AT breakfast the next morning, a commotion in the foyer drew everyone's attention. Bruce saw trunks piled up, and next to them, Regina Fox and Freddie Reardon were dressed to travel.

"But you can't leave," Theriot was saying. "I asked you to come up specially. Everyone was told you would be here! The party won't be a success without you."

"Sorry," Freddie said. "But when Regina makes her mind up, there's nothing to be done."

"She's in charge? She's *your* mistress!"

Regina gave Theriot one cutting look. "Freddie," she said, "I'll wait in the carriage. Now I'm positive the air here is unhealthy." She turned to go, and saw Bruce standing there. "Goodbye, dear Theodore!" she said, with a wave. "Look me up when you get back to London…with or without your wife."

Bruce gave her a crooked smile and watched her go. Having Regina out of the picture relieved him, even though it turned out her brief presence had helped his disguise. Furthermore, the unexpected departure of Lord Freddie Reardon and his mistress clearly caused a bit of consternation for Theriot, and Bruce took some pride in that.

The two agents settled into their respective roles. For the most part, Bruce had overcome his initial distrust of Sophie. His attraction to her didn't diminish, but he was able to contain it. Most of that, he admitted, was due to Sophie's strategic retreat from baiting him.

He still noticed her, of course. She had the charisma to dominate a room when she wished. He loved to watch her work. And he realized with a slight shock that he was learning from her. Sophie's methods of distraction and misdirection were intriguing. She was very effective at gleaning information from men, naturally. But she had an appealing directness with other women too. Lady Danielle warmed to her considerably after she expressed admiration for Danielle's skill at French.

They were learning to work together. And yet, Bruce withheld the morsel of information that Charlie had given him about Volange coming to the house. Partly, he wasn't sure how to bring it up, afraid he would end up admitting he had doubted Sophie. And he knew if there were even the slightest chance Sophie was sympathetic to France, seeing her interact with Volange would be enlightening.

So he said nothing. And Volange never arrived.

The days ticked by for both agents, neither of whom enjoyed the diversions offered. Everyone at the house seemed to consider their time there as a sort of indulgence of vice. The evenings were bawdy and raucous, always with new entertainments of varying degrees of crudeness, as well as a glut of beverages and other substances designed to create a feeling of blissful unreality. In the afternoons, women and men spent hours lying prone on couches, lost in opium dreams. Prostitutes arrived at the house one evening, and several male guests vanished shortly after.

Bruce could only comprehend the individual aspects of the party. The whole thing overwhelmed him and made him sick. He understood vice very well, but he didn't understand how all these people could lose their ability to act like adults for days on end. Perhaps Sophie was right about them thinking it was their only chance to live out their fantasies.

The daily rides were becoming necessary for Bruce to preserve his sanity. He cherished the opportunity to escape the house and his role. He rarely felt so oppressed by an assignment, but the very air in the house was noxious. And the people inside were worse.

Each time, he rode the borrowed horse to the very edges of the estate, often stopping by the hidden cottage with a few items he carefully concealed while leaving the main house. He never saw anyone following him, but Bruce left nothing to chance.

Everywhere he rode, dark fringes of the forest bordered the poorly tended fields. The land was virtually unworked, proving that their host had no interest in maintaining the property or acting like a proper landowner. It convinced Bruce of Sophie's theory. Theriot was little more than a swindler, ready to vanish as soon as he got hold of all his marks' money. But until the host revealed his grand plan, they could do nothing but play along. Charlie's warning of Volange's arrival weighed on him too. The two agents should be there to see what they could glean about the plans of their host and Volange. But another player meant more danger, both for him and for Sophie.

* * * *

One morning almost a week after they arrived, Theriot took Sophie aside and discreetly told her she should take care to look fabulous that evening. When she asked why, he only said a special guest would join them. Remembering Pisces's brief message, Sophie wondered if it would be Arceneau himself.

She told Bruce as soon as she could. "Tonight will be vital," she said. "We'll finally hear the plan Theriot has been teasing us with!"

When she was finally ready to go down for dinner, Sophie did look fabulous. The sweep of her hair cascading down one nearly bared shoulder to graze the top of her brilliantly dyed gown, the diamonds around her neck…she would draw every eye.

Bruce dressed very plainly compared to her, though she thought he still looked like the finest man at the house. Perhaps it was simply because he actually behaved like a gentleman, and not like most of the guests, who acted more like spoiled children.

They walked down the stairs together, each wondering what the ultimate plans of Theriot would be. Sophie was also curious about the guest, who she surmised was key to the main swindle Theriot would propose.

But when Sophie saw the newcomer, in the center of a

group of guests in the main room, she stopped short at the doorway. "Oh, no."

Bruce halted beside her. "What is it?"

"I...forgot my fan," she said. It was a ridiculous excuse, and Bruce plainly knew it. But he steered her around and guided her through the hallway to a quieter location.

Sophie was glad he was there. Her limbs started shaking, and she clutched his arm. When they reached a private corner, Bruce turned her to face him. "Your fan is hanging from your arm. So what's wrong?"

"I just need a minute," Sophie said, her voice trembling. "Why is he here? God, why is he here?"

"Who?"

She closed her eyes. "Volange."

"The important guest? You know him? By sight?"

She nodded. "Holy Virgin, I didn't think this could happen." She opened her eyes again. "Julian shouldn't have sent me."

"Does Volange know who you are? Personally?" Bruce asked intently.

"In a way. I've met him several times. I was dressed as a boy each time, and I used a different name then. But... oh, Lord."

Bruce held her by the shoulders. "Calm down, dove."

Dove. Sophie held the word in her mind, trying to summon all the good, safe, joyous feelings the name implied. Only a very few people in the world had called her by that name, and she trusted them all. "Say that again," she whispered.

"Calm down, dove," he repeated.

She took a long breath, then said, "I am calm."

"What did you think would happen?" Bruce asked, examining her. "He couldn't possibly recognize you now. Look at you! You're as perfectly feminine as any woman could be. And everyone here thinks you're Madame Cassou, so why would he dream of you being some lad he met a handful of times in another city?"

"He's terrifyingly astute."

"No one's *that* clever. You're letting your fear run away with you." He paused. "What did he do to scare you like this?"

She shuddered. "I can't tell you now. But trust me when I say that no one in the world frightens me as much as he does."

"You can go upstairs again. I'll say you're unwell."

"No! What use am I if I hide in a closet?" Sophie said. "I can do this. At least I had some warning."

"I'm sorry…are you sure you're all right?" he asked, keeping close to her.

She was a little surprised at his concern. "Yes. In fact, we should go now. What if someone saw us turn around?"

With Bruce close at her side, Sophie held her head high when they reentered. Luckily, no one remarked on their behavior.

Sophie saw Volange and tried not to panic. Theriot introduced him as a friend and strong supporter of Theriot's ambitions, to which Volange merely smiled.

Alain Volange was a slender, dark-haired gentleman with a distinct military bearing, though he never said anything about having served at any point. He spoke little—

always in French, because he despised English—but his eyes missed nothing. He joined conversations as an observer, offering subtle encouragements to keep others talking and vague nods to convince them he had agreed.

He spoke graciously to Sophie when they were introduced, his voice smooth and inviting. Sophie kept up her façade of the witty social butterfly, but she also ended the conversation as quickly as possible.

Fortunately, Theriot was eager to announce his plan. Going through the gathering, one by one Theriot summoned all the important guests to a separate parlor. Some fifteen people gathered there, plus Volange, who looked on from a secluded perch in a corner.

A few servants offered drinks to everyone. By now, the guests' preferences were well known, and Sophie was not surprised when she was handed a glass of red wine from Burgundy, and Bruce was handed scotch.

"Sip slowly," she murmured. Knowing Volange, she wouldn't put it past him to have put something else in the drink. "Better yet, don't have any at all."

"Noted," Bruce said.

At last, Theriot was going to reveal his plan. He was excited. Anyone could tell that. He paced from one side of the room to the other, as if he couldn't sit down.

"Everyone is here," Volange said at last. "Begin. We've all been waiting."

"Excellent, excellent." Theriot smiled. "Friends. Comrades, I'd say, if I were a *sansculottes*. But no, we're above that. Far above that."

He walked to the center of the room and looked

everyone over. "Friends, I asked you here for a reason. Not merely to enjoy yourselves with like-minded souls who understand what's important in life."

"Wine, women, and song," a drunk Deverall chimed in.

Annoyed at the interruption, Theriot said, "What's important is order. Order based on status. Prestige. Blood. You are all here because you know this. Blood is what tells the worthy from the unworthy. You all have a lineage, traceable back for generations. You have, or had, lands in France before they were taken from you all…first by the rabble, and then by this self-appointed Emperor. What right does he have to sit on a throne? The Corsican doesn't have an ounce of royal blood in him."

"He has an army," Bruce said, his voice calm.

Theriot nodded, conceding the point. "That he does, Cassou. And he knows how to use an army. So what is to be done?"

"You think we *can* do something?" Lady Danielle asked, curiosity in her voice.

"I know it, my lady," their host said. "Not you alone, despite all your beauty. And not Deverall alone, despite a link to the real kings of France. And not Mr Baden here, with his connection to the influential men of Europe. Not Madame Cassou, with her wealth. Not any of you. And not me, with all my knowledge of the Emperor's plans."

He kept talking, offering praise to each guest and condemnation for the current state of France. Sophie watched as the man worked his audience to be ready for his real proposal, something so preposterous that he needed his marks to be well-prepared before he could spring the trap.

"Alone, we can do nothing," Theriot said. "But together, we can do the unthinkable. We can correct the travesty that occurred when the king was murdered. We can restore the monarchy and all our ancestral rights with it!"

"We are not an army," Deverall said, though he sounded interested.

"Working together, we can *buy* an army. And once that army is raised, we will control where it goes and who it attacks."

Another guest spoke up. "You want us to get into the mercenary business?"

Theriot waved a hand. "Mercenaries are just tools. I'm proposing a new use for them. Previously, soldiers fought for one side or the other…no matter who paid. We are doing something different. We're going to use our funds to put a thumb on the scales. We'll use our force to decide which side will win a battle, or capture a city."

He named the sum he wanted each guest to contribute to the cause, to be paid to him in tidy, discreet quarterly installments. Sophie blinked at the amount. She would never see that much money in her whole life.

The other guests muttered a bit, but no one appeared completely shocked at the proposal. Theriot was still spinning his air castles. "Once our strength is recognized, the smarter side will listen to our terms. Whichever will fulfill them gets us on their side. And they'll win the war, which means we'll get what we all want…the restoration of the French monarchy and the recognition of our rightful places in history."

"Easier said than done," Bruce muttered. "What if the paid army has bad luck?"

"I have an insurance policy," Theriot said.

Volange suddenly shifted. "No need to…"

But Theriot plowed ahead, his eyes glittering. "Friends, we are *not* alone in our desire to restore the kings of France. A wise member of the British Cabinet has secretly pledged to support our cause! He will speak in our favor and steer things our way in the highest echelons."

Volange looked infuriated. Theriot was not supposed to have let that information out to everyone. But Sophie exulted. His admission meant the information the Zodiac needed had to be real, and it had to be in the house—an insurance policy meant tangible proof, which Theriot would no doubt keep close. And Sophie possessed the skills to retrieve it.

Chapter 16

♏

THERIOT QUICKLY ADJOURNED THE MEETING, declaring the night's entertainment would begin soon. He didn't want guests to question his offer too much just yet. He wanted them to talk to each other, convince each other, and dream of more extravagant lives.

No doubt everyone would be whispering about the proposal Theriot made. Some would be assessing the cost, but others were already trying on crowns in their minds. Theriot's offer was absurd, but extremely flattering to his marks. The plan was a confidence scheme, but some would be seduced by it.

Bruce took Sophie's untouched wine glass out of her hand, and placed both their drinks on a table. He'd only sipped his once. He watched the increasingly foolish actions of the other guests.

"Charming crowd," he muttered, as they walked to the main room, where guests were gathering to join in dancing, which was already underway. This part of the evening, at least, was perfectly proper.

"Careful, dear," she whispered. "Your contempt is showing."

"Point taken. I'm not sure how much more of this I

can endure."

"A few days," she said, squeezing his hand. "We'll get what we came for, and we'll make our escape."

"I'm counting down the hours," he replied. "This whole thing is mad. Theriot has very little appreciation of how to strategize during a war."

"I take it you don't believe that the purchase of one puny mercenary force—supplied by Arceneau, naturally—will be of much use."

He snorted. "It's the stupidest idea I've ever heard."

Sophie thought a moment. "Do you think it's a coincidence that none of the other special guests have a military background, or any similar knowledge?"

"Maybe. It doesn't really matter if Theriot's idea will ever work. What matters is that he can convince the others to pay up. Even if he only gets a few guests to do so, that's potentially thousands of pounds."

"He'll give some of that to Arceneau to 'hire' the army…just in case the marks want some proof to keep paying up. But Theriot gets his cut, and Volange will be paid," Sophie said. "Still, a success, considering. Everyone will walk away with several thousand, and the marks will have no way to retaliate or mention it to the authorities without being called traitors. It's smart."

"But whether he intends to go to war or not, his trump card is real—the cabinet member who will betray us all. We have to get that document," Bruce said quietly.

"I have a plan for that," she said, "I've been stringing Thom—"

Before she could add anything more, Volange caught

her eye from across the room, and nodded politely. Sophie held her breath, then smiled back. Madame Cassou wouldn't fear him, so Sophie couldn't either. "Sorry, darling," she murmured to Bruce. "I'm needed stage center."

"Are you sure?" he said.

Sophie barely nodded, despite her trepidation. "I can't run away, so I have to fight. And this is how I fight."

"Be careful, dove."

* * * *

Bruce saw Volange approach his wife—false wife—but he could do nothing without breaking character, so it was up to Sophie to take matters into her own hands. He felt a sharp sense of guilt after seeing her reaction to the man's appearance. It was obvious she wasn't working with Volange. He could have given her much more warning, and reduced the risk they both took.

Volange bent over Sophie's hand and murmured something Bruce couldn't hear. She laughed charmingly at whatever it was and then allowed the dark haired man to lead her to the dance. Bruce was proud of her. He knew how bone-shakingly scared she was, but not a flicker of it showed now.

Bruce watched as the couple danced in the line. Sophie was perfect as a noblewoman, he had to admit. She was sparkling, witty, and drew every eye. Even Volange seemed enchanted.

When Volange escorted Sophie off the floor at the end of the set, it was to the opposite side of where Bruce stood. He lost sight of them for a moment.

Before he could move to catch Sophie again, their host was standing at his side. "Volange has taken a liking to your wife, it seems."

"Yes, well. She's a charming woman," Bruce said.

"Just be careful. Volange is a man who takes what he wants...no matter who it belongs to." Theriot looked rather envious himself.

"Does that include people?"

"Anything and everything has a price. And Volange has the means to pay...lucky bastard. If I had one tenth his wealth..."

"Where does his wealth come from?" Bruce asked, curious to know more about the man who plagued Sophie.

"If rumors are correct, he is involved in several criminal enterprises. He works for Arceneau, you know." A few other men joined them to listen to the host's tale.

Bruce feigned ignorance. "Who?"

"Arceneau. One of the most successful men in the underworld. He was born in France and has bases in Paris, Calais, London, Naples...anywhere one finds heavy trade and bribable authorities."

"Oh, well then." Bruce forced a laugh. "He has many options there."

"Too true. Regardless, he is a man to be reckoned with. He has wealth and connections beyond most princes."

"All through smuggling, if I understand you?"

"Smuggling is only the beginning," the gentleman named Baden said. His voice dropped to a whisper. "I heard the war might be over, except Arceneau manages to keep all sides supplied with materiel to keep it going. He has no loyalty to any king or country. He serves himself."

"How very independent," Bruce drawled. "I wonder that he is not mistaken for an American."

His comment raised a general laugh. Bruce felt confident his interest didn't seem out of the ordinary. He let the others take over the thread of the conversation. He couldn't think clearly anyway, ever since he saw Volange sweep Sophie out the doors. Her head was held high, but even from that distance, he could see she ached to turn back…but she dared not.

Bruce wouldn't relax until she was in his sight again. He had to let her work…after all, he'd never expect her to dash after *him* in the same situation. And so he waited, one eye toward the garden, and only half an ear listening to the babble around him.

* * * *

Volange kept Sophie very close to him. After a dance, he asked her to join him outside, and she allowed him to escort her there. She didn't even glance back to see if Bruce noticed her movement. She had to trust he did. She was not used to trusting anyone.

And then she was in the darkened space outside, more intimate and more isolated. If Volange realized who she was, this was a better place to either confront her or get rid of her. No one was there to see.

But her companion kept the conversation on the topic of the war and the house party. Perhaps he couldn't see through her after all.

Eventually, he said, in French, "So you have heard Theriot's proposal."

Sophie just nodded.

"And your opinion?" Volange asked, his eyes alert and even amused.

"It is a very…grand plan," she hedged, glad she could speak French when discussing the delicate subject. "Ambitious."

He laughed, noticing her equivocation. "*Precisement*, my dear. Very grand. Perhaps too grand?"

"I have no love for the Emperor," she said with absolute truth, "but…"

"But you are a practical woman, are you not? You don't relish the idea of throwing good money away on a dream."

"To earn a great reward, one must take great risks. I understand ambition. But I have made no decision yet."

He tilted his head, as if considering her words carefully. "Might that mean you are open to hearing another proposal?"

She looked at him, and allowed interest to show in her eyes. She said, "It would depend very much on the particulars of the proposal."

He leaned toward her. "I am a businessman. My—partners—and I are always looking for investors."

"Do you offer a reasonable rate of return?"

"Spectacular rates, for those who can accept the risk."

"I do not fear risk. I came to this house, after all. We could all be branded as traitors if someone knew what was being discussed here."

"Ah, talk is just talk. Theriot is very good at talking. But is he a man of action?"

Sophie let a smile hover on her mouth. "You speak like one who knows."

"I do, dear," Volange said, his hand suddenly caressing her lower back. "I know many things."

"Well, when you see fit to share the details of your proposal, you will find me attentive...though I make no promises," she added coyly, despite the fear running up her spine.

He took his hand away, having tested her to see if she would flinch or shy away. "So confident. I love that quality in a woman. You don't seek your husband's advice on this little matter?"

"My fortune is my own. He is well aware of the reality of the situation." Sophie tossed her head to the side. "I believe a woman equal to a man. Why should I ask permission for anything?"

"You are exquisite," Volange murmured, his gaze turning distinctly amorous. "I have half a mind to steal you away at this very moment."

Sophie laughed, even as her guts turned cold. "I should be cross with you if you did. You ought to know a lady can not simply take off at a moment's notice."

"And you are a lady," he replied. His tone suggested just enough doubt to make her shiver.

"As much as you are a gentleman," she said. "And a true gentleman shows courtesy to all ladies, does he not?"

"Then I should be a gentleman and let you return to your husband," Volange said. Then his eyes turned speculative. "But you know, you look so familiar. Haunting, almost."

Sophie said, with a light laugh, "I have been told so many times. Even by Madame Baden a few days ago, who was convinced I was the ghost of her old friend!" She decided to risk some bolder flirtation. "If you find that you can not forget me, sir, you must let me know somehow."

His eyes flickered. "Oh, I shall never forget you."

Sophie felt a surge of triumph. Even if there was a threat in his words, she knew she captured his interest. And once she had a man's interest, her success was assured.

Shortly afterward, he escorted her inside, once again the charming gentleman. Volange handed Sophie back to Bruce with an old-fashioned bow. "You are a lucky man, sir."

Bruce pulled Sophie to his side, perhaps with more strength than necessary. "You have no idea. Whole new worlds of possibility opened the moment I first laid eyes on this lady."

Sophie rolled her eyes. "Such flattery. Have you had too much to drink?" She felt Bruce's embrace tighten around her and felt suddenly safer. Volange's touch had chilled her.

"I may want more," he said.

"Excellent," she said. "I'll have a glass, too."

Bruce excused them both, and steered Sophie toward the room where food and drinks were laid out. "Are you all right?" he muttered as they walked.

"I'll survive," she said. Then, without knowing she was going to say it, she added, "I'm glad you're here."

She was suddenly giddy with relief and pleasure. Her nerves were as frayed as if she had been on stage alone for her very first performance. But she performed well! Volange didn't suspect her true nature, and she had already laid the groundwork to learn more about his private plans. The Zodiac would learn so much, and all because of her work.

Well, Sophie amended, Bruce was helping out in his supporting role. She never could have faced Volange if he hadn't reassured her. Moved by a sudden sense of shared secrets, Sophie stopped him, then stood up on her tiptoes and twined her arms around his neck. She kissed him softly, intending only a brush of her lips across his.

But he tasted rather good, and Sophie lingered on his mouth, tasting his lips with her tongue. After a moment of surprise, he held her close and kept her there. Sophie didn't mind. She closed her eyes, focused completely on the kiss, deepening it when he responded. If only her job was to seduce him. That would be delightful.

Sophie pulled back, inhaling. Her train of thought was dangerous. But she tried to smile as she said, "It went well, and you helped."

"I'm glad," Bruce breathed. He still held her with one arm around her waist. He smiled too, but then his voice was cold. "But don't do that again."

She wavered. "The kiss?"

His voice was low, secret. "From you, I require a kiss from a dutiful wife. No more." He released her. "Remember why we're here."

"I'm well aware of that," she shot back, only training keeping her voice low as well. Since when did a man get angry when he was appreciated?

Putting the incident aside, he secured more wine for them both, and they continued to play out their characters.

* * * *

By the end of the evening, Bruce saw Sophie was actually trembling with the effort of keeping up her persona as Madame Cassou. After a week together, he recognized many of her tiny tells.

He moved closer to her when they had a moment alone. "Do you need to escape?" he asked.

"I'm quite well," she said coolly.

"No, you're not. You're thinking of your mother."

"What?" Sophie was startled. "How do you know that?"

"Whenever you drift off, you touch your chest here," and he touched the same spot on her body with one finger, "as if you should be wearing a pendant there. But you're not. Just the cross, and that's too low."

"Do I do that?"

"You told me once you had lost a necklace long ago. It must have been your mother's, or you wouldn't be so sentimental about it. So why are you thinking of her now?"

"Why does anyone think of her mother? I miss her, I suppose."

He paused and looked around the room. "We're done here for the evening. Let's go to our room."

Sophie looked like she was about to protest, but then merely nodded. "Yes, dear."

She must be exhausted to not argue with him, Bruce thought.

In the room, they barely spoke as they took off their evening clothes. Bruce had established early on with the maid Maggie that she would not be needed to assist Madame to prepare for bed. He expected total privacy. Maggie never intruded again. She probably gossiped—it was a good story to tell of the besotted Cassou and how he saw to his wife's needs before bed. Either that or everyone thought the couple couldn't keep their hands off each other. Bruce didn't care which, so long as they got a few precious moments to drop their personas.

Sophie took off her wig and placed it carefully on a carved form in a large box. She looked tired when she climbed into bed. But when Bruce followed, she turned to face him.

"What's on your mind?" she asked. In the darkness of the room, and the forced intimacy of sharing a bed—though they never touched after the first night—the murmured conversations felt natural. Perhaps all husbands and wives talked like this at night, Bruce thought. Though they probably discussed their children, rather than espionage tactics and enemies.

At the moment, Bruce had only one question. "Why does Volange scare you so much?"

Sophie looked away. "Remember the night we met? Julian told us about the assignment, and I mentioned Arceneau had men who would kill for the fun of it?"

"Yes."

"Well, Volange is the man I was thinking of. He goes out of his way to hurt people. It's not efficiency, it's a sickness inside him."

Bruce didn't want to press her, but he needed to know more. "Can you explain?"

"When I was living on the streets, I never joined any of the gangs, but many did. And at the time, Volange ran a few of them. It wasn't an accident that his gangs prospered while the others faded."

"How so?"

"He killed the leaders of the other gangs, as an example to others. But the way he killed them, you could tell he enjoyed it."

"How do you know how he did it?"

"He issued *invitations*," she said. "Once, he got a lot of the kids in one place with the promise of food. And he did give out food. But before, he made us watch as he killed one boy."

"Sophie…"

"He used a chemical, something in a solution," she said, speaking over him. "It looked like milk. He made the boy drink it, and he started screaming that he was burning up inside. His face turned red, then black. We watched him die. And Volange just stood there, grinning the whole time."

"You don't have to…"

"He likes all sorts of chemicals. Guns and blades too, but any drug…oh, he loves drugs. He had a girl for a long time, a sort of pet he kept so far gone on opium that she'd dream standing up."

"Sophie, stop."

She didn't. "Tonight, when we were all handed our drinks while Volange stayed at the back…I wondered. He would think it such a joke, to have a whole room of people at his mercy."

Bruce took her face in his hands. "Dove. Stop it. I shouldn't have asked. I'm sorry."

"You should know," she said, her voice broken. He hated that sound in her voice.

"Tell me how you joined the Zodiac," he said, to distract her. "You never really said."

"It's rather convoluted," Sophie whispered back, blinking.

"We have hours, dove."

"Very well," she began, trying to recover. She shifted, and sat up in bed. "It was in 1795. I was working in Paris. Mostly as an actress, but also as a dancer…and a bit of pickpocketing on the side, though just to keep sharp. Anyway, I developed an act. It grew quite popular among a certain set. I was invited to perform at these private events that became all the rage one summer in Paris."

"You joined the Zodiac because you went to a party?"

"Actually, yes. I was dancing at one of these affairs, and I saw a man watching me. An older gentleman, all in black like the others—but there was something a little off about him. He was interested in me, for some reason. After my performance, I saw him again. And again. He was waiting for me to come over to him. And I did. Like iron to a lodestone.

"He smiled and told me I was magnificent. He said I looked much older than fourteen."

"You were fourteen?"

"Three years at the theater after Mama…yes, I guess I must have been fourteen."

Fourteen. Something stabbed through Bruce. Sophie wasn't a coquette playing at espionage as a lark. She'd been through more of a war than he had.

"What is it?" Sophie asked, noticing his silence.

"Nothing. Go on."

"Well, he said we were kindred spirits. He said, Sophie, you should come home with me. He knew my real name, even though I advertised myself as Serafina still. I was fascinated.

"Now I wasn't an innocent, and I knew exactly what it meant when older gentlemen invited a girl 'home' with them. But to play along for a moment, I asked him where his home was. He learned over to me and whispered 'England…come with me, Sophie. Neither of us belongs here.'

"He was an infiltrator! An impostor. And he *was* a kindred spirit. He promised that if I came back to England with him, I'd be fed, clothed, kept safe, and given any profession I wished."

"And you accepted."

"What choice did I have?"

"I'm not judging you. I might have done the same in your position."

"Ah, but you're a man. So you would have had other options."

Sophie suddenly looked down at her hand, as if surprised to notice that, at some point, Bruce had taken her hand in his own. She didn't pull it away, though.

"He took you to England..." Bruce prompted her to continue.

Sophie nodded. "I won't say he was like a father. I never had a father. But he was like a marvelous old uncle. He kept his word. He was kind to me. He took me shopping for new dresses. He found me a safe place to stay, with a proper chaperone. He sent me tutors and made sure I kept up with my ballet and magic tricks. When I said I wanted to join a theater in London, he had no objections.

"One day, though, he introduced me to a new tutor, a gentleman who didn't look like anything much. But my benefactor said this tutor was the best at his subject, and if I chose to study it, I could have no better teacher in the world.

"That subject turned out to be spycraft, and my so-called tutor was none other than Julian Neville. He taught me many many things. Combined with what I knew from the streets and the theater, I knew no spy could match me for skills. And in due time, Julian told me about the Zodiac. I told him if he didn't let me join I'd kill him. He said that was fair—because if I didn't accept the invitation, he'd kill me."

Bruce listened to her story as if it were a fairy tale. A dark tale, true, but one that might still end happily.

"So you joined," he said. "Do you ever wish you'd chosen differently?"

"If I chose differently, I'd be dead," she said, once

again sounding like herself. "So no." She smiled at him. "And you're stuck with me...till we're done with the assignment."

He nodded, wishing she didn't sound so happy about the last part.

Chapter 17

Ω

As Sophie expected, the morning after the revelation of his plan, Theriot cornered her. He was eager to hear her answer to his insane plot. Sophie actually couldn't wait for the meeting. She had several things to ask, and she had to ask them all in a way that would keep her real interest hidden.

He began innocently enough, asking if she was enjoying herself. Sophie knew that he would angle for a way to get her in a compromising situation. He moved closer and closer to her, until she couldn't pretend not to notice his intent.

"My dear, you must have faith in me. As I said last evening, I have assurances from sources *inside* the British Cabinet that Britain will support my moves against the Emperor. Of course, they don't know what I will do once I get to the palace!"

"But can you trust those sources?" she asked. "Words spoken once can be easily forgotten."

"But these words were not spoken, beautiful. I have the promise in writing."

"You must show me!" she said, making her voice astonished and breathy. She had to get her hands on the letter, preferably when she was alone with Theriot. "I'd do almost *anything* if I saw proof."

He stopped his advances. "I can't show you."

"And you ask me to trust you." Sophie pulled away from him and returned to a haughty attitude. "All I hear are empty promises. A woman doesn't like that."

"But Marianne, I don't have the letter any more. It was delivered to me not long ago, but I passed it to Volange for safekeeping last night. He's very careful with all such things." He looked frustrated about it.

Not Volange! Sophie cringed inwardly. How could fate possibly be so cruel as to force her to seduce *him*? "You have given it to Volange," she murmured, keeping her outward composure. "Why did you give it away?"

"I had no choice. I answer to Arceneau, and Volange works for him. He is a persuasive man," Theriot said, not looking at her.

Sophie had a guess as to how Volange "persuaded" him to give the letter over. It probably involved the threat of extreme pain. In fact, if Theriot tried to extort money from his supposed employer, he was lucky he was still alive.

"He won't let it out of his keeping, believe me. He wouldn't even tell me where he's hiding it, as if I couldn't be trusted. But he has his orders, too. The letter is real, and safe."

"Do you promise me?"

"I do, Marianne."

Remembering her role, she playfully batted his arm. "You should have told me at once and put all my questions to bed."

"Speaking of bed…"

She laughed. "Not so fast. You held out on me. Now I hold out on you. I'll request the funds from my bank… then we'll celebrate, yes?" She kissed him, keeping her attitude playful.

Theriot reacted much as she expected him to, and Sophie was nearly lying on the desk by the time she extracted herself from his embrace. "Later," she said. "I have an image to maintain, Thomas."

"I don't care," he said.

"My husband does, and he keeps an eye on me." Sophie straightened her skirts and gave a silent prayer of thanks that she could use Bruce as a shield. "I will let you know as soon as the funds are in my possession."

"I can't wait."

"I know, sweetheart," Sophie said. "But all the same, you'll have to."

Making a strategic retreat, Sophie waited for Bruce to return from his ride. She had made a major discovery, and she couldn't wait to share it with him. The letter was with Volange, so there weren't many places it could be. In fact, Sophie was certain he'd have it ready to hand in his own room, hidden but easily retrieved in case Volange had to flee quickly. Sophie understood how people who lived in the shadows thought, since she'd done it herself. She just had to devise a way to get into his room while he was occupied.

However, hours passed before she saw Bruce. Only when Sophie walked into the bedroom to change for dinner did she unexpectedly find Bruce waiting for her.

"I thought you'd never get here," he said, grinning like a boy.

"I should say the same thing! Besides, I didn't know you were expecting me at a certain time."

He handed her a loosely wrapped package. "I got you something."

"What is this?" she asked in surprise. For the moment, she forgot her news of the letter.

"The quickest way to find out is to open it."

Sophie pulled at the ribbon. The wrapping paper fell to the bedcover as Sophie exposed the velvet-covered inner box. She opened the hinged lid to reveal not one, but three necklaces. "Oh!" she said, completely nonplussed.

One was a ruby cross worked in gold, on a gold chain. The other had sapphire arms and a diamond in the center, with silver filigree. The third pendant was a silver locket, with an elaborate cross etched onto its oval surface. "Where did you get these?" she asked in disbelief.

"I bought them," he said, with a careless shrug.

"But these are expensive!"

"You need them for your costume, dove. I have money enough. I'll send the bill to Aries if I'm feeling poor."

"But why did you do it at all? I didn't mean for you to buy anything."

"It's just a little help for you to look the part for the rest of the time. We are not going to be thwarted by a lack of jewelry. We're too invested for that."

Sophie took off the cross she already wore and pulled

the locket out, ignoring the more expensive and elaborate crosses for the moment.

"Put it on," he urged.

Sophie did, but her fingers fumbled with the delicate clasp. She sat at the vanity to try again.

Bruce moved behind her. "Let me." He bent and took the chain away from her. He fastened it while Sophie waited, her hands sliding to her lap. Bruce ran his fingers under the chain so it lay properly. "There."

Sophie stared at herself in the mirror. The locket was not quite in Cassou's style, but Sophie found the gleaming silver oval flattered her.

"I like it," she said, the words coming out in a whisper.

Bruce was still standing behind her, leaning over her shoulder with a pleased smile. Then, without warning, he dipped his head and kissed her skin just below the chain, where her shoulder rose to meet her neck.

A wash of heat shot through her, but the kiss was over as soon as it began. He straightened up and regarded her reflection again. "You wear it well," he said.

He picked up the box with the other necklaces. "Here. Put these with your jewelry and I'll dispose of the box. I don't want any maid coming across it and wondering why all your jewels are new."

Sophie nodded, still a bit shaken. "Yes. Thank you," she added quickly. "You didn't have to do this."

He glanced at her. "It's nothing."

Sophie looked away. He was right. It was nothing to him. So why had he kissed her for no reason?

"Speaking of presents, I have one for you," she said, returning to the more important subject. "You should be very pleased with me."

Bruce gave her a puzzled smile. "More than usual?"

She drew him closer. She had to rise on tiptoe to circle her arms around his neck, but she wanted to be able to whisper her secret to him. "I know where the letter is."

His arms tightened around her waist. "Tell me more, dove."

"Volange has it in his possession," she said, keeping her voice low, even though they were alone. "Theriot told me Volange took it from him, and won't give it up. He's obviously going to pass it to Arceneau when he leaves here. So we don't have to find a way into Theriot's rooms after all."

"But how do you expect to get to Volange?"

"He's interested in me. It won't take more than a day or two to secure an invitation to his rooms."

Bruce pulled back to look at her. "That's far more dangerous, dove. Theriot is mostly harmless, but Volange is a killer. And anyway, considering how you feel about him…" He trailed off.

"I can do this," she said. "I thought about it all day. I was scared of him, but this is too important to let emotions rule me. I'll get that letter."

"While I wait around and do nothing," Bruce said sourly.

"Not nothing." Sophie smiled at him. "You'll protect me."

"How am I supposed to protect you in a situation like

that?"

"Knowing you're close will help. You'll come if I call, isn't that right?"

"Count on it," Bruce muttered, even as he released her.

Sophie turned away before she realized she meant every word. She had come to rely on Bruce.

Chapter 18

Ω

THE NEXT DAY BROUGHT SOPHIE endless frustrations. She had to fend off Theriot's attentions while encouraging Volange's, and in the meantime she had to deal with her own increasingly complicated feelings toward Bruce. To his credit, he let her work. He stayed largely out of her way—just what she told him she wanted at the beginning.

Yet working alone was not always ideal. She found herself thinking of what Bruce might do in a certain situation, and wished she could ask him about one thing or another instead of guessing. What was worse was the fact that Volange proved a difficult man to seduce, if only because he was difficult to find.

She finally managed to get him alone, after waiting for him to conclude a meeting with someone who had just arrived at the house. She pretended to only be passing by the open door, but she moved languorously, and he saw her.

"Marianne!" he called, taking the liberty of using her supposed Christian name. Sophie let it pass; indeed, she wanted to encourage familiarity.

She stepped inside the room, which appeared to be in use as a sort of office. "Yes, Monsieur Volange."

"Alain, please," he said, with a smile that would have been inviting if Sophie didn't know his true personality.

"Alain," she said, as if savoring the name. Catering to his prejudices, she spoke in French. "What mysterious business are you conducting in here, so far from the fun?"

"I am ensuring the fun will continue, Marianne," said Volange. "Some interesting goods arrived today, and just in time." He gestured to a large box on the floor near the desk. "We're going to have a little party after supper tonight."

"I thought this whole month was a party."

"This is special. Have you ever used nitrous oxide?"

Sophie knew what the stuff was, having been to a few gatherings of theater types where the novel substance was available. She tried it once and found the effect most alarming. But she thought it best to seem ignorant. "I've heard it mentioned by friends," she said. "They praised it highly."

"Your friends were right, my dear. It's wonderful. Delightful. It brings joy and peace."

"I do look forward to it, then," she murmured. "You will show me how it's done, yes?"

Volange leaned forward, pulling Sophie into his embrace. As before, she had to strive to ignore the natural fear he stirred in her. When he kissed her neck, she shivered, but he took it for pleasure. Sophie gasped, letting him continue. Physically, at least, he was attractive, so she could respond to him as long as she didn't think too much about who he was. Judging from his reaction to her touch, he noticed nothing unusual.

"You are so often guarded by your husband," he said between kisses.

"I have a role to play, Alain," she said softly. "In many ways, it's useful to have the protection of a husband."

"I suppose," he grumbled. "But this is better."

Sophie giggled when his hands covered her breasts. "I like it better, but I think we should find a more suitable time to…conclude this, yes?"

"Tonight," he said.

"Tonight is the nitrous party," she pointed out. "You would not deny me that."

"You'll love it." His eyes gleamed. "It's a unique experience."

"We'll see." Sophie withdrew from his embrace, not only to keep him unsatisfied but also to preserve her own appearance. "I've often been promised unique experiences, and been disappointed."

"Not this time," he swore.

"You promise?" she asked coyly.

Volange smiled again. "When you try this, you'll forget who you are."

"How very intriguing." Sophie exited with that line.

Once she was alone, her mind raced. The substance Volange would offer the guests was designed to loosen inhibitions…and tongues. If she and Bruce were to survive, they both had to be on their guard.

Sophie retreated to the bedroom until Bruce returned from his daily ride so they could discuss the evening's plans. She went to the window and watched, hoping to catch a glimpse of him before he returned to the house itself.

Why am I behaving like a woman in a melodrama? she wondered. Mooning about and waiting passively for her beloved…that wasn't a thing Sophie ever did. Yet here she was, looking out the window while holding the locket he'd given her. Ridiculous.

She hadn't opened the locket. Why should she? It had just been purchased, and only for a prop. There was nothing that could have gone inside. But as she mused, she played with the locket and her fingernail caught the hidden catch. The locket popped open and a tiny folded paper fluttered down to the floor. Curious, she picked it up and unfurled it.

The strip of paper contained one line: *All the world's your stage.* Below the slight misquote of Shakespeare was a little symbol that most people would dismiss as a scribble. It was actually the astrological symbol for Scorpio. Bruce had written it for her and signed it with his secret name.

Sophie folded the note again and replaced it in the locket. She snapped it closed, and stared out at the scene through the glass. *It doesn't mean anything,* she reminded herself. Bruce only bought the necklaces because they would help her cover be more convincing. But he hadn't needed to buy a locket. And he hadn't needed to write a little secret note in it for her to find. And he certainly hadn't needed to kiss her so sweetly when he put it on her.

Sophie could not afford to be touched by this, or by anything Bruce did. She had a task to do in this house. He had to help her complete it, and nothing more.

By the time Bruce returned to the room, Sophie was in command of herself once again.

"We have a slight problem," she said.

"Only a slight one?" he asked, removing his coat. "That's a relief."

"Tonight after dinner, Volange plans to introduce the guests to nitrous oxide."

"Sounds hideous. It's a drug?"

She nodded. "I've tried it once before. My crowd are always looking for diversions of that sort. It's a gas, inhaled rather like a hookah."

"How powerful is it?" he asked, his expression tight.

"The more you breathe in, the more it affects you," she said. "It makes one relaxed…and suggestible. I've also heard that it tends to induce honesty."

"That could be a slight problem."

"Avoid taking any. But if you must, try to only inhale the least possible amount. You may think it's not doing anything to you until it's too late. It sneaks up on you."

"You say it makes people more open to suggestion?"

"Yes."

"Then Volange will undoubtedly suggest you break your imaginary marriage vows tonight."

"I'm counting on it," Sophie said. "He nearly did so this afternoon, but I put him off. I want him to invite me to his room. I need to be able to search it after he sleeps."

Bruce's expression was impossible for her to interpret. "Be careful."

She smiled. "Naturally. I'm not a reckless person."

The way he laughed at that made Sophie wish dearly

that she could kiss him, instead of the man she was here to pursue.

For the gathering, Sophie wore the most provocative gown in Marianne's trunk. It was a dark red silk, with a low-cut neckline and a loose shape that was decidedly French. Sophie wore the ruby cross instead of the locket, fastening the chain so the stones nearly rested in the little valley between her breasts. With the wig's curls brushing her bare shoulders, the flashing jeweled pendant, and the sensual fabric of the dress, Sophie was dressed as a seductress ought to be.

She watched for Bruce's reaction when she stepped out to be inspected. His eyes widened fractionally. "You should certainly get Volange's attention tonight," he said mildly.

What did she have to do to get his? Sophie wondered. Putting aside those first few encounters, Bruce seemed indifferent to Sophie altogether. And just when she was beginning to think that she rather liked him after all.

He was dressed quite plainly. The man he was impersonating was not a dandy, and Bruce himself had no proclivity for flashy dress. A well-tailored jacket over a linen shirt, and understated, narrow pants were all he needed. He looked deceptively simple. Only a careful examination of his expression revealed that he was thinking behind that façade.

"Shall we go down?" he asked her.

She nodded, and he escorted her through the halls to the gathering they both dreaded.

Guests were already enjoying the evening's diversion.

Several people lounged on sofas in the drawing room, and at least one couple was engaging in behavior that would be embarrassing on a London street.

Volange saw Sophie and Bruce enter, and immediately gestured for them to come over.

"You are just in time," Volange said by way of a greeting. "I've opened a new bag of the gas. You shall be the first to try this one—after me, of course."

He demonstrated how to inhale it, then gave the tube to Bruce. "Take a deep breath. A man of your size won't be affected by a little puff."

Sophie watched Bruce accept the offer. Hiding her concern, she saw him take what seemed like a very deep breath.

"Careful, dearest..." she murmured, in spite of herself.

"Oh, don't worry, dove," Bruce said, laughing. "I don't feel a thing." He took another breath, while Volange watched with a growing smile.

"You'll feel the effect in a moment. Why not have a seat?"

Bruce nodded, and turned toward the grouped couches. Sophie tried not to stare after him. Hadn't she warned him about this?

But Volange was watching her now. He offered the tube to Sophie. "A breath of paradise?"

Sophie knew she couldn't avoid taking the drug, so she inhaled it as lightly as she could. Even so, she knew it would affect her. As indeed it did. She felt lightheaded, and giddy. Volange urged her to breathe in another dose, and she did, knowing that he was watching her very closely.

"I might faint," she murmured in slow, slurred French.

Volange smiled. "You may want to sit down for a moment." He leaned over, his breath hot on her cheek. "I'll find you later, lovely." He used the darkness of the room to run a hand down her side, and then between her legs. Sophie was grateful for the fabric of the dress. It rendered the violation barely tolerable. *Well, at least I know he's interested...* she thought with a giggle. Damn, the gas was affecting her already.

"Yes. I should…sit…" she managed. Volange released her and she swayed toward the grouped couches. A few lanterns glowed on a low table in the middle, the light refracting through the colored glass in rainbows. Other than that, it was dark.

As Sophie looked around, the colors in the room seemed to deepen. Everything looked more beautiful. *It's just the drug,* she reminded herself. *Nothing has changed. Be careful, dove. Be careful.*

Bruce sat on a long divan, watching her with dark eyes.

Sophie walked toward him. "What are you looking at?"

He didn't say anything. He only smiled a little and beckoned her closer. His eyes were darker than usual, the pupils larger.

"Enjoying yourself?" she asked, trying to keep her voice light.

"Come here," he said. His voice was relaxed, and his tone held much more meaning than what the simple words implied.

She obeyed.

He put his hands on her waist and drew her down on his lap. Without thinking about the wisdom of it, Sophie settled there. His perusal of her took a long time, but she found herself enjoying it. She wanted him to be pleased with her. But when his hands drifted upward along her side, inching closer to her chest, she recalled her duty.

"Volange expects me…" she began to say.

"Forget him," Bruce said bluntly.

He sounded lucid enough that Sophie couldn't tell how much of the gas he'd inhaled. At first, she thought it had been a lot more than what she'd taken, judging by his languid attitude and his frank appreciation of her body. Now she wasn't sure.

"So—" he began.

"So what?" she said quickly, leaning forward to cover his mouth with hers. The fool was about to say her real name in front of everyone.

This was not a wifely kiss, that was certain. But she had to stop him from talking. Bruce's lassitude faded instantly. He tightened his arms around her and kept her kissing him with a few flicks of his tongue. Sophie's body flushed and she arched her back, bringing her chest against his. The drug worked to make all sensation much more potent.

A low moan filled the air. It took her a moment to realize it was Bruce who made the sound. His hands slid up her back and settled so he could hold her firmly against him, not that Sophie had made the slightest effort to pull away.

He broke the kiss again to take a breath. Sophie took the opportunity to whisper in his ear, "Are you all right?"

He laughed. "I feel better than I have in days, dove," he said. "It's a shame we aren't alone right now."

"Oh, don't let that little fact stop you," someone said.

Sophie looked over to see Volange watching them. She felt dirty, thinking of him watching her kiss Bruce. She buried her face in Bruce's shoulder.

"Now you've made her shy," Bruce said, sounding incredibly put out.

"Another puff of the gas will cure that," Volange said.

"Darling?" Bruce asked her in the same tone. "Would you like a little more of that nice...nite...what's it called?"

"Nitrous oxide," Volange said.

"Nitrous oxide," Bruce repeated, with the sort of precision drunks used to show they weren't drunk. "Why don't you?" Belying his words, one hand gripped her thigh almost painfully hard. Sophie realized he wasn't completely lost to the substance. He didn't want her to leave him.

"If you think so, dear," she responded faintly, feeling torn. She had to allow Volange to get her alone if she were to advance the plan.

"Here, my lady." Volange offered the tube again. Sophie sipped at it slowly, trying to look as if she was breathing a lot more than she was.

"My dear Volange," she breathed, "I fear this is very...potent."

He grinned. "A fine quality, my lovely." He took the bag back from her, his hands covering her own. "And you are lovely, I think."

"Why, thank you," Sophie said, giggling in spite of herself. "I try so hard to be lovely, you know." The drug made her sound like an idiot.

"You succeed." Volange held out a hand. "Come with me. I want to show you something in the next room."

"But…" She glanced at Bruce, reluctant to leave him.

He squeezed her thigh once more, then deliberately pushed her up and away from him. "You go on, dove. Just hurry back. I'll be waiting." He wasn't going to rescue her from Volange, because rescue wasn't what she needed.

Sophie allowed Volange to walk her to the adjoining salon. This room was also dark, but empty except for them.

"What is it you want to show me?" Sophie asked, giggling again.

"I want to show you power."

"What do you mean by that?"

"Kiss me," he said, lowering his mouth onto hers.

Sophie allowed him the liberty, and responded as well as she could, considering her state and her secret rage. "Alain," she gasped, when she managed to pull away and take a breath. "My husband is in the next room! He'd be enraged if he knew what we were doing."

"He's practically asleep. And not deserving of you, Marianne. God, you move like a dancer sometimes!" he said. "I've been watching you since you arrived, dreaming of seeing you naked."

"Shh," she hissed. "Someone will hear you."

"I want you, Marianne. Now."

"Now?" She frowned, trying to hold onto her invented personality. "Am I a girl fresh out of school, to be bedded in the corner of a library?" Sophie felt how excited he was. "You may need more than a single night to work that off, Alain," she whispered provocatively.

"Then I'll have you every night."

She rolled her eyes. "My husband is not a fool."

"He is if he doesn't keep a siren like you under lock and key. You don't need him. Not with your wealth. He won't leave this house if that's how I want it. I could do that, you know. There's a veritable dungeon below the old wing."

"There is not!" she said with real surprise.

"It's the oldest part of the building. Perhaps it needs a new prisoner. I could dispose of your man, and then tie you up and keep you here as my slave, Marianne. Would you like that?"

"You're scaring me," she whispered, again with absolute truth. But she made sure to smile.

He saw her expression and grinned in triumph. "Scare you? No, I excite you." He pressed himself against her. "You will come to my rooms."

"Yes," she said. "Whatever you say."

"That's right, dear. Whatever I say."

"Tomorrow night," she said quickly. "I'll make sure my husband won't know a thing. Then I'll be all yours."

"Tomorrow night," he repeated. "You won't ever forget it."

Sophie was very sure that was true. But she doubted he'd remember a thing, because the seduction would be her work, and she had several tricks to play.

She would find the letter he'd hidden in his room. Within two days, she'd be gone from this house and all the people inside it. Glorious, glorious thought. She and Bruce would return to London…and never see each other again.

Sophie felt a little cold seep into her body. Tonight would be the last night they'd talk in the darkness, because tomorrow she'd be seducing their enemy. And once done with the assignment, they had nothing to hold them together.

Once she escaped Volange, she all but fled back to Bruce. Her nerves were strained from her act, and she needed a respite.

Bruce was exactly where she left him. Sophie could have sworn his gaze sharpened when he saw her, but when she reached him, his eyes were dull from the drug. "Where've you been, dove?" he asked in a low, lazy tone.

"With Volange. He *finally* asked me to come to his rooms," Sophie muttered. "I'm to meet him late tomorrow night. I told him that you'd be snoring away at that point."

Bruce accepted that information without saying anything for a moment. Sophie wasn't sure he quite understood what she said. Was he completely under the influence of the gas?

"Dearest?" she asked, wishing she could say his real name.

"Dove," he said suddenly. "Come outside with me. I

need clear air."

Sophie nodded. That was actually an intelligent suggestion. Together, they slipped out of the house and into the gardens. Luckily, no one was particularly attentive, bent as they were on their own pleasures. Bruce kept walking until they could barely see the house.

She glanced back to see if anyone was following. They stopped near a massive oak tree, the branches of which spread out so much that the shadows were deep underneath the leaves. Sophie pulled him near the trunk, out of sight of the house. "I think the air is clear enough here."

He leaned against the trunk and looked at her. "I want to kiss you."

"Or perhaps the air isn't clear yet," she said. "The drug will wear off eventually."

"It's not the drug," he said.

"You once told me you only kissed me to prove a point."

Bruce laughed. "And you believed me?"

"At the time, yes." Sophie didn't like where this was going. And she didn't like that she wanted to hear him laugh again.

"Then you're a fool, dove."

"I'll leave you alone to recover."

"Don't." He put out one arm to stop her from turning away. "Stay with me."

Sophie knew she should leave, but something in his tone kept her there. "Don't ask me for anything," she warned.

"Just stay," he repeated. He closed his eyes and took a deep breath. "God, it's hell in that house."

She agreed wholeheartedly with that statement. "Tomorrow night I'll have the letter, and it's done. I guarantee it. We won't even wait till dawn."

"We'll get back to London within three days," he said. "I'm going to tell Aries he can't send me anywhere for at least a fortnight."

As they talked, he'd somehow drawn her closer to him. Sophie leaned against him before she really knew she was doing it. But when his arms circled her waist, she knew she had to leave. "Bru—"

"Don't say my name," he said, bending his head. His mouth was close to her ear. "It's dangerous."

"That's what's dangerous here? You're still under the influence of that gas."

"You're right. It does induce honesty."

"Then don't keep talking."

"Excellent idea. Kiss me."

"I told you not to ask me for anything."

"I'm not asking. I'm suggesting, very strongly, that you kiss me."

"No," she said.

"Please."

"You don't want me," Sophie reminded him. "When your head clears, you'll remember that."

"Let me deal with that." His arms tightened. "One kiss."

"Why?"

"Because you're remarkable."

"Remarkable?" Sophie almost laughed. "Well, at least you didn't say beautiful."

"Beauty is passing," he argued. "You're far more than that." He brought one hand up to her mouth, and traced her lips. Sophie let him, too intrigued by the intense expression on his face to stop him. Sophie's experience never included lip tracing, and she found she liked it.

His finger drifted to her cheek, and then her jawline. His touch was rapidly getting more than merely pleasant. Sophie's body, already weakened by the drugs and the drama of the evening, began to respond to him. Her skin warmed and her nerves tingled. She wanted desperately to moisten her lips, in anticipation of his kiss. But despite all the warning signs, she still didn't pull away. It felt far too good, after days of constant tension.

Bruce sighed when she leaned into him. She realized he must be feeling the same way. *That* was why he was devoting such attention to her in his current state. He merely sought a release. "I should go," she said at last. Her voice carried no conviction.

"A kiss first," he insisted.

Before she could convince herself not to, Sophie tilted her head up to kiss him.

When her lips met his, all other thoughts fled. While just as eager as the one she'd endured from Volange in the gallery, Bruce's kiss wasn't demanding. He gathered her closer and enjoyed her.

What did he want? He wanted something beyond the simple kiss he asked for. There was always something else. Sophie struggled to think what it was, even as he pulled back to study her face.

"There's such a thing as too much dedication," he said then.

Sophie blinked, befuddled. "What does that mean?"

"You're terrifying, dove. Did you know that?"

"Why?"

"Do you need anyone?" he asked. "You'd go into battle all alone, wouldn't you?"

"Bruce, you're not making sense," she said. "You're confused by the drug. You should sleep."

"You shouldn't have to do this," he said. "We'll figure out something else."

Sophie suddenly stiffened. "What are you saying?"

"Don't go to him tomorrow night."

She said, her voice hot, "Are you trying to stop me from doing what I came here to do? Is this some kind of trick to make me fail?"

"No. Just…do something else."

"Such as what? It's what I have to work with, Bruce. I'm not strong. I can't intimidate people into working with me. So I seduce them into submission. It works surprisingly well."

"But it makes you little better than a—"

Her eyes blazed. "Than a what, Bruce? First you taunt me, then kiss me, and now you think you can judge me? I suppose you never used your charm to get a secret out of a woman, hmm?"

He looked away for one second. She hissed in triumph. "I see. And how many women? But you would never think to call yourself what you were just about to call me. It's different, isn't it? Because you're a *man*. And men make the rules."

"That's not what I meant."

"Because you know why I really terrify you," Sophie pushed on. "It's because we're *not* different. We both lie and cheat and steal, but we justify it because we're doing it for others. But at the end of the day, we're both professional liars. But I'm a woman, so there's an easy word for you to use that makes me seem different from you."

"Dove," he began.

"Don't call me that any more! I don't care if you don't like the person I am. But don't pretend the reason you don't like me is how I use my own body. Because we're the same kind of person, and you know it."

With that final, vicious sentence, Sophie stormed off, leaving Bruce behind to sleep off the effects of the drug and his own maddening prejudices. He wasn't different from other men after all. She was lucky, really. She almost confessed something absurd back there. Thankfully, he revealed his true feelings first.

"He can rot there, for all I care," she said aloud, to make the words sound true.

Sophie made her way back to the bedroom and made a nest of the sheets, burying herself beneath the fabric, hoping he wouldn't return until she was unconscious.

This was the first night he wasn't there to talk to in the darkness, and she hated how lonely she felt.

Chapter 19

℩

THE NEXT MORNING, SOPHIE WOKE up to find Bruce stretched out next to her, his long frame taking over much of the space. He lay on his stomach, above the covers and only partially undressed, as if he'd barely made it to the bed before collapsing. Her temper back to normal, she regretted leaving him behind. Who knew how long he'd remained outside, his mind clouded by that gas?

Sophie sat up. She ought to get out of the bed and start thinking of the day—and night—ahead. As she shifted, he stirred.

"Dove," he said, his voice rough.

"Yes?" she asked.

"Are you awake?"

"Are you?" she asked. "You look half dead."

He groaned, rolling onto his side. "I must have had more of that gas than you did."

"A safe wager." Sophie said no more, wondering if he didn't remember their heated exchange last night.

He opened his eyes and considered her, clad in only the expensive lace-trimmed shift of Marianne Cassou. He said, slowly, "We kissed."

She nodded. It was no good to deny it. "In the parlor.

Volange was watching us."

"After I took the first breath of that vile stuff." He shook his head. "But I don't remember much beyond that."

Sophie spoke cautiously. "Later…we went outside to clear our heads. Then I left the garden to go to bed. You stayed. You may have fallen asleep out there." She didn't mention the second kiss.

He frowned. "I remember the sky getting light. I must have got back here somehow. Lord, I'll never breathe that stuff again. My head is pounding."

"Because you're parched. I'll get you something to drink," she said gently. After all, he wasn't to blame for the effect of the gas. They both had to maintain their roles as hedonistic idiots.

He wrinkled his nose. "Ugh. More wine? Tell me there's scotch."

"I can ring for some."

A short while later, Maggie entered, bearing a tray with scotch and a pot of strong tea. Sophie, now wearing her wig, nodded gratefully. "I don't suppose there was a recent London paper downstairs?" she asked. Bruce had requested the most recent edition every day so far.

Maggie shook her head. "Not seen it this morning, ma'am. I did look. Perhaps another guest asked for the last one. Not that most are awake yet. They had a late night." She looked at the floor, red coloring her cheeks, all too aware of what went on. Sophie dismissed her with a gracious nod, wishing she could spare the girl the worst excesses of the party.

Bruce recovered quickly enough after he took a sip of the scotch. He dressed, looking quite composed for a man who slept part of the night in a drug-induced stupor under the moon.

Sophie took tea, fortifying herself. "Do you remember that I said tonight I'll be…occupied?"

Bruce nodded. "Late, you said. I'll be sure to give the impression of the drunk lord and be out of your way."

"I'll find you as soon as I retrieve the letter."

"You're sure…" he trailed off.

Sophie glared at him. "Sure of what, exactly? My success? As you so enjoy pointing out, I have done this before."

He looked as he were about to argue, then said, "Just be careful."

She paused, a bit mollified. "I always am."

After checking to see that Sophie needed nothing for the upcoming night, he said, "I'm going to ride for at least part of the day. That will give you an excuse to seek out other company tonight." If he had any lingering qualms about Sophie's seduction of Volange, he didn't show them. "Good luck, dove."

She smiled. "Thank you."

Bruce left to go for his ride, despite gathering clouds that hinted at rain. The day looked like it would be hotter than usual.

Sophie chose to stay in the room for the morning, away from the others. She was always nervous when she had to put herself on the line for the Zodiac. Around noon, she rang for more tea and some toast to be brought up, hoping the ritual would calm her.

A new maid brought in a tray with tea, sugar, some bread, and a plate of little cakes.

Sophie watched her, comparing her motions with Maggie's. "Where's our usual maid?" she asked, putting a bit of haughtiness in her tone.

"She was feeling poorly this morning," the blonde replied.

"She looked well enough when I rang earlier."

"Uh…it was a sudden fit," the blonde girl said. "I'm to take over her duties till she returns. My name is Harriet, ma'am," the new maid said as she left.

Sophie drank the tea without sugar. The little cakes were covered with slivered almonds, and were far sweeter than what she typically ate. Still, she devoured them, realizing she had not eaten anything at all that day.

After the snack, she spent a few moments clearing her head. She had a task, and the Zodiac counted on her to complete it.

As the afternoon came on, she dressed with care for the evening dinner. She had to be dazzling to complete her seduction and get the information she needed. Her shift was a fine cotton, almost transparent. It was trimmed with lace, and drifted over her slight curves like a caress. She was almost sad to put on the stays. They were hard to tighten properly—she kept getting dizzy—but she finally managed to tie them up, forcing her breasts to well up slightly.

The dress went on next. It was also light, but Sophie found herself sweating a bit as she adjusted the buttery soft silk of the gown. Lord, it wasn't that hot, surely? The fabric should keep her cool. At least the color was cool, a watery blue green so entrancing a nymph would envy.

She found her matching fan, a gorgeous creation of carved ivory panels threaded with coral ribbons. She waved it slowly in front of her face, reveling in the tiny breeze. Despite the now overcast sky outside, it was deadly hot. She took a sip of cold tea, noticing that her throat itched.

"Don't let me take ill," she told herself. "A runny nose never helps a seduction."

She had just put on her wig and was playing with the curls, finding the most pleasing arrangement, when Bruce entered the room.

"Sorry to intrude," he said. "It was starting to rain, and I cut short the ride."

"Just as well. You can tell me how I look."

"You don't need me to tell you you're stunning."

"Are you sure?" she asked. Anxiety spread through her, making her tremble. She'd never been so nervous, so shaky before. What if she wasn't alluring enough? What if Volange got bored? "I have to look *perfect*."

He walked closer. "I assure you, you look perfect." Then his brow furrowed. "You look a little flushed though. Are you nervous?"

"Yes," she admitted. "But what's worse is that I don't feel well," she said, putting a hand on her stomach. "I wish I could...lie down."

"You're sweating a bit, dove. Is it that bad?"

She nodded. "Yes. I...oh," A sudden wave of heat

assaulted her. Her body shook. Bruce put his arm around her, his careless expression vanishing. "Sophie, are you actually ill?"

"I'm…going to be sick."

She was sick. Suddenly, violently sick. A wave of nausea brought her to the chamber pot, where she lost the small meal she ingested earlier.

"Oh, this is a problem. If Maggie took sick, perhaps I'm sick too," she muttered. She wanted to lie down. She wanted to sleep. "Bruce, I'm not quite right. Help me."

"You're asking for help?" He grabbed her by the shoulders and moved her to the edge of the bed. "Sit. I'd be flattered, except I know this means something has gone completely wrong."

Her sickness was only the beginning. A bitter, chemical odor mingled with the all too organic stench. She watched Bruce lean over and smell the bile. "Oh, don't do that…" she began. "I've just taken a turn…"

His eyes were serious as he turned back to her. "Did you eat or drink anything this afternoon? Before I got back?"

"A maid brought tea to the room, after Maggie was ill. I didn't eat much. Just these sweet little almond cakes…" Her eyes widened as she understood his implication. "I didn't ask for them. They were just there, on the tray—" She clutched at his arm as a new wave of pain passed through her. "I'm stupid."

"No, you were tricked," he said. "I've got to get you out of here."

"No! We'll be exposed."

"Sophie, you were poisoned. That means we're already exposed. I don't know how bad it will be, but we can't trust for you to be cared for here." He stood up. "We're leaving."

"But I have to go tonight, or we'll miss our chance to get the information."

He pushed her back. "You can't get it if you're dead!" Bruce looked out the window, where rain began to pelt down from the sky in earnest. "This is a terrible time to sneak out of a house," he muttered.

Sophie clutched her stomach as another, nastier cramp seized her. "You should go alone," she said, once the spasm passed. "I'll just…"

"No." He moved swiftly to pull her off the bed. "You'll walk out of this house with me, and we'll get to the stables."

"I'll fall," she protested. Walking seemed like such a bother.

He put one arm around her waist. "Then I'll pick you up and carry you." He started walking. "Come on. We don't have much time."

Sophie blinked. "I think it's too late." She raised a hand to put it on Bruce's arm, but she had no idea if she managed to actually do it. Images swam before her eyes, and she knew nothing else.

Chapter 20

♎︎

SOME TIME LATER, SOPHIE WOKE up again and saw only vague shapes and a fire burning low. She had no idea where she was. It could be the great house. It could be an inn. It could be a room in hell. She did know that she was on a floor. "Bruce?" she asked, her voice faint. The warm air smelled odd, like burnt bread.

His voice came from beside her, just beyond her vision. "Right here, dove."

Sophie tried to turn to see him. All her muscles were horribly cramped, making movement impossible. "This isn't going to end well."

"Quiet, Sophie," he said. "You're not going to die." He shifted so he was holding her.

Sophie sagged against him. "I am going to die." She knew it. Her insides were boiling. Dark, wiggling shapes intruded at the corner of her eyes. "Don't let me scream."

"Too late for that," he said, "but no one heard."

"I'm sorry."

"Don't be sorry." He shoved a piece of charcoal toward her. "Here. You need to eat this."

Weakly, she shoved it away. "No." Why would he give her such a thing? Maybe it wasn't Bruce. Maybe it was just a demon who looked like him. "That's not food."

"Eat it," he insisted. "Trust me, Sophie. It will help."

He held her mouth open and force-fed her what turned out to be a chunk of burned bread. She managed to chew and swallow the ashy-tasting mess, and then immediately felt her stomach rebel. "You're trying to kill me," she hissed.

"I'm trying to *save* you. The charcoal might help take the poison out. Trust me."

"I have to throw up," she said, just as she gagged again.

"Good. Do it. Get it out." He turned her over. She catted into a bowl on the floor, filling it with blackened flecks of charred food and—hopefully—the poison.

Bruce didn't let her rest. He made her eat more charcoal and ash, giving her enough water to get the substance down. Over the next hour, she catted four more times, her muscles spasming until she couldn't sit up on her own. Bruce shifted her around like a life-size doll, moving her to the pallet, to the wash bowl, back again. He sat her up or lay her down, depending on how she felt. She was powerless.

"Where are we?" she whispered after the last purge.

"Doesn't matter, love," he muttered. "Just get the poison out and we'll talk about everything later."

"I don't have a later," she said. She was so tired. Her muscles all ached, far worse than the most horrible illness she'd ever had. "I'm so sorry, Mama."

"Mama," she babbled, now seeing her mother mounting the steps of the guillotine, resolutely not looking for her daughter, terrified someone would connect the two. "Mama, come back."

Once again, Sophie saw the blade flash down. Saw her mother's head drop into a basket like a rotten fruit. The crowd cheered a bit, but it was already late in the Terror, and the enthusiasm just wasn't the same. Sophie was enraged. Her mother died at the hand of the executioner and no one even cared? What did her death even matter?

Recklessly, Sophie approached the guard afterward.

"That's my mother," she told him. "I want her body. I want to bury her…"

"You want to be with her? Very well, child." The guard laughed. She wasn't strong enough to keep his hands off her, to keep him from pawing at her barely-there bosom or from finding the locket and snapping it off her neck. "I'll put you right by your mother, you little whelp of a traitor."

He hit her hard with the butt of his dagger, nearly knocking her senseless. Then he flung her into a pit with all the bodies, some without heads and some with—just the normal victims of the day. Sophie never knew how cold flesh could get. She didn't see her mother anywhere. She couldn't see anything through her tears.

Sophie tasted ash in her mouth and felt chunks of wet dirt rain down on her. She tried to scream once, but clamped her mouth shut when the dirt fell in. *Mama's dead. You're on your own.* The thought came to her, clear and cold. *Save your breath if you want to save yourself.*

She closed her eyes, and drifted off into darkness.

* * * *

The night passed with agonizing slowness. Bruce tended Sophie, all the while watching her condition deteriorate. Minute by minute she succumbed to the poison in her body. He knew of only one way to try to neutralize the poison, a barely-remembered lesson from his days on campaign. He had no idea if it would work, especially considering he didn't know what sort of substance she'd been given. He might be killing her himself.

Hours crawled by. His anger soared as he confronted new horrors that he could do nothing to prevent. Sophie sweated profusely, then became feverish. Her eyes dilated and she spoke to people who weren't there, people who were dead and dying. Her mother. A friend. The man she called Abraham. She even talked to Aries a few times, reprimanding him for getting her into this mess. Occasionally, her eyes would focus and she'd mutter Bruce's name, but within seconds, she'd slip back into her nightmares.

She cried and laughed, then got sick or taken with a seizure. When her body stilled again, Bruce tried to feed her water or wine, and then force-fed her more charcoal and ash, until she had no strength to fight him, or to fight the poison in her body.

Later, she completely lost consciousness, and he couldn't revive her, even for a moment. He hoped her nightmares had stopped too. He had no idea what to do other than wait. Her heartbeat fluttered. Sometimes it was so faint he thought she was dead...except for her fevered skin. But then she would whimper or moan a little, and he sighed in relief. He cradled her, holding her head up so she couldn't choke herself. He rocked her when she moaned, and when that seemed to calm her, he was terrified to stop, so he kept at it, listening to her breathing, shallow but steady.

What would he do if Sophie didn't recover? Bruce spent his time contemplating revenge. It didn't lessen his anger, but at least it gave him something to focus on. If she worsened, if she died, he would wait till everyone in Carterhaugh gathered for dinner, and he'd just set the place ablaze. He didn't even care who poisoned her. Kill everyone, and she'd be avenged.

But Sophie would still be dead. And who would care for her then?

"I'll take you home, Sophie," he said to her, hating himself for the morbid turn of his thoughts. "I'll have you buried at home with my family. Beloved Sophie."

Beloved Sophie. Hearing his own words, he went quiet. He had said it without thinking, which made him realize the simple truth. In the short time since they'd been thrown together, he'd got to know her as he had no other woman in his life. And he wanted to keep her in his life.

But she was dying.

Chapter 21

♎

SOPHIE WALKED, THEN CRAWLED THROUGH nightmarish places in her past. She wavered between life and death, but something kept pulling her back toward life.

When she came to, she lay curled up by a fireplace, naked except for a blanket tucked close around her. She was draped over Bruce, who sat on the floor against the post of the large bed. He held her so she couldn't have choked in her sleep, or accidentally rolled too close to the hearth.

She breathed shallowly, trying to assess whether she was dying. She was as weak as a newborn kitten. Her muscles simply would not react to her inner commands. Bruce said nothing, but he wasn't completely asleep. With one hand, he traced circles over her back, his fingers putting enough pressure on her skin so she could feel it, but not to disturb her rest.

"Bruce?" she asked.

He inhaled, waking up fully. "Sophie? How do you feel?"

"Dreadful," she admitted. "How long has it been?"

"Since I found you? Maybe a day and a half. You slept for the last several hours."

"How did you know I'd wake up?" She blinked, trying to see him in the darkened room. She had no idea what time of day it was.

"I didn't know," he said. "I kept feeling for your heartbeat. It was fast for a long while. But I think you got the poison out."

"Where are we?"

"A cottage not far from the house. All that riding I was doing wasn't for fun. I found this place and very carefully brought a few items here each time, just in case. And a good thing I did. I knew you wouldn't make it to a doctor, even if I could find one to trust."

"You and your planning." She wanted to laugh, but it took too much effort. "What will we do about the assignment?"

He frowned. "We'll talk about that when you feel better. Clearly, something went wrong."

She bowed her head. "Volange knew. I must have let something slip..."

"Don't make assumptions, Sophie. We don't know what happened."

"We know someone found out about me," she said.

Bruce gathered her up in his arms. "I'm glad to hear you talking, love."

"Dove," she corrected.

"That's what I said," he amended. "You may not feel like it, but you should eat something. Do you think you can manage broth?"

"Depends on who cooked it," said Sophie.

"I have a little food here. You can eat the bread and

broth. I haven't tried the next bottle of wine yet, so don't touch it."

"What do you mean?" she asked.

"I mean that from now on, you don't eat or drink anything unless I do first. Understand?"

She would have protested, but she was too famished. She ate all the remaining bread and most of the soup, watching as Bruce opened the wine bottle and poured out a small glass.

"You're trying that?"

"If I say I'm dizzy, offer me a second course of charcoal, will you?"

Despite the seriousness of the situation, she smiled. "I'd be glad to. You have to tell me where you learned that trick."

"When I saw action with my company, one of the surgeons traveling with the army became a friend. He'd been over the whole world—or at least it seemed to me. He told me about all sorts of odd little facts he picked up in his travels. He was very interested in how medicine was practiced elsewhere. He told me that the Chinese had long used charcoal to treat various poisons. Something about the composition of the charcoal acts like a wick or a sponge. It draws all the poison into the charcoal and renders it harmless. A man could drink a full glass of poison and not see any effect as long as he ingested charcoal quickly enough."

"What's the name of your physician friend? I owe him a sincere thank you."

"Fisher. But you can't thank him, I'm afraid. He

passed away. An accident, while he was on his way to help someone."

"Oh, I'm sorry."

"So am I, for losing a good man too soon. But he helped save a lot of lives, including yours. And that's nothing to be sorry for."

Sophie finished the food and wished there was more. But she was also extremely tired, as if she had been walking for miles in the sun. "I'm going to sleep again, Bruce…" she said. She didn't even hear his reply.

She woke up to the sound of rushing water. She blinked, and saw Bruce had found a metal tub somewhere and had dragged it inside. He was just filling it.

"You awake?" he asked.

"I am now." She straightened up, feeling more alert than before, though still incredibly weak. "Is that mine?"

"You asked for a bath."

"I did?"

"While you were falling asleep. So I found you one."

She wrinkled her nose. "I feel like I've been swimming in mud. Worse."

"This should help." He headed toward the front door of the cottage. "I'll be back in a half hour or so."

"Where are you going?" she asked, anxious.

"Nowhere. But I know you like your privacy."

"Actually, I may need help to get in."

He returned and helped her to the bath. Sophie took off what little she was wearing. She had never felt less seductive in her life, and blushed to think of what his impression of her would be, seeing her nude like this. She was too skinny, and her skin was disgusting. As for her hair…what could be less attractive than the filthy, cropped cut on her already meager frame?

He helped her step into the steaming water, and let her sink down into the tub.

"Thank you," she said. "I don't suppose you smuggled soap into this place."

"It was already here, actually."

"Excellent. Hand it over."

"No," he said. "I'll do it. You concentrate on keeping your head above the waterline."

He washed her face with a cloth, then scrubbed the rest of her. Sophie accepted that she wasn't able to do much more than not drown. Letting Bruce wash away the sweat and dirt from her ordeal was necessary.

She said, "I must look hideous. I'll never be able to seduce that man at this point."

"I think the seduction plan won't work any longer, anyway," he replied, squeezing water out of the cloth. "But trust me, you'll be as alluring as ever once you recover."

She would feel better about his assessment if he looked the slightest bit interested in her himself. "How alluring is that?" she asked. Before she could say anything else, though, he put a hand around the back of her neck.

"Take a breath and slide down," he ordered.

"What?"

"I have to wash your hair."

"Oh." Taking a deep breath, Sophie slid lower, her head slipping below the surface. She felt Bruce's hand supporting her so she wouldn't fall too far. With the other hand, he quickly ran his fingers through the short locks of her hair, working soap into her scalp. Then she rose to the surface. Water streamed down her head and back into the tub.

"Much better," he said, smiling. "You needed that."

"I'm sure. Help me out, please," she ordered.

Bruce stood, and held her hands while she stood up carefully. She looked down at her body, then laughed softly. "Well, you once said you wanted to know what I really looked like. Now you know. What do you think?"

He kept his gaze on her face as he wrapped a sheet around her. "I think you look like a sign of the Zodiac. Sorry it took me so long to recognize that."

"Are you apologizing?" she asked.

He looked down, then right into her eyes. "So you're a woman. It doesn't mean you're not a fighter. They attacked you, and that means they attacked me. We'll get the bastard who tried to kill you, Sophie. I promise."

Sophie smiled. "Determined words." But not the words she wanted to hear. God help her…had she found the one man she actually wanted but couldn't have?

Bruce ordered her to bed. She lay wakeful for quite a while, her mind racing. By the time she fell asleep, Bruce was still absent.

It was dark when Sophie woke again, her head completely clear for the first time in days. Bruce was awake. He faced away from her, sitting in a chair drawn up to the window, though it was night outside. His left hand lay on the arm of the chair. Despite all that had happened, he still wore that gold ring on his finger.

Sophie gazed at him, her eye snagged by the false wedding ring, when he twisted around in the chair.

"Sophie?" he asked, focusing on her. "Are you feeling better?"

"Yes," she said, smiling to reassure him. "Thanks to you." She got up, twining the sheet around her body, and crossed the room to him. "How do I look?"

He stood up and gave her a once over with appreciative eyes. He reached out to take one of the strands of her cropped hair in his fingers. "Your hair curls," he said, absently.

"It's getting long. I'll have to cut it again soon to fit well under the wig. You know you're one of the very few people in the world who've seen my real hair."

"It becomes you."

Trying to keep a sudden nervousness out of her voice, Sophie said, "You didn't sleep by me last night."

"No." He pulled his hand away.

"There's not much point in my being recovered if you're running yourself down. You don't need to stay up every moment. I'm much better now."

"It's not that."

"What, then?"

"I don't trust myself around you," he said. "Especially not now, when you're yourself all the time."

Sophie never heard more charming words. She laughed, then leaned in and kissed him. She only stunned

Bruce for a moment. Then his arms circled her and held her close to him, and the embrace itself was dizzying in its sweetness.

She twined her arms around his neck, pressing herself closer. Taking a quick breath, she whispered, "So I *can* still seduce you?"

At her words, he pulled away, even though she could sense his reluctance to do so. "I didn't think...I'll stop."

"Why?"

He looked away. "You've made your opinion clear before."

"That was before," Sophie said. She did not move away from him. "I've...ah, reconsidered."

He watched her, his breath quick. "Maybe the poison affected your brain."

"Don't mock me," she said. She felt horribly vulnerable. "I'm serious, Bruce. I...I don't know how to ask you for this." She curled one hand around his forearm, feeling how tense he was.

"Why not? We both know you've done this before."

Sophie looked down, seeing her own skin and the plain sheet she wore as her only clothing. Was this how she thought to seduce him? She had only one thing that would appeal to Bruce. Her honesty. "Yes, I have. But never just because I wanted to."

"Oh." He reached out to touch her chin, making her look at him. "And you do now?"

She nodded, searching his face. "With you. Please? I need to know that...I'm alive."

Somehow, he understood her true meaning. Without

another word, Bruce took hold of the sheet, using the fabric as a way to keep her next to him. His clothes pressed against her bare skin, but she didn't complain. She was too busy being thoroughly kissed. Bruce's mouth and tongue were everywhere, exploring her neck and shoulders until Sophie's gasps revealed the most sensitive places. Pleased with her reaction, Bruce lingered just below her ear, his lips barely brushing her skin.

She swayed a bit, and he quickly swept one arm around her back, holding her even more firmly to him. His hand nestled in the curve of her back, then drifted to cup her bottom.

He groaned a tiny bit. "I could take you right here, dove. You're already destroying me."

She knew it. She felt how hard he was.

"I wouldn't mind," she whispered, "but there is a bed just over there."

He laughed, and the sound wrapped itself around Sophie, surrounding her with warmth. "So there is. Once again, you prove you're far smarter than I am."

Sanity restored for a brief moment, he led her back near the bed, lowering her so she lay the wrong way across it, her feet still touching the floor. He loosened the sheet and then freed her from it. Sophie reached out to pull him down with her.

"No," he said. "Give me a moment."

Sophie watched as he removed his clothes. He didn't rush, but at the end, everything lay disregarded on the floor.

Sophie had seen him nearly naked before. It didn't

stop her from appreciating him all over again. His height made the breadth of his shoulders more remarkable, and the well-formed muscles rippled beneath skin that was tanned all the way down to his waist. She didn't notice the color of his skin then, because she saw his erection, which he made no effort to hide from her.

"You've had a moment. Please come here," she said.

He caught her slight smile and returned it. Then he bent over her and kissed her on the mouth, taking his time. Sophie caught his lower lip and teased him with her tongue, delighted when she heard him stifle a groan.

Bruce laid one hand on her bare stomach, lightly enough to let her change her mind. He didn't fully trust Sophie's desire for him.

She didn't change her mind, though. "You can touch me," she invited.

He spent a very long time touching her, at least by Sophie's rather dazed reckoning. He learned her body, pausing when she breathed in a little deeper, discovering what she liked, often at the same moment Sophie learned it herself.

He said he wanted to make her happy. She wasn't happy. She was euphoric. No drug in the world could work on her like his touch did. Sophie forgot everything else and became raw desire.

She reached out and touched his hard length. He let her stroke him for one delicious moment, but then stopped her. "Damn you, Sophie. That's far too good. Are you trying to kill me?"

"I'm trying to please you, but I don't know you well

enough to know what you like," she said.

"You're a fast learner, sweetheart," he said, shifting so she couldn't tease him further. "I refuse to let this be over too quickly."

Sophie shifted too, unwilling to lie on her back any longer. She pushed Bruce down onto the bed. He let her do what she liked. He couldn't say no to her now. Especially not when she sat over him, her legs astride him, her center excruciating close to his painfully hard erection.

"I know you like this," she said, her eyes sparkling wickedly. "You always tried to get me on your lap when you kissed me."

"I'd have to be insane to not like this, dove," he said, completely taken with her command of the situation. His hands skimmed her body, from her legs up to her breasts.

He watched as she leaned over him and laid her body over his, her slight, sweet breasts brushing against his chest. He'd give anything to have her like this every night of his life. But he only had one night.

Thinking of that, Bruce put his hands on her waist, keeping her body tight against his.

Sophie tilted her head to smile at him. "What would you like me to do?"

He had no idea. Virtually anything she did would destroy him at this point. He wanted so badly to be inside her, but he also didn't want to rush her.

"I want to see you come undone first," he said, his voice rough. "That's what I want."

Sophie lost her coy smile, feeling suddenly shy. She wasn't used to hearing that. She straightened up, determined to give him exactly what he asked for. "Then I'd like you to touch me," she said, her voice low, almost pleading.

She didn't have to ask twice. He slid one hand down to the curls at the center of her, touching her as gently as he could. Sophie's skin began to flush, and her breathing grew quicker with every stroke.

Seduced by her response, he slipped one finger inside her body, and was rewarded with her soft voice calling his name. She was warm, wet, and her hips pushed against his hand in perfect time to his strokes.

"Please," she said, her eyes closing.

He'd never seen her so absorbed, so focused, and it was now happening because of what he was doing to her. Bruce felt a fierce sense of possession come over him. He needed Sophie.

"Come for me," he hissed.

Her eyes flew open, fixed on his own.

"I...I want to." And Sophie realized that she truly did. She wasn't playing any part but herself. She desperately wanted Bruce to see her enjoy their coupling, to know that she wanted him.

She leaned forward to put her hands on his shoulders, lowering herself over him. "Can I kiss you?" she asked.

"Only if you come," he said, a new tension in his voice. "So tell me what to do."

"Just keep..." Sophie couldn't put the word together. She preferred to let her body speak for her. She shifted, her hips moving faster. He responded with a harder touch, willing her to lose herself.

With a soft, short cry, Sophie did. Her body shuddered, and then relaxed. "Please kiss me now," she begged, leaning down again, too weak to sit up.

He found her mouth and kissed her deeply, his tongue tangling with hers. He stroked her once more, and Sophie cried out again. He swallowed the cry as he withdrew his hand. Sophie's body shook a little, and then she lay content against him.

"Bruce," she said, "you have to tell me what you want."

"I have what I want, for now," he said.

But that wasn't the only thing he wanted.

"Sit up, love," he said. Sophie straightened up, her expression both curious and knowing.

He put his hands back on her hips and lifted her slightly. Sophie knew exactly what he needed. She shifted so his shaft touched her center. She watched his eyes close briefly, an expression almost like despair on his face.

"You do want me, yes?" she asked, her nerves flaring. She couldn't stand the thought of him turning her away now.

In answer, he held her body as he thrust up within her. Sophie moaned as he filled her, and then sighed.

"Sophie, you're perfect," he said.

She saw how taut his muscles were, how much he'd held back for this moment. She loved the feel of him inside her. It felt familiar, as if they'd been lovers before.

"Tell me what you'd like now," she said, smiling at him. "Now that you have me."

Bruce wanted to take his time, but he doubted that

he'd last. Sophie was too overwhelming. "Come down here," he said, barely trusting himself to speak. "Come here and twine yourself around me."

She smiled, and lost no time. Her arms twined around his neck. He held her fast with one arm, and rolled so she was again below him. Sophie didn't mind at all. She liked him above her, his body blocking the whole world out. She wrapped her legs around him before he could ask.

"I need you, dove," he said.

Sophie pulled him closer, putting her lips against the pulse at his neck. "You have me."

They were so attuned to each other that her breathing soon matched his. She came undone once more with a long, soft sigh. He kissed her once when she opened her eyes after the release.

She smiled at him, thinking he was the most beautiful person she'd ever seen. "I'm so glad we're on the same side," she said.

He laughed, the low sound warming her like nothing else. "Sweet Sophie," was all he said.

When he moved, rolling onto his back and bringing her to his side, she blushed again. He was as spent as she was. She had been so consumed with her own experience that she hadn't even known, which never happened before. How marvelous, she thought, to simply feel these things, to not worry about anything but the pleasure of being with someone. And not just someone, but him.

Sophie wanted Bruce to stay with her. She wanted to play like this again, free of any obligation except for pleasing him and being pleased by him. She tucked her head onto his chest, feeling the steady rise and fall of his breathing. If only things could be that simple.

"Bruce?" she began to say, then stopped, uncertain what she wanted to know.

"Yes, dove."

Had she pleased him? Who seduced who? Was it possible to go on as before? Could they still work together? Had he lost his regard for her? Too many questions.

"Sophie?" he prompted.

She blurted out, "Where do we stand with each other?"

"We stand with each other," he replied instantly. He put one arm around her shoulders and kissed the top of her head.

"What do you want?"

"I want you to be next to me when I wake up."

"Is that all?"

"Is that all?" he mimicked. "Just the one thing I've never asked a woman before."

They lay together on the bed, Bruce cradling her shoulders as she slept on his chest.

Sophie woke briefly in the middle of the night to find her body cupped against his. He was asleep, his breathing even. She didn't try to move away. It was curiously comforting to be so close to him. To feel his chest against her back. Sophie sighed, and caught the golden glint of the ring on her finger before sliding back into sleep. Momentarily forgetting why the ring was there, she smiled. She was so glad she had decided to marry him.

Early morning light seeped into the little house. Sophie opened her eyes, feeling languid and unwilling to move, possibly because she was still curled into Bruce's body. She couldn't see him, but he wasn't asleep. His hand slowly traced the curve of her hips, down to her knees, and then back up again to her waist. Sophie reveled in it without feeling any need to respond immediately. That was a delicious sensation, the lack of urgency, the absence of concern.

He must have heard a subtle shift in her breathing, because he moved his hand to wrap around her belly. "Awake, dove?" he asked.

"I am now." Despite her own height, she felt completely enveloped. She turned her head to look at him, and he laid a kiss on her mouth. Then he kissed her again, with more intent. Sophie responded to him before she even knew what she was doing. His mouth was warm against hers, and his hands quickly found how to arouse her with almost no effort.

"Bruce," Sophie murmured when she took a breath. "We shouldn't. It won't be like last night…" She trailed off when he turned her body to face his.

"Why should it be?" he asked, dipping his head to kiss the spot behind her ear. "I nearly lost you, dove. I will literally never have enough time to devote to you."

Pretty words, she almost said. She hadn't intended to become entangled with Bruce. But here she was, submitting happily to everything he offered. And each time he touched her, she found herself less likely to turn away. Now, with their bodies entwined like this, Sophie had nothing to say, she had nothing to think, other than to match his moves with her own.

He kissed her insensible. He asked her what she wanted, and then he indulged in whatever sensual act it was—a kiss or a touch or a stroke—until Sophie cried out and begged him to let her recover a little.

He wasn't above tickling her, either. Whenever Sophie's emotions threatened to take over, he seemed to touch her just right to elicit an involuntary, utterly non-seductive giggle.

"Bruce," she demanded after one such assault, "don't tease me."

"Why not? You teased me often enough."

"That was different."

"I suppose it was. You hated me then, didn't you? A blundering lord, judging you at every turn." He pulled back to look at her, his eyes shadowed.

"I didn't hate you. I just…You being there made things difficult. I thought it meant you were there to watch me, as if I couldn't be trusted." She blushed. "I was always attracted to you."

"You hid it well." But he smiled, and kissed her again until she sighed in pleasure. He moved to whisper in her ear. "I prefer it when you don't hide it, Sophie. You're glorious when you tell me what you want."

"I want you," she said, blushing more.

His expression was worth everything they'd been through.

She touched him and kissed him too while he told her outlandish, flattering things that made her laugh. But there was something different in his eyes. It made her breath faster and her skin tingle when he spoke them.

Sophie turned pliant and yielding under his touch. When they joined, it felt perfectly natural. She unspooled slowly, until her body was his. She came undone while he watched her face with an intensity that astonished her.

Then he withdrew from her and quickly lay beside her. He had his own release, sighing when Sophie moved to hold him, stroking his skin, moist with a sheen of sweat.

"You didn't worry about that last night," she said, feeling a bit shy. She hadn't even considered the risk of pregnancy last night, though she usually took care to reduce her chances of it. She'd been too in the moment.

"I should have," he said. "I can't do that to you, dove. The risk…" he trailed off.

"I'm used to all kinds of risk," Sophie said, trying to keep her voice light.

"If things were different…" he began.

She frowned. Different how? If she were a lady, he'd marry her to avoid a scandal? If they weren't together by circumstance, he never would have slept with her?

"Never mind. It's not important," she said. She didn't want to hear his musings. She had enough to occupy her mind.

But Bruce, as if sensing her retreat, turned again. Effortlessly, he swept her around so she lay beneath him, wrapped in his arms.

"What are you doing?" Sophie yelped.

"It *is* important."

"What is important?"

"Us. How we think of each other."

"And how is that?" she asked.

"You tell me, dove."

"We're…allies."

He laughed as he pulled away from her. "Allies? That's a cold word."

"Friends, then." She hastened to add, "I'll never forget that you saved my life."

"That's not what I'm concerned about."

"Then what? What do you want from me, Bruce? What could I offer you that you need?"

"I wish you'd stop talking in terms of trade, Sophie."

"It's how I see the world," she snapped. "And you'll never change that."

Before he could start arguing that topic, she slid out of the bed. "As you just proved, I'm feeling like myself again. It's time we returned to the real reason we're here." She found her clothes, now clean and neat. Lord, he'd washed her clothes for her while she was sick. She pulled the shift over her body. "If Volange is still at Carterhaugh, so is the letter. We have to get it back."

"Do you have a plan?" he asked, watching her dress.

"Plans are your purview. I thought that was why you were chosen." He certainly wasn't there just for her pleasure.

"All right, dove." Bruce got up as well. His expression was similar to the one she remembered from the first time she saw him, cynical and calculating. "If a plan is what you want, that's what you'll get."

Chapter 22

♏

As Sophie dressed with careless grace, Bruce watched her move around the room as if nothing had changed. Well, for her, perhaps nothing had. But he couldn't think about Sophie the same way again, and he had no intention of forgetting about her.

But she did have one valid point, which was that they both had an assignment to complete.

"What we need," he said out loud, "is to know what's happened since we left."

Sophie looked over at him in obvious relief that he was no longer discussing *them*. "With a proper change of clothes, I could—"

"No," he said shortly. "You're not showing your face to anyone until it's necessary. Besides, you're not as re-covered from your ordeal as you seem to think."

She looked about to protest, then shrugged. "So how would you go about it?"

Bruce thought it would be damn useful to have some-one like Jem or one of Lady Cordelia's other reformed servants. They'd be able to listen for below stairs gossip, and news of the suddenly disappeared Cassou couple. Unfortunately, he had no trustworthy contacts to ask about the goings-on at Carterhaugh.

If only he could go down to a public house and nose about.

Bruce paused, struck by the thought. There was no reason why he couldn't. True, he couldn't stroll down in the persona of a lord—neither Cassou nor Forester would get the sort of answers he needed. But Sophie wasn't the only person in the world who could act.

"I'm going to the village," he said. "And you will stay here and rest." He found suitably bland clothing among his smuggled items. He wouldn't look local, but he wouldn't look like a lord.

"What if you don't come back?" she asked, her eyes dark.

"If I don't come back, it will be because I'm dead," he said. "So if I don't return by…sundown, you do as you see fit."

His thoughts were in turmoil as he headed toward Bromthorpe, the village close by Carterhaugh Manor. He no longer considered Sophie as a possible traitor, of course. Her dance with death convinced him that, if anything, she was someone the French agents feared. However, he personally considered the assignment thoroughly botched. Bruce racked his brain for a clue to what alerted Theriot or Volange that their guests were not who they claimed to be. He had no lead, though, which was maddening. Had Sophie's disguise been imperfect? Had he let something slip? Was it possible that Regina Fox revealed his identity after all? Perhaps Volange had somehow remembered Sophie's face. It was impossible to tell.

Bruce despised the thought of returning to Aries empty handed. He agreed with Sophie. They had to try once more.

He wished Sophie agreed with him on other matters. No amount of intimacy seemed to break Sophie's walls down. Why should he have expected it to? Sophie made it clear she placed no value on what went on in a bed. Bruce was torn by his own reaction to her; he knew that he shouldn't get ensnared by Sophie, who was as unpredictable as fog. He refused to believe she could be so detached, though. There was something else going on. But Bruce didn't have the luxury of time to find answers.

In the village, he reached the public house and entered, matching his tone and behavior to the people already inside. His disguise could never alter his actual height, but Bruce knew how to slump and look considerably less imposing than he usually did. He walked with one foot slightly turned. Rough clothing and poor fit further concealed his true form.

He didn't talk much among the folk, but he kept his ears open. They knew him for a stranger, but Bruce had a pocketful of ready tales for these situations. When asked, he gave a false name, and a story with just enough detail to allow others to relax.

After a few moments of casual interrogation, he diffidently mentioned a relation who lived in the town…a cousin, once removed, by the name of Maggie Sawyer. How was she getting on? Married yet? He remembered her as a bright young thing.

The reaction to his query was unexpected.

"Poor Maggie! You know her, then?" one patron said.

"She's not in trouble, is she?" Bruce didn't have to fake the concern.

The man leaned closer, eager to share the news. "The poor girl, she's like as to go mad! She was employed up at the great house until a few days ago, but then…"

"What happened?"

"She came running home, bearing tales of debauchery and worse. Such foreign people, all behaving scandalously and acting like devils. But what made her leave, that's the shocking part. She said one guest—a woman—died and was taken from the house even before a doctor or undertaker could be called! Miss Maggie won't step outside her family's home until the swells all leave the manor. Three other servants quit the next day. It's not a place for proper folk."

Bruce thoughtfully paid for the man's next drink. He said he would stop by and pay his respects to the family. The man offered directions before Bruce could even ask.

The Sawyer house was off the main thoroughfare. Though modest, it was kept in good repair, and the neighbors eyed him carefully as he walked up the front path.

At the door, an older woman greeted him.

Bruce had thought about how he would present himself to the family. He didn't want to alarm anyone, least of all Maggie, who had simply got caught up in events. But he couldn't tell the whole truth.

"Mrs Sawyer?" he asked in low voice.

"Yes," she said.

"My name is Mr Green, and I am here to inquire after

Miss Maggie Sawyer."

"Why?"

"I am acting in an official capacity, ma'am. If she can relate some details about what happened at Carterhaugh Manor, she is due some compensation."

She was about to shut the door, but the word *compensation* caught her interest. "What sort of compensation?"

"The magistrate offers a reward for any information concerning the death at the house. I can pay it to the young lady today, if she is able to speak to me about it."

"You'd best come in." She showed him to a small parlor and left to fetch her daughter, warning him that Maggie wasn't likely to talk since she was so upset.

But Maggie did appear in the parlor, trailing after her mother.

She took a moment to recognize him, but when she did, her eyes rounded. "Sir!"

"Good afternoon, Miss Sawyer. May I have a few words with you…alone?"

She nodded slowly. Her mother left the door half open.

Maggie sat down, staring at him. "I never thought to see…they sent me downstairs that morning. Told me another girl would take my place upstairs. And then all the news was that Madame Cassou died…but it was such a confusion. And you and her were both gone…no one really knew. Is she dead, sir?"

"She was very, very ill, but she is mending."

Maggie sighed in relief.

"Maggie," he said. "I can't explain much, but it's essential you tell me what happened after we had to leave. Every little detail, even if it doesn't seem important."

Maggie nodded. She told him that in the morning the housekeeper abruptly ordered Maggie and another maid, Harriet, to switch duties for the day. Maggie stayed below stairs, while Harriet responded to any summons from guests, including requests for food.

She also mentioned the news of a wrapped body leaving the house without the supervision of either a doctor or a clergyman.

"Did you ask Harriet what she did that day?" he pressed.

"I never saw her after that morning, sir, because I quit and came home. I was told she was let go for impertinence."

Bruce didn't frighten the girl by sharing his theory of the body that left the house. When Madame Cassou inconveniently disappeared, Volange probably got very angry…and he wouldn't want the maid Harriet to talk about anything she might have noticed.

Thankfully, Maggie hadn't quite put those two elements together. "Will you see Madame Cassou again, sir?" she asked curiously.

"I will see her later today," he said.

"If you'll wait a moment, sir, I have something of the lady's."

She went upstairs and returned within moments. She handed Bruce the puzzle box. "I didn't steal it, sir. You see, Mr Theriot was interested in all the things in the room. And that Volange gentleman was *furious* when you left. They kept saying something about the news from abroad. And I'm sorry to say they took all the lady's jewelry. I swear it, sir. I didn't steal a thing. But I thought the box might be special and I didn't want him to take it. He asked me if anything was missing, and I said I didn't know. I didn't open it. I can't even see how to open it."

Bruce held the little box carefully, impressed by the girl's instincts. "That was well done. Thank you, Maggie."

"I'm sorry I couldn't save the jewels, sir."

"No matter. She'd give up ten times the worth of those jewels for this box."

"But the lady said one necklace was special, sir. Made out of the stones from a Bible."

Bruce laughed. "The lady was fibbing a bit about that, Maggie. She knows how to tell a good story though."

After requesting her continuing silence regarding his identity, Bruce paid Maggie a generous sum for her information.

Her mother, who had rejoined them by that point, nodded in satisfaction. "That will help us, considering my poor girl can't work in *that* house anymore."

"Your mother is quite right. I advise you, Miss Maggie, to remain here at your family's home for at least another week. With luck, the business at the manor will be concluded by then. But you shouldn't step onto that estate again."

Maggie nodded vehemently. "Indeed, sir. I shall not."

Bruce reached the door when Maggie added, "Please pass my best wishes to the lady. I hope she will be well."

After hearing Maggie's tale, Bruce went back to the public house, hoping to riffle through the collection of newspapers that always gathered in such a place. He had a hunch concerning how the truth came out.

Among the stacked papers, Bruce found a fairly recent London edition. As soon as he found a quiet spot, he skimmed the newspaper. He hadn't got past the front page when an item snared his gaze.

Cassou Scandal Continues: Aristocrat held in wife's death.

Stunned, Bruce read on. The article related the news from Vienna, where the aristocratic couple had been staying. Cassou had apparently caught his wife in a compromising situation with another man. In a fit of rage, he killed them both. Neither his title nor his wealth was likely to save him, for the crime was gruesome and very public. He was being held in Vienna pending further developments. With international relations already strained in Europe, the case would likely be mired in politics.

Bruce checked the date on the paper, and then the date of the actual incident. The news of the real Cassou couple might well have reached Carterhaugh Manor by the morning Sophie was poisoned. Volange must have learned of it and knew that he had impostors at his gathering.

Thus, he took steps to eliminate the woman as fast as possible. Bruce probably would have been attacked the same day, except for his unexpectedly early return from his ride. If the rain hadn't threatened, Sophie might have been dead by the time he got back to the house.

Nevertheless, if this was all Volange knew, it meant he

didn't know who Bruce and Sophie really were. The secret of the Zodiac was safe.

He was still reading when a babble of voices interrupted. More news started tongues wagging. "After all that's gone on, that Theriot gentleman wants to hold a ball! As if nothing ever happened!"

Several people expressed opinions as to where the gentleman could go. But a few others noted he had brought plenty of money to the village, and perhaps after the ball was concluded, he would return to wherever he came from.

"We've got no proof of wrongdoing. Just stories."

"But a wealth of stories!"

Bruce listened carefully to the gossip being shared. When he headed back to the cottage where Sophie waited, it was with a flame of hope in his heart.

Chapter 23

$$\underline{\underline{\Omega}}$$

SOPHIE WAITED IN THE LITTLE house after Bruce left. He promised to return as soon as he learned something, but once he was gone, Sophie was struck by a melancholy that she couldn't escape from.

Everyone she had ever cared about left her. Why would this time be different?

She leaned absently against the door frame, watching the world outside. A warm late summer morning greeted her. The dark, dusty green of trees rustled in the slightly hazy air. The first flush of the birds' dawn song was long over, but Sophie heard the twittering of dozens of birds in the trees around the cottage. It was a beautiful, peaceful scene, and she should be happy.

But she wasn't.

"What do I expect?" she asked herself out loud. She'd cheated death. She had, for the first time in years, spent an entire night with someone for no other reason than that she wanted to. She'd been treated well—very well, she thought with a sudden blush—and Bruce seemed to think no less of her the next day, even if his attitude was rather too…well, romantic.

But it was all an illusion, Sophie reminded herself.

They were here for a specific purpose that had nothing to do with their happiness. And they lived dramatically different lives. What future might they have together? Sophie knew they would both find other people to occupy their lives as soon as they parted ways. Bruce would marry a lady of suitable standing. Sophie would continue her life as an agent, and shift herself to accommodate each new assignment. Within weeks, neither Sophie nor Bruce would be the same person they each were this morning.

She shook her head. How had she got so maudlin? She had other things to worry about.

She went back into the cottage. She got everything in order before Bruce came back. They might need to leave the place without warning. He had worked to prepare this place if they needed to hide. She owed him the courtesy of keeping the place tidy.

As she did, she found the locket Bruce gave her. He'd put it on the mantel to keep it safe. Sophie put it on. Though it was meant to help her play Marianne Cassou, she now thought of it as hers.

As the hours passed, Sophie grew increasingly anxious. He'd so casually tossed out the notion that if he didn't come back, it was because he was dead. Sophie didn't care for that idea at all. She had no way to tell if Bruce was walking into danger or not. What if someone recognized him? What if he said the wrong thing?

She worried, and then noted her concerns were precisely the same as the ones *he'd* had the first day of the assignment. Try as she might, Sophie couldn't pretend she was indifferent. If Bruce didn't return, she didn't know what she'd do.

She was on edge all day, and when she heard a man's footsteps approaching, she almost flew to the door.

"Where were you? What happened?" She didn't hide the eagerness in her voice.

Bruce was smiling with his success. "I think we have another chance!"

"Tell me," Sophie demanded.

He saw the bundle of items near the door. "What's that?"

"Our things," she said. "Just in case we needed to move quickly."

"You're not planning on running away."

Sophie stiffened. "Running away is not a thing I do."

He moved closer to her, reaching out to touch her shoulder. "I'd find you, you know."

"Is that a threat?" she asked, forcing a light laugh. She decided to go out of her way to be as agreeable as possible. She hated the thought of hurting Bruce, even if she didn't think their relationship had somehow changed. When they returned from this assignment, he would forget the intensity of emotions that temporarily drove them together.

"It's a promise, dove," he said.

She swallowed nervously. To distract herself and him from the subject, she said, "Please tell me what you found. I've been in agony."

He related all he'd learned. "And for the final piece of good news," he concluded, "I've found out that Theriot is throwing a party in a few days. A masquerade."

"Indeed?" Sophie asked, brightening. "That sounds promising. We can get in undetected if we're masked."

"But there's a catch. There's something odd about the party. Only victims are invited. But I have no idea what that means."

"Victims…I know!" Sophie said in a rush. "He's resurrecting the *bal des victimes*. Of course he would. His crowd of madmen probably miss the excitement."

"What?" Bruce asked, looking puzzled. "What victims does he mean?"

"You've never heard of the *bal des victimes*?"

He shook his head. "The Victims' Ball? It sounds rather morbid."

"You have no idea. After Robespierre died, Paris went insane. For years, everyone lived under the threat of instant execution. Aristocrats had the most to fear. Very few of them managed to convince Robespierre that they whole-heartedly supported his vision of the future. And why should they? The whole idea of hereditary class depends on the world staying the same, year after year.

"So when the aristocrats were finally free to claim their identities again, all sorts of things happened. These dancing societies developed. Fancy dress balls. They were the height of fashion. But to get in the doors, you had to prove you were a victim of the guillotine."

He raised his eyebrow. "You had to be *dead*?"

"Nearly. You had to be a close relation to one who died under the blade. Some balls required papers. Others, only for another guest to vouch for you."

"And people wanted to go to these?"

"Oh, it was *the* thing. Men dressed like condemned prisoners. Women wore cross-back dresses to highlight their necks, and a red ribbon around their throat in case anyone missed the point. They were like martyrs who never quite had to be martyred. So they danced and dined and dreamed of how glorious it was before Robespierre ruined everything."

"A true danse macabre."

She nodded. "I acted as the entertainment at several of these—I told you before that I danced at them. Professional dancers were often hired to show the other guests the steps in a set. I danced with the men on the floor, but I also did a little performance reenacting a death by guillotine. With ballet. They loved it."

"Your mother?" he asked in low voice.

"My mother what?"

"Your mother was executed," he guessed. "That's why you were allowed in."

"How do you know that?"

"You talked a bit while you were sick."

"It's true." She didn't want to say more, and her expression must have conveyed that.

"Dove," he began. "You don't have to explain…"

"There's nothing to explain," she said, repressing her memories. "People die. What could I do to stop it? She would have wanted me to live."

He took a step away from her, letting the matter drop. "For this masquerade," he guessed, "they'll dress the same way as in the old parties."

"Undoubtedly. Which means we will dress that way

too. We'll blend in and be able to move through the house to Volange's rooms where the letter is hidden!"

"First we have to get in. Tell me what we'll need for clothes to get past the front doors. You know they'll be looking for us."

"They'll be looking for *you*. For all anyone knows, I'm dead." Sophie tried to say it without emotion, but something in her burned upward. She wasn't used to personal rage. But the poisoning was personal, and she wanted revenge.

Sophie looked up to see Bruce wearing a strange smile.

"What?" she asked warily.

"I have a little present for you," he said.

"What is it?"

Bruce shrugged. "Just a small thing. Don't you want to guess?"

"Not particularly."

"Then I won't make you. Close your eyes, love," he said. "And hold out your hands."

Sophie obeyed. He put a familiar object into her hands.

"My puzzle box!" she breathed, her eyes flying open. She never expected to see it again. "How did you get it?"

"You have the maid Maggie to thank. She grabbed it after I got you out of the house, and kept it safe. She gave it to me when I saw her in the village."

She remembered the day she got the box, as well as the dark period in her life that followed, when the reminder of the little box was nearly all she had to hold onto during the worst times. She looked up at Bruce, who regarded her with both curiosity and…something else. "Thank you," she said, her voice raw. "I can't tell you how much this means to me."

"I'm glad you have it back."

"Did you open it?" she asked. If anyone could figure it out, Bruce could.

But he shook his head. "It's not mine to open."

* * * *

After learning of the coming masquerade, Sophie knew exactly what they both should wear for costumes. She planned for Bruce to be nearly invisible. With luck, Volange and his underling Theriot wouldn't even know Bruce was in the house. Sophie's costume would have a different effect. Once seen, no one would ignore her.

Bruce went out and got everything Sophie requested, no matter how odd or expensive it might be. How he procured them, she didn't even pretend to know.

"You managed to get a bolt of silk of such quality without going all the way to London. How?"

"Sophie, I'd go out and find you Death himself and take the gentleman's robe if that's what you wanted for your costume," he replied, his light tone only belied by a certain tightness around his eyes. Was he tired?

"We're almost done with the assignment," she assured him.

"I know," he said. "But first we have to get into the party tomorrow evening. You have the fabrics now, but I couldn't kidnap a seamstress."

"You don't have to," Sophie said. "You already have one."

The arrival of the fabric and props restored Sophie's good humor. This was what she excelled at. She cut and sewed diligently to complete everything by the evening of the masquerade. The outfit she would wear was far simpler in cut than the current fashion. Her costume would echo the lines of classical simplicity that had been so in vogue after the Terror. She thanked her stars it would also be so easy to make.

When she was done, she laid her costume aside, ready to make a few alterations to Bruce's costume. It was also simple, in its way, and she knew it wouldn't take long to assure a proper fit.

He stood patiently as she worked. "Sorry I wasn't able to get a proper outfit in such a short time. Tailor surely wasn't in the job description when Aries assigned you."

She shook her head. "Well, you're lucky to have me to fix everything."

"I am," he replied. His voice cut through her bantering tone, and Sophie cast him an uneasy look. His expression was unreadable, but serious enough to alarm her.

"You're also lucky I don't stab you with these pins," she said, taking refuge in flippancy.

"I am," he repeated. Something flickered in his face. Disappointment? Resignation? She didn't know.

Sophie ducked her head again, focusing on the task. "There. Take the jacket off carefully. I'll finish the seams and you'll look as tailored as any gentleman in London."

He obliged. Handing the jacket to Sophie, he asked,

"I've modeled my outfit, yet yours is a mystery. When will I see it?"

"When you escort me to the ball," she said. "You don't need to know anything before then."

"Why do I get the feeling that you're holding out on me?" he asked.

"Because I am," Sophie said with a smile. Then she picked up the puzzle box. "Now listen. When we arrive, we'll have to work separately. I'll distract the guests with my act, and you'll search Volange's rooms. Remember, he's tricky. The hiding spot will be clever and unexpected. When you find the letter, tuck it into the puzzle box. That will give us a very slight protection if anyone comes after us to get it back."

"The only flaw is I don't know how to open it."

"I'll show you now," Sophie said.

"You were quite fierce about keeping the secret before."

"It's just a toy," she said, shrugging. "And now it can be a tool." Settling herself on the edge of the bed, she gestured for him to sit beside her.

Bruce did, watching her every move. The rich wood-grain of the carved box was dark against the pale skin of her hands. Slender, quick fingers brushed over the surface of the box and suddenly the lid slid open. "See?" Sophie asked.

"I see that it's open. But you know you moved too quickly. Do it again."

She repeated her gestures, her hands now moving slower. Her fingers fluttered over the carvings in the box's surface, and he again missed the key gesture.

"Slower," he said.

Sophie obliged, snapping the lid shut. As she began the sequence again, Bruce put his arm out to stop her. "One step at a time, dove."

"Hold the box like this," she said. "Then, press the flower on the side panel, like so."

"Yes," Bruce said. "Go on."

"Now slide this little knob that's carved like a leaf over, just a tiny bit. You'll feel the catch."

"I see."

Sophie took a breath. "And then, you'll feel the seam of the lid here," as her finger traced a barely perceptible line around the top, "so push gently outward and..." The lid opened. "Done."

"Remarkable," he said.

Sophie handed him the open box. Bruce took it carefully and closed the lid. In his larger hands, the box really did look like a toy. Moving without haste, he repeated her movements. As the lid opened, he smiled. "Not impossible, once you know the secret."

Sophie shook her head. "It's just a trick. You can easily fit a folded paper in the space. And once you close it, no one will know what's inside. You can let the guards tinker with it all they want. They can't open it without knowing the pattern."

He picked up a small object from the box. "What's this?"

It was a curl of hair, the burnished chestnut shade nearly the same as the box itself. "It was my mother's,"

Sophie said. "All I have left. I never had a picture of her."

Bruce closed the box and put it back in her hands. "Put the box somewhere safe, Sophie," he said.

He kept his hand on hers though, and when she turned to him ask him why, he kissed her gently on the mouth.

Sophie, unprepared for the move, froze up for a second, but then warmed to him. Her lips parted and she felt his tongue taste her lips. But he did nothing more.

"What's wrong?" she asked. "Why don't you go on?"

"Why don't *you*?" he asked, his voice challenging.

"Ah, I see." She leaned back to put the box on the table, and then returned to him, twining her arms around his neck. He wanted her to come to him. She whispered, "What would you like?"

"More than you can give me," he replied.

Sophie frowned. "Then what are you asking for?"

"I'm not asking for anything, dove. You don't have to do a thing. Leave the bed."

"I don't want to," she said, before she thought better of it.

His expression was one of wary hope. "Why not?"

"Because…because I want this."

"Why?"

"Because you make me happy. No other reason."

"Good. There shouldn't *be* any other reasons, dove."

She kissed him, and they forgot everything else as they fell into each other. Within moments, they shed each other's clothing and lay entwined on the bed, exploring the limits of their passion. They found none, and when both reached their peak, they moved as one. Afterward,

Sophie curled up, her head resting on Bruce's chest. She heard his heartbeat slow down to a normal pace. She felt his hands trace her skin lazily, and she wished dearly that the frail happiness she felt right then could last beyond the next few minutes.

She was afraid to ask him what he thought about what had just happened. Sophie never succumbed to passion. She didn't have impulses like that. And yet, Bruce had only to kiss her and she unraveled in front of him. But he didn't need anything from her. So what did he think she was?

Not just a partner or a plaything. If that were true he wouldn't hold her afterward, which he seemed to like to do. Sophie didn't complain. She could hear his heart and his breath, and when she shifted, he shifted with her. Before Sophie could decide what she ought to do—get up, or at least untwine herself from him—she drifted off. Her last conscious thought was that it felt quite lovely to feel his hand on her head, toying with the strands of hair. Then she sighed, and fell asleep completely.

* * * *

Bruce knew the precise moment Sophie gave herself up to sleep. She didn't say a word during or after their coupling, letting her body speak for her as she so often did. He didn't want to break the silence either, in spite of the flood of questions he wanted to ask.

He was afraid of his own feelings, which hadn't diminished at all. If he'd ever thought that his attraction to her would fade after he bedded her, he was wrong.

From the first meeting, he knew Sophie was special. She was infuriating and challenging, true. She was as feral as a cat, ready to take on the world. But he wanted her to believe that life didn't have to be a series of endless fights. And more importantly, he wanted to show her it wasn't always necessary to fight alone.

Bruce contented himself with the thought that she at least let him be this close to her. He tightened his arm around her and was rewarded with a contented, sleepy murmur. She didn't open her eyes, but he felt her relax further. He was rapidly sliding into sleep himself, and within minutes, he drifted off, still holding Sophie close.

Chapter 24

♎

THE NEXT EVENING, SOPHIE DRESSED for the masquerade with all the ceremony she'd once put into her theater roles. She pulled the gown on and let the fabric settle over her body. It fit perfectly. Her recent sickness and pale skin made her look ethereal. She tied a red velvet ribbon high on her neck, where it glowed like blood.

She then dropped a large dose of belladonna into her eyes, making her pupils widen so her eyes looked like black pools, completing the otherworldly effect. The halos the belladonna caused whenever she looked at a bright light were the price to pay, but Sophie could endure it for the several hours while the belladonna lingered.

Finally, she tied the ribbons of her mask around her head. The mask was a simple creation of red lace. It didn't totally conceal her features, but the effect was to intrigue, not to hide.

"Sophie? We don't have all night," Bruce called through the door of the little room.

"I'm coming out," she said. Sophie stepped into the main room and kept her eyes on Bruce's face.

His reaction was priceless.

Bruce's jaw dropped when he saw her. "You're not

going out in public like that."

Sophie's outfit—if it could be called that—left little to the imagination. It was a gown, of the same sort of filmy, *dishabille* style that was so popular during the time of the Terror. The thin fabric grazed the curves of her body, and the low neckline stopped a finger's breadth above her nipples. The hemline was also ragged and several inches higher than usual, to better display her feet and ankles. She wore a ballet dancer's slippers, and the hidden slits in her skirt would allow her full movement later. She was scandalous, and she knew it.

"Jealous others will see?" she asked.

"Yes." From his expression, jealousy wasn't the only sin he was committing. Sophie felt him raking her body with his eyes. "You'll start a riot in that...I can't even call it a gown. It barely *exists*, it's so thin."

Sophie smiled, her reddened lips parting. "I am the distraction, Bruce. We *need* everyone to be looking at me."

"Oh, there will be no doubt about that. How will you keep from being ravished?"

"I can handle myself, Bruce. I know how to deal with men who get too interested in me."

"Is that a warning?" he asked.

Sophie reached out to him. "Not to you. You're different."

He took her arm and pulled her closer. He tilted her face up slightly so he could look at her. "Promise me you aren't just humoring me, Sophie."

"You're being silly," she said. "Haven't I shown I trust

you?" Sophie knew her feelings toward Bruce had become complicated, but they could not afford to ignore the primary objective. "We're partners."

He nodded, then bent to kiss her. Sophie let him, drawing as close as she dared to him, feeding off his heat. She wanted nothing more than to lose the costumes and false identities and just be with him. She slipped her hands under his dark jacket and followed the contours of his torso through the fine fabric of the shirt. She knew he'd make love to her if she asked, and she very much wanted to ask. "Bruce, we shouldn't..." she murmured once she caught a breath.

"We should," he protested. "But not now." He pulled away, his desire for her plain. "Have to stop a war, you know."

The wry comment heartened Sophie. "Later," she purred, deliberately making her performance farcical. "Let us save our nation first."

"Oh, very well," he said, rolling his eyes. "You aren't wearing your wig."

"I don't need it tonight. I'm wearing my hair *a la victime*, just like they did during the Terror. No long hair to get caught up in the blade, you see. Very chic, yes?"

"If disturbing and morbid are chic, then yes."

He held up a long black cloak. Sophie stood still as he draped it around her. She drew the hood up. It would conceal her until the time was right to make her entrance.

He turned her toward him and gave her a last, light kiss, as if he were unwilling to let her go. Then he stepped away. "You look amazing. Scandalous and provoking, but amazing. How do I look?" He straightened the shirt and the jacket, the dark layers blending into each other.

"Boring," Sophie said honestly. "You're perfect."

Bruce was dressed in a typical gentleman's garb, but all his clothes were black, and the overall effect was too monotonous to grab the average person's attention. "Don't forget your mask," she said. "I know there are women at Carterhaugh who would happily throw their husbands off a cliff for a night with you. A few of them even told me so."

"That sounds attractive." He grimaced. To complete his costume, he put on a black velvet domino. It made him anonymous, though his eyes were still so obviously his that Sophie knew she could pick him out of a crowd of a thousand men. But others would not. Combined with the mask, the dark clothing, and his naturally black hair, he'd fade away in the candlelight of the ball.

"Excellent. You'll be able to move freely while everyone is watching me," she said. "So you must *not* watch me."

"That will be the hardest part of this whole thing."

Sophie raised an eyebrow. "Oh, will that be the hardest part?" she asked, with a suggestive laugh.

"Don't come one step closer if you want to go anywhere tonight, Sophie," he warned.

"But I must come closer to you. We're riding together to Carterhaugh."

"Cruel," he murmured, almost too softly to be heard. As Sophie slid a small knife into a specially made sheath she wore high on her thigh, Bruce checked that he had both his pistol and his own dagger safely tucked away.

"And the puzzle box?" she asked, watching him.

"In my pocket. It's perfectly safe, dove."

"You have a strange view of what perfectly safe means."

"Look who's talking, Mademoiselle Guillotine."

With that, the two spies left for the Victims' Ball.

Chapter 25

♏

THEY MADE THEIR WAY TO the village, where they hired a spare rig. No one knew who they were, and when the carriage joined all the others on the drive to Carterhaugh, they were indistinguishable from everyone else.

In the end, Bruce wanted to laugh at how simple it was to gain entrance to the ball. Many additional guests had been invited, swelling the ranks of attendees to nearly two hundred. Everyone was masked and dressed in fantastical garb. Some people weren't emulating the style of the *bal des victims*—they had likely only been told it was a grim masquerade. Others wore dark mourning clothes and masks like skulls or veils to shroud the face. Those few ladies who wore lighter colors stood out. And there were uniformed men circulating among the crowd. Most guests mistook these figures for footmen. Bruce knew them for guards.

"Are you ready?" Bruce muttered to Sophie as they walked down the hall to the ballroom. For all that he tried to be confident, he was not keen on the part of the plan that required them to separate for a time.

But there was no other way to distract Volange and Theriot. With Sophie at center stage, no one would look for anything else. She smiled at Bruce, and a jolt of pure excitement went though him. *I'm about to glimpse a performance of a lifetime*, he thought. "Are you ready for another turn as Serafina the Brave?"

She beamed when he used her old stage name.

"*We* are ready," she whispered back. "And we'll get what we came for. Together."

Bruce covered her hand with his own, a subtle gesture to let her know he stood by her.

Unlike the other ladies, Sophie kept her cloak on all the way to the ballroom. She paused at the head of the stairs, waiting to be announced. The man who did the honors called out the only name she would give him: Madame Guillotine.

When he shouted the words across the air, everyone turned and looked. With a name like that, who wouldn't? Her calm eyes fixed on the audience, Sophie let the dark, loose cloak fall to the stone stairs at her feet, where the soft folds pooled around her.

Bruce watched the crowd's reaction from several feet further back. He had to give Sophie credit as a director. She knew how to make an entrance. All eyes were riveted to her. Theriot looked shocked and pale, perhaps wondering if his masquerade had somehow conjured this peculiarly French spectre of Death. Even Volange, standing near Theriot, was unable to move for the moment.

All the guests were stunned. Even those who didn't understand the meaning behind her costume noticed the costume itself. The scandalously thin, revealing gown would have been shocking on its own, but with the rest of the costume, people only saw a mysterious, alluring, and somehow frightening figure. The short hairstyle made her look even more remarkable, and the meaning of the red velvet ribbon around her neck was all too obvious.

Sophie descended the stairs with a dancer's grace, the balls of her feet lightly pressing down first on each step. She cast her eye on guest after guest. No one held her gaze for long. She laughed low in her throat and called several by name, telling them they had an appointment with her.

A few women gasped in fear. Several men laughed nervously. Only one dared reach out a hand to touch Sophie, but she spun away before he could actually reach her.

Watching the performance out of the corner of his eye, Bruce doubted that anyone connected this Lady Death with the missing Madame Cassou. She looked and acted completely differently. Even the way she held her head up was uniquely Sophie. In the excitement of her entrance, no one asked Bruce for his name, and he wisely moved to the side, where he blended in with several other men in similar attire.

He continued to watch Sophie's progress, in case something went wrong. After a few moments, as she cut a path through the crowd to the dance floor, it seemed the guests had decided she was hired entertainment. Indeed, she was heading directly for the still stunned Theriot, as if she expected him to dance with her. It appeared her plan was working perfectly, so he had to take the next step.

Moving unobtrusively, he slipped around the perimeter of the ballroom, watching others watch Sophie. He sighted Volange, who was staring hard at the slender beauty. If anyone guessed the truth, it would be him.

Bruce wondered if he could possibly get away with killing the man in plain sight. But no. He had to find to the letter. He left out of a side door and moved toward the wing of the house where Volange stayed.

Naturally, the door to Volange's room was locked. Bruce pried the lock open with more force than finesse, not caring that it would be obvious the room had been searched.

Volange was a man of simplicity. His room was nearly bare. He had a secretary desk in one corner, with several locked boxes stacked next to it. Just as he was about to work the top box open, though, he had thought. *Misdirection.*

Volange knew all about misdirection. He let Theriot appear to be the leader of the plan to unseat the Emperor. He was smart enough to know people were after what he had. The most important papers would be hidden elsewhere.

Bruce left the boxes alone and moved methodically, searching for another cache of papers. He ransacked the desk, opened drawers, peered under rugs, working around the room from left to right, always making sure he hadn't missed any spot.

Sensing time slipping by, he tried to rein in impatience. He reached the far wall, where a small stack of books sat on a table. The top one appeared to be a diary. Bruce flipped through it, wondering that Volange would keep such a private thing in the open. Then he reminded himself: misdirection.

He quickly looked through the rest of the stack. A history of the city of Paris, written in French. Two volumes of poetry, also French. A King James translation of the Bible.

Bruce paused. Volange wasn't a pious man. So why did he travel with a Bible written in English (a language he claimed to despise), especially when it was the one book a person might expect to find in any home in Britain? Bruce snapped the book open and fanned the pages. Nothing fell out, but he sensed he was on to something. The Bible was out of place, hidden in plain sight. He examined the book more carefully. The binding was thick and the end papers bubbled out, as if poorly glued on. One corner of the endpaper was loose. He pulled it back and saw another sheet of paper below it, its color and texture different from the book's.

"There you are," he murmured. He gently pulled out the little sheet of paper. He unfolded it, scanned the contents, and knew he'd found the prize.

A sound behind him alerted Bruce one second before the attack. He whirled around to see one of Volange's guards with pistol in hand. Dropping the book, Bruce swung to the side, catching the man's outstretched arm.

He used all his weight to leverage against the other man, twisting his arm in the process. The man dropped the gun and gasped out a pained sound. Bruce was not in a merciful mood, though, so he continued to push the man into the floor.

As the guard's knees buckled, he took in a huge breath, preparing to yell for help. Bruce didn't let him. He punched hard, an uppercut that caught under the guard's chin. His eyes rolled up, and he sagged silently into a heap, like a marionette whose strings had just been cut.

Bruce checked that the man was still breathing, then dragged him into a far corner and bundled him into a sheet, tying it so it would be hard to get free quickly.

Then Bruce retrieved the vital letter. He folded it up into a square and slipped it into the puzzle box. They had what they needed now. Bruce had to return to Sophie and get them both out of the house before anyone else grew suspicious.

He ran through the halls back to the ballroom. When he arrived, though, he was already too late.

Chapter 26

IN THE BALLROOM, SOPHIE PLAYED her fantastical role. She shouldn't have been able to pick Bruce out in the crowd, but somehow, she knew when he was in the room, when he wasn't. A pain needled her when she saw him pass a guard before leaving the ballroom to find the letter they so desperately needed. If Bruce died, if he was even scratched, Sophie didn't know what she would do next.

Sophie had always been wary of falling in love. As it turned out, she never came close. Until now. The warnings Julian once gave her before an assignment…he should have warned her this time. She had tried to despise Bruce, but it was futile. The more time they spent together, the more she learned about him, the more she liked him. She respected him. Then she loved him. And now he depended on her to distract everyone while he worked.

When Sophie reached Theriot, he asked, "Who are you?" in a strident voice.

She smiled. "Call me Madame Guillotine."

He took her offered hand before he knew what he was doing. "You're cold!" he gasped.

"Then warm me with a dance."

She made him partner her, after the music resumed.

She laughed and spun around her enemy, but a terrible feeling began to build in the pit of her stomach. Bruce was in danger. But she could do nothing except keep up her act and wait for him to return. She left Theriot after one pass, and danced with other gentlemen as they tried to guess who or what she was. Sophie kept one eye on the doors Bruce had vanished through.

Suddenly, the music halted. The musicians had been slashed into silence by Volange, who was holding a thin sword like a conductor's baton.

The audience murmured and shifted, sensing the abrupt change in mood.

"Madame Guillotine," called Volange. The few guests standing between Volange and the vision in question hastily moved aside.

She gave a graceful, courtly curtsey, which had the side effect of showing nearly the whole length of her legs.

"You call for me, Monsieur Volange," she said in French, projecting her voice easily. "A bold move."

"I wish to dance with you, my lady."

"Be careful what you wish for," Sophie warned, even as she advanced toward him. She stopped a few feet away. "Let the music begin again…if you would dare dance with me."

He did not signal the musicians to resume, but instead pointed his sword toward Sophie's neck. "I know who you are," he said quietly.

She tipped her chin up higher. "Given a thousand thousand years, sir, you could never understand who I am."

"You wear the red ribbon of a victim, my lady Death, so I understand more than most. For one thing, you are not Madame Guillotine."

Sophie said insolently, "I congratulate you on not believing in a metaphor."

"I also know that you are not Madame Cassou, however skillfully you played her."

"Another revelation, sir. We both know Madame Cassou is dead, a true victim who will not be attending any more balls."

"Then who are you?" he mused.

"Whoever I wish to be, Volange. To you, though, I am well-suited to the role of Death...dance with me, and you'll die. I promise you that."

She dared not let her gaze slip from Volange. If... *when* Bruce returned, she would have a chance to get away. But the net was closing in.

Volange had less patience than she bargained on. "Hold her!" he directed.

Two men who had advanced behind her while she spoke to Volange now lunged toward Sophie and grabbed her by the arms.

She didn't try to get away, but gave each man a haughty stare. "Touch me again, and I'll feed your guts to crows," she hissed. They didn't release her, but they also didn't laugh.

"She's not magic, you fools," Volange growled. "Just a flesh and blood woman." He stepped up to her and jerked off the red lace mask.

Volange studied her face, trying to place her and failing. He'd never seen Sophie's real face, only the various masks she'd worn.

Still, he had the upper hand. "You are a most intriguing woman," he said at last, softly. Only Sophie and the nearby guards could hear his words. "Most…distracting."

Volange went on, "That was your role, was it not? To distract us all?" The softness of the French language made his question almost gentle. "You did quite well tonight. But I'm a suspicious soul. As soon as I could, I sent a man to find your partner, whoever he is. In fact, he might already be dead."

"Your man?" Sophie asked lightly, despite the chill in her heart. "I wouldn't be surprised."

Volange looked annoyed, but only said, "I wonder who you work for, dear." He ran a finger along her jaw. "Something tells me you are a most committed woman. You would do almost anything to further your cause, wouldn't you?" He dropped his gaze quite obviously to Sophie's filmy gown.

Sophie kept her voice calm. "You must not confuse that with having no standards." She deliberately gave him her most disdainful look.

"Tell me your name," Volange hissed, heat in his voice.

"As I said, Madame Guillotine will do for you," Sophie purred in her pure Parisian accent.

"Appropriate, Madame. For I will take your head."

As he spoke, the sound of a gunshot burst out. The guard holding her right arm suddenly slumped down, dragging her with him. The other guard released her, more out of surprise than anything else.

Sophie looked up to where the shot had been fired. Bruce stood at the top of the grand stairs, black as Death himself.

"Hello, dearest," she murmured.

"Dove!" Bruce shouted. "Go!" He held the gun in one hand, and with the other threw her the puzzle box. Sophie sprang up to grab it, narrowly beating out Volange, who was faster to react than the other guard.

With the precious object in her hands, Sophie dropped to the floor. Without being told, she knew Bruce planned to fire again, using another gun he'd taken from a guard.

The crack of another shot confirmed her guess. A shout of pain sound near her: the remaining guard. Sophie didn't wait. Hearing Bruce shout once more to urge her on, Sophie ran, her scandalous costume allowing her full freedom of movement. She plunged through the open doors to the gardens.

She glanced back to see if Bruce got caught, but could see nothing. Guards trailed her and she couldn't afford to wait. They were outnumbered. Bruce wouldn't be pleased if she allowed them both to be caught.

She ran past the main gardens toward the fields beyond. On the lawn, she was pushed suddenly from behind as a man collided with her. Sophie lost her balance and hit the ground, but she twisted around to kick the man before he could overpower her.

It was Volange, his face contorted in fury. He grabbed for her, but Sophie rolled out of the way. "How the hell did you live?" he asked. "I gave you enough poison to kill three men."

"But not enough to kill one woman," Sophie snapped. While he scrambled for her, she lashed out with the little knife she pulled from beneath her costume, hitting his face. Volange screamed in pain and clutched his cheek.

Sophie stood up warily, her breathing hard. She looked toward the house. More men were running toward them, so Sophie couldn't finish Volange off. He was already getting up, ready to reach for her again.

She made sure she still had the box, then ran off into the darkness. Volange snarled behind her, but she was faster than he was. The plan called for Sophie and Bruce to rendezvous at the cottage if they weren't able to escape together…and, if one agent was caught or killed, the other would return to Aries immediately.

That was the part of the plan Sophie had no intention of following.

Chapter 27

♎

INSIDE THE HOUSE, BRUCE LAY prone on the ballroom floor. Three guards held him. He was well and truly caught, just as he knew he would be. His plan was to get the letter to Sophie, not to get out himself. He prayed that Sophie escaped safely with the puzzle box. She was too smart to come back at this point. Sophie never let sentiment get in her way.

It wasn't long before a familiar voice spoke. "Put him in the stone room."

Volange had returned, holding a hand to his face. He looked ragged. Red seeped from under his fingers. More important, he didn't have Sophie or the box. So Bruce could be perfectly content, even when a sharp-toed boot connected with his temple, making everything go black.

When Bruce woke up again, he was lying on his side in some dim room he didn't recognize. He saw only a stone wall in front of him. Every part of his body ached. He instinctively moved to stretch, but his arms wouldn't work. Were they broken? After a moment, he realized no, his wrists were tied behind his back. His ankles were tied up too. The cramps from being confined in such a position on the cool stone of the floor were already agonizing. And that didn't even get into the bruises from the initial attack.

He groaned as he rolled onto his other side. The pain worsened, but he saw more of the room, which distracted him.

It looked like a dungeon, but it was surely just a basement room below Carterhaugh. Apparently, he hadn't seen every part of the house during his explorations. The area was about fifteen feet square. A heavy wooden door in one wall had a grate in it for a guard to peer through. There was virtually nothing else in the room. Bruce shifted again, trying to ease the cramps in his muscles.

His actions, minor as they were, still caused someone to shout on the other side. Bruce expected the door to burst open immediately, but nothing happened for minutes, or perhaps an hour. A terrible thirst crept up on him. His throat was dry and he didn't even know if he'd be able to speak to the person who might eventually come to interrogate him.

For that was what would happen. He'd be interrogated by someone. He'd either stay strong and not tell them what they wanted to know…or he'd break. Either way, he'd be killed at the end. That actually helped, a bit. He had to remember that spilling his secrets would buy him no mercy, no matter what they promised.

He would not have the death of others on his conscience. Others like the agent Libra. His Sophie.

When the door finally did open, Bruce had no warning. Two of Volange's men approached Bruce. He flinched before he could stop himself; he expected another beating.

"Help him up," a voice said in French. Volange entered, followed by another guard who was carrying a plain wooden stool. He put the stool the center of the room, and the other two men dragged Bruce toward it.

He was bigger than either of them, and he did nothing to make their task easier. They dropped him twice before managing to get him to sit on the stool. He took a perverse pride in that.

"Thirsty? Hungry?" Volange asked, still using French.

"Bugger off," Bruce growled. He didn't bother to translate.

"You first. If you're wondering how you ended up here, we got word about the real Cassou—he and his wife had been detained in Austria. She was a little too indiscreet, it seems, and he killed her! So it's a bit odd that both the gentleman and lady managed to also be here for the party."

Bruce said nothing. That was old news.

Volange leaned in. "It's pointless to pretend. I know you're a spy. I know you work for the British Crown. I know you stole a very important letter from me. I know that letter is now in a pretty box. I also know it isn't going anywhere. No, the lady remains close by. Do you want to know why I know all that?"

Bruce said nothing. If Sophie was nearby… He didn't even look at Volange.

"I know because someone told me. Can you guess who? Here's a hint: it's someone very, very close to you."

Bruce closed his eyes. *Sophie. He meant Sophie*, he thought.

Volange, watching him carefully, laughed a bit. "You guessed, didn't you! She's a beautiful thing, isn't she? A little skinny for my taste. But what a face! And what a mind! She's *smart*, that one. Smarter than you. She had you dancing to her tune, despite all the clues. She's French, you idiot! Did you really think she was on your side?"

Bruce did. But had she been laughing at him this whole time? No. Sophie wouldn't do that. Volange was lying, already toying with his head. He tried to cling to reason. "If she were on your side, she wouldn't need me to get the letter at all," he said, despite his resolution not to talk.

"If she were on your side, she wouldn't have lied to you since the moment you met her," Volange said flatly. "But she's on *her* side. That letter is worth a lot to the right people. Of course she wanted to get her hands on it."

Bruce didn't believe him. He knew Sophie, and he trusted her. Volange was the one who lied.

"What time is it?" he asked. The next day? How far to London did Sophie get already?

"You ask for information, yet you don't share any with me." Volange shook his head. "That's not how it works."

Bruce looked down again. He refused to get drawn into a new game.

"You are hungry," the other man said. "And I don't want you to starve." Volange was already directing his men to bring in some food and drink. "I'll have them untie you to eat. Try to escape, and you get a bullet in the head."

Food. Bruce was suddenly far too interested in food to escape. But he had learned one thing about French cuisine. "You eat some of it first," he croaked out.

A gleam in his eye, Volange nodded to one the guards.

Shrugging, the guard ate several healthy-sized bites of the meal, enough that Bruce got angry and jealous. "Drink," he hissed.

Grinning now, the guard took a long drink of the wine, and let some slosh onto the floor.

"Happy now?" he asked, slamming the drink down.

Bruce didn't answer. Now untied, he devoured the rest of the food and every drop of the wine. He didn't even care when they retied him, this time with his arms in front.

"I'll let you think on your predicament," Volange said. "Later, I'll have a number of questions to ask you, and I assure you that I am most interested in obtaining the answers." He smiled. "I will be as persistent as I need to be."

Bruce knew exactly what he meant.

They left him alone again. The torture had already begun. Bruce's thoughts turned black as he contemplated everything that happened in the house. Could she betray him? Was Sophie really that good an actress? She played him perfectly if she was. The initial pride, then the temptation to keep him interested. Then the vulnerability. Maybe the poison was all a trick. Some chemist's blend that looked far worse than it was. He was an idiot for letting down his guard. And all because of her pretty face and big eyes.

No. He had to be rational. Why would Sophie engage in such a complicated scheme when a simple plan would do? Besides, she was Sophie. He trusted her. His head ached, and he was thirsty again. The wine had left a strange, metallic taste in his mouth.

His mind continued to whirl. But how did Volange know about her? He must have talked to her on the night of the ball. And right now, she could be anywhere. If she was trustworthy, she would already be on her way to find Aries, to get help. If she wasn't…he had no hope. Which was the truth?

Bruce had too little information. He couldn't even think clearly, especially when he kept seeing Sophie when he closed his eyes.

She wasn't a traitor.

She was a traitor.

He spun from one conclusion to the other until he thought he'd go mad. And the hours slipped past. Volange seemed perfectly content to wait, keeping Bruce alone.

Chapter 28

♎︎

SOPHIE WATCHED AS SEVERAL OF the guards blundered through the trees. She debated her options while she held completely still, waiting for her chance to bolt.

She could hide out in the woods on the estate, or press her luck by returning to the cottage. But Sophie was creature of the city, and the idea of burrowing down like a woodland animal didn't appeal to her.

There was no city to hide in around Carterhaugh, of course. But there was a village. Once Sophie saw the last of the guards move away, she slipped like a ghost through the trees. In fact, she might be mistaken for a ghost in her filmy white gown.

It took quite a while for her to reach Bromthorpe. She had to conceal herself and wait several times while carriages or horses went by. But eventually she reached the street where the Sawyers lived, recognizing the house from the way Bruce had described it when he met Maggie earlier.

It was late, but she knocked on the back door. Once, twice. She hoped no one in the neighboring houses would see her. She knocked again.

"What do you want?" a man's voice shouted from

inside.

"I need to speak to Maggie!" she called. "Please, it's important!"

"She doesn't speak to strangers in the middle of the night."

"I'm not a stranger, I'm…"

Before Sophie could finish, the door was yanked open and an older man peered out. "Who are you and what…" Abruptly, he averted his eyes. "…what are you *wearing*?"

"It's a long story. If you can just wake Maggie and tell her Marianne Cassou needs—"

"Ma'am!" a voice shouted. It was Maggie, wearing a loose wrapper. A woman who must be her mother joined her. "Ma'am, what are you doing here?"

"Please, Maggie. I need your help." Sophie's teeth started to chatter, as much because of her exhaustion as cold.

"Let the woman inside," Maggie's mother said, sympathy overriding anything else. "She can explain herself after she gets warm."

Sophie was quickly wrapped in a blanket. The whole family wanted to hear what happened, and Sophie wasn't sure what to tell them.

"Miss Maggie," she began, "I can't tell you everything about what went on at the manor, but I can tell you that Theriot and another man who is staying there, Volange, are both trying to hurt me."

"I know that, ma'am. They tried to poison you. And your friend said the magistrate would take action."

"Well, yes. Tonight, we confronted them. They didn't

take it well. I ran out, but my companion is still there, and I'm afraid for him."

"Oh, ma'am," Maggie said. "I'll help you if I can. But you look near dead! You need to rest, and there's nothing we can do tonight."

The worn out Sophie had to agree. She let Maggie take her upstairs, where she could sleep. Maggie shared the bed, promising Sophie that everything could be sorted in the morning.

By the time Sophie woke up, she had a plan. Despite Maggie's misgivings, Sophie returned to Carterhaugh that day, dressed as a boy. She had to listen to servants' gossip and learn where Bruce was. She would discover a way to get him back, even if she had to kill to do it.

* * * *

Bruce was nearly asleep when the door opened again. Volange was alone this time. He propped Bruce up into a sitting position.

He wasn't even fully awake when he realized he was drinking something. It was wine—he thought. It had an odd taste, like the first drink. But he needed to drink something.

"Excellent," Volange said. "I don't want you to die on me. I have so many more questions."

"I won't tell you anything."

Volange was unimpressed. "Of course you will."

He appeared to be reluctant to torture Bruce physically. But he talked about Sophie. He described her body—in great detail—and laughed about the letter and her daring costume on the night of the ball. He promised Bruce that Sophie would come down and visit him herself, just as soon as he gave Volange the information he needed.

"Don't you want to see her again? What if I said I'd let you alone with her in this cell? Just for a few minutes? You could do whatever you like with her...I don't even care if she's breathing at the end. Just tell me the things I want to know."

Bruce didn't. At first. But he couldn't think well. He dreamed sometimes, and he talked to people in his dreams. Then he woke up in the middle of a dream and saw Volange watching him avidly. He held a paper and pencil.

"Tell me more about the Zodiac," he said.

Bruce refused, and Volange laughed. Then he left Bruce alone in complete darkness. He lay there, helpless to do anything but think.

Charlie told him not to trust Libra. Bruce remembered his friend's whispered warning when he delivered the message about Volange. Charlie was right. Sophie and Volange were both deadly, and in league with each other.

Bruce laughed at himself. Of course! It all made sense now. He saw the situation clearly at last. Sophie's slyness. Charlie's warning. Julian's concern about assignments gone wrong. There was a mole in the Zodiac, and the mole was Sophie.

As he lay alone in the darkness, Bruce built his case up in his tortured mind, piece by piece. His thoughts were fractured, and he too often remembered Sophie's eyes, or her laugh. It almost made him forget the truth, which

Volange had revealed to him.

He thought a few days had passed, but he couldn't be sure. Lights would appear, then go away. He was fed regularly, though never enough to keep him from being hungry. He hated the fact that he wanted to eat. He knew there was something wrong with him, but he couldn't put two thoughts together properly. Volange's words kept filling his brain, ever more persuasive.

Volange questioned him more several times. Bruce might have told him more—he wasn't sure. But he didn't tell Volange what he truly wanted to know, because the man kept coming back.

At last Volange lost his patience and sliced Bruce a few times with a blade. Face. Arms. Side. Bruce felt the pain acutely, but didn't care. He was stronger than Volange. For now. If Volange killed him, Bruce would still win, because Volange would have learned nothing.

"You're tougher than she said," Volange hissed at the end. "If you're useless to me, I'll let you die. And then you don't get to see her again. Ponder that."

Volange left him alone and bleeding. Bruce sat there, staring into the darkness, thinking of his future. *The estate and the title would go to Ash,* Bruce thought, his brain clearing for the first time in days. Ash would ruin it— spend all the money and destroy the name of Allander completely. Bruce felt a brief stirring of anger at that thought, but not enough to pull him out of the darkness.

Sophie would get away with betraying the Zodiac, he thought then. That roused him enough so he sat up. If Volange killed him now, Bruce would never get to Sophie and force the truth out of her. Revenge might be worth living for.

He sat up straighter. He thought of Sophie and her lies. Her stories spun out night after night as the two agents lay together, all while she was laughing at him inside.

He thought of ways to kill her, but ultimately discarded all of them. Sophie couldn't die. He'd take her to Aries, and Aries would take her to the Astronomer. Sophie was a traitor, and she deserved to be treated like one. But he'd be satisfied knowing she was found out by him…

* * * *

Outside, Sophie was watching the house from the stables. She'd been there for two days, starting the morning after the party. Dressed in men's clothing, she resembled any other boy. Volange and his men stopped looking for her after the first night, assuming she'd long since escaped.

Sophie wondered if Volange actually thought she'd leave Bruce behind. But after she considered it, it made sense. Volange didn't care about other people—he never understood loyalty. But Sophie did.

Bruce had to be in the house, because Volange was there too. She saw him step outside from time to time, to ride somewhere or walk around the grounds. She was certain Bruce was being held in the so-called "dungeon" Volange had mentioned while he was influenced by the nitrous oxide.

Sophie gnawed at her lower lip. Even if she rescued Bruce from the house, how could they return to London?

She had almost nothing to her name. No money. No clothes. She couldn't simply hire a hack for the entire journey.

She absently touched the silver locket, now hidden beneath her clothing. She wore it as a reminder—until she got Bruce back safely, it was her only link to him. She might be able to sell it though. Would it be enough?

Before she could think further, a hand clamped down on her shoulder. Sophie whirled to face her attacker.

"Get away from me," she hissed as she pushed someone away. A long, lanky someone. "Jem?" she asked, astonished, seeing the same driver who had first taken her up to Carterhaugh. "What are you doing here?"

"Looking for you," the young man said. He winced. "I suppose I shouldn't have snuck up on you. Where's your partner?"

"Inside, though not as a guest." Sophie was frustrated. "I've been trying to think of a rescue plan. Everything has gone awry."

"I know," Jem said. "That's why I'm here. I have a message for you. The people you're pretending to be are in the newspapers. It's too dangerous to impersonate them any longer. Aries says to end the assignment, no matter what."

Sophie took a deep breath. "That would have been an extremely helpful message several days ago."

"I was sent as soon as the rumors were verified. But when I finally got here, you were already gone...and I couldn't ask after you, because I didn't know where you were or what other names you were using! So I've been hiding, hoping to run into you."

"And at last you have." She remembered when Bruce told her Jem was employed indirectly by the Zodiac. "Better late than never."

"Sorry, my lady."

"Oh, stop it, Jem. I'm not a lady."

He surveyed her short hair and unusual garb. "You don't look much like one now, for certain."

Jem's arrival, late as it was, sparked some hope in Sophie. With him around, there was a possibility of formulating a plan.

"Tell me you drove a carriage up, Jem."

"Aye, my la—. That is, yes. I did. And Aries gave me some cash, should it be needed. And a few weapons."

She smiled. "Excellent. Come with me, Jem. It's time to plan an assault."

The very next evening, Sophie and Jem returned to Carterhaugh. She was wearing a guard's uniform which Jem filched from the manor's laundry earlier, and she carried a pistol. Jem drove the carriage that would take them back to London—with Bruce.

Her plan was a desperate one. Bruce would have done better, she was sure. Right before she left the Sawyer's home for the last time, she told Maggie she'd repay her for her help.

"Just be careful, ma'am," Maggie said. "I don't need a reward."

"How about employment…after this is all over?"

Maggie pursed her lips. "Would it be dangerous?"

"Only if you want it to be."

The girl smiled. "Well, I do need work. I'll think about it."

"Do that." Sophie checked the darkening sky, then her gun.

"Good luck," Maggie said.

They reached Carterhaugh by carriage, and she told Jem to wait on the road just out of sight of the house. "We'll be back as soon as possible," she said.

She made her way to the manor and snuck inside. Her first goal was to find Volange. She had planned so many things to say to him. She had questions. She wanted him to know who she was. The previous night, she lay awake, deciding exactly what to say. Around three, the perfect phrase occurred to her, and she slept like a baby for the rest of the night.

With all the guests long gone, the manor was quiet. Sophie got through the halls with little trouble. As she suspected, at that hour, Volange was in the room on the main floor that he'd commandeered for his own use. The door was open, but Sophie rapped on the wood as she entered.

Volange glanced up, noticed only the guard's clothing she wore, and looked back down at whatever he was writing. "Yes? Do you have a report?"

"No," she said.

"Then what the hell..." Volange started to say, then trailed off.

Sophie held the gun out straight, and took a deep breath. She'd made sure it was ready to shoot before she came in. As she exhaled, she fired.

The sound of the shot was loud. Definitely loud enough to summon others. Sophie didn't have much time.

Neither did Volange. He stared at a growing patch of red on his chest. She'd aimed well.

"Who…" he started to say.

"Someone who knew you from Paris," she replied. "I hated you then, and I hate you now. That's all. I did have some questions, but it's more important for me to know you're dead."

Sophie walked closer. She watched him sag back into his chair, then go limp. She moved even closer to check his pulse. There was none.

Sophie heard sounds in the corridor. People were coming. She glanced at the desk. She had so little time!

If she couldn't have the information, no one could. Sophie gathered all the papers she saw and stuffed them into the fireplace. She picked up a lamp and threw it in as well. The glass broke, and oil coated the papers. The flames spread quickly.

The sound of approaching footsteps made her turn. *Out the window*, she thought, shoving a glass panel open. Thank goodness she wasn't wearing a dress.

She dropped to the ground outside, hidden in the evening's shadows. Now, she had to get back inside by another door and find Bruce.

As she gripped the gun and started to move, Sophie laughed to herself. She whispered, "To think he once called me reckless!"

Chapter 29

♏

BRUCE HAD NO SENSE OF time any more. The door to the cell opened again, though he hadn't heard any footstep outside in the hall. It wasn't Volange who entered, just one of the other guards.

"Another session tonight? Where's your boss?" Bruce muttered.

"Aries would be here if he could," the guard replied.

Bruce blinked. The guard was grinning at him. Narrow face, short, dark hair. Smile so sweet it nearly killed him. Sophie.

His heart flipped. Against all reason, he was deliriously happy to see her. "What are you doing here?" he asked. Was she another dream? Then, remembering the truth, his fury swiftly returned.

"What do you think I'm doing here? I'm rescuing you. God, you look terrible." Kneeling down, she kissed his forehead, then efficiently got him out of his bonds. She put her hands around him to help him stand.

"Hurry," she said. "We only have a minute or two before someone notices that not all the guards are where they should be."

"This is another trick. I'm not going with you," he

said, forcing himself back from her.

Sophie stopped. "Bruce, it's me. It's really me. Sophie." Her eyes searched his face. "You know me."

"I know who you are," he confirmed, though in a cold tone.

"Good," she said, relief covering her features. "Then let's get out of here. There's only one good way out. We can't let them block it."

He didn't move. "You're working for them."

Sophie punched him. Not a slap. A solid blow that came out of nowhere.

Bruce took another step back and raised a hand to his jaw. "Ow."

"Did I hurt you? Good." Sophie glared at him. "What the hell happened to you? Volange drugged you, didn't he? I am on your side. If I wasn't, why would I try to get you out of here?"

It was an excellent question, and Bruce didn't have a response. "You're doing something to trick me. And where did you learn to hit like that?"

"Bloody hell," she said, sounding remarkably English. "He definitely gave you something. I've never heard you sound so stupid. Move now. Chase me out if that's what it takes. We can fight when we get outside. But for God's sake, *move*."

A shout from the corridor caused them both to freeze. "Oh, no," Sophie whispered. "We'll be trapped."

The worry in her voice roused something in him. "We can run," he said.

She looked at him hopefully. "Yes. Run to the end of

the corridor, then up the stairs and to the left. There's a door at the end. Go through it. You'll see the outside. Run. I'll be right behind you. Don't stop for anything."

"I won't," he said grimly.

Sophie pushed Bruce through the door first, directing his steps from behind. He wouldn't be able to keep up his pace. It had been too long since he moved normally.

She was only a step or two behind. At the first doorway, she shoved him through, then followed and slammed the door shut behind her. A shot rang out just as she finished.

"Close," she commented, her breath barely quickened. "Keep running. We're not safe yet."

She moved up so she was beside him. Then she pulled him along as they ran to the driveway of the estate. Bruce knew Sophie could easily outrun him. She was quicker and stronger than he was right now. So why was she helping him? Didn't she know he'd throttle her as soon as he got the chance?

"That carriage," Sophie said, pointing far down the lane. "That's ours. Jem's driving."

More shouts came from behind them. Time was running out.

With an end in sight, though, he found a hidden reserve of strength. His longer legs helped him outstrip Sophie for a moment or two. He reached the carriage just before she did. He yanked the door open. He heard Sophie yell instructions to Jem, who whipped at the horses before Sophie even finished climbing inside.

But she was undaunted. Scrambling into the carriage,

she pulled the door shut behind her, her momentum putting her on the floor rather than in a seat. She lay there, knees up, and suddenly burst out laughing.

"My goodness, I'm sick of this place. Would you like to go to London, darling?"

Bruce stared at the bizarrely dressed woman on the floor of the carriage. Perhaps he was still dreaming. Sophie left him to die, then let him out of a prison, then offered him a ride?

"You're the strangest traitor I've ever met," he said.

Chapter 30

♎

SOPHIE'S LAUGHTER DIED IN HER throat when she heard him say that. "Bruce, talk to me. What did they do to you?"

"Told me the truth," he said.

She scrambled onto the opposite seat, keeping her eyes on him. "Listen to me. You have to forget anything Volange might have told you in there. You're not well."

He grimaced. "I am better now that I'm not in chains. I'd thank you for it, but you're the one who helped put me there."

Sophie's heart lurched. "Bruce, you're not making sense. Lord, you're *bleeding*. And you can barely sit upright…"

Indeed, Bruce was already sagging down in his seat, the exertion of the run having sapped him. Sophie pulled a basket toward her and opened the lid. "I brought food…"

"You taste it first," he said.

"Darling, it's safe." But she ate some of everything she handed to Bruce. He took each thing unwillingly, but he was too hungry to stop.

He must be addled from his torture, Sophie decided.

She'd seen a few bottles and powder packets outside his cell door. Very likely Volange had drugged Bruce's food and drink, testing out various substances to either confuse or hurt him. At the end, Volange hurt him more plainly. She saw several visible wounds on Bruce's skin. They were badly cleaned, or not cleaned at all. He risked getting scars.

"Look at you. I'll patch you up," she said.

"Volange is going to follow us," he said. He looked exhausted.

"I doubt that. Volange is dead," Sophie said, putting her chin up. "By the time Theriot organizes any real group —if he even bothers—we'll have enough of a lead to be safe. I gave instructions to Jem. We're traveling straight through. We'll switch horses as often as we need to."

He watched her suspiciously. "How do you know Volange is dead?"

"Because I shot him," she said simply. "Remember when you warned me it might be difficult? Well, killing him was quite satisfying." Sophie pushed him back against the seat. "Just be calm. I'm going to clean you up."

He was in no condition to stop her. Sophie recalled when she'd been helpless, and was glad that she could repay him so soon...though she didn't like to think of their relationship in terms of trade any more. Why had he said such a thing, calling her a traitor? Delirium?

Sophie tended to every physical wound she could find, wiping the blood off and doing her best to bandage him. Bruce let her, though he didn't speak. Sophie kept touching him after she finished patching him up, hoping she could reassure him of her loyalty just by her actions.f

He didn't push her away, so she sat next to Bruce on the seat.

"Do you have the puzzle box?" Bruce asked finally.

"Of course."

"May I see it?"

Sophie fished it out of the bag nearest to her, and handed it to him. Bruce took the box in his hand, but made no move to open it.

"What's wrong?" she asked.

"Nothing now." He smiled tightly. "I'll take this box to Aries, and everything will be over."

"Of course it will," Sophie said worriedly. "We'll both see Aries. I'm coming with you."

Bruce only shook his head, then fell into an exhausted sleep. Sophie watched him, feeling as if something had gone terribly wrong. She tried to believe Bruce would be himself again when he woke, but some little dark place in her heart warned her it was not so simple.

* * * *

Jem wasted no time. By switching horses every few hours, they reached London within a day.

The sun was just setting when they pulled up to the building where Aries waited, and lights were coming on in windows all around as people lit lamps and candles. Sophie didn't even consider going anywhere else first. The assignment had taken longer than they hoped, and who knew what was going on in Europe at the moment?

She tried to help Bruce walk inside, but he shrugged off her assistance. Perhaps his pride made him want to walk in on his own two feet, she thought, her brows knitting together.

They entered the Zodiac offices in silence. Miss Chattan was there. She took in their appearance with a worried glance, but just told them to go in.

"Sit down," ordered Julian. He looked them over. "You both look like corpses," he said flatly.

"To be expected," Sophie said. "We were both killed a few times."

Sophie related the events of the assignment in an abbreviated way. Bruce added almost nothing, but he laughed at odd times, causing Sophie to watch him in concern. At the end, Bruce handed over the puzzle box. Julian tried to open it several times before handing it to Sophie in frustration.

"Do the honors," he said.

Sophie opened the box and handed over the note. She said, "Volange had this in his possession—he took it from Theriot, probably after Theriot tried to force him to pay for it. It's just what you expected. A promise to support anti-imperial movement in France, signed with the cabinet member's own hand and sealed with his stamp. I'd say you have what you need."

He looked at the name at the bottom of the letter. "Lord Shearing. Not my first guess."

"Related to the King, through his mother's side," Bruce said, the first words he spoke in a while.

"That won't save him," Julian muttered. "Thank you.

Both of you.”

Neither of them said anything. Julian looked up, as if only just aware of the tension in the room. “The link to Arceneau is key, and we should pursue it. With Volange dead, the whole operation will likely be in disarray. I’d like to send you both to France as soon as possible.”

“Together?” Sophie asked.

“That was my intention, yes. Though not as the Cassou couple. How much time will you both need?”

“You should ask my companion here. He’s worse off than I am.” Sophie hesitated to say more. She was unsure of Bruce’s mental state, but she didn’t want to speak for him.

“She shouldn’t work alone,” Bruce said bluntly. “She shouldn’t work at all, until she can prove she’s not a mole.”

“Mole?” Sophie repeated. “What are you talking about?”

“Don’t act so surprised. Think about it. Documents going missing. Capricorn dead. Pisces nearly killed. Volange knowing about the Zodiac…There’s a mole,” he said.

“And you waited until *now* to mention it?”

“If I mentioned it earlier, *Libra*, I might have woken up with a knife between my ribs. If it’s any consolation, while I don’t trust you, I don’t doubt your skills.”

“You don’t trust me?” she asked.

“You were born to be a double agent,” he said. “Your loyalty is suspect by your very birth and nature.”

Sophie said nothing, but only because she couldn’t

accept that she had just heard those words. From Bruce. The one man she'd dared to trust fully.

"Sophie?" The concerned voice was Julian's.

Sophie turned to Julian, saying, "He was held by Volange for a few days before I could get him back. He must have tricked Bruce into believing…well, I don't know. He may have been drugged. He was so strange when I got him out, but I hoped it was just exhaustion. It appears to be more than that. Please tell him there's no mole among us."

Julian glanced at Sophie, then Bruce. "Unfortunately, I can't. The evidence suggests there *is* a mole."

"Of course," Bruce said triumphantly. "It's her."

"Be silent," Julian told him.

"I should have left you behind," Sophie snapped at Bruce.

"Likewise."

He may as well have hit her. Sophie took a step back.

She focused on Julian. "You really think one of us is working against the country?" she asked him, steadfastly ignoring Bruce.

Her superior nodded. "Unfortunately, I think it could be possible. Several assignments have gone badly. I've lost agents. At first, I ascribed the failures to bad luck, but a pattern was already emerging. However, I had no proof, and I don't accuse people without proof."

"If only everyone followed your example," she said, trying to maintain her composure.

Julian went on, "Virtually all the bad luck occurred on assignments that either directly or indirectly involved

Arceneau."

"So you knew the risk was greater on the assignment we just completed."

"Yes. That's precisely why I sent two agents. And why one of them *had* to be you, Sophie." Julian's eyes bored into her. "Who else would understand Arceneau and his tendencies better than you? Who would be aware of how Volange thinks…thought, rather."

She nodded, very slowly. The door was only a few steps behind her. Bruce stood close to the desk, and Julian stood behind it. Sophie was faster than either of them.

"I see your thinking, Julian," she said. "But I don't agree with your logic. You should have told me. You and your damned secrecy."

She turned and fled. Sophie heard Bruce growl something and begin to go after her, but she didn't wait.

Within moments, she was outside. Sophie kept running, keeping to the more shadowed side streets and alleys.

Alone in the city…how familiar the feeling was. This was where she belonged. In the dark, alone, thinking by herself and for herself. Sophie shoved aside all thoughts of the man she left behind in the building. He lied to her, and never trusted her. Thank God she never told him she loved him. How he would have laughed at that.

He thought she was a traitor. If there was a mole, *he* was the one ultimately responsible for Sophie's near death, and her entanglement with Bruce. She worked alone…and now she had something to work on.

She would find the mole.

She would bring him to the Zodiac.

And she would prove herself the better agent.

Armed with a new assignment, Sophie walked alone into the deepening twilight.

Chapter 31

♏

BRUCE HAD BARELY REACHED THE door when Julian's cold voice caught him.

"Let her go."

"She's going to get away!"

"Let her. If there *is* a mole, Sophie isn't it."

"You don't know what Volange told me!"

"Then do report the details." Julian indicated the chair. "And sit. I'm sick of craning my neck."

Bruce sat. Julian didn't. He asked question after question, gleaning the whole story of the assignment from the moment Bruce and Sophie began traveling north together, to the poisoning, to the masquerade, to Bruce's capture, Volange's mental torture, and then Sophie's subsequent rescue. Bruce left out the part where she seduced him, not wanting to admit to that weakness. But Julian listened carefully to the account, and something in his attitude suggested he missed nothing.

"You admit Sophie saved your life when she stole you back from Volange," he finally said.

"A trick to cover her treason!"

"I don't think so." Julian's eyes were flat, angry.

"My God, is everyone charmed by her?"

"Why are you so convinced Sophie is the enemy? If she were a double agent, she would have left you behind. You already served your purpose in getting her inside the manor."

"Volange said…"

"Oh, well, if the cold-blooded killer who tortured you for information said so, that must be the truth. To think we didn't just go ask him at the beginning of all this," Aries said in a cutting tone. "From everything you told me, Volange said very little. He suggested things. But he told you nothing you didn't already know."

Bruce sagged in his chair. "He'd show up at strange times, and just talk. Questions, yes, but he also just said things, and I couldn't stop thinking about them…"

"How was the food?"

"What?"

"The food. What did he feed you? What did you drink?"

"Just…the usual." Bruce paused. "It wasn't poisoned. The guard ate some."

"But he wasn't questioning the guard. He questioned you. He might not have poisoned your food, but—"

"It was drugged." Volange, according to Sophie's stories, had a predilection for such tactics.

Julian was nodding. "Almost certainly. He was trying to make your mind more malleable, and quickly."

"I should have starved."

"I'm not sure that would have been a better outcome."

"And now Sophie's gone. She never told…did she?" Bruce was still confused, trying to sort out fact and fiction in his mind.

"If Sophie were in his confidence, she would have told Volange your real name. Your sign. Did Volange ever mention the Zodiac?"

"Ye-es," he said, slowly. "But I could have told him that while I was under the influence of the substances he gave me. So much of the time was hazy." Bruce stood up and paced to the window. "He told me Sophie gave him information. And I eventually believed him, because…her whole attitude. She did everything she could to get rid of me at first."

"She's an independent woman," Julian noted. "She didn't appreciate being told she needed protection. Which she did…considering the parties involved."

"Sophie said she was afraid of him," Bruce said unwillingly. "She acted as if she was afraid of him, even when she resolved to seduce him."

"She wasn't lying about that. I know what sort of things Volange did to his enemies in Paris. But Sophie actually saw him work. She was incredibly brave. One of the reasons I trust her is because I know what she's endured."

Bruce winced, remembering Sophie's stories. But he wasn't quite ready to give in. "Chattan didn't trust her either," he said quickly.

"What?" Julian's eyes widened. He moved over to the door. "Miss Chattan? A word?"

The young woman stood up. "Yes, sir." She walked into the office and looked at Bruce. "You look like you should be dead," she said.

"It's how I feel too," he said. "Miss Chattan, you don't trust Libra. Say why."

She tipped her head. "Libra has been an excellent agent. I don't mistrust her."

"Yes, you do." Bruce closed his eyes, trying to recall the exchange Charlie overheard. "You think Julian has a blind spot concerning her."

"I…don't." She looked flustered.

"Because she's French?" Bruce pressed.

"God, no!" Chattan's lips were a thin line. "Julian does have a soft spot for Libra, but not because she's French!"

"Then why?"

Chattan dropped her eyes. "Just because of the kind of woman she is. She's…alluring."

Julian was staring at Chattan. "What are you talking about?"

"You clearly have very strong feelings about her," Chattan said, her voice growing hotter.

"Of course I do! I trained her. Not to mention, if I send her out on an assignment and she doesn't come back, I have to answer to my predecessor."

"And that's all?" Chattan asked.

When Bruce heard the jealousy in her voice, everything became much simpler. Chattan didn't like Sophie, but it was because she feared the agent had a hold over Julian…who Miss Chattan cared for herself.

"Wait," he said, before the woman had to confess something more. "I think Pisces just misunderstood. He thought you had doubts about Sophie's loyalty."

Chattan glared at Bruce, probably glad she could focus on that. "If that were so, I certainly wouldn't let Julian send her on an assignment!"

"When did you talk to Pisces about this, anyway?" Julian asked curiously.

"You sent him up with the message about Volange's arrival—just after we left."

Julian blinked in confusion. "I didn't send him anywhere."

"Then what was he doing at Carterhaugh?" Bruce asked, just as he realized the truth. The letter. That was why Charlie had been at Carterhaugh. He had connections in the cabinet. He brought the letter from the cabinet member to Theriot—Sophie said the letter arrived just when they got to the house. Charlie was the only messenger they trusted, because he was as corrupt as they were. Pisces, Charles Wolverton, his friend and a full-blooded Englishman, was the mole.

Coming to her own conclusions, Chattan gasped, in outrage more than surprise. "He lied about nearly dying on that last assignment. A trick to throw us off."

Julian said, in a disturbingly calm voice, "We have to find Charlie. Immediately."

Bruce nodded. "I'll do that. But first I have to find Sophie." He should have trusted her. He allowed an enemy to get into his head. He valued Volange's word over Sophie's. And he failed *her*.

He'd watched as Sophie's eyes went cold when he accused her. She'd stood very still, and seemed to wrap herself up in disdain, separating herself from him, from the Zodiac, from the world. She fled, and he would never see her again.

Unless he could show her he believed her by finding the real mole.

Chapter 32

$$\Omega$$

ONCE SHE IDENTIFIED HER GOAL, Sophie recovered her equilibrium. She went to her own rooms first, to wash off the grime and dress in a more appropriate manner. The landlady heard her as she passed by her door, but Sophie had only to call though a greeting and a promise to share everything in the morning.

That was very likely a lie. Sophie shrugged. It seemed to be a night for lies.

She changed into an outfit suitable for a lady and selected a favorite wig, one much darker than what she'd worn for the assignment. In her reticule, she concealed a small gun. She knew where to go to begin her own hunt.

Despite the hour, when she called at a certain house in the quiet neighborhood of Quince Street, she was received like any other lady of quality.

She told the maid, "I apologize for the timing. But will you tell Lord Thorne that I must see him? It is extremely important."

"Your name, ma'am?"

"Miss Sophie Bertrand."

"And shall I tell him what this concerns?"

"Yes." Sophie gave the girl a cool smile. "Tell him it

concerns astronomy."

A few minutes later, the girl reappeared and ushered Sophie to a small room at the back of the house. A gentleman stood there, waiting for her.

"Good evening, Miss Bertrand," he said, taking in her appearance. He glanced at the maid. "That will be all."

The maid nodded and closed the door behind her.

"Do I know you?" he asked bluntly.

No," Sophie said. "But you will."

She took a moment to survey the man. She had seen him once before, but in very poor conditions. He would have been striking in any setting. He was a few inches taller than Sophie, though considerably less tall than Bruce. He was also far handsomer. His features were well-balanced, and everything about him suggested that he knew his effect on others.

"Are you done?" he asked, amused.

"You look far better than you did in Calais," Sophie said, skipping any preamble. "I am glad to see it."

Lord Thorne blinked at that. "How do you know about…who are you?"

Before Sophie could answer, a woman with black hair and a warm expression swept into the room. "Sebastien, I had to ask—" She halted on seeing Sophie. "Excuse me. I didn't realize we had a guest."

"Not a guest, exactly," Thorne said, his voice tight. "A matter of business, darling." Thorne's eyes hadn't left Sophie.

"I can see that." Lady Thorne turned to go, offering Sophie an apologetic smile. But when she looked longer, something caused her eyes to widen. "I know you."

"My lady," Sophie began, not knowing what to say. The other woman's certainty was no accident, and revealing the truth might help Sophie. "You might remember—"

"My heart," the other woman gasped suddenly. "*You're Jacques*!"

"What?" Sebastien asked in confusion.

"Jacques. You remember, Sebastien. The boy who who helped me during that terrible time in Calais. I told you he warned me about Arceneau. Except it was no boy at all. It was you." She beamed at Sophie, who ducked her head.

"It was only right, my lady."

The man was less impressed. "Cordelia, don't get involved in this, please."

"I swear it was her."

"That's crazy. She's just agreeing with you to suit her own purposes...whatever they might be."

Cordelia's eyes flared. She turned back to Sophie. "What did you give me, the very first time you saw me?"

"A glass bottle filled with water," Sophie answered promptly.

Sebastien's eyes rounded. Cordelia must have told him of the strange young man called Jacques who had given her water in a bottle during her captivity, and how she realized he'd given it to her because glass could be a weapon of last resort. There was no way Sophie could have known that unless she'd been there.

"You *were* the boy," Sebastien said. "You helped Cor. I swore that I'd give that man—person—anything in my power."

"It was me," Sophie said. "And if you acknowledge your debt, then help me now."

Sebastien looked at her, weighing his options. Then he nodded. "Tell me who you really are, and why you're here."

Sophie took a breath. "I'm Libra," she said quietly. "You are Sagittarius. We both work for Aries, and I come to you because something happened to Scorpio on our assignment, something that places the Zodiac in danger."

"Christ." Thorne leaned back against the desk. "You're Libra? Libra is a woman?"

"Yes."

"I didn't know that."

"Few do. I happened to be in Calais when your then-fiancée was captive there. In my disguise as Jacques, I was infiltrating one of Arceneau's operations."

She could see him coming to terms with the concept of a female agent, which he did with admirable swiftness. "Very well. What happened to Bruce…Scorpio, that is?"

"He was tortured, and tricked into thinking that I'm a double agent. He thinks I betrayed him."

"Did you?" he asked calmly, coldly.

"Of course not! I would have died for him."

His expression changed slightly. "Past tense?"

"He doesn't trust me, and apparently never did. Something went wrong, and I need to clear my name."

"Why come to me?" he asked skeptically, "Why not go to Julian?"

"I just came from Julian! He doesn't think I'm a mole,

but he's not the one I need to convince." She sighed. "I know you and Bruce are friends…not just fellow agents. I hoped you would understand…"

Cordelia, who had been listening avidly, now stepped up to Sophie. "Everyone's emotions are running a bit high at the moment. Miss Bertrand clearly has a story to tell, and you, my dear," she said to Sebastien, "should hear all the details."

"What do you suggest?" he asked his wife.

Cordelia smiled. "What any proper woman would do. I'm going to ring for some tea. Then we'll talk."

Chapter 33

♎

ACCEPTING CORDELIA'S DIRECTION, SOPHIE SAT down and related nearly all the relevant details of the assignment. Tea—and a blessed amount of food—was brought in by a silent servant. Thorne listened to her story with a minimum of interruption. Cordelia, who remained in the room, said nothing at all.

"All right," he said finally. "If you're telling the truth, I grant you that Bruce overreacted. If both can settle on the fact that neither of you is the mole, we can move on to discovering who it is—if there is one."

"What should I do?" Sophie asked.

"You should stay here." Sebastien looked at her. "If you came here directly from Carterhaugh, that means you haven't had a proper rest in days. I'll go hunt down Bruce and bring him here. This is a matter to resolve together."

"Go to Julian's office first. He may still be there."

Thorne left to retrieve Bruce, promising to return as soon as possible.

Once he was gone, Cordelia smiled a bit tremulously at her. "Did I say thank you for what you did? I always wanted to. I would prepare little speeches, in case I met Jacques again."

"What speeches?" Sophie asked.

"Most of them didn't get much past thank you, in fact," Cordelia said. "I have my whole life now. I have my husband and my family. And I came so close to not having anything."

"I know the feeling," Sophie said.

"I'm sure Bruce will realize he's made a mistake."

"I hope so," Sophie said absently.

"What's wrong, dear? When you see Bruce again, everything will be explained. I'm sure he knows in his heart you could never betray anyone."

"His heart is quite closed to me," Sophie said, before realizing she said far too much.

"Oh." That was all Cordelia said, but Sophie felt she might as well have poured out her whole story to the other woman.

"I just want to clear my name," Sophie added hastily.

"Of course," Cordelia said, not believing her.

"And that's what I've been thinking about all evening," Sophie said. "I didn't betray Bruce—but someone did. Someone worked against both of us. And I should be able to figure out who it is. Like an answer on the tip of your tongue, understand?"

"Would it help to talk it out?" Cordelia asked hesitantly.

"Perhaps. Soon."

Cordelia let her alone, telling her to ring if she needed something.

Sophie stayed in the room, lost in her own thoughts. If only she could think clearly about the whole situation, instead of hearing Bruce's accusation over and over.

The leaks Julian described had been too wide ranging to be the result of a simple theft or innocent slip of the tongue. "So. Who could it be?" And here Sophie was driven to a halt. The few agents she knew personally had to be innocent. She wasn't the traitor. Bruce wasn't. Sebastien couldn't be either.

"Not Libra. Not Scorpio. Not Sagittarius. Not Aries."

And not Miss Chattan. The woman didn't care for Sophie, but she certainly was loyal to Julian, and to the Zodiac itself. Eight left. Sophie broke down again. The way the Zodiac worked meant that she didn't know who the rest of the agents were. The secrecy they all relied on was now hindering her search.

She did know Capricorn died about a month ago. Not him, obviously. That left seven.

She knew Pisces came to visit the house where Bruce and she had been sent in order to give a message.

Pisces. Something about what that agent told Bruce. Something she overheard.

He'd made a mistake.

Somewhere in her brain the clue was hiding. Something he'd said, a tiny slip. What was it?

I knew that with the three of you in Calais, the plans would be found.

Sophie went still.

The three of you.

"Oh, no," she whispered. The truth flared in her brain. When she overheard the words, she assumed he'd meant the two men and Cordelia, who they intended to rescue.

But he didn't mean that at all. He meant there were three *agents* in Calais, something only a mole could have discovered.

She had to find Pisces, who Bruce called Charlie Wolverton. And she would rather go to hell than wait for Bruce to return, filled with doubts about her.

Sophie stepped into the hall, and found Cordelia walking toward her.

"Are they back?" the other woman asked, confused.

"No," Sophie said. "And I'm not waiting. I know who the mole is."

"Who?" Cordelia asked, her eyes wide.

"Pisces." Quickly, she explained her theory, her words rushing over each other in her eagerness. Cordelia kept asking her to repeat herself.

Finally, Cordelia said, "If you're right, you can't leave now. They'll be back soon and you can all go together."

"Together?" Turning, Sophie felt the weight of Bruce's silver locket around her neck. Remembering his cold words again, she snapped it off in a flash of rage. "I work alone. If Bruce happens by, do tell him that I am returning his property. It was just a prop he bought. I don't need it anymore, and I don't expect I'll see him again."

"Sophie," Cordelia began. "Please wait…"

But Sophie dropped the locket onto the nearby table and left the house. She knew exactly what she had to do.

Chapter 34

♎

IT WAS CHILD'S PLAY FOR an agent like Sophie to discover where Charlie Wolverton lived. As a gentleman of London society, he was not one to hide.

Sophie knocked on the front door of Wolverton's charming, expensive house as if she had every right to do so. An older woman answered the door, and—tellingly—she did not look particularly surprised to see a strange woman standing there, even as the hour advanced to ten o'clock.

"Mr Wolverton is home, I trust," Sophie said. She didn't wait to be invited in, but simply moved past the woman and into the gracious marble floored foyer.

"I'll tell him he has a guest." The woman sighed. Again, the fact that she didn't ask for a name told Sophie much about the sort of company Charlie kept.

Charlie himself came down a moment later, his expression curious. Sophie got a look at him for the first time. In truth, he was…adorable. Light hair, warm blue eyes, an open expression, and well-chosen evening clothes made him appear to be a picture perfect gentleman. No wonder he made a successful mole.

"Ah," Sophie said, smiling in her most inviting way.

"I see you are about to go out. May we speak in private for a few moments, Mr Wolverton? I think I may have some little piece of information you'll be interested in." Oh, did she ever.

Charlie looked her over with an appreciative glance. "Please follow me up to my study."

Sophie walked up the stairs, not following too closely. She was sure Charlie didn't suspecther, but if Sophie had learned anything, it was that she could rely on no one but herself.

In the study, he turned and surveyed her more closely.

"Who are you?" he asked.

"I'm a woman with information to your benefit," she said, keeping her tone light and teasing. "You do have a habit of collecting other people's secrets, don't you?"

He frowned slightly, trying to place her. "Who have you been talking to?"

"People with influence."

"Ah. People in high places?"

She laughed. "Very low places, in fact." She took a breath, then said in French, "Arceneau and I have a history, you see."

He relaxed slightly, thinking her another opportunist. "Interesting. And you say you have information that will interest me. I warn you, I'm more interested in selling than buying."

"I know," she said. She took a few nonchalant steps so she stood between Charlie and the closed door.

He turned to a small cabinet and pulled out a bottle. "May I offer you something to drink?"

"Not at the moment, Pisces."

He stopped. "How do you know that name?"

"Oh, I know some things about you, Charlie Wolverton, that no one else knows." She smiled sweetly. "For instance, I know what you said to Scorpio up at Carterhaugh Manor. You said: *I knew that with the three of you on the case, the plans would be found.* A little flattery to keep Bruce from thinking too hard about your presence. Initially, I thought you referred to Bruce, Sebastien, and Cordelia, who had the plans in her head. Bruce probably thought the same.

"But you meant Scorpio, Sagittarius, and Libra. You knew there were three *agents* in Calais at the same time. And you found out that information in your work as the Zodiac's mole. I only know because I was the third agent."

"Of course. You're Libra." Turning around, he drew out a knife from under his coat. "You're also alone."

Sophie didn't blink. She raised the pistol she'd held behind her skirts. "So are you, Charlie."

He lost his smile. "You look quite serious with that gun."

"How long has this been going on?" she asked.

"Two years, give or take. I first met Arceneau while I was on an assignment. He convinced me I was going about things all wrong. He wasn't the enemy of England. The Emperor was. And if Arceneau could keep his business going, it would cost Bonaparte more and more money to buy the arms Arceneau sold."

"And kill more men in battle, you idiot."

"Arceneau sells to all sides," Charlie protested. "In the grand scheme, my involvement changed nothing."

"That was your rationalization?"

"I can't stop the war. No one person can."

"One person can try," she said.

"But you don't understand…"

"Of course I do. You betrayed our country. You're a sign of the Zodiac, Charlie. You were *chosen*."

"You say that like it's an honor," he spat. "But all it means is that we take the risks while those who are truly in power sit snug in their palaces. You think they care who dies on a battlefield? Of course they don't."

"Charlie," Sophie said. "You're no political radical. Spare me the pedestal. Why did you do it?"

"Money, mostly." He shrugged. "Sorry if that's mundane, but it's true. I'm going to be married soon, and I don't want to stay with the Zodiac much longer. It's too risky, for too little reward. I want to live the sort of life I deserve to, which will be quite expensive."

"You're a peer."

"Yes." He laughed. "But no one knows how indebted my estate is. I've kept it quiet—very quiet. The sale of the documents I acquire keeps me ahead of my creditors."

"So you have more documents!" Sophie said, pouncing on his slip. "Where are they?"

"Not here," Charlie snapped, annoyed at his own admission.

Sophie merely raised her arm so the gun was pointed at his head.

"Wait, wait, wait," he said quickly. "I'll tell you. I

have a hunting lodge not far away. Been in the family for years."

"And?"

"I'm the only one who goes there now. It's where I keep all the little items that fall into my hands. And cash as well, if that's what you're interested in."

"I'm interested in bringing proof to the Zodiac," Sophie said. "So we're going to retrieve some of those items, and then we'll meet with Aries."

"What if I don't care for that idea?"

"Then I shoot you. Whatever else you might be, Pisces, you're good at staying alive. So I don't think you'll walk into a bullet while you have a chance to change your fate."

Charlie hadn't taken his eyes off the gun. "Aries won't be in the mood to negotiate."

"Neither am I. Let's go downstairs and call your carriage out, shall we? We're going for a moonlight ride. How romantic."

Keeping the gun concealed beneath her wrap, Sophie walked Charlie downstairs. She would get what she wanted from him, and then she'd prove to the Zodiac that she could always work alone.

Chapter 35

♏

BRUCE HAD JUST TURNED TO go when someone knocked on the outer office door.

"Answer that," Julian told Chattan, "And try to look as if everything is normal."

"What if it's Wolverton?" she asked.

"I doubt we'll be that lucky."

It was not Wolverton. It was Sebastien. He related his news—Sophie arriving unannounced at Quince Street and demanding his help in clearing her name. "And since she turns out to be the agent who located my fiancée, I feel I have to do it."

"What?" Bruce asked.

"Remember that skinny errand boy who kept going in and out of the house we were watching in Calais?"

Bruce remembered how familiar Sophie looked with her short hair and the cap she wore the first night at Carterhaugh. "That was Sophie. I'm an idiot."

"I refrain from comment."

Julian looked at them. "If you are both determined to be involved, you'd best listen." He explained the revelation of Charlie's betrayal. At the end, he said, "Go find Charlie and bring him here. But you should go to Libra first, and let her know she's safe." Julian added, staring hard at Bruce. "You owe it to Sophie."

"I owe her more than that," he admitted.

The two agents returned to Quince Street. In the carriage, Bruce realized how nervous he was. "She won't talk to me."

"Why?"

"Besides the fact that I betrayed her trust?"

"A legitimate concern," Sebastien said drily. "Having just met her tonight, I can't pretend to know how she'll react. But we'll find out soon enough."

On that point, Sebastien was wrong.

They entered the house to find Cordelia waiting for them, pacing anxiously. "Where were you?" she burst out.

"What happened? Where's Miss Bertrand?" Sebastien asked.

"She's gone! She went after the mole."

"Alone?" Bruce asked, unable to keep the tension out of his voice.

Cordelia sent him a withering look. "And just who could she have gone to, my lord? You didn't prove yourself the best of allies."

Bruce had absolutely nothing to say to that.

Cordelia realized the gravity of her accusation, and she immediately put one hand out toward him. "I didn't mean…I'm sorry, Bruce."

"Not as sorry as I am," Bruce said.

Sebastien moved to join his wife. "When did she leave here?"

"Just over an hour ago."

"And did she say she was going to find Charlie?"

"How do you know who it is?"

"We just put it together," said Bruce. "But how did Sophie know?"

"She overheard a conversation you had with Charlie at Carterhaugh. She remembered something he said, and that's how she realized he knew more than he should."

Bruce tried to think clearly. "What did he say?"

Cordelia explained Sophie's reasoning that Charlie's offhand comment about "three of you" referred to three agents instead of the trio of Sebastien, Bruce, and herself.

"And she went after him." Before Bruce could say more, he saw something glint on the nearby table. Sophie's locket, the one he'd given her to help the disguise.

"She left this?" he asked Cordelia.

"She said it wasn't hers."

She *didn't* care. For the first time in a very long time, he was frozen with fear. Not since he'd been a child had he been so paralyzed. So unable to think.

How could he have done that? How could he have betrayed her? Without warning, a flash of pain made him wince, and then a heat washed over his back. The scar was aching. He was again a terrified young boy, waiting for the punishment he knew he deserved.

You'll never amount to anything. The title will be wasted on you.

That was what his father said, right before he brought the poker down on Bruce's bare back.

Heedless of his inner turmoil, Cordelia was speaking to her husband. "Might I recommend you two go after her?"

Sebastien was nodding absently. "I'm still having difficulty believing he could be the mole. He's…Charlie. I went to school with him."

"Then he should be able to clarify things," Cordelia was saying, "particularly if Sophie is there too."

Sophie and Charlie in one place, Bruce thought. The woman he loved was going to meet the traitor. Bruce tucked the necklace and chain into his pocket. "We need to go."

The two men raced to Charlie's rooms in town. His nervous housekeeper said he wasn't in, but Bruce allowed for no refusals. He made his way through the rooms. Neither Charlie nor Sophie were there.

Sebastien asked, "Did he take Sophie somewhere else?"

Bruce shook his head. "Sophie doesn't let anyone take her anywhere. Maybe *she* made him go somewhere else."

The housekeeper had trailed after them, and now stood in the doorway of the study, looking distressed. Bruce turned to the lady and asked when Charlie left.

"Not more than an hour ago." She looked at him with wide eyes. "He said he and the lady were going to his hunting lodge."

"What did she say?"

"Nothing, sir. She just sort of smiled. And when I told Mr Wolverton to drive safely, she laughed."

"That's Sophie," Bruce muttered. "I'm going after them."

Chapter 36

♎

SOPHIE NEVER TOOK HER EYES off Charlie, even when the coach got moving and he was too busy driving to do anything else. They travelled in silence until the carriage emerged from the city onto a quieter road leading northwest. The signs of humanity thinned out, lending a deceptive calm to the night.

Charlie hesitated for a moment when the road forked, but after a quick glance at Sophie, he sighed and chose the right-hand road.

"Remember to go straight there," Sophie said. "No detours."

"Where would I go?" Charlie muttered, his eyes on the road. "You've got your finger on the trigger, and even if you're not an expert, you won't miss at this range."

"Well reasoned." Sophie wished Charlie had the grace to look defeated. She could tell he was far from resigned to his fate.

"Join me," he offered unexpectedly. "Arceneau would take you in a heartbeat."

"I'd rather die than join up with you."

He nodded, his eyes still on the road. "That's what I thought you'd say. True agent of the Zodiac, you are." He sounded rather sad.

"Even though I'm a woman?"

"And foreign born."

"Both traits, I'm sure, that you mentioned in your findings as a mole."

Charlie held up a hand. "I did learn one of the signs was a woman, but I didn't know which one. Even in the notes I read, nothing connected your name with the name of Libra."

"But you told someone that an agent was going to Carterhaugh."

"I told Theriot—for a price. It's the sort of thing I'm expected to know about. But I didn't say the Zodiac had a female agent."

She snorted. "As if I believe that."

"It's the truth. Would I lie at this point?"

Sophie smiled. "You've lied at every other point."

"Give me a modicum of credit. It would have given them an advantage, knowing a woman was working as a spy. You know why I didn't tell them?"

"What reason could you possibly have had?"

He paused. "It would have been ungentlemanly."

"You're joking."

"Not a bit. I couldn't bring myself to say a lady was on our side."

"How chivalrous, even though I'm *not* a lady."

"You're not exactly, are you?" Charlie said, unexpectedly laughing.

Without warning, he jerked the reins, and the horses reacted. Sophie had to take her eyes off him for a split second, and that was enough.

Charlie reached for Sophie and knocked her off balance.

Sophie felt all her memories of living in the streets wake up. Back then, she had fought dirty and rough, because she fought to survive.

Charlie was several stones heavier than her, but he was born a gentleman. He didn't see her coming. She kicked out with both feet, using her hands to brace herself against the seat.

He was fell sideways, jerking the reins along with him. The horses whinnied nervously at the mixed signals and started to veer to the right.

Sophie lunged forward, hurling herself at her enemy.

But Charlie recovered from his surprise and pried the gun from her hands. By then, their scuffling utterly spooked the horses. With a curse, Charlie tried to pull the reins to assert control over the animals.

While he was distracted, Sophie used a precious second to knock the gun out of his hand. It fell and clattered onto the floor of the open carriage.

"Stop it! The horses will go crazy!" Charlie yelled. "Are you trying to get us both killed?"

"I'll trust the horses with my life before I trust you."

Sophie only had a moment. He kept glancing between her and the horses, trying to decide where the bigger threat lay. She couldn't beat him with bare hands. She had to get the gun back and stop him.

Charlie knew what she needed, too. He yanked the reins again, so the horses pulled hard to the right, trampling off the narrow lane and into tall grass. The gun slid toward Charlie's side of the carriage.

If she lost sight of the gun, she would lose. She dove after it, sliding under Charlie's feet.

He didn't expect that, but he reacted fast, kicking her hard in the stomach. Sophie cried out, and the gun slid further toward the edge.

"You…are…annoying me," Charlie hissed. Sophie twisted upward, but he had already moved. He kicked her again, catching her ribs. She felt a searing pain, and instinctively lashed out, going for the nearest weak spot.

Charlie howled when Sophie's teeth sank into his leg. He lost control of the horses. Sophie was thrown clear as the carriage surged forward and then toppled over on its side.

She hit the ground hard and lay stunned for a moment. Something rock-hard jabbed into her lower back. Her head spun. But she couldn't stay on the ground. Charlie would be coming for her.

Sophie rolled to the side and tried to heave herself off the ground, but her arms gave out the first time. She lifted herself again, and just as she got onto her hands and knees, she saw the object that nearly broke her spine.

Then a huge weight slammed into her. Charlie shoved her down, face first in the dirt.

"Get off me," she hissed, anger overtaking her pain.

"Not yet." Charlie laughed wildly. "I have to kill you first."

Pain shot through Sophie's back—deep, deep pain that was blinding in its intensity. A knife. She couldn't even scream.

"Got you," Charlie sighed. He moved off her, and Sophie tried to breathe. She choked instead.

"What, you're still alive?" He moved again.

She tried to roll out of the way, but only managed to flip onto her back again. Charlie plunged his knife into her shoulder instead of her heart.

This time Sophie screamed.

Sophie clawed at the ground, trying to find something to fend him off. She wouldn't survive another attack.

Her hand touched something cold.

"Oh, Charlie," she gasped, her breath coming in rapid waves. "I'm so sorry."

He paused for half a second. "You're sorry? For what?"

Half a second was all she needed. Sophie gripped the pistol and pointed it toward Charlie. She pulled the trigger just as he saw what she held.

The barrel was almost touching his chest. The flash of the gun illuminated his body and his astonished, ashen face. He collapsed onto her. Stifling her horror, Sophie shoved him off with the last of her strength.

Charlie wasn't dead. He made gasping sounds like words and clutched at the air. Sophie didn't listen. Tapping the last of her reserves, she crawled away from him. She found the gun and tossed it about ten feet and one lifetime away from the rapidly fading man.

She had to get to the horses. She could ride back to town. She could get help.

Sophie laughed hysterically when she saw how very,

very far away the horses were. She'd never make it. She crawled until her arms gave way under her, and fell on the suddenly sloping ground. She couldn't stop herself from rolling down the embankment. Thorns and brambles caught at her skin and clothes. She landed in a cold, wet patch of mud, the final insult. She heard a stream trickling nearby.

It would be a long climb back up to the road. Sophie's heartbeat fluttered. She needed to rest first. Closing her eyes, she gave herself up to the pain.

Chapter 37

BRUCE RODE ALONE ALONG THE route he'd been given. Sebastien offered to go with him, but Bruce told him to report back to Aries. "I'll find them soon enough. They've less than an hour's lead." Though an hour could be a lifetime if he was too late.

The road to the hunting lodge was nearly deserted at that time of night. While the route led through farmland, the night sky provided enough light to ride swiftly. But soon the road cut through woods, which surrounded him in darkness, forcing him to slow down.

When the track split, offering no indication as to which way each branch led, Bruce thought he'd scream in frustration. He wheeled his horse around the small clearing where all the roads joined, his eyes fixed on the ground. Bruce took a breath. "Go right," he muttered. He didn't know why he chose it. He'd simply have to act by instinct.

He urged his horse onward, pressing the beast as much as he dared. The new path was still shadowed by trees, and he knew he risked injury to the horse or himself if he hit a pothole or stone. Still, he couldn't slow down.

One heartening fact was that the road was certainly wide enough for a carriage. He kept riding, praying his instinct was leading him to Sophie rather than away from her. He'd betrayed her once already. He couldn't stand to do it again.

The outline of an overturned carriage suddenly made him pull up. His horse snorted with annoyance and confusion.

He rode carefully toward the broken vehicle. No one was inside. "Sophie?" he called out. "Charlie?"

A slight sound caught his attention. Something had moved near the trees. "Hello?"

The sound repeated. A cough.

Bruce dismounted and headed for the source of the noise. He saw a man's body lying among the grasses. At the sound of Bruce's footsteps, the man's eyes flickered open.

"Forester…" Charlie's voice came out weak. He clutched a hand to his chest, but Bruce could see it was hopeless.

He bent down near the dying man.

"She's stronger than she looks," Charlie whispered, his smile thin and bitter.

"Sophie? Where is she? By God, if you hurt her…"

"Hurt *her*…" Charlie managed a feeble laugh, an odd bubbling sound in it. "The bitch was the end of me."

"You deserved no less," Bruce growled.

"Had my reasons…" Charlie struggled to speak, but began to cough again, the blood trickling from his mouth. "Saved the cost of a hanging, anyway…"

The man's confession did nothing to assuage Bruce. "Where is Sophie?"

"Tougher than I thought." Charlie's voice cracked. "Never thought a woman—"

"You were a fool for thinking of her as a woman and not an agent. She can do everything we can do, and more." Hadn't Sophie given him that very warning, the first night?

Charlie was fading fast. Perhaps he'd only been waiting till someone got to him. "Forester. Don't tell my family what I became." As death gripped him, his eyes grew wide. For the first time, Charlie seemed to realize what he had done. "Promise... They'll hate me."

A bloody hand reached up in a desperate bid to hold on to someone, anyone.

Bruce took hold of the already chill fingers.

"I promise," he said. But it was too late. The breathing had stopped, the eyes were fixed on the moon. Charles Wolverton was dead.

And Sophie was missing.

* * * *

Charlie's body had a strange pallor in the feeble moonlight. Bruce let go of the body of his onetime friend, and stood up. If Charlie was here, Sophie must be too.

He cast about, searching for some sign to indicate which way she had gone. The broken carriage's horses were both still in the vicinity. Sophie wouldn't have walked to get help if she could have taken a horse.

"Sophie!" he called out in the darkness. There was no answer. "Sophie!"

Bruce walked back toward the carriage, wondering if he'd missed something. But before he got halfway there, he heard another odd sound.

He held absolutely still, listening. It might have been some animal, or it might have been a person.

The sound wasn't repeated, but Bruce thought it came from the line of hedges growing out of the ditch beside the path. He switched direction. "Sophie?"

As he reached the ditch, his eyes were drawn to a pale root lying above the dirt, half-hidden under the branches.

No, not a root. A limb. A woman's arm.

He half-fell down the embankment, skidding in the dirt. He reached out to touch the arm, Sophie's arm. The flesh was cold. He cleared away the branches and debris that covered her when she landed.

Sophie lay unmoving, her face up to the sky and her dress tangled in the thorns. The wig she had worn now perched in some branches like a bird's nest. A dark splotch stained the light fabric at her shoulder. Another obscured her side. The smell of blood mingled with the soil. Short, dark locks of hair lay tangled over a moon-white face. Her eyes were closed.

He stared at her broken body. It was not only Charlie, but he who had done these things to her. If he hadn't turned her away, she would never have faced Charlie alone.

Another slight sound caught his attention. He fell to his knees beside her. Had that been a faint rattle of breath?

"Sophie, please be alive," he begged, and was rewarded by the sight of her chest rising and falling ever so slightly. "I'll get you to a doctor. Just don't leave me," he said. Her skin was as cold as the air, but her pulse beat faintly under his hands. He picked her up as gently as he could, horrified by the dark stains spreading across her gown where Charlie's dagger had pierced her.

The roots and mud conspired against him. He lost his footing again and again. He had to clutch Sophie with one arm while he dragged them both up the steep slope. Through it all, Sophie remained unconscious and frighteningly still.

Once he laid her back down on the grasses by the road, he had no idea how to move her to a safer place. This road was sparsely traveled, particularly at night. The chances of anyone coming to help were remote.

The carriage was unusable. Bruce hated to do it, but he had no other choice than to ride his own horse back to town, holding Sophie the entire way. It might hurt her further, but he couldn't linger.

So he rode. He was utterly alone on the track. He clutched a limp and lightweight Sophie close to his body. He wrapped her in his coat, hoping it would keep her warm. Though only in a shirt, he was sweating with exertion.

The first twinkling lights of the outer suburbs of London acted as a beacon.He headed directly to the Quince Street house, the closest place he could trust. A few windows were alight, even in the pre-dawn hush.

Sophie's arrival was handled with wonderful aplomb. Though totally confused, Cordelia's servants carried out every order given by their lady, who was awake and completely in control. A surgeon was summoned and instructed to stay until the lady's condition was beyond his ability to aid.

Bruce hovered outside the bedroom where Sophie lay. When the surgeon emerged from the bedroom, his coat stained red, Bruce stopped his pacing and arrowed toward him.

"How is she?"

"I stitched the wounds and administered a dose of opium to dull the pain. She lost a great deal of blood, I'm afraid. Perhaps enough to be fatal." The surgeon looked troubled. "I cannot tell you if she will live, my lord."

"But surely I can do something for her. I can't just wait."

"As I told the woman attending her, keep her warm. Offer her weak tea or wine, if she'll drink anything. Broth would be excellent too. If the wound festers…" he trailed off. "If you are a man of faith, I suggest prayer." He shrugged. "I have left a little opium by her bedside. It's in syrup, so stir a dropperful in a drink and get her to take it if she's in pain. I'll call again tomorrow to check the bandages."

Bruce nodded absently.

"No one has told me what happened," the surgeon noted pointedly.

"We are still discovering the details," Bruce returned, his voice suddenly sharp and cold. "Thank you for coming. Good night."

Bruce entered the bedroom, now blazing with light, since every lamp had been lit for the surgeon to see Sophie's wounds. He was only vaguely aware of the scurrying around him as the maids put the bedroom to rights.

"Can you douse some of the lights?" he asked, sitting

in the chair drawn up near Sophie's bed. "She can't rest like this."

"Yes, my lord," one of the maids said, then paused. "If I may ask…what is her name, sir?"

"Why?"

"I thought her husband should be alerted."

Bruce blinked "Her husband?"

"She's wearing a wedding band."

Bruce glanced at Sophie's hand and saw she was still wearing the false wedding ring. "Miss Bertrand is my fiancée," he said, wonderingly. "I have the matching band."

"Oh," the maid said again, confused as to why they both wore bands if they were not yet married. But she also knew she was not to ask questions.

Bruce waited in the dimmed room. At some point, Cordelia's butler, Stiles, materialized with a glass of whiskey and a cup of coffee. Bruce gratefully gulped both down. Sophie had not stirred. Whether it was her wounds or the opium, something kept her body weak and still. Bruce looked hard to reassure himself that she was still breathing.

"Has Thorne returned?" Bruce asked.

"Not yet, my lord," Stiles said. "And milady has retired. I'll let him know you're waiting in this room. Will there be anything else?"

Bruce only shook his head. The other man left, closing the door gently. With a sigh, Bruce turned back to Sophie, taking her cold hand in his own and watching her for any signs of life.

Chapter 38

m̖

BRUCE MUST HAVE DOZED. HE felt a hand on his shoulder and opened his eyes to see Sebastien nearby, looking ragged. Cordelia was there as well, on the other side of the bed, hovering anxiously over Sophie. The curtains were drawn, but a single shaft of bright sunlight leaked in.

"What time is it?"

"Nearly noon," Sebastien replied.

Bruce nodded, his eyes bleary.

"How is she doing?" Cordelia asked, her bright eyes missing nothing of Bruce's appearance.

"I don't know," he said. "I don't know."

Sebastien coughed. "Charlie's body was recovered from the woods, following my report to the local magistrate," he said, not looking at Bruce.

"Yes," Bruce said shortly. "What's our official story?"

"He and Miss Bertrand were attacked by highwaymen. The authorities are satisfied with the tale, and they are searching most diligently for a small gang in the vicinity."

"Good luck to them," Bruce said sourly. "Has Charlie's family been told?"

"They'll soon be notified of his death, and given the

official story. They didn't know he was an agent, and they don't know he was a traitor. We'll keep it that way."

"He was sorry, at the end," Bruce said quietly. "He begged me to keep his secret."

"It will be kept, though not for his sake." Sebastien's expression was cold.

"He was going to be married," Cordelia added, almost as an afterthought. "Next year, I think." Her green eyes were distant, perhaps thinking of the young woman who would never know how or why her husband-to-be had died. Or what his true nature was.

"Has anyone found out the extent of his work?" Bruce asked Sebastien, who merely shook his head.

"Too soon. We don't know exactly who he was in contact with, other than Arceneau and Volange. Nor what his final aim was, if not simply money."

"Sophie might be able to tell you more, if—when she wakes," Bruce said, his voice catching. "She must have tried to get some details from him. He intended to kill her that night, so he may have said more than he meant to."

"You haven't slept properly," Cordelia said. "Why don't you now? I'll sit with Sophie."

Bruce was about to dismiss her offer, but a wave of tiredness swept over him, and he couldn't stifle a yawn.

"Yes, get some sleep," Sebastien agreed. "Cor can watch over Miss Bertrand as well as you can."

Bruce nodded and stood up. "Very well."

"Sophie, dear, it's me," Cordelia said in a soft tone. She took Sophie's hand and rubbed it gently, as if trying to erase the chill. "I'm going to sit with you awhile, darling." She pulled up the chair Bruce had been using.

"You'll call me if she wakes?" Bruce asked.

The look Cordelia shot him spoke volumes. "Go to sleep, my lord."

"Yes, ma'am," he said, sheepishly aware that she had dismissed him as if he were a child. In the guest room he was shown to, he fell onto his bed without removing his clothes. Oblivion kindly chased away any dreams he might have had.

He woke up sometime in the evening. Without thinking, he headed directly for Sophie's room. As Bruce approached, he heard Cordelia speaking in a low, conversational tone. His heart leapt at the thought of Sophie awake again, but when he reached the doorway, he saw nothing had changed. Cordelia sat by the bed, holding Sophie's hand, speaking gently about mundane matters, as if Sophie could hear her.

Well, perhaps she could, on some level. She seemed more restful now, less fevered.

Cordelia heard him enter the room, and turned around.

"No change?" he asked.

"She still sleeps. Her eyes open sometimes."

"Yes, the doctor said it happens. Patients can blink and move, but they are not truly awake." Unconsciously, he reached out to Sophie and touched her face.

"Perhaps she's waiting for something."

"What?" asked Bruce.

"I don't know. But her body is recovering. It's her mind that suffers."

Or her heart, Bruce thought. "You should go find your

husband. I'll stay with her now."

"She's very lucky to have you," Cordelia said.

"I doubt she'd agree."

"You saved her life. Twice. Surely that gives you some credit with her."

He shook his head. "If she hates me, she has every right to."

Cordelia looked at him sadly. "I hope you can discuss it with her when she wakes." She headed toward the door.

"If she wakes."

"She said a word," Cordelia said, looking back at him. "Just once, about an hour ago."

"What was it?" he asked, suddenly alert.

"Your name." Cordelia closed the door as she left.

Bruce sat by Sophie, just looking at her for a long moment. "Did you, Sophie? Did you say my name? Were you cursing me?"

The figure on the bed was silent.

"Sophie, please listen to me," he whispered, leaning close to her head, his hands still tight around hers. "You have to wake up again. I can't live without you." He paused, collecting his emotions. "I love you, Sophie. Please just live. I'll make amends for what I did to you, I swear it. Just live."

He waited, breathless, willing her back to life. But she lay still.

Sophie seemed to come to the surface of a great ocean. She'd been underwater for so long she had almost forgotten there was a surface, but little things began to call her back. Twinges of something like pain in her side.

A flash that might be daylight, if she opened her eyes… although she had no strength to do so. And from somewhere, a voice speaking. Calling to her? She doubted it. Who would call to her? She remembered one thing about the surface world—she had been unhappy there. Alone.

But the voice went on. She drifted, hearing a word or two come clearly, only to be swept out by a tide of darkness again. She heard her name once. Then twice.

"Sophie," the voice said. Why did that voice fill her with dread? But she also longed to hear it again.

"Sophie, please." *Please what?* she wondered. What did the voice want? And then she remembered something else about the world she left. She knew something. Something very important to tell.

"Sophie, come back to me," the voice said again.

Who was it? Why did it sound so familiar? What was her secret? Should she tell the voice?

Yes, surely that was what she was meant to do. Once she told the voice her secret, it would let her go into the ocean of darkness again, and be at peace.

"Sophie," the voice called.

She struggled against the clinging darkness. "Traitor," she whispered. "Traitor."

A pressure on her hand. "Sophie," the familiar voice said. "Sophie, you can wake up now."

"Traitor," she whispered through dry, cracked lips. "I know who…."

"You found the traitor, love. It was Charlie, we know. Don't slip away."

Sophie opened her eyes, and saw the one person she

both needed and hated to see. Everything rushed back to her. "What are you doing here?" she asked Bruce. Her voice came out cracked and harsh.

He looked so strange. So intense. "I brought you here, Sophie," he said. "You killed Charlie on the road, remember? I found you afterward."

"Charlie's dead?" she asked.

"Yes. Don't feel bad."

She shrugged, or rather tried to shrug. Her shoulder ached fiercely. "I don't feel bad about it at all. He tried to kill me."

"You survived."

"How very fortunate," she said.

"Sophie…"

"Where are we?" she interrupted. She did not want to speak with Bruce.

"Lady Thorne's home in Quince Street. You remember coming here after leaving the Zodiac offices?"

"Ah…yes," she said. "Right after you accused me of being the mole. That does stick in my memory."

"I was wrong."

"Too bad it took Charlie's body to convince you."

"He told me himself, right before he died. But that's not what convinced me. I should have trusted you all along. Sophie, please forgive me."

She stared at him, her emotions swirling. "If I forgive you, will you find me something to drink? All the blood loss has left me rather parched." She hadn't meant to sound so callous, but rage was quickly rising in her heart. She didn't want a mere apology from Bruce. She wanted…

He had already seized some wine that had been placed at the bedside. "Here."

To her consternation, Sophie found her hand shook so much she could barely lift the glass.

"I'll help," he began, reaching toward her.

"I don't want your help," she hissed, her anger sharpening as she found a target. "You're the last person in the world I want help from."

He didn't argue. Sophie hated that he didn't argue. He just stood up and stepped away. "I'll send someone else, then, more to your liking."

She watched him go, and wished she knew what she wanted.

Chapter 39

Ω

SOPHIE HAD NO LACK OF attendants, including the surgeon, her benevolent hosts, and their small army of servants. Everyone told her to stay in bed. Indeed, once Sophie decided to rejoin the world, the others had to work hard to convince her that healing would take a while.

Sebastien told Sophie flatly that he owed her a life, and if she were as rational as she claimed to be, she should bloody well take advantage of the care he and his wife could provide. Sophie did not have a smart response to that, so she only nodded stiffly.

Bruce said very little, when she saw him at all. She took the advice of the physician and remained in bed—though it made her anxious—mostly due to the fact that Bruce could not very well barge into a lady's room under normal circumstances.

Cordelia was usually the person to tend her in her convalescence. Sophie and Cordelia were like night and day, but Cordelia had shoved all pretense aside and welcomed Sophie in like a long-lost sister.

She even offered her own clothes to wear. Trying on gowns was an activity Sophie could only manage with the assistance of Cordelia and her lady's maid, Bond. It did, however, help to pass the time.

They were of similar height, though Cordelia had a fuller figure, and Sophie reveled in the luxurious fabrics Cordelia must wear on a daily basis. She surveyed herself in one gown of pure white linen, the lines conspiring to make her look elegant and the shade making her skin glow. Even with her shorn hair, she felt pretty. If only Bruce could see her…she faltered, her smile fading. She did not want to dress for him.

"Something wrong, dear?" Cordelia asked. She was sitting in a plush chair, watching the proceedings. She had an open notebook on her lap, and several sharpened pencils next to her. But she wasn't working on anything. Instead, she was gazing at the dress. "I rather like that cut on you."

"The dress fits well," Sophie began. "It's simply…" She paused. "I don't need to be watched all the time," Sophie said, taking a different tack.

Cordelia smiled. "I have found any association with the Zodiac seems to result in always being watched over…whether one likes it or not."

"No one watches over me," Sophie declared.

Her statement was immediately refuted by Bond, who murmured, "You're stepping on the hem, my lady. Shall I unbutton the dress and press it for you?"

"You're more comfortable being the watcher, aren't you?" Cordelia asked. Her eyes were calm, and Sophie didn't like the wisdom in them.

She shifted as Bond helped her out of the new dress. Her bandages made bending difficult. "I got my fill of watching at Carterhaugh Manor."

"Carterhaugh…" Cordelia repeated, her tone becoming speculative. "Named after the poem, I expect."

"What poem?"

"Tam Lin, the Scottish ballad. Do you know it?"

Sophie shook her head. "What's Tam Lin?"

"Who, rather. He's a noble knight who falls from his horse one day, while riding through the forest of Carterhaugh. He is ensnared by the faerie queen, who plans to sacrifice him to the dark powers she owes allegiance to."

Sophie thought immediately of Bruce, a once noble knight who had certainly been captured by dark powers while they were at Carterhaugh. "And what happened to him?"

"He had the great fortune to have gained the love of a remarkable woman. Janet, who meets him one day in the forest, gives her heart to him. She is the only one who can save him from the faerie queen."

"How does she do that?"

"On the night Tam Lin is to be sacrificed, he is led down a road to where he will be killed. At the crossroads, Janet leaps out of hiding and holds him in her arms. Cursed by the enraged faerie queen, Tam Lin suffers a series of horrible transformations. He appears to be one monster after another. But Janet is both brave and wise. She keeps hold of him and will not let go, no matter how horrible he appears. And when the cock crows at dawn, Tam Lin becomes himself again, for Janet broke the spell."

"And they live happily ever after," Sophie guessed.

"For many long years."

"A tale for children."

"I think it's a beautiful poem," Cordelia said, unperturbed. "It is far too easy to mistake appearance for reality—something you know well, Sophie. It takes a brave person to keep hold of what's important, despite all the difficulties."

Sophie turned her head away. Cordelia didn't tell that story by accident. But Bruce wasn't some enchanted knight under a curse. Though many of her memories were cloudy, she did remember his words to Julian. He willfully, knowingly betrayed Sophie, hiding his own distrust until the moment when it hurt her most. Why would she want to hold onto that?

"I'm tired," she said. "I don't want to talk any more."

Cordelia stood up immediately, and signaled Bond to follow her out. "Get your rest, dear."

After Cordelia left, Sophie stewed. She wasn't tired at all. Her blood raced as her body healed. She couldn't stand to be cooped up for much longer. And what did Cordelia mean by her words? Why should she play Janet? Bruce wasn't under a spell, he simply wasn't the man she hoped he was.

Cordelia was just meddling, in a kind-hearted but foolish way. How easy for her to say those things. She had her fairy tale ending when her beloved saved her life and then married her without hesitation. They were not the same, Sophie and Cordelia.

And yet Cordelia treated her so kindly, as if Sophie were family. That was not a thing Sophie was used to. It had happened exactly once before in her life, when she was spirited away from Paris and given a new chance. Sophie was too worldly to expect a miracle twice.

She sat down on the bed. Her body still hurt, and she considered taking another dose of opium to dull the pain. She started to open the bottle when she remembered the bottles she'd seen by Bruce's door.

He *had* been enchanted, though by chemicals rather than magic. Volange never passed up a chance to play with people's minds that way. Perhaps she was blaming Bruce for something that wasn't entirely his fault. Then again, no one forced him to call her a traitor in Julian's presence—was that just the aftereffects of the drugs or his real feelings coming to the surface? If only she knew what he truly thought. But how could she ask him without risking more than she was prepared to stake?

Chapter 40

♎

THE NEXT MORNING, SOPHIE DECIDED she would no longer hide in her room. She was physically much better—though she still tired easily. But she could join the others downstairs and make her plans for the future…a future she was not particularly looking forward to.

She rang for a maid to help her dress. Bond appeared soon after, accompanied by Cordelia.

"I intend to eat breakfast downstairs," Sophie began.

"Excellent," Cordelia replied quickly.

Sophie had expected resistance. "You're encouraging me?"

"I actually came to tell you there will be a meeting of sorts later today. Mr Neville is coming by, and I gather that all of you—meaning you, Forester, and my husband—will discuss what happened. Do you feel strong enough?"

"Yes, of course." Was she strong enough to talk with Bruce? Well, it had to happen sometime.

"I'll be there to divert attention most of the day, in case it's necessary." To make her point, Cordelia wrapped her arm around Sophie's waist, the sort of affectionate gesture an older sister might make toward a younger. "We are friends, after all."

"Are we?" Sophie asked a little coldly.

Cordelia sighed. "It's hard, you know. I love my husband, but to most people, I can't even hint that I'm aware of the things he's involved in. So to know a woman who does understand such secrets…that would be quite wonderful." She paused. "Can I ask you something, Sophie?"

"Yes."

"When you were Jacques, watching me while I was a captive of Arceneau…were your orders merely to help me?"

Sophie paused. "As much as I could," she allowed herself to say.

Cordelia continued, her voice gentle, "But you were supposed to kill me, correct, should it become necessary?"

Sophie stared at her. Cordelia did see a lot more than she seemed to. "I…" Then she said, "I'm glad I never had to decide that."

It was not an answer, and Cordelia knew it. "I see. Well, you are still welcome any time."

"How can you *say* that, knowing what I am?" Sophie burst out.

"I accepted a certain amount of risk in marrying Sebastien. What's a little more for another friend?"

Friends. Sophie struggled to reply. "That's kind of you. But I'm not… You'd regret having me as a friend."

"That is my decision, dear." Cordelia smiled again, with an edge that suggested she would no longer tolerate disagreement. "Now, shall we go down and join the gentlemen?"

In the bright room where a modest breakfast was laid on a sideboard, the women found both Sebastien and Bruce were already sitting down, engaged in a fierce discussion of recent events. Bruce had full plate of food, though he was too involved in the talk to eat. Sebastien had two separate cups of dark coffee in front of him, and his energetic attitude suggested he'd had a few servings already.

"If someone cleared out the stash of documents Charlie hoarded at the lodge, we have to assume this sort of thing will happen again!" Sebastien said, taking a long drink of coffee.

Bruce shook his head. "Charlie was no idiot. If he had a hiding place at the lodge, it was well designed, and hidden from everyone else. I'll wager any papers are still there."

He turned his head when he saw Sophie enter. "Good morning," he said, without inflection.

She nodded to both men as Cordelia helped her to a chair. "We should also consider the possibility that he was lying to me about having more documents," she said, as if it were perfectly natural to join such a discussion over breakfast. "What appeared to be a slip of the tongue may have been intentional…he persuaded me to leave the house with him. He doubtlessly intended to kill me. No one would have been the wiser. You would have assumed I merely ran off."

Bruce watched her carefully, considering her words. "Maybe. But I still think he had materials for blackmail—

or sale—hidden somewhere. You said he was at it for two years. I doubt he only stole one document at a time."

"All while he worked in foreign affairs in the government," Sebastien added, with a sigh. "How could he have gone undetected for so long?"

"Because he also passed information on to the Zodiac," Bruce reminded him. "Julian trusted him as a source."

"Which brings us back to what we need to tell Julian today," Sebastien pressed. He turned to Sophie. "I'm going to argue for a more united Zodiac—we ought to work together rather than separately."

"Julian will object," Sophie said. "Tradition has it the signs always worked alone."

"Forget tradition. What do *you* think?" he asked.

"I think," Sophie said, without looking at Bruce, "that both methods have their dangers."

Bruce started to say something, then stopped.

"What?" Sophie asked.

"You're right," he said finally. "But I know which I prefer."

* * * *

Sophie managed to avoid speaking with Bruce privately all morning, and used the excuse of needing a brief nap before the meeting to escape to her room. Now, again clad in one of Cordelia's gowns, she made her final preparations before going down to where Julian and the others waited. She wanted to look as though she belonged in the Zodiac, able to hold her own with the men in the room.

She no longer had a wig to hide her sheared hair, and she found she didn't particularly want to hide her head after all. She had few enough opportunities to show her true colors.

The gown suited her well. The fabric was a finely woven, lightweight worsted wool dyed scarlet. Most women would consider it too bold. Sophie loved it. Fine red satin piping at the neckline kept the look clean. The slightest flouncing where the dress fell to the floor suggested a softening of the simple lines. She wore delicate black leather slippers and white gloves, both also loaned to her from Cordelia. Deliberately, Sophie wore no jewelry at all.

After the meeting with the Zodiac concluded, she would hire a coach to take her back to her rooms in London, and then…perhaps Aries would have another assignment for her soon. Sophie feared being idle and alone in England. Nations were racing toward war. She couldn't stand to be against the wall, watching while others played the game.

A knock at the door brought her back to the present.

"Yes, I'll be finished shortly," she called, expecting it to be one of the maids.

Instead, Bruce cautiously opened the door. "May I come in for a moment?" he asked.

Sophie's heart jumped violently. "There's no need," she said, pitching her voice low to avoid a tremor. "I was just coming down."

"I wanted to speak with you in private before we saw the others." He entered the room, but didn't approach her.

She took a silent breath. "Speak, then."

"Sophie, I was wrong. I said it before, and you have every reason to doubt me. But don't let us go downstairs as enemies. Please. I don't know how long it will take me to regain your trust, if you'll ever let me do that. But it's important for me to tell you that I *will* try."

"What does my opinion matter?" she asked. "Why should you care if I trust you?"

"Because I love you," he said.

Sophie's heart did something very strange then, something she didn't have words for. "You what?"

"I love you." He walked toward her, as if he couldn't stay away. "I knew it that night you fought the poison. You were so far beyond me that I thought I'd go insane if you...left. Then you recovered, and I was too scared to tell you how I felt. The time was never right, even when we..." he trailed off. "I don't suppose it matters. Even if you felt something in return—"

"I did," she said.

"You did?"

She straightened her posture in an attempt to appear, well, stronger. "I don't make a habit of sharing my bed, and certainly not telling others my past or my thoughts. I told you because I wanted you to know who I am. I've never spoken about that to anyone else, but you were... never mind."

"I was what?"

"You seemed different," she said. She chose her words carefully, afraid to choose the wrong one. "You worried about me. You watched over me. You treated me as a partner, instead of a foolish girl. And you never tried to force me to bed, even when I taunted you…rather horribly, I admit."

"I'd say tantalizing rather than taunting," he offered. "And the only horrible aspect was having to stop."

"Bruce," Sophie began desperately. Before she could think of a reason not to, she stepped closer to him and put her arms around his neck.

He didn't need any encouragement to draw her in, and when she kissed him, she nearly forgot all the intervening damage since the last time they'd been this close, just before the Victim's Ball. Sophie wished this was all that mattered, because she wanted to stay like this, enjoy the sweetness of touching him, and the promise of more to come.

She didn't know how long they remained like that, but at last little trivialities like breathing and reality intruded. She took a long breath when he ended the kiss, and turned her head so she could rest against his chest. She whispered, "If lust was the only consideration, this would all be very simple."

Bruce folded her into a gentle embrace, mindful of her still-healing body. "Lust is an inadequate word for what you do to me, dove." He very slowly stepped away, obviously unwilling to do it. "But I'd rather have your trust again. I love you too much to dishonor you by suggesting anything less."

She knew what honor meant to him. It must have cost him to say those words. "I believe you love me. And I admit I care…greatly for you. But what does that mean in practice? We're not in the same world. There's no reason for us to meet again, unless Aries has another brilliant assignment for us both—assuming he even wants to go that route."

He looked uncharacteristically nervous. "You could marry me. That would give us a reason to meet again."

Her jaw dropped. "*Marry* you? You're a peer of the realm. I'm the bastard daughter of a French stage actress."

"You're whoever you need to be, Sophie. You've been a dozen people in your life, you've changed and died and been reborn whenever it suited you. That's how you survive. What makes you think you can't do it again?"

"You want...what? For me to pretend to be a lady? High born enough to be suitable for a man like you?"

"Not a man like me. Me alone." He looked at her appealingly, willing her to believe it. "It would be a confidence scheme of epic proportions, but..."

Sophie bit her lip, pondering the idea despite herself. "How reckless do you think I am?"

He brought her closer to him. "Just enough to risk the rest of your life."

"A life of lies."

"What would the lie be?" Bruce asked, his voice hot. "Just another name. You'd have a real marriage, a real love. What else can I offer you to show I'm sorry? Please. So what if I know a little more about you than everyone else?"

"You're joking." How many names will I have in my life? Sophie wondered.

He produced a small box. "I got this for you."

"A ring? We already have wedding rings, from our first false marriage." She tried to be sarcastic, but didn't quite manage.

"Open it and see."

She opened the little box. It wasn't a ring at all. It was a small, heavy silver locket on a chain. But where her prop locket had a cross inscribed on it, this one had an engraving of a dove. "What's this?" she asked.

"Just a gift. I know nothing can replace the locket that was stolen from you all those years ago, but I wanted to give you something. Even if you don't…even if we never see each other again."

Ignoring the odd catch in his voice, Sophie pulled the locket out. It didn't look like her original, but it somehow felt strikingly like it. She opened the locket itself. "It's empty," she said, a bit sadly.

Bruce stepped closer again. "It's up to you to fill it, Sophie. You can do whatever you want with it. A miniature of your mother, maybe. Or one of me for remembrance…if you can stand to have such a handsome portrait around your neck all the time." His voice grew more earnest. "Or save it for the portraits of our children. It's your choice."

She raised an eyebrow. "Our *children*?"

He grinned crookedly. "I don't dream small, Sophie."

"You're assuming a lot." She didn't smile back.

"That's what dreams are for. Not all good things are illusions. You can start again. And I'd love for you to start a new life with me. I owe you for what I did before. And I would make it up to you. Please say you will. I'd be delighted and honored…and happy."

"I…" Sophie swallowed. Her heart wasn't beating quite properly. She knew he was sincere. But she did not like that he thought he owed her a marriage, or anything at all. "I have to think about it."

His mouth tightened. "You're going to say no."

"I said I'll think about it." She sharpened her voice. "And now we have other work, do we not? You may escort me downstairs, if you want to make yourself useful."

"You won't even try the necklace on?"

She put the box down. "Not yet."

Chapter 41

♎

THE THREE SIGNS OF THE Zodiac met with the first sign, Aries, in a small room in the Quince Street house. Miss Chattan was there as well, taking notes. Cordelia, well aware of the nature of the event, stayed away from the whole discussion.

Sophie watched her retreating figure, noticing how relaxed the woman was. Cordelia, it seemed, had got an ending that was not an illusion.

"Sophie?" Bruce asked from where the men were sitting.

She turned back and joined them. "I'm here."

Sebastien took the lead. "We need to know more about the Zodiac's activities. All the agents' assignments."

"Exactly what Charlie thought," Julian noted acerbically.

"That's my point," Sebastien argued. "Charlie's betrayal went undetected for as long as it did because almost none of the agents know the identities of the others. And more to the point, the idea of working alone may not be as useful as we previously thought."

"The Zodiac has operated this way for decades. Agents are specifically chosen for their ability to work without support…or needing guidance at every turn."

"But the world is changing," Bruce interjected. "New innovations in war, shifting alliances. We have to be able to communicate with each other to be effective. Or at least to know it's an option."

Julian asked Bruce, "Do you agree with your friend then?"

"I do. If I knew more about what the other agents were supposed to be doing at the time, I would have known Charlie wasn't at the house by your orders and what he said was false. I would have known something was wrong sooner, before…" he broke off, looking at Sophie.

So did Julian. "Libra? What do you say?"

Sophie kept her eyes on him while she spoke. "I was a successful agent for years, not just because no one knew who I was, but also because no one even knew there was a female agent working for the Zodiac." She paused to gather her thoughts. "It was the best sort of protection, and I know there will be other situations where total se-crecy is required. I liked to work that way."

Sophie took a breath. "However, if you'd sent me in alone at Carterhaugh, I would have failed." She would have died. "Knowing I had support," she said, glancing at Bruce, "made it possible to complete the assignment."

Julian shook his head. "That assignment was an anomaly."

"Or the beginning of a trend." Sophie held up one hand. "It was also helpful that I knew who Sagittarius was, even though I learned through happenstance."

"By intervening in yet another assignment," Julian

said.

Miss Chattan raised her hand. Everyone looked at the normally reticent woman in surprise.

"Yes?" Julian asked.

"Keep in mind," she said, "Libra was the one who let the Zodiac know where Cordelia was. More agents working together means more eyes. Personally, I think Sophie is right."

Sophie couldn't hide her surprise. Chattan had never agreed with her before, but now the other woman offered her a slight smile.

Julian sat back and put his hands behind his head. "So what does this brave new world of espionage look like? Do we have meetings where our enemies can find us all at once?"

The others shot back suggestions. Ideas and arguments were floated and discarded. Sophie began to lose interest in the minutiae. She kept seeing Bruce and hearing his unexpected proposal.

She stood suddenly. "I must get a little air. I'll be in the garden. Do inform me if a life-altering decision is made in my absence."

The men, who had risen automatically when she had, made apologies. Bruce asked hesitantly if she needed help.

Shaking her head, she made her way out through the glass doors to the yard. After walking toward the lovely garden that lay beyond, she paused.

She leaned against the cool stone wall of the house, and looked out at the world around her. This was as alien a place as the moon must be. The house was gracious, in the truest sense. Not as old as some, but old enough to whisper of generations past.

So what am I doing here? she asked silently.

* * * *

After Sophie left, the men continued to discuss the issues at hand. Julian was slowly, grudgingly coming around to the idea they proposed. The near loss of Sophie as an agent was most likely the reason for his change, even more so than the revelation of Charlie as a traitor.

Bruce confessed he'd been swayed by his prejudices when Charlie appeared. "I had no reason to think it was wrong—even though it was unusual. But Charlie was a friend, so I buried any doubts. Meanwhile, I resisted trusting Sophie, because she wasn't British and I didn't know a thing about her."

"The foreigner was more loyal than the native son," Julian said, his expression ironic.

"I was wrong to think that couldn't be the case, but if the Zodiac agents worked together more—"

He broke off when a footman entered. "Yes, Jem?" Sebastien asked.

"Apologies for interrupting, sir, but there's a gentleman waiting who insists on seeing the viscount."

"Someone's here to see me?" Bruce asked, confused. Very few people knew where he was.

"Yes, my lord," Jem said. "His Grace, the Duke of Walsham."

Julian also looked surprised at that name, but said,

"Best go see what it's about."

Bruce strode to the parlor, intensely curious. He had met Walsham a few times, and had liked the man, but he was of his father's generation. They had nothing in common that Bruce was aware of.

In the parlor, Walsham looked the same as ever. Disdainful of the newer fashions, he still dressed in a powdered wig, breeches, and a brocade coat. It fit him well, Bruce had to admit.

"Your Grace," he said, bowing slightly. "This is a surprise."

"I imagine so. Thank you for seeing me."

"The honor is mine," Bruce replied. "Though I'm not sure to what I owe the pleasure."

The duke bowed his head. "Not all pleasure, I'm afraid. My visit concerns Miss Bertrand, as she is known."

"Sophie?" he asked. What possible connection could the duke have to Sophie? And how could that connection be strong enough to bring the man out to this house, where almost no one knew Sophie was?

Walsham didn't enlighten him. "My sources suggest you've taken a rather personal interest in her," he said. Something in the older man's gaze made Bruce very glad he didn't have darker intentions toward Sophie.

"That's one way to put it," Bruce said. "The short version is that I owe her my life. I'll leave the details for her to tell you...I'm afraid our versions of the tale will differ."

"Is she well enough to come down, or may I visit her upstairs, if that is more convenient for her?"

"No, she's quite recovered from… How did you know
—"

The older man finally chuckled. "You young people
are not the only ones good at discovering things, my boy.
I can see you burning with curiosity. But if you will send
Miss Bertrand here, I will be most grateful. I was quite
worried for her." The tightness around the old man's eyes
hinted at concern, and perhaps anger.

"At once, sir." Bruce left to search out Sophie. He
found her sitting outside under a canopy shading her from
the late summer sun. The marks of her recent injuries
were nearly faded, and she looked more beautiful than
ever. He took a breath before disturbing her. "You have a
visitor, Sophie."

She looked over blankly. "I do? Who is it?"

"The Duke of Walsham."

Surprise and delight covered her features. "Really?"
She looked years younger.

"Is that a thing I could make up? How do you know
him?" Bruce couldn't help asking.

"Come with me and you'll see." Astonishingly, she
held out a hand to him, as if their troubles were forgotten.

He would have followed Sophie into hell when she
looked so happy.

Chapter 42

$$\underline{\Omega}$$

Excited as a child, Sophie let Bruce take her to the parlor. "Your Grace!" she said, curtseying low.

"My dearest Sophie, how dare you be so formal with me." Showing total disdain for class or gender relations, he embraced her in a gentle hug. Sophie responded with more feeling, twining her arms tight around his neck.

"Oh, I'm so happy to see you!" she said, truly delighted. "I thought you were still abroad, or I would have…"

"No matter, dear. I returned before I expected to." He patted her back and released her, holding her at arms' length. "I am so relieved to see you, my dear. I feared the worst."

"She's far stronger than she looks," Bruce said quietly.

"How very true," the duke agreed. "Our Sophie is a marvel, is she not?"

Bruce only nodded. After a moment, he asked, "But how do you know Sophie? Who are you?"

"Apart from a mere duke, you mean?" His eyes twinkled. "Shall I tell him?" he asked Sophie.

At her assent, he said, "Well, I first met Sophie at a very strange party in Paris…when I used to be known as Aries."

Sophie enjoyed Bruce's surprise.

"You were Julian Neville's predecessor?" he asked.

"Indeed I was. It took me a long time to find someone I could trust to follow my position in the Zodiac. Julian proved himself to both me and the Astronomer, but before he assumed the first sign, he worked under my command. Gradually, I let him take more responsibility, including the training of this magnificent young lady." He smiled again at Sophie, and she felt as if she were washed in sunlight.

"You were the man who got Sophie out of Paris," Bruce said. "The gentleman who supported her in London until she joined the Zodiac herself."

"Ah, she told you about that, did she?"

"I heard a bit."

"She has not shared the details of her life with many people." He paused. "Will you give us a moment alone, Forester?"

Bruce excused himself, his face filled with curiosity.

Sophie said, "I'm *so* glad to see you. But how did you know I'd be here?"

"I may not be a sign of the Zodiac any more, dear, but I meddle when I like. Julian knows how concerned I am about you, and he told me about your recent assignment. The poison and then the attack by… Well, I won't honor that traitor by speaking his name. You were always so daring, but two brushes with death in the same assignment hints of recklessness."

"I…I had help."

"Forester was with you?"

"He was. He saved my life. More than once." Saying that to her oldest friend made Sophie feel better, as though a weight was lifted off her.

"You returned the favor by stealing him back." Walsham was obviously very well informed about the details. "And I heard there was some…misunderstanding regarding your…ah, loyalties?" he added carefully.

"It wasn't Bruce's fault," she said quickly. Several thoughts that had been warring inside her mind fell into place. "Please understand he was tortured. You know Volange had a penchant for drugs. I suspect he used something on Bruce which could have turned him against me."

"My dear. How horrible for you."

"I never felt so abandoned," she confessed.

"And like the Sophie I know so well, you were bound and determined to prove yourself worthy, and so chased down a traitor by yourself."

She looked at him sheepishly. "I let my anger get the best of me."

"It came out well in the end, at least," he said.

"Did it? I feel…very shabby."

"Dearest, how can that be? You performed above and beyond all expectations. And Forester clearly thinks the world of you."

"He asked me to marry him."

"Indeed?" Walsham's eyes lit up. "I thought him a man of good taste, but it is heartening to hear it confirmed."

"I will refuse him."

His face fell. "Oh. Why, if I may ask?"

Sophie shook her head. "You already know. You know my birth, my life. I'm not the sort of woman he ought to marry. I'd have to become someone else yet again, and this time I'd have to act the role for the rest of my life! His title, his estate, and his commitment to keeping his family name alive...all of that is foreign to me. He requires a true lady."

The duke's expression hardened then. "Nonsense. You are one of the finest ladies I have ever been privileged to know, my dear."

"Not by blood. Love is all well and good, but he'd soon regret his decision. You don't know him. He's very determined to do things the proper way. I'm sure he's only offering marriage because we...ah..." She trailed off, suddenly aware of the intimacy she'd been about to confess.

Walsham only smiled. "I see. But I think you do him a disservice in assuming he didn't propose for nobler reasons."

"It doesn't matter. Society would discover my birth, or even my past as an actress...not to mention my less than pristine moral fiber," she added bitterly. "I'd be vilified, and Bruce would be mocked. I'd never do that to him."

"Because you love him."

Sophie nodded, afraid to say more.

"Supposing you were a lady of noble birth. Would you object to his proposal then?"

"I'm not, so what does it matter?"

"Humor me, dear Sophie."

"I suppose it would help because it would provide a

bulwark against other rumors. But I don't want to leave the Zodiac!" she burst out.

He looked affronted. "Is retiring from the Zodiac a condition of the marriage?"

Sophie paused. "Well, Bruce never said that. I just assumed…"

"If he proposed to you, Sophie, knowing all he knows about your life and your temperament, perhaps it is because he wants you just as you are."

She looked at him a little shyly. "Perhaps I should discuss the matter with him again. I might not have been completely…open to his argument."

"Perhaps," Walsham said in a dry tone. "In the interim, I would like to offer one small piece of information that may aid your decision." He offered her a folded parchment. "Here. I planned to give you this today in any case."

"What's this?" Sophie opened the paper to find a page of notes, written tidily in the Duke's own precise hand.

"Your lineage. You're Sophia Renee Eugenie Bertrand de Garnier, the daughter of the last Comtesse de Garnier."

"That's quite a mouthful. How did you dream that name up?" Sophie asked. Then she recalled where she'd heard such a name before. "Wait! Madame Baden insisted I looked just like a woman she called the Comtesse de Garnier. She was right after all!"

"In such ways, the truth tends to out." He shook his head. "When you were formally offered a sign in the Zodiac, it was because we had already learned a lot about you. Your mother was an actress in Paris, but that's not how she started out in her life." His voice tightened with anger. "An affair with the wrong sort of man brought her to Paris, and forced her to turn on her reputation."

Sophie's jaw dropped. "She was really a comtesse?"

"Yes. She hid her past from nearly everyone, though her execution at the hands of Robespierre and his committee implies that someone uncovered the truth." Walsham looked fierce at that thought. "She was part of the class the Revolution despised. But she hid it to protect you…as best she could. I'm sure she never envisioned the horror the Revolution would bring."

"And my father?"

He bowed his head. "I can't give you that name, I'm afraid. As is often the case, he left before she knew she carried you." He paused, still not looking at her. "If he had known, he would have stayed, or found some way to…" He trailed off. "Don't listen to me. No one can change the past."

"You knew about my mother's history for years, but you never told me?"

"What purpose would it have served? I thought it better to conceal it unless it became necessary…though you would have been informed after my death. I made sure of that."

"So I am a lady, or I might have been."

"You always were, name or no."

Sophie stared at the paper. Then she looked at the duke. "Will you wait here a moment? Just a few minutes?"

"As long as I need to, dearest."

Sophie flew to find Bruce. He had retreated to the small study, where he was sitting with an untouched drink before him. He stared out the window at the garden.

"Bruce!" Sophie called, her nervousness making her heart beat too fast. "May I ask…would you allow me to remain in the Zodiac if we married?"

"Allow?" he echoed, looking at her. "As if I could stop you."

She stood up straighter. "Understand what I'm saying, Bruce. I use charm. At some point, I will need to seduce a mark. You'd hate me after that."

He looked at her for a long time. "Would you hate me if I did the same? I'm not offering to give up my place in the Zodiac, either."

Sophie frowned. "I…don't know." The thought of Bruce with another woman did make her see red, but how could she demand something of him that she was unwilling to give? "It wouldn't hurt as much if it was something you had to do for the Zodiac."

"Honesty. That's one of the things I like best about you. It always has been." Bruce took a sip of his drink. "We're both oddities. No one else lives the sort of lives we do, so who else can we rely on? I've done things any ordinary person would find unconscionable. I've lied, I've cheated, I've taken lives."

"So have I. I know why you do those things."

"That's my point. I found you, Sophie…a soul that actually matches my own. We're not conventional people. We can't expect a conventional partnership."

"So you would understand…if I, well, broke my vows?"

"If you did it as Libra. All I'd ask is that you be honest with me. Just as I'd be with you."

"As bizarre a bargain as that is, it's honest." Sophie kissed him soundly. "Oh. One more thing. My mother was really a comtesse," she added breathlessly, as Bruce took her in his arms. "So I may outrank you."

"That's the least of my problems." He kissed her back, then said, "Sophie, I made a hash of it before…proposing to you that way. I didn't mean that you shouldn't be yourself. I just didn't know how to ask…I've never asked such a thing before. I don't want you to play a part. I want you to be who you want, with the hope that such a person would be content with me around. If I asked you to marry me again, would you say yes?"

"I would," she said, "if you asked to marry Sophie Bertrand. If we are really going to attempt this, I must be myself…whether others accept who I am or not."

"Of course."

"So…would you ask again?"

He took her hands in his, speaking slowly as he put the words together. "Sophie, will you please help me live? Be my wife, and my partner, and watch my back, and let me love you and trust you and keep you as safe as I possibly can…even if that means not safe at all?"

Dazzled, Sophie took a breath, then smiled. "I will do that, Bruce, provided you do the same for me."

She wasn't sure if she kissed him, or if he kissed her then. But she was sure she found her match.

Epilogue

♎

IT WAS A MATTER OF wild speculation among the society gossips when the Viscount Forester announced his engagement to a heretofore unknown lady, the mysterious Comtesse Sophia Renee Eugenie Bertrand de Garnier, who he had apparently met abroad and who captured his heart.

Sophie heard a few of the rumors as she recovered fully and prepared for her move to Bruce's estate, where they planned to marry in a few weeks.

One matron—who had a long red nose and three unmarried daughters—said she was quite sure she'd scoured the *Almanach de Gotha* from cover to cover, and never found the woman's name.

Another rumor suggested the so-called comtesse was a penniless fortune hunter who somehow gulled the viscount into marrying her.

A gossip column in one newspaper guessed the wedding would never take place. As soon as the comtesse learned of various scandals in the Allander family's past, she'd throw the viscount off.

Interestingly, on the same day the gossip column appeared, another column devoted to London theatre noted that the actress Sarah Finn had announced her retirement from the stage. Her reliable comic performances would be missed.

If anyone drew a connection between these two events, they kept the fact to themselves.

"Bond, these gossips would die if they knew the truth of the matter," Sophie said. She laughed as she put the latest newspaper down beside her.

"They wouldn't believe a word of it if you gave a public lecture, ma'am," the maid replied. Lucy Bond was attending her as a lady's maid until Sophie had settled in her new home and could select one of her own. It was another gracious act by Cordelia.

"I suppose we should be thankful for that," Sophie said. "What do I have to do today?"

"Milady's dressmaker is visiting so you can be measured for a new wardrobe, and you must select which gown you'll wear for the wedding. In the afternoon, the viscount intends to take you for a ride in the park."

"Showing me off," Sophie said.

"Telling a story, ma'am," the maid corrected. "The sooner the *ton* recognizes you as a lady like them, the easier the rest will be."

Sophie smiled at the maid. The young woman had a past almost as shady as her own. "Well said, Bond. Let's get me dressed and ready then!"

"Oh, yes, ma'am! I have just the outfit in mind."

* * * *

Not many days later, Bruce took Sophie to his home. She made an instant impression on the household. From the butler on down, all the servants were mightily taken with the delicate Frenchwoman. Sophie took care to present herself as a cool, collected soul who would never be suspected of any scandalous behavior—and certainly nothing so scandalous as a history on the stage.

Sophie liked the estate right away, and it didn't take long for her to feel as if it were meant to be her home. She had a lovely guest room overlooking the western fields. She wouldn't move into her actual bedroom until the wedding day, when she would truly be the mistress of the house. For the sake of appearances, they had agreed to restrain themselves until the wedding night. Sophie didn't like the wait.

The day of the wedding drew closer. Sophie sat in a parlor and looked over the guest list. The ceremony itself would be attended by only a few close friends. There would be a larger party at the estate for the household and village immediately afterward, though. Sophie blanched slightly at the thought of meeting so many new faces in such a short time, particularly because they would be neighbors and others who she would likely see for many years—she had to be convincing. She wouldn't be slipping away from this role.

Bruce found her. "You look worried," he said.

"Just a little anxious. It's an important role."

"It's not a role, Sophie." He kissed her lightly, though it was clear he wanted to do much more. "You just have to be yourself."

"Which self?"

"The one you want to be."

She kissed him back, and it took a moment before

both of them recalled propriety enough to separate. She loved the way he held her close to him, with his hand on the small of her back.

"Mmm," she said, "I miss you."

"We can remedy that," he said.

She reluctantly moved back, before he could become too convincing.

"By the way, did you ever hear from your brother after you wrote to him?" Sophie asked.

"Only an eloquent silence. He obviously hasn't forgiven me," he said. "However, I did receive a note from Miss Fox."

"And what did she have to say?"

"It's here somewhere." He found a folded letter on the table and passed her the note to look over. "She congratulates us both on our impending union, regrets that her social position precludes her from attending, and wishes us the best."

"That's all?"

"She urges me to not give up on Ash."

Sophie looked over the letter from the scandalous Miss Fox, written in a bold and flowing hand that mirrored the writer perfectly. "She says she will prevail on him as well. I suppose the two must be very close, for her to care so much."

He said, "Regina has never been as mercenary as she presents herself. I fear she may secretly be a romantic."

"You speak with authority on the issue," Sophie said in a tone of mock censure.

"Well, I've known her for many years. She's just one

of the many disreputable connections I made over time."

Sophie smiled. "And now you're marrying another one."

"Not soon enough."

"One more week," Sophie said. "For a man who claimed he didn't plan to marry for years, you're quite impatient."

"I know what I'm missing now." His eyes raked over her, and Sophie felt her body reacting.

"A week is a rather long time," she whispered.

"Long enough to fall in love," he agreed. "Tell me you're thinking what I'm thinking."

Sophie smiled, wondering if the giddy feeling would ever fade. "We would have to be discreet."

"Of course." He reached for her.

"And we have to wait until tonight."

Bruce made a sound of mock frustration. "Must we?"

She leaned in and whispered, "You can use the time to think about what you'd like to do with me."

He kissed her, then said, "What do you think I've been doing all this time?"

Sophie laughed softly. "I can't wait to see what you've come up with."

"I think you'll be pleased," he said, already looking pleased himself.

* * * *

A few days later, guests began to arrive. First among them were Lord and Lady Thorne. Sophie greeted them both warmly, as if she hadn't just seen them a week prior.

"I have good news," Cordelia said as the two women met in the hall before the evening meal. "I sent a letter to the Miss Sawyer you mentioned, and she replied straight away."

"What did she say to the proposal that you engage her?"

"She agreed to travel to Cheshire next week. She was very excited to have the opportunity to work among quality people, as she put it. She was grateful for Madame's recommendation."

"So that's sorted."

Cordelia nodded. "We're heading directly back to Cheshire after the wedding. Miss Sawyer will take her place in the household. I'm sure she'll be a fine addition."

"Good," said Sophie. "I didn't like to think she'd lost her place and wouldn't have a reference just because she crossed our path." She smiled. "Once she's been through some training, perhaps she can take over as my lady's maid."

* * * *

On the morning of the wedding, Bond dressed Sophie in the exquisite gown she had chosen. It echoed the classical lines that were still in vogue, and the embroidered white muslin was so sheer that a pale pink petticoat was quite necessary. Sophie wore her new silver locket around her neck. Bond convinced her that her natural hair would be thought incredibly chic, especially as a short, sheer veil softened the look.

The ceremony took place in the village church, and

Sophie remembered very little about it, other than Bruce's smile when he told her she was with him now.

The whole village cheered as they left the church. They rode back to the estate in an open carriage so everyone could admire the bride in her finery.

"I may as well be invisible," Bruce noted, though he sounded untroubled by it.

"It's just they know who you are already."

"Please. It's because you're the most striking lady they've ever set eyes on."

The post-wedding celebration took place on the lawn of the estate. Nearly the whole village showed up, and it was fortunate there was plenty of food and drink. Sophie was beset by well-wishers, and soon stopped trying to remember names or faces. She simply gave herself up to it, and hoped Bruce would eventually steal her away.

* * * *

Bruce watched with both pride and delight as he saw Sophie moving among the guests with a grace suggesting she was born for this. She charmed the household, the neighbors, the village…and him. He grinned to himself as he recognized how besotted he was.

The Duke of Walsham, who had come up from London the night before, walked up to him.

"I must congratulate you, sir," Walsham said. "I've never seen Sophie look so happy. She's even more beautiful than her mother. I'm sure her state owes a lot to you."

"I'll do my best to keep her content. You'll come after me if I don't, isn't that right?"

"Let's hope it doesn't come to that." Walsham chuckled, but added nothing more.

Bruce was about to move on to another subject when something clicked in his brain.

He said, "You've known Sophie a long time. You met her in 1795, when she was fourteen."

"Indeed. A fortunate day for us both," Walsham said.

"By that point, her mother was already dead and buried. How did you know what she looked like, enough to call Sophie more beautiful than her mother?"

Walsham sighed. "What if I said she was a famous actress?"

"Not that famous," Bruce said flatly. "And Sophie already mentioned she had no portrait of her."

"Did she. How regrettable. A tidy explanation that I can, sadly, no longer use." Walsham's expression, especially around his eyes, was so like Sophie's that Bruce couldn't believe he'd never noticed it before.

"You knew who she was that night at the party," he said, choosing his words carefully. "You went to Paris to bring her back."

"Yes."

"But you never told her the truth."

"I have made many mistakes in my life. I know I've chosen poorly, but truly I never intended to hurt anyone." He took a deep breath. "Trying to correct some of my mistakes has occupied much of my time in later years." Walsham's gaze was locked on the figure of Sophie, who was currently speaking animatedly to a few of the other guests. "To tell her the full truth and risk losing her again…"

Walsham looked so pained that Bruce took pity on him.

"Of course, it's not my secret to tell," he said. "And I am good at keeping secrets."

"I would appreciate that," Walsham said. "Maybe someday…"

"Not soon. I wouldn't want Sophie to think she owed her place in the Zodiac to blood, rather than the fact that she's extraordinary."

"She most certainly is. Hush now. Here she comes."

The men fell silent in exactly the sort of way that made her suspicious.

"What are you two scheming about?" she asked.

"We were talking about you," Walsham admitted.

"Oh, dear. What did you decide?"

"We agreed that you are extraordinary," Bruce said quietly.

"How sweet…and convenient."

"It's absolutely true," Walsham said. "Now, if you'll excuse me, I'll go talk to some of the other guests…and give you both a respite." He kissed Sophie lightly on her cheek and then left.

Bruce said, "It is true, you know."

"That I'm extraordinary?" she asked. "Well, then I'm not the only one who is."

Bruce lowered his voice. "I think," he said, "at this point in the festivities, no one will mind if we slip away."

"How remarkable." Sophie smiled at him, her heart beating faster. "That's exactly what I was thinking, love."

ABOUT THE AUTHOR

Elizabeth Cole is a romance writer with a penchant for history. Her stories draw upon her deep affection for the British Isles, action movies, medieval fantasies, and even science fiction. She now lives in a small house in a big city with a cat, a snake, and a rather charming gentleman. When not writing, she is usually curled in a corner read-ing...or watching costume dramas or things that explode. And yes, she believes in love at first sight.

Find out more at: elizabethcole.co